BEFORE SHE COULD STOP HIM, HE HAD TORN THE INSERT FROM THE FRONT OF HER GOWN. . . .

"Quinn!" she gasped.

"Shut up and look at yourself!" Roughly he turned her to face the mirror. "You're the most beautiful woman in London. No one can take that away from you."

He was right. Never had she looked better, even though the gown was now scandalously revealing. As she stared at her reflection something heavy and cold fell into the warm valley between her breasts. It was a plain square-cut topaz suspended from a long gold chain.

Quinn chuckled as he fastened it. "In case they're so blind they miss your assets, this will draw their attention back to their oversight. Pick up your chin, Highness. With you in that dress and me at your side, they'll know for certain that neither of us gives a damn what they think!"

Also by Susan Elizabeth Phillips

RISEN GLORY
GLITTER BABY
FANCY PANTS

THE COPELAND BRIDE

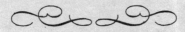

*Susan Elizabeth Phillips
and
Claire Kiehl*

A DELL BOOK

Published by
Dell Publishing
a division of
Bantam Doubleday Dell Publishing Group, Inc.
666 Fifth Avenue
New York, New York 10103

ISBN: 0-440-11235-4

Printed in the United States of America

Published simultaneously in Canada

One previous Dell edition

October 1989

10 9 8 7 6 5 4 3 2 1

KRI

To Julie and Gail . . . thank you.
To Linda, who said, "Of course you will."
And, without question, to Sandra Choron.

Prologue

"Noelle, *ma petite*, if we just hang on a bit longer, things will get better, you'll see."

Daisy Dorian was sitting at her cluttered dressing table carefully brushing into fashionable disarray the short blond ringlets that curled too youthfully around her face. With her littlest fingers she touched her lips lightly with coral and then, satisfied with the result, pouted prettily into the mirror.

The seven-year-old child sitting nearby gazed at her mother. She knew she had never seen anyone so beautiful. She did not notice the lines at the corners of Daisy's blue eyes or the puffiness under her chin, nor did she realize that the blond curls were a shade less bright and the upper arms a touch less firm than they had been. More than anything, Noelle wanted to look like her mother when she grew up.

"*La bonne chance* is finally going to smile on us," Daisy concluded. "Why, just today I overheard Mr. Lackland discussing the casting for *Hamlet*. I tell you, Noelle, he looked quite hard at me when he was discussing Ophelia."

Noelle giggled happily and ran to kneel beside her mother, careful not to touch Daisy's last good gown, a somewhat worn but still attractive pink confection.

"What a wonderful Ophelia you would be, Mama." She placed the accent carefully at the end of "Mama" just as Daisy had taught her, for Daisy, in the mode of the day, admired all things French. "Just think how exciting it will be when you are famous."

She jumped up and threw her thin arms above her head. "Daisy Dorian appearing at Covent Garden with Mr. John Philip Kemble! Or maybe you and Mrs. Siddons could do *As You Like It*. She can be Celia; I want you to play Rosalind."

Daisy smiled fondly at her daughter and replied that she very much doubted whether Mrs. Siddons would agree with that casting.

Ignoring her mother's pessimism, Noelle danced enthusiastically around the small, shabby room. "I loved it when you told me that story. Especially the part where Orlando finally meets his Rosalind in the Forest of Arden and everybody gets married." She dropped to the floor, her eyes wistful. "I would so love to see a wedding. Maybe someday you can get married, and I could be in your wedding. Do you think I could, Mama?"

Daisy set down the musky cologne she had been dabbing in the hollow of her throat and turned to her daughter, who was regarding her solemnly. She experienced a familiar warmth as she gazed at the beautiful topaz eyes and the little elfin face surrounded by golden brown curls cut as short as Daisy's own.

"Aren't you happy, *enfant*, with just the two of us?"

"Of course I'm happy, Mama. But if you got married, I would have a father, and we shouldn't have to worry about the bills we can't pay." She paused thoughtfully. "And we could live in a beautiful house, and I could have a pony."

Daisy's laughter tinkled gaily. "Why, you little minx! You don't give a fig about my getting married. You just want a pony. Besides, you do have a father as you very well know. He just doesn't live with us."

"I know, Mama, and he is noble and handsome and rich!"

And I'm not precisely sure who he is, Daisy silently added, giving her hair one last reassuring pat. But it was no doubt true that he had been all three of those things.

That was such a happy time in her life. All those rich and titled gentlemen bringing her flowers and buying her trinkets and sharing her bed. She inspected her face critically. Now it was not so easy; the years had passed much too quickly.

"Don't plop so when you sit, Noelle. Lower yourself gracefully." She had spoken more sharply than she intended. "Remember, *chérie*, you have the blood of kings in your veins."

Anticipating her mother's next admonition, Noelle straightened in her chair, being careful not to lean against the back. "I do wish I could see him just once."

As much to herself as to Noelle, Daisy admonished, "I'm sure you do, *ma petite*, but it's so silly to waste time wishing for things that are impossible and worrying about what may or may not happen. It's much better to have fun: to dance, to play cards or buy a new hat."

"But you do have to worry or you won't have the money to buy the hat, Mama. And that's why I'm so happy. Not only will you be famous when Mr. Lackland lets you play Ophelia, but we'll be able to pay all our bills and even give Mrs. Muspratt the rent money so she'll stop looking at me with her nasty old face all pinched up."

Inwardly Daisy cursed herself for mentioning Ophelia to Noelle. She was such a solemn little thing, so intent on Daisy establishing herself as a famous actress. However, even Daisy's cheerfully optimistic nature would not permit her to place any great store in a brilliant future on the stage; at thirty, she was getting a bit long in the tooth. Besides, when Francis Lackland was watching her, he had undoubtedly been remembering the enjoyable tumble they had had the previous night on the floor of his sitting room.

Daisy's life as a demimonde had begun at fifteen when she escaped her tyrannical yeoman father by running away to London. She promptly lost her maidenhood to an elderly baronet who bought her muslins and silks that she had made up into slim, clinging gowns. She wore gold bracelets on her bare arms and ostrich plumes in her soft curls. He adored her; she made him feel young again, gay and carefree.

Soon after Daisy's eighteenth birthday, he died. She wept for a day and then resolved to make a career for herself in the theater. Although she was hired immediately for her beauty, managers were understandably reluctant to advance her beyond minor roles when they heard how thin her voice was, how lacking in dramatic range.

In the past few years even the smaller parts had become scarce, and her debts had climbed alarmingly. She found herself dependent upon the largess of her admirers. Unfortunately, the men who now sought her favors were no longer the charming and wealthy gentlemen of the *ton*. Instead, they were tradesmen and clerks, men who worked hard for their money and guarded it carefully.

Thinking of money always made Daisy's head ache, and now she stood abruptly and smoothed her pink frock. The new edging of white lace at the neck and hem was quite successful, she reflected, hoping, at the same time, that no one would recognize the refurbished garment.

"I'm going out, now, *chérie*. Tuck yourself in as soon as I leave." She kissed Noelle on her soft, dimpled chin. *"Bonsoir, enfant."*

"Bonsoir, Mama." Noelle closed the door behind her mother and then climbed into the bed they shared, pulling the covers up to her chin. She was asleep almost instantly.

It was only a few hours later that Daisy raced through the streets back to her lodgings. The night had turned bitter, and the raw wind tore viciously at her cloak. She rounded the last corner and rushed up to the house, clutching the key in her numb fingers. Fumbling clumsily with the lock, she finally turned it only to have a gust of icy wind catch the door. Daisy clutched at it desperately, just saving it from crashing into the wall and rousing the vigilant landlady. Breathlessly she climbed the stairs, her feet noiseless on the wooden treads.

She let herself into the sitting room and, without taking off her cloak, began tossing the few belongings she had not yet pawned with those of her child into a large valise and a bandbox decorated with a pleasant scene from Regency Park.

Only after she was done did she cross the room to the child curled peacefully in their narrow bed, her breathing deep and even. "Noelle, wake up." She shook the small child gently and whispered, "Wake up, sweetheart."

Noelle's lids opened heavily, then closed, and then opened again.

"You must get up and dress quickly." She pulled the covers off the child and began tossing clothing at her. "Put these on. You'll have to dress warmly, child. It's bitterly cold outside."

"What's happened, Mama? Where are we going?" Noelle's clear voice cut into the silence of the room.

"*Shh!* There's not time to explain now. Hurry! We must leave very, very quietly." Daisy thrust the sleepy child into her garments, handed her the bandbox, and then led her quietly down the stairs and out into the bitter night. She carried the heavy valise herself.

Wordlessly Noelle followed, clutching her mother's cloak. The bandbox bumped against her thin legs. When it was caught by an icy gust, it fought against her, the silken cord cutting deeply into her fingers. Sometimes she stumbled; once she slipped on an icy puddle and landed painfully on her hip. But she did not protest. The fear in her mother's face drove her on.

They fled across cobbled streets and dark lanes, through frozen alleyways and past stinking tenements. The cold crept through Noelle's clothing until she was shivering violently. She began to whimper softly, but still she did not protest.

Finally they reached the river. Spanned by a massive stone bridge, it stretched inky black and uninviting on both sides of them. Noelle followed her mother onto the bridge and then, abruptly, Daisy stopped and stared at her surroundings. She seemed confused, disoriented.

"It's the river, Mama," Noelle prompted hesitantly.

"The river?" Daisy's eyes were vague; they chilled Noelle far more than the cold. She stood there quietly, unnaturally still.

Noelle looked around her. Four square recesses were set into each side of the stone bridge. In one of these an old crone huddled; in another, two urchins slept. Noelle led Daisy to one of the empty niches and gently pushed her down against the cold stone wall where there would be some shelter from the bite of the wind. She crouched next to her.

"Mama, what has happened?"

Daisy looked at her blankly.

"Tell me what has happened," Noelle pleaded.

The shadow lifted from Daisy's eyes. It was replaced by a terror so stark that Noelle recoiled.

"Newgate!"

The name of the infamous debtors' prison hung between them like a death sentence. "They are coming for me. This very morning they are coming to take me to Newgate. The watchman on Oyster Lane is my friend. He overheard two men talking. I'm to be jailed for my debts."

Daisy clutched Noelle to her and began to cry bitterly. "We can never go back," she said, sobbing.

The next day they found crude lodgings in a drab, crowded tenement. By pawning Daisy's few remaining belongings, they were able to buy food and pay their rent in the months that followed. Finding work, however, proved impossible for Daisy.

She was afraid to inquire at any of the theaters on the chance that she would be recognized, but she had no other skills and was so frivolous in appearance that no one would take her on for heavier work.

Gradually she began to lose interest in her own life, caring only about her daughter. Where before she had been a loving, if somewhat careless, parent, now she was obsessed with everything Noelle said and did. She harped at her to watch her diction, walk properly, behave like a lady. Terrified that Noelle would pick up the strident accent of the streets, she forbade her to play with any of the swarms of ragged children who glutted the chokingly overcrowded tenements.

They were empty-eyed urchins, many with swollen bellies and festering sores on their bodies. In Noelle, who looked and spoke so differently from them, they found a target for their own wretchedness. They called her "Highness," bowing when she passed them and then sticking out scrawny legs to send her sprawling headlong onto the slimy streets. They mocked her speech and assaulted her with obscenities.

Noelle ran to her mother, but Daisy could not seem to comprehend what was happening. Noelle was a pariah, out of her element and unable to defend herself. Helplessness was something the others understood. Seeing it in her, their abuse intensified. They chased her through the streets, hurling filth from the gutters at her.

Finally, when a group of boys held her down and urinated on her, something inside her snapped. Dry-eyed and furious, she fought them. She was beaten badly, but not before she had done some damage of her own. From that day on she no longer heeded whether there was only one or an entire group. She took them all on. Each time she lost a fight, the incident repeated itself again and again in her mind, Noelle learned from her mistakes, determined not to repeat them. She found that, if she could survive the initial brutal assault, she could outlast her antagonist. Having been better nourished than the other children, she had a wiry strength that drove her on after they were exhausted. She began to choose her opponents more carefully, refusing to be drawn into a fight she knew she couldn't win.

By the end of her first year among them, they had learned to leave her alone and even accorded her a grudging, if distant, respect. They still called her "Highness," but no longer to mock her. It was the only name they knew her by; her real name had been lost to everyone but her mother.

In time Daisy's tiny horde of money was exhausted. For two days they had no food.

In the evening of the second day, Daisy pressed her lips to Noelle's hair and slipped out into the night. She had nothing left to pawn, nothing left to sell except herself. The next morning she returned, bringing with her two savory meat-filled pastries, a bag of new potatoes, and half a plum cake.

Daisy's unexplained disappearances continued, and gradually Noelle became used to them. Sometimes Daisy returned with food or coins, sometimes empty-handed. Once she stumbled in almost unconscious. Blood dripped from the corner of her mouth, and her eye was badly bruised and swollen shut. Noelle cleansed her gently and helped her onto the rough sacking that formed Daisy's bed.

When she pressed her mother for an explanation, Daisy only smiled at her vaguely and murmured, "Don't fret, my pet. Remember, you have the blood of kings."

At night the eight-year-old child sat by her mother's sleeping form. Hugging her knees with her thin arms, she thought about what Daisy had said. Surely only wonderful things should be happening to a little girl with the blood of kings. She shouldn't ever be dirty or hungry or have to wear such ugly clothes.

Something cold clutched at Noelle's heart. What was going to happen to them? She looked at Daisy. Although her mother was only thirty-one, the past year had prematurely aged her. Her skin was rough and lined, her shiny curls were now drab and tangled, covered by an old gray shawl. Daisy had lived on hope and pleasure, and now that the dreams were gone, she was barely able to survive.

One morning, before Daisy was awake, Noelle donned a shirt and a pair of canvas trousers she had found. Biting on her bottom lip, she used a dull knife as she concentrated on sawing off her hair until it was as short as a boy's. She picked up a rough piece of sacking, quietly let herself out of their dingy cellar, and walked to the river.

A group of urchins were scattered across the bank, searching for pieces of coal dropped by the bargemen. They were the mudlarks, young scavengers who collected bits of coal to sell to the poor and pieces of metal that brought a farthing a pound as scrap.

Noelle watched the boys from a distance and then began to search the banks herself. She realized she had started too late; only the smallest pieces of coal were left. She picked them up anyway and tied them securely in the sacking she had brought. Soon she noticed the boys rolling up their breeches and wading barefoot into mud that came up to their knees.

Noelle settled herself on the bank and began turning up her own breeches. She looked up to see a gangly red-headed boy about her own age approaching her.

"Yer new 'ere, ain't ya? Name's Sweeney." He thrust out a coal-blackened hand.

Noelle took it gingerly. "I'm N–N–Neal," she stammered. "Neal Dorian."

Sweeney's green eyes twinkled mischievously. "Neal? That's a right queer name for a girl, it is."

Noelle's heart sank. How had he found her out so quickly?

As if reading her thoughts, the boy grinned and said, "It's yer walk. Yer take them bloomin' little steps. Bloke 'round 'ere'd die first afore 'e'd walk like that, 'e would."

Something about the boy's friendly face made Noelle decide to trust him. "I knew they'd run me out if they suspected I was a girl. Do you think any of the others noticed?"

"Them?" He dismissed the others contemptuously. "Oh, they'd 'ave noticed sooner or later, but they miss a lot, they do. Got no imagination. The way I see it, the only way ter get along is ter 'ave a bit of imagination. That way ya can anticipate, if ya get me meanin'. Stay one step ahead of the rest."

Noelle listened avidly to Sweeney's philosophy and thought him very wise and worldly. "How did you ever learn so much?" she asked with admiration.

"Just bein' 'round and keepin' me eyes open," Sweeney responded, tucking his thumbs into the waist of his tattered breeches.

Noelle's eyes lit up with hope. "Do you think you could teach me? My mother's sick." She hesitated. "Not quite right in the head." It was the first time Noelle had admitted it, even to herself.

"So yer got a mum, do ya?" Sweeney thrust his chest forward proudly. "I've been on me own since I were a babe. Learned all there is ter know about gettin' on." He regarded her critically. "First we'll do somethin' 'bout that bloomin' walk of yers. Can't 'ave me chums findin' out I'm 'elpin' a girl become a mudlark. Then I'll 'ave ter show ya the best spots. Teach yer 'ow to get the coal out of the mud wi' yer toes. Got a lot of work, we does. Don't expect yer'll ever really fit in, not with yer fancy way of talkin', but yer'll get on. Who better 'an Sweeney Pope 'imself ter teach ya!"

That day he taught Noelle where the coal was most likely to rest on top of the muck and where she would have to sink her legs into the ooze and feel for the lumps with her feet.

By the afternoon Noelle was caked with mud and soaked through to her skin, but she was pleased with herself. With her toes she could distinguish a lump of coal from a stone. She had found a small handful of iron rivets and nails and even one precious piece of copper. But, most importantly, she had acquired her first friend.

From that day on, Sweeney took Noelle in hand. He was a stern teacher, explaining everything to her once and then expecting her to remember it from then on. Together they walked the streets of London. For a penny they would hold a horse or sweep a path across a street so that the fashionable pedestrians would not soil their shoes. They became part of the world of the street people: the costermongers, porters, and prostitutes. Once Sweeney obtained a box of bootlaces that the children then hawked at two pairs for halfpence. Sweeney taught Noelle all he knew; in return, he received her total adoration.

With the arrival of cold weather, Daisy began to bring men back to her lodgings. The first time it happened Noelle was awakened by the sounds of Daisy's cries. She jerked up fearfully. "Mama, what's wrong?"

"Shh! Noelle, go back to sleep." Noelle did not miss Daisy's pleading tone.

A man's voice, ugly and menacing, growled from the direction of the pile of rags that made up Daisy's bed. " 'Ere now, who's that?"

"It's just my little girl. Pay her no mind. She won't bother us again."

"Good. I'll give 'er a cuff if I 'ear any more from 'er. Now, turn over."

"No!" Daisy's voice begged. "Not like that. Please!"

"Turn over, yer bitch!"

Noelle heard the sound of a stinging slap and the rustle of the crude bed. Daisy screamed once and then began whimpering. The pitiful sounds continued until well after the man had gone, but Noelle did not go to her mother's side to comfort her.

Instead she lay motionless, remembering all the obscene banter she had heard from the other mudlarks. Without realizing it, her quick mind had stored away every crude remark, every filthy gesture. Now they all came back to her, and for the first time she understood what happened between men and women. With that knowledge came shame and humiliation so intense, she trembled. She pressed her thin legs together tightly and clutched her arms to her chest. No one would ever use her so!

The following morning Noelle awakened at dawn, a cold ache surrounding her heart. Quietly she slipped on her trousers and shirt and prepared to let herself out of the cellar room. Involuntarily her eyes went to her mother.

Daisy lay facedown on the bed, her naked back exposed. There were ugly bruises on her shoulders and raw marks that looked like bites on her back. Three coins lay scattered on the scarred wooden table. Noelle picked them up and held them in her palm, the bitter tears running down her cheeks as she stared at them. They would eat well tonight, but the price had been too high.

Daisy's condition deteriorated. Sometimes she would sit for days in a dark corner of their hovel, only getting up to relieve herself or to eat a few bites of bread. Other times, when Noelle returned from the riverbanks, Daisy would be gone, reappearing with a man long after her daughter had gone to bed. Sometimes the men paid, sometimes they didn't. Daisy did not seem to notice.

These were the worst moments in Noelle's young life. She lay in bed with her small fingers shoved deeply into her ears, trying to block out the grunts of the harsh men who heaved over her mother. Sometimes they would strike Daisy, making her whimper with pain. Other times she lay soundlessly enduring whatever they did to her.

Noelle became desperately afraid of men. She recoiled if a man brushed against her. When the friendly old peddler who sold apples greeted her, she rushed past him with her eyes averted. Other than Sweeney Pope, she had never known the kindness of a male, and now, except for him, she feared them all.

Tragically her friendship with Sweeney Pope was cut short. On her ninth birthday, Noelle stood outside the forbidding stone walls of Newgate as crowds pushed and shoved past her, peddlers hawked their wares, and carriages clattered by. Inside, a hangman slipped a noose around the neck of Sweeney Pope. The child was executed for the theft of two oranges, his death to serve as an example to others of the bad end that came to those who did not obey the law.

When Noelle was ten, Daisy stopped eating. "Please, Mum," Noelle begged, her eyes large and solemn, "just eat this. Just two bites, that's all." Noelle tried to press small morsels of food on her.

"Eat it for me," Daisy murmured, staring listlessly as a rat darted into a corner. "You have the blood of kings, my precious one. You will be so beautiful some day, so beautiful." Her frail voice faded. She began to cry pitifully.

In early April, on a balmy day full of the promise of spring, Daisy died. She was buried in an unmarked grave in Potter's Field. Only Noelle stood beside her grave.

Tall for ten, all elbows and knees, she wept silently, tears streaming down her thin face, her nose running. She had loved her mother desperately, but she vowed she would never be like her. She would make her own way; she would survive.

PART ONE

Highness

Chapter One

Noelle Dorian was possibly the best pickpocket in Soho. This distinction was not given lightly and, indeed, had often been the subject of much debate in the illegal gin shops that flourished in the area.

"I'm tellin' ya, no one can 'old a candle to 'er." The speaker, a fat, balding man clad in a greasy smock, waved a tin mug in the air to punctuate his remarks. " 'Ighness is the best I ever seen, and, believe me, I seen 'em all in me time."

"No, there yer wrong." Absentmindedly his scabby-faced companion picked a louse from his hair and squeezed it between his thumb and forefinger. "Oh, 'Ighness is good, that I'll not deny. But she can't match Gentleman Jack, the way 'e was afore the Runners caught 'im and seed 'im 'ang. She's too picky, she is. You watch 'er. She won't go right into the 'Aymarket after the toffs. 'Angs on the outskirts, so ter speak, where the toffs ain't as likely ter be and where pockets ain't as well lined with the ready."

"Aye, yer may be right there, me friend. No doubt but wot Gentleman Jack took in more than she does, but 'e wasn't as smart as 'Ighness, not by 'alf." The fat man pounded one filth-encrusted fist on the table. "Blimey! I never seen anything like the way she decks 'erself out like a whore and swings 'er arse up ter some unsuspectin' bloke! Except fer 'er tits, she's plain as a pikestaff, but I don't mind tellin' yer, when she leans over and they 'ang out of the top of that green dress . . ."

At this point the speaker abruptly stopped and pulled a much-abused handkerchief out of his pocket to mop a film of sweat that had suddenly appeared on his brow.

"Ha!" his companion hooted. "Gettin' yerself all 'ot over the 'Ighness's tits, are ya? A bleedin' lot of good it'll do ya. Fer all that she looks like a whore, ya can bet there's not a man 'as ever touched 'er. Even if she did let ya near 'er, she'd treat yer same as th'others. Rub 'erself against yer while she talks real quiet like about 'ow she wants to meet ya at the Cock and Pheasant fer a good tumble. All the while goin' through yer pockets and takin' what she pleases."

"The Cock and Pheasant!" The fat man was so overcome with merriment, he choked on the cheap gin he had been swilling, spraying it in droplets over his companion as he tried to catch his breath. Recovering himself, he refilled his mug and continued. " 'Ow many times 'ave we 'ad one of them poor blokes come up ter us axin' us where the Cock and Pheasant might be?"

"Last one that axed me," his companion responded, once more digging his fingers into his scalp, "I tole 'im ter try Drury Lane, I did. Blimey if I was gonna be the one ter tell 'im there weren't no Cock and Pheasant anywhere and 'e'd better check 'is pockets."

At that very moment the subject of the gin shop discussion was huddled in a dark, peeling doorway near Glasshouse Street, trying to find some protection from the night's drizzle. Although she was near the Haymarket, as the gin drinkers had predicted, she had not ventured out into the actual bustle of that famous center of London's nightlife, for the memory of Sweeney Pope's tragic fate had never left her. As a pickpocket, the risks were great enough without hobnobbing with the upper classes. Besides, the blue devils, as the members of the newly created police force were called, were vigilant about protecting the *ton*.

Underneath her damp, shabby cloak Noelle wore a once-elegant emerald-green satin gown. The material was now faded and badly stained under the arms and across the skirt, the black lace trim tattered at the deep rim of the bodice. In some places it was evident that the tired seams of the garment had split open. Although Noelle had sewn them together again, the uneven stitches and bright yellow thread offered mute testimony to her ineptness as a seamstress.

Even though she was not quite eighteen, she looked ten years older. The tiny elfin face that Daisy had loved so much was smeared with scarlet rouge; the topaz eyes, no longer luminous, were dim and darkly outlined with kohl. She was tall but excruciatingly thin, with hollow cheeks and a dirty neck. Her complexion was almost cadaverous, an effect that was heightened by her unfortunate hair. In an attempt to keep it free of vermin, she had cropped it just below her earlobes. Since she had no mirror and only a knife to do the cutting, it was ragged and uneven. It was also orange. Not a deep auburn or a warm chestnut, but a hue that most closely resembled a string of withered carrots. When she had first made up her mind to pose as a prostitute, she had decided to alter her hair to make herself look older. But repeated use of the unstable dyes had resulted in a noxious frizz that was now sorrowfully decorated with a single, limp ostrich plume.

Her appearance was so unappealing that at first glance it was difficult to tell how posing as a whore had helped her become such a successful pickpocket. But a more careful assessment revealed a certain sensuousness about the mouth, an appealing huskiness of voice, and, of course, pushing themselves above the top of her plunging neckline, the swelling breasts that had become an object of speculation among men and boys throughout Soho. All of these qualities hinted at the great beauty that poverty had stolen from Noelle Dorian.

At the moment Noelle was trying to decide whether she should stick it out a bit longer, in the hopes that the drizzle would let up, or return to her room. Just a little longer, she decided, for the truth was she was short of cash to pay the rent for her lodgings. She had been careless not to have watched her pennies better; now she stood in danger of losing her privacy, and she couldn't bear that. The room was tiny and squalid, but at least it was not in a cellar and she was alone.

She grimaced as she thought of the years after Daisy's death and the damp hovel she had been forced to share with as many as fifteen inhabitants crowded together at one time. Most were orphans like herself, some younger and some older. She remembered twelve-year-old Meg Watkins standing guard over her infant to keep the rats from feeding off his tiny body while he slept. And Bardy, the old man who had befriended them, guarding their meager possessions while they were out scrounging for food. He was nearly blind now, but he still lived in the hotel, and Noelle saw him as often as she could manage.

She had come up in the world since those early days. Not far, but enough to have her own room and a bit of food. And there's nobody who's going to make me give that up easily, she told herself as she peered down the narrow street in search of a likely mark. She knew she should be better off than she was, but she couldn't seem to set any money by. She was an easy touch. She smiled to herself as she thought of the little street urchins who now lived in the hovel from which she had escaped. Their bellies were fuller than hers had been because of the money she slipped Bardy to feed them.

At the sound of wooden wheels clattering on the cobblestones, Noelle looked up to see Billy the ragman approaching, pushing his grumbling cart down the deserted alley. She sighed, knowing the inevitability of what was coming.

"Well, if it ain't 'Ighness 'erself." He doffed his muddy cap and bowed mockingly. "And wot would 'Er 'Ighness be doin' so far from Buckingham 'ouse on a night like this? King Willie decide 'e don't want a pickpocket in 'is bed? Or did 'e just get tired of stickin' it ter a block of ice?"

Noelle stared stonily past him.

"Won't talk ter the likes o' me?" He abandoned his pushcart and shuffled up to her. "Someday, 'Ighness," he said, leering, revealing the rotted stubs of his front teeth, "yer gonna find out that yer ain't no different from the rest of us. Yer 'igh and mighty airs don't mean nothin.' "

Noelle leveled a cold glance at him. "Leave me alone," she retorted, clipping each word precisely.

Billy thrust his face inches from hers. She recoiled from his foul breath.

"I seen the way yer strut up ter them toffs, shakin' yer tits at 'em, leadin' 'em on so's all they think about's the fun they're gonna 'ave 'tween yer legs." He fingered himself obscenely through his filthy trousers. " 'Ow 'bout rubbin' up 'gainst old Billy, 'Ighness?" He stuck out one clawlike hand and reached toward her breast.

Noelle leaped back from him, pulling a lethal-looking knife from her pocket. She jabbed it in the air, stopping barely an inch from Billy's throat. "Get away from me, Billy, before I take a slice out of your filthy face." Her voice was menacing; her face a mask of determination.

He leaped back angrily. "God damn yer, bitch. One of these days somebody's gonna get yer, and ya won't soon forget it." A thin trail of spittle leaked from the corner of his mouth.

"Get away from me, you scum, or I'll fix you so you'll never put your dirty hands on another woman!"

Something in Noelle's face caused Billy to retreat hastily to his cart. He'd pushed the Highness too far. He thought of Jim Wheeler with the jagged red scar across his cheek. Others had found out too well what happened when they tangled with her. Muttering under his breath, he hobbled quickly down the alley, the cart creaking ominously at its unaccustomed speed.

Noelle was trembling as she slipped the sharp knife into the top of her boot. How much longer could she hold out against Billy and the others? She knew she was playing a dangerous game. Noelle shuddered as she watched two old hags with their leering faces and thick lips pass her. They'd been young once, but they'd sold their youth for a few pence and then spent the takings on bad gin.

How could they sell their bodies? Nothing, not even starvation, was as horrible as that. The memories of the men who had abused Daisy crowded unbidden into her mind. She had found her own way to get even with them, she thought grimly. It was not accidental that she had decided to pose as a prostitute. Each time she left a man lusting hungrily after her but ignorant of his empty pockets, she felt as though she had, in a small way, avenged Daisy's death.

The sound of deep laughter caught Noelle's attention. At the end of the narrow alley two men stood, caught in the soft yellow glow from the lone streetlamp. Noelle's breath quickened. She knew by their dress that they were gentlemen. What were they doing so far from the pleasures of the Haymarket?

She thought carefully. One of the reasons she was successful was that she did not take chances. Toffs were bad luck; she had made it a rule to stay away from them. Only once had she broken that rule, but he had been old and feeble. She had also been well rewarded, she reminded herself. The pockets of the upper classes were filled with silver. Expensive watches rested at the ends of golden fobs. Their silk handkerchiefs alone could fetch as much as a shilling from the pawnbrokers in Drury Lane.

Of course there were problems. Many of these gentlemen now carried paper bank notes in their pockets instead of silver. She bit thoughtfully at her bottom lip. Trying to use one of these bank notes was tricky. None of the street peddlers would take them, and despite the upper-class accent she had struggled so hard to maintain, she would have no luck passing the paper on to a more respectable merchant without raising suspicion. Of course, she could always sell the notes to the pawnbroker, but her practical nature rebelled at that because the amount received for the notes was always significantly less than their face value. Silently she laughed at herself. Here she was worrying about getting rid of the paper money before she even had it.

She looked again at the two men. Although she couldn't see them clearly, she sensed they were young. She needed money so badly, she just might risk it. I've been lucky so far, she reminded herself—but no, that wasn't quite true. It hadn't just been luck; she had been careful. She had not taken foolish chances. And setting upon two rich young gentlemen was foolish. She stood there indecisively, then reluctantly began to turn away just as the shorter of the two stumbled, barely saving himself from falling onto the muddy cobblestones.

Why, he's drunk, Noelle thought, her interest caught anew. That does change the odds a bit, doesn't it?

Sidestepping a pile of rotting garbage, she moved from the doorway that had provided such poor protection from the drizzle and stealthily crept closer to the men, finally concealing herself in a small recess between two buildings.

The shorter of the two turned. He had a boyish face with full cheeks and small merry eyes. Unruly sandy hair peeked out from under a tall beaver hat.

"Quinn, old boy," he addressed his companion, "sorry to be such a deuced poor guide, but I'm afraid I've got us lost." He punctuated this pronouncement with a loud hiccup. "Bradley's Hotel should have been right here." Gesturing vaguely into the night air, he took a final swallow from the bottle he held before passing it on to his companion.

"Don't worry, Tom." His companion's voice was deep and strong, the American accent unfamiliar to Noelle. "At least we'll both be spared an unpleasant evening with Simon." He drank deeply from the bottle.

Noelle strained to see the face of the speaker, the man called Quinn, but he remained turned away from her. He was even taller than she had first imagined. Powerful shoulders thrust against the seams of his coat. He was hatless, and the raindrops in his raven-black hair sparkled in the glow of the streetlamp.

"Come now, Quinn, your father's not a bad sort," Thomas expostulated, lowering himself unsteadily onto an adjacent doorstep. "The old boy could have left you home in America to run the company. Instead you're here, renewing our schoolboy friendship and enjoying London's elegant nightlife." He laughed uproariously at the irony of his own poor joke.

"I wish to God he had," Quinn replied sourly, handing the bottle back to Thomas. "All he's done these past three months is lecture me about my unsuitability to be the heir of Copeland and Peale."

Noelle's ears picked up at this reference. She had no idea that Copeland and Peale was a small but prestigious builder of oceangoing ships; she only knew that such an imposing name undoubtedly meant money.

If I could just see his face, she thought. I've no intention of taking him on cold sober. She shuddered slightly as she again observed his broad, powerful shoulders.

Quinn continued bitterly, "My God, I think he's gone crazy. He can't seem to look to the future. He's going to ruin Copeland and Peale with his damned pig-headed stubbornness."

Privately Thomas thought Simon wasn't the only stubborn one, but he wisely kept this opinion to himself.

"He refuses to put up any capital for experimentation. The initial studies I've done on hull shape are staggering, but they need to be extended. We could revolutionize the China trade, but Simon refuses to take them seriously. Even conservatively, Tom, Copeland and Peale ships could make the New York to Canton run in one hundred and ten days and be back in less than ninety."

"Ninety days?" Tom didn't bother to hide his incredulity. "It's impossible! I don't blame Simon for being skeptical."

"No, it's not impossible," Quinn insisted. "With some radical hull revisions, our ships will do ten knots or better. Unfortunately, I'm not the only one doing experiments with hull shapes. If Copeland and Peale isn't to be hopelessly outdated in fifteen years, we need to start now—more hull experiments, a model, and then a ship. I don't know how Simon can be so blind. I've a mind to get out now and start on my own. He's going to bankrupt us, the bastard, or, at the very least, turn us into second-rate shipbuilders."

Thomas's eyes widened at the venom in Quinn's tone. "Now, now, old boy, have another drink. With more of this good rum in you, things won't seem so bad."

As Quinn turned to take it, the full glow of the streetlamp fell on his rugged face. Noelle drew in her breath sharply. The American was young, in his mid- to late twenties, and incredibly handsome, but it was an unconventionally rugged handsomeness, foreign to Englishmen. His skin was bronzed. The black hair Noelle had observed earlier tumbled over a broad forehead. His cheekbones were high; his nose strong, narrow at the bridge; and the line of his jaw clean and hard. Dominating all was a pair of piercing eyes, black as chipped onyx.

The tiny hairs at the back of her neck prickled. Her instincts, finely honed from living by her wits for so long, warned her that this was not a man with whom to trifle.

"At least Simon should be pleased at the way you've been received socially. With half the hopeful mothers in London pushing their unmarried daughters at you, you've become the catch of the season," Thomas remarked, not without envy.

Noelle looked at Quinn more sharply. She tried to imagine why rich ladies with beautiful clothes and plenty to eat would possibly want to marry this menacing stranger. He was undoubtedly handsome, but couldn't they sense the savagery in him? Wives were property, owned by their husbands. They would have to be daft to put themselves under this man's control.

"Believe me, Thomas, it's not something I'd wish on my worst enemy!" Quinn took a thin cheroot from his pocket and lit it. "All those overdressed, overstuffed matrons pushing their whey-faced daughters at me. It's enough to turn a man against women!"

"By Jove!" Thomas hooted. "Quinn Copeland a misogynist! That'll never wash, old boy. No, from what I've seen, you're a marked man, marked for the parson's mousetrap!"

"Shut up, Tom," Quinn growled. He pulled deeply from the bottle, swallowing the rum as though it were water.

Thomas grinned, enjoying Quinn's discomfort. "You can tell me. Which one of our high-steppers are you going to choose as your bride?"

"Dammit, Tom, not you too!"

"Oh, Simon's been at you, has he?"

"For years," Quinn responded, leaning indolently against the lamppost, the smoke from his cheroot curling around his black hair. "At one point he told me he was no longer requesting that I marry, he was ordering it."

"That's rather heavy-handed, even for Simon, isn't it?"

"I thought so," Quinn replied sardonically.

Even in his befuddled state, Thomas sensed there was more to the breach between Simon and his headstrong son than disagreements over either the management of Copeland and Peale or Quinn's marital status. "If he wants a Copeland bride so much, why doesn't he marry again himself?"

"You miss the point, Tom. Simon, like many Americans, is a self-made man. He rose from being a carpenter's apprentice when he was thirteen to one of the greatest shipbuilders in the world at forty. Now, at fifty, he wants to forget that he was ever a carpenter's apprentice. He wants the name Copeland to be as respected as Winthrop or Livingston or Franklin. Although he won't admit it, he has visions of a Copeland dynasty, oldest son to oldest son. But for this dynasty, he needs a woman. Not any woman, naturally. Only someone of impeccable breeding can be the next Copeland bride." Quinn flicked the last of the cheroot into a puddle where it hissed sibilantly as it went out. "Of course, he also believes the right wife will settle me down and make me respectable."

Thomas snickered, his words beginning to slur together. "See it all now. Quinn Copeland, august citizen, pillar of the church, cornerstone of the Copeland dynasty, arrives home promptly at six o'clock. Kisses the pudding-faced wife at the door."

"Pinches the maid," Quinn interjected, grinning lecherously.

"God's life, no, man!" Thomas exclaimed with mock horror. "Not in front of the children!"

"All six of them," Quinn said piously.

"Six! You forgot the twins!"

"Eight?" Quinn roared, pitching the now-empty bottle into the overflowing gutter. "Damn it, Thomas Sully, you've gone too far!"

With an unsuccessful attempt at dignity, Thomas raised himself from the stoop. "I'm not the one who went too far. She's *your* potato-faced wife!"

"You said pudding-faced. Make up your mind!"

"Pudding, potato—either way you'll only be able to make love to her with her nightgown covering her ugly face!"

"You're talking about my wife, you bastard," Quinn bellowed as he playfully cuffed his already staggering companion.

Noelle observed the two of them trading friendly obscenities and throwing harmless punches at each other. They were oblivious to the damage the drizzle was inflicting on their beautifully tailored garments. Could feed a family of six for a year on what those clothes must have cost, she thought. The Englishman was as drunk as a blacksmith on payday.

She studied the American again, his head thrown back in laughter, rain glistening on his chiseled face. Her uneasiness would not leave her. Then she thought of the solitary room she desperately wanted to keep and the money she needed to do so.

Noelle made up her mind. She would give the American wide berth; Thomas Sully was her mark.

Drawing two breaths to calm herself, she stepped out of her hiding place and walked toward them, wiggling her scrawny hips provocatively and smiling seductively in perfect imitation of the women she had watched so often.

The two men, arms thrown around each other's shoulders, had broken into a lively, if somewhat bawdy tune:

> "What is a friar wi' a bald head?
> A staff to beat a cuckold dead?
> What is a gun that shoots point blank,
> And hits between a maiden's flank?"

They broke off their song as Noelle approached them, stopping several feet in front of Thomas. Resting her hands brazenly on her narrow hips, she smiled boldly at him.

"Evenin', Guv'nor. 'Ow 'bout a bit of fun?" She broadened her vowels and dropped her consonants with ease, a practice she had astutely adopted so that she did not stand out from the rest of the prostitutes.

"Well, well," Thomas slurred drunkenly, "if it isn't one of London's fairest flowers, a fashionable impure, gracing us with her presence." He doffed his tall beaver hat and bowed deeply in front of her. The movement would have been gallant had he not spoiled it by belching loudly at its conclusion.

Noelle giggled coquettishly. "Gor, sir, ain't you the one." Looping one of her arms through his, she moved closer to him, preparing to pick her moment carefully. He smelled of tobacco and rum, a not altogether unpleasant combination. Deliberately she pressed her body next to his, tilting her shoulders forward to reveal more of her breasts.

Looking at him through partially closed lids, she whispered seductively, "Yer a fine lookin' cove, y'are, Guv."

Quinn snorted with amusement.

"What the devil are you laughing at?" Thomas challenged, shooting Quinn a superior glance. "This young lady is undoubtedly one of the more experienced judges of men in London."

"I don't doubt she is experienced, Tom," Quinn retorted, a smile playing lazily at the corners of his lips, "but I question how discerning she is."

Noelle felt a small stab of shame at their jests. What do you expect? she chided herself. You want them to believe the worst.

The American's eyes raked over her impersonally, taking in the tawdry ostrich plume stuck in her frizzled hair, the painted cheeks, and her partially exposed breasts.

Noelle's face burned under his gaze. I must ignore him, she told herself; do what I'm here to do and get away quick as I can.

She squeezed Thomas's arm to distract him. "Oh, ain't you the strong one. There are them that says yer can tell a lot 'bout a man from the size of 'is arms."

She flirted outrageously as, with lightning speed and a feather touch, she extracted a heavy watch from his pocket and unobtrusively slid it into one of the large pockets she had sewn into her gown for just such a purpose. Keeping her eyes on Thomas, she continued her charade, all the while looking for any sign that he was aware of what had happened. He was grinning drunkenly at her, obviously enjoying her flattery. Conscious of the comfortable weight of the watch deep in her pocket, Noelle began to feel easier about the encounter. Still, she cautioned herself, she must do nothing to raise his suspicions.

"I can tell yer a flash cove with the 'igh-flyers, I can," Noelle bantered, tickling his lapel with her forefinger. "I don't mind sayin' I've earned my fair share of compliments too, ducks." Her pink tongue flickered across her vermilion lips. "Let me show yer wot I mean."

Eyeing her full breasts, Thomas was momentarily tempted, but the sight of her sunken cheeks and garishly painted face immediately brought him back to his senses.

"My dear lady, you tempt me beyond belief. If I only had the

time, I would be delighted to partake of the pleasure you offer."
Ever the gentleman, he tipped his hat to her.

Noelle giggled, whether from amusement or relief, even she
could not have said. "Yer a rare one, Guv'nor, y'are." She waved
three fingers coyly at him in farewell. "Anytime yer want me, just
look fer me at the Cock and Pheasant."

Turning her back on the two men, she sauntered away, swinging
her hips gaily. Her spirits leaped as she furtively caressed the
smooth, solid object lodged deeply in her pocket. She had done it!
This watch would do more than pay her rent. She could buy a new
dress, perhaps even a hat.

Absorbed in her reflections, she was unaware of the footsteps
approaching her until it was too late. Fingers like steel talons bit
painfully into the thin flesh of her emaciated arms, jerking her to a
stop. The sodden ostrich plume flew from her hair and landed in a
rain-swollen ditch. Her heart racing, she spun around to find the
American staring coldly, his eyes frozen black flints.

"Not so fast."

"Beggin' yer pardon, sir?" she stammered.

Effortlessly he pushed her against the damp stone wall behind
her, cutting off any avenue of escape. Now his large hands rested
lightly on her shoulders, but she was not deceived. She knew that
her slightest movement would once again bring the pain of those
steely fingers biting into her tender flesh.

"Well?"

Gathering her scattered wits, she kept her voice steady. "Gor,
sir, yer needn't be so rough. If yer was wantin' me, just tell me
so." She tried to smile coquettishly. "Say 'alf an hour at the Cock
and Pheasant?"

"That's not what I'm after, and you know it."

Thomas, gasping in astonishment at Quinn's actions, hurried to
catch up with them. "I say, Quinn, what's this about?"

Without taking his eyes from her, the American ran his hands
down her sides to her waist.

She began to struggle. " 'Ere, now, don't you be touchin' me
like that."

The hands went back to her shoulders and then moved to the top
of her bodice. She gasped as he cupped her breasts, and her
struggles became more frantic. With his forearm, he pinned her
against the wall so he could continue his leisurely search of her

body. Finally he found what he wanted. Thrusting his hand into the hidden pocket, he pulled out the gold watch and dangled it accusingly in the air inches from Noelle's stricken face.

"In addition to being a whore, she seems to be a first-rate pickpocket."

"Good God!" Thomas was unable to conceal his embarrassment. "She played me for a fool."

Quinn handed Thomas his watch, then looked at Noelle impersonally. "Don't be too hard on yourself, Tom. She's an accomplished thief. I've seen this trick pulled before, but even at that, I almost missed it. She's probably been at this game for years."

Noelle stood frozen in a blind, nameless panic. What a fool she had been! She had betrayed herself by not following her instincts. At her first sight of the American, she had known he presented too great a risk. *"One of these days somebody's gonna get yer and ya won't soon forget it."* Billy the ragman's prophetic words came back to her.

Suddenly she remembered the knife tucked safely in her boot, the one place the American's burning hands had not searched. How could she get it out? She looked up at the two men, her eyes wide and pleading.

"Please, 'elp me. I'm feelin' so sick. I feel like I . . . ." Closing her eyes, she fell to the ground, being careful to tuck her boot under her full skirts as she landed.

"Dash it, man. What a bloody pickle this is turning into! Leave her here so we can continue our drinking in a more congenial atmosphere." Thomas began to walk away.

"Not so fast, Tom," Quinn interrupted. He looked down at the still form at his feet. The side of her face was pressed against the edge of a rain-swollen pothole; the spiked ends of her hair dipped into the muddy depression. He felt a flash of pity for the sorry creature and looked around for a drier place to deposit her. He spotted a doorway protected by an overhang.

Through half-closed eyes, Noelle saw the American begin to lean over her. Before he could touch her, she tore the precious knife from her boot, leaped nimbly to her feet, and thrust it menacingly in front of her.

"Not one step farther, or I'll cut out yer cold-blooded 'eart, I will, and dangle it in front of yer scurvy face!"

"I don't think so." He gave her an odd, twisted smile, his momentary pity forgotten. Slowly he began to circle her, his arms flexed at his sides.

She backed away, holding the knife up like a talisman to protect her from evil. She looked like a small animal fighting for survival: hair in wild disarray, enormous eyes shooting murderous sparks, scarlet mouth compressed with determination.

Relentlessly he advanced on her, his weight easily balanced on the balls of his feet.

Was he insane? she wondered frantically. She had a knife, and he was unarmed, yet he seemed to have no fear. And then, as her heel touched something solid, she knew why. He had backed her into a wall!

Insane with rage, she lunged at him, ready to thrust the knife into his mocking face. But her upraised arm presented an easy target. With one swift motion he grabbed her wrist and twisted it mercilessly. Yelping with pain, her hand involuntarily opened.

Incredulously she watched the knife arch through the air and then tumble downward. The clatter of metal on cobblestones signaled her defeat. With disbelief she stared at it, its shiny blade already dulled by the muddy raindrops.

Uproarious laughter shattered the moment. Noelle's eyes flew to Thomas. He was doubled over, tears of drunken merriment streaming down his red face.

"Half the bucks in London wouldn't dare cross you," he guffawed, gasping for air, "but this little strumpet, not weighing much more than seven stone, has the unmitigated gall to take you on all by herself." He slapped his knees, jovially. "What a great story this is going to make at Watier's."

Quinn flashed his companion a crooked smile as he tightened his grip on Noelle's arm. "Don't be so quick with your tales, Tom. I might be forced to share your experience. I'm sure everyone will enjoy hearing how she relieved you of your watch."

As he spoke he reached down and picked up the knife. Noelle wanted to weep with frustration and fury as she watched it disappear into his pocket.

"Aha! I daresay you're right." Thomas chuckled. "Still, it might be worth the embarrassment. How she went after you! She was just as determined to escape from you as you have been to escape all those unmarried females. You're two of a kind!"

"The devil we are!" Quinn retorted.

"Of course you are. You can't deny that. You're both totally unprincipled in your dealings with the opposite sex. You two deserve each other." Thomas smiled mischievously. "Now, she'd be a fitting bride for you."

"In a pig's eye, you bastard!" Quinn grinned, amused at his friend's baiting.

"I can see her now on your wedding day: a beautiful gown, a lovely bouquet, and a knife held between her teeth." They both roared with laughter. "And the father of the groom beaming with delight to see his only son and heir so well married."

Quinn's laughter froze. Slowly a look of cold calculation crossed his face, and with it, a tremor of fear and apprehension shot through Noelle.

"That's it," Quinn said, his voice barely above a whisper. "That's the answer. I'm going to marry her."

Noelle stared at him in stunned disbelief.

"You're what?" Thomas cried.

"Don't you see, Tom?" Quinn explained, his excitement growing. "It's the perfect answer. I'm going to marry her."

"Are you insane?" Thomas shouted. "She's a whore!"

"Of course she is. That's the point." Still maintaining his iron grip on Noelle's thin arm, he slapped Thomas exuberantly across his shoulders with the other hand. "Picture Simon's face when I introduce him to my wife, the Copeland bride on whom he had pinned his hopes. It's the perfect revenge . . . for so many things."

A shadow crossed his features, and Noelle shuddered with dreadful premonition.

"By Jove, I think you're in earnest."

"Of course I am. Really, Tom," Quinn added with mock seriousness, "I'm disappointed in you. Marriage is no joking matter."

"Damn, man, it won't serve. You could have any of a dozen beauties. Why in the name of all that's holy do you want to stick yourself with a whore for a wife?"

"Use your head, Tom. If I married one of those blue bloods, I'd be gratifying Simon's fondest wish, and I have no intention of doing that or of spending the rest of my life shackled to one woman."

Thomas looked at Quinn blankly.

"Don't you understand, Tom? With this little trollop as my wife, I escape all of that. Look at her! Do you think Simon would chance anyone's discovering she's his daughter-in-law or give me an argument about packing her off?" He smiled sardonically. "I'll be legally married without the burden of a wife. And there'll be nothing Simon can do about it."

"Damnation, Quinn, don't be a fool!" Thomas exploded. "He would have the marriage annulled within a week."

"Yes"— Quinn hesitated thoughtfully—"that's a problem. The weak link in a perfect arrangement. The marriage has to be binding."

He turned to Noelle, distaste etched clearly on his face at the sight of her dirty neck and cropped hair, now releasing great, muddy droplets from the ends of the carrot strands. "I'm going to ask you a question, and God help you if you lie to me. I want the truth, do you understand?"

Noelle nodded mutely, but inside she was almost ill with the force of her anger and her fear. Why couldn't she fight this man? How had she let herself be drawn into this situation?

His eyes, dark and ominous, bored into her. "Are you diseased?"

She looked at him without comprehension.

"Diseased, girl! Do you have the French pox?"

Her face reddened with humiliation. She began to stutter an indignant denial, then stopped herself abruptly and gave him a wide, cunning smile. "Yes, sir, that I am. Cruelly diseased."

Before she knew what had happened he was shaking her viciously. "Don't toy with me. I demand the truth."

At the sight of the stubborn set of her jaw, he released her. "Never mind. You've already answered my question. She's not diseased, Tom, and, at least, her teeth are good, so, somehow, I'll consummate the marriage. Then Simon will have no way of annulling it without my consent. And you can be sure I'll never give him that."

Grinning, Thomas shook his head in disbelief and then grabbed Quinn's hand and began to pump it. "I'm on, old boy. Damnation! Of all the pranks we've pulled together, this one is the topper!"

Noelle stared at them incredulously. The American expected her to marry him, to give her body to him! She was livid with rage, directed as much at herself as it was at him. Enough of standing here like a ninnyhammer while he tried to take over her life!

"You bastard!" she shrieked. "Who the bloody 'ell do you think you are, telling me what to do. Nobody tells me anything, do you 'ear? And I wouldn't marry you if you was the friggin' King of England!"

Thomas looked at Quinn doubtfully. "Are you quite sure, old boy? I know it seems a good scheme, but I think it's only fair for me to point out that we're both rather drunk. Besides, she seems a bit—rough around the edges."

"Rough around the edges!" Quinn hooted with laughter. "Only you, Tom, could put it so tactfully. But the lady does seem to need some courting."

Taking Noelle firmly by the arm, he led her struggling form to the stoop of an apothecary shop closed for the night. "Sit here." Without giving her a chance to refuse, he pushed her down onto the step.

Although Noelle's fear was rapidly overcoming her anger, she was determined not to let him see how he intimidated her. Gathering her dignity about her like a suit of armor, she sat stiffly, almost primly. He hovered over her, resting one elegantly booted leg next to her skirts.

"Listen to me," he began, not ungently. "This marriage can only be to your advantage. I'll pay you well. All I'm asking from you is twenty-four hours of your time to go through the wedding ceremony and then spend the night performing your wifely duty." He lifted one eyebrow wryly. "You should be good at that."

Despite her fury at his effrontery, Noelle instinctively clung to the protective anonymity of the accent of the streets as she ranted at him through clenched teeth. "I won't do it, and I don't want yer bloody money. Nobody tells me wot to do, least of all someone like you!"

"What possible objection can you have?" Quinn was genuinely astonished by her refusal. He was offering her an opportunity that would change her whole life for the better. She would make more money with this one night's work than she'd ever dreamed possible.

But Noelle did not care if he offered her a royal fortune; the memories he brought back of the men who had used Daisy were too terrifying. No money, no comfort, no security, no luxuries, were worth submitting her body to this barbaric man.

"I don't 'ave to give you my reason. Yer nothin' to me, nothin', do you 'ear?" In final defiance she spat at him, hitting him full in the face.

As soon as she had done it she regretted her action. She could almost see the cold fury flowing through his body. Instinctively she braced herself, waiting for his attack.

His eyes raked her face mercilessly. "That was a mistake." Slowly and deliberately he removed his handkerchief and wiped off the spittle. "You no longer have any choice in the matter. Unless you want to be taken before the law for theft, you will do as I say."

"You can't make me." Her defiant words had a hollow ring.

"Oh? I think I can. Do you know what will be in store for you if I turn you over?"

Noelle's face paled. Those who made their living dishonestly feared the harshness of the English judicial system above all else.

"If you're lucky, it will be the gallows. If you're unlucky, transportation to Australia."

She drew in her breath sharply, her heart sinking at the thought of the stories she had heard of the convict ships.

As though reading her mind, he continued relentlessly, speaking of the men and women packed by the hundreds into the holds of the ships; of men turning into snarling animals and using the women freely. He talked of food, foul and filled with vermin; of the water, undrinkable; of disease running rampant—smallpox, dysentery, and cholera. For those who survived the trip, the nightmare was just beginning. The conditions at Botany Bay were harsh and inhumane, devastating to the human spirit.

Confident of her reaction, he waited patiently, watching the play of emotions on her face. Even Thomas was quiet, although visibly paler from Quinn's recitation of horrors.

Noelle's stomach pitched. He had her trapped. Her only hope lay in retrieving the knife he now held in his pocket. But you had your chance before, she reminded herself, for all the good it did you. Waving that blade and making threats won't work this time. This time you bloody well better be ready to kill him.

Noelle rose from the step. "You don't give me much choice, do you?" Although her words were those of capitulation, her look was defiant. "All right. I'll do wot you say."

Ignoring her eyes, which were blazing with hatred, Quinn turned to Thomas. "I'll need a special license tonight. Can you get it?"

"Special license?" Thomas puckered his forehead in thought and then snapped his fingers. "Yes. Yes, I believe I can."

"Also, I'll need a minister who won't ask too many questions. Know of anyone?"

"I've heard of a fellow. Not terribly respectable, mind you, but officially ordained."

"Good. Now we need a place to keep her while we make the arrangements."

"How about my parents' house? They're in the country, and the house is empty."

"And the servants?"

"They took everyone with them except the gardener, and he's off visiting his sister for the week. We can put her in the attic. It's at the back of the house where nothing can be noticed."

"Attic! I won't be locked up!"

"It sounds perfect." Quinn flashed Thomas a reckless grin as he gripped Noelle's bony wrist forcefully. "Come on, Tom. Let's be off."

Chapter Two

The Haymarket, linking Piccadilly with Trafalgar Square, was one of the most notorious locales of London's nightlife. Here, London's most fashionable citizens mingled with its least accepted. Curricles and tilburies barely missed the dust carts and brewers' drays that clattered down the street. Thieves, footpads, and pickpockets conjoined with the rich and powerful, each feeding off the other.

Prostitutes, gaily clad in ribboned and feathered bonnets, approached merchants' clerks and stonemasons. Although many of the women did not speak English, there was no language barrier in their trade; in rented rooms on the small streets near the Haymarket, they called out false endearments in French, Flemish, and German.

Barefoot children, some as young as six, clutched shoeblack boxes. Frequently they turned somersaults on the pavement as they scampered alongside carriages and cabs, trying to solicit customers.

Running patterers in greasy caps and patched breeches screamed scurrilous accounts of scandals and murders as they tried to hawk their penny papers. An enterprising urchin displaying "The Scarborough Tragedy" titillated bystanders with the highlights of the gallows confession of one Dempsey Tuttle, an unsavory baker who reputedly toasted his victims in a brick oven along with the day's batch of bread.

Quinn skillfully maneuvered the sporty phaeton through the evening traffic, finally pulling out of the carnival atmosphere of the Haymarket onto Regent Street. He and Thomas ignored Noelle as they debated the merits of the pair of matching grays Quinn had recently purchased.

Although it was the first time Noelle had ever ridden in a

carriage, she barely noticed its fine appointments. Instead, she could not seem to take her eyes from the American's hands as they clasped the reins. They were broad and powerful with long fingers, squared at the tips. She thought of them as they had slid down her body, searching for the fateful watch; of the one moment they had cupped her breasts. What would it be like to be naked under those hands; to have them touching the rest of her body, exploring secret places?

She wanted to cry, scream, fling herself from the racing carriage, but sandwiched as she was between the two men, she could do none of these things. Instead, she turned her thoughts to her knife. She had to get it back! If he had only put it in the pocket nearest her instead of the opposite one.

The carriage had come to a quiet street lined with tall trees and elegant homes. Quinn turned into an alley that ran parallel to the street and stopped the rig behind one of the homes, its outline blurred by the dark and the evening's drizzle. He sprang out lightly and then held up his arms to Noelle, who glared at him defiantly and vaulted agilely over the side. He chuckled softly.

Noelle allowed herself to be led through a rear door and into a small room where several coats hung on wooden pegs. A pair of abandoned pattens lay on their side in a corner.

"Wait here while I get some light," Thomas instructed. He returned almost immediately, holding a brass candelabrum with three flaming candles. The flickering lights threw deep shadows on the planes of Quinn's chiseled features, giving him a diabolical look. The chilling illusion did not go unnoticed by Noelle. She shivered in spite of herself.

"This way." Thomas gestured toward a flight of narrow wooden stairs obviously used by the servants and led them to the attic landing. He stopped in front of a stout oak door and then unlocked it.

As the door swung open Noelle dimly perceived sloping ceilings and mysterious conformations. Thomas entered, and the light from the candelabrum fell on odd pieces of furniture, battered trunks, and dust-covered bundles.

Quinn pushed Noelle into the room, making no effort to enter himself. Panic, as relentless and uncontrollable as the forces of nature, overcame her. She stumbled over to Thomas, frantically clutching at his arm.

"Please don't leave me 'ere," she begged, her lips trembling.

Thomas, uncomfortable under her frightened gaze, looked away and mumbled, "Don't worry. We shan't be gone long, and this will keep you company until we return." He placed the candelabrum on a scarred desk top and rushed from the room, the sound of his footsteps fading into the darkness of the hall.

Raising her ravaged face, Noelle looked into the arrogant countenance she hated so much. He regarded her impersonally, his overpowering presence filling the doorway.

Even after the door had slammed, separating them, she could still feel his eyes boring into her. No longer rational, she threw herself at the door.

"No!" she screamed. "Don't do this to me!" Her frail fists beat futilely against the barrier. "Please, somebody help me!" It was useless. She rested her cheek against the door and sobbed. Her strength ebbing with her spirits, she slid into a crumpled heap at the base of the door.

It had happened. A man was threatening her, controlling her. Feeling the panic rising again in her throat, she jerked up from the floor.

"No!" she exploded. "I'm not going to let this happen to me."

She scanned the room. The candles had burned to three sputtering stubs; she had to move quickly.

For the first time since she had entered the room, she felt a small stir of hope. Set high in the wall across from her was a small window. In one corner of the room a child's rocking chair with a broken seat lay on its side. She rushed to it, wrenching off one splintered rocker, then crossed to the window. Raising her arms high above her head, she thrust the rocker through the glass. Jagged pieces showered over her, one making a thin cut on her cheek, another embedding itself in the back of her hand. Ignoring her wounds, she looked about for something to stand on. Precious minutes elapsed as she struggled, trying to move some wooden crates. It wouldn't do; she couldn't budge them.

Straightening wearily, she noticed bookshelves lining the wall adjacent to the door. She hastened to the shelves and loaded her arms with the dusty volumes, stacking them underneath the window. When the pile reached her knees, she cautiously climbed on top. Avoiding the glass lying on the dusty sill, she peered out the window and took in great lungfuls of cool, crisp air.

The rooftop sloped sharply away from her, its edge disappearing into the bleak, silent night. She removed the last shreds of glass from the frame and tried to angle her shoulders through the opening, but it was too narrow to accommodate them. She climbed down off the pile of books and removed her bulky coat, but it did no good. No matter how she contorted her body, she couldn't get through the small window.

She screamed with frustration, then shouted into the darkness, "Help! Somebody help me! Is anybody there? Please!"

She waited, praying for any response. Again and again she screamed. The night mocked her with its silence.

Once more she lowered herself back into the attic room and sat on the pile of books she had stacked so hopefully. Quinn Copeland! He had caged her like an animal.

In a wild rage, she dashed across the room to the door and slammed it with her fists, cursing and sobbing. Abruptly she stopped and stared at the door. Then, her pulses racing, she bent over and peeked through the keyhole. A slow smile crept across her face.

Purposefully crossing to the pile of books, she ripped a page from a large volume. She spotted a thin quill lying on the floor next to the broken desk. Taking them both to the door, she lowered herself to her knees and slid the paper underneath, carefully aligning it with the knob. Barely breathing, she gingerly poked the quill through the keyhole. Only when she heard a faint plop from the other side did she let out her breath. Cautiously she pulled the paper back into the room. A large brass key rested on top.

She let out a whoop of joy and pressed the key to her lips. With trembling hands she fit it into the lock and turned it. The tumbler clicked. Free at last, Noelle flung open the door triumphantly.

He stood indolently on the other side, his dark eyes crinkling with amusement. "Very clever," he drawled. "I underestimated you."

Wordlessly he led her down the narrow stairs and out of the house. Instead of the open phaeton, there was an enclosed carriage waiting for them in the dark alley. A driver, his bulky form muffled in a cloak, spoke softly to the patient horses.

The interior of the carriage was empty. She clutched her hands tightly, the torn fingernails biting into her palms. Where was Thomas? she wondered. The door of the carriage shut firmly, and

Quinn settled himself beside her. She slid to the end of the seat, putting as much distance between them as possible. Quinn did not seem to notice. With unseeing, haunted eyes he stared out the window of the coach.

Noelle shivered with cold; she had left her cloak in the attic room, and her thin dress offered little protection against the night chill. Now she would give anything to be back in the room from which she had struggled so hard to escape. Although it had been her prison, the small attic room had also been her sanctuary, her last bastion of hope of escape. And now she was alone with this savage stranger who was intent on controlling her destiny.

Involuntarily Noelle's hand stroked the soft black leather of the seat. She had never seen anything as grand as this carriage. Red silk curtains trimmed in black fringe hung at the windows. Outside were shiny brass lanterns, sparkling with the rain that clung to them. She peered into the night beyond, but the streets were unfamiliar. An idea was beginning to take shape in her mind.

She turned to the American and smiled shyly. "I'm right sorry I been causin' ya so much trouble."

For a moment he looked at her blankly, as though he had forgotten she was there. "Oh? Why this sudden change of heart?"

"Well"—she was thoughtful—"I could say it's because yer a 'andsome devil, and I've taken a fancy to ya, but yer'd never believe that, would ya, ducks?" She looked at him guilelessly. "The truth is, I been thinkin' 'bout that money yer said ya was gonna give ter me. 'Ow much would ya be thinkin' about, if ya don't mind me askin'?"

"How much do you think you're worth?"

"It's 'ard ter say." She regarded him levelly, coyly patting her hair, which was now stiff with dried mud. "Some 'as said I'm worth a king's ransom, but I don't know as I'd go that far."

"How modest of you," he replied, his tone clearly signaling his disinterest.

There was a slight tremble to her voice. "Maybe the best thing ter do would be ter give ya a sample of what I've got ter offer." She lowered her eyes, looking at him through her lashes. "Then ya could judge fer yerself. Work from experience, so ter speak."

He leaned lazily into the corner of the carriage, making no move to touch her.

Gathering her courage, she slid over to him and tilted her

shoulders forward, revealing more of her bosom. As she smiled in poor imitation of a temptress, she slid her arms slowly around his shoulders, then tilted her head back and pressed her lips to his. They were hard and dry, and he instinctively recoiled from her kiss.

Summoning up her wits, she pushed her body against his, moving her fingers over his neck and back, simulating passion. Gradually she led her hands to the pocket where he had placed the dagger. It was empty! With growing alarm, she slid her hands over his chest. The knife was gone! Furious, she pushed herself away from him.

His eyes were ruthless. "You didn't think I'd be stupid enough to keep it, did you? Your knife is lying in a gutter in Soho. I underestimated you once. I'm not going to do it again."

With all her force, she swung at the arrogant face. He drew back, his head barely avoiding her flying fist, and imprisoned her wrist, cruelly twisting her arm behind her back. Grabbing her jaw with his free hand, he pulled her face toward his.

"I've had enough! One more episode like this and I will personally turn you over to the law. Do you understand me?"

Noelle mutely nodded her head in defeat. He released her, and they rode the rest of the way in silence, bitter resentment churning inside her.

The minister was a tall, angular man with ferret eyes and an oily smile. Noelle knew immediately that she could expect no help from him; he had obviously been well paid to do his part. He picked up a tattered Bible and inquired the name of the bride.

Thomas looked blankly at Quinn, realizing they'd never bothered to find out her name. Quinn turned to the despondent young girl next to him. She was suddenly aware of three sets of eyes watching her, waiting for her response.

"Noelle Dorian," she mumbled.

Quinn smiled crookedly at the absurdity of the pitiful street creature with the elegant French name while Thomas snorted loudly, then attempted to conceal his rudeness with a cough.

Noelle's cheeks burned. They were laughing at her! God, how she hated them both.

The marriage ceremony passed in a blur. Noelle was conscious of nothing except a dark stain on the cracked wall behind the minister's head. It reminded her of a rat sitting on its haunches. Reality leaped back at her when the American took her hand and slipped a thin gold band onto her finger.

Outside, the rain had stopped, leaving the night air fresh and crisp. Waiting for them were the carriage and Thomas's curricle. "I say, Quinn, you two can't go off without letting me drink to your happiness. Sorry I forgot the crystal." Producing a bottle of brandy from the floor of his rig, he saluted Quinn with it and grinned broadly. "May your time together be short and your revenge sweet." He took a swig and then passed the bottle to Quinn, who drank deeply.

Quinn turned to Noelle and regarded his bride with the detached, impersonal air she had come to expect. "Will you have a drink?" he inquired.

"I'd die of thirst before I'd drink with you," she sneered defiantly.

"Suit yourself." He dismissed her indifferently and turned to Thomas.

"I'll accept this excellent brandy as your wedding present, Tom. I'm going to need it tonight much more than you."

Quinn mutely guided Noelle to their carriage. As they pulled out of the narrow street she heard a clock toll the single hour—a death knell for her old life. Noelle Dorian had been replaced by Noelle Copeland. She should be elated by her good fortune; Daisy would have rejoiced to have had such luck. Instead, she felt debased, used, terrified of the savage man to whom she was now so permanently joined. And this hellish night was not finished with her yet.

Her thin fingers clutched her skirts convulsively as her ears rang with the remembered sounds of her mother's pitiful cries and the obscene noises of the men who had writhed over her. This was the fate in store for her, and she knew he would have no mercy.

The appearance of the mismatched pair at Quinn's respectable lodgings did not go unnoticed. The venerable patrons of the tap room stared incredulously at the tall, dashing American escorting the filthy creature in an emerald satin dress.

Ignoring their stunned expressions, Quinn strode purposefully to the innkeeper, never loosening his grip on Noelle's arm. "Hastings, I'm going to my room, and I want plenty of hot water sent up immediately."

"Certainly, sir," the robust Hastings responded in hushed tones, "but if I may say so, sir, this young . . . lady, sir, is . . . well, sir . . ." He sputtered with embarrassment, unwilling to offend his wealthy American lodger but determined to have his say. "She's not the sort who is normally welcomed in establishments such as this." He spread his plump arms. "Mr. Copeland, what you do for pleasure is none of my business, of course, but—"

"You're absolutely right, Hastings; it's none of your business. Now, send up the water."

Quinn turned on his heel and led Noelle upstairs to his room. He opened the door and, none too gently, pushed her in.

In the corner of the comfortably furnished room was a small carved chest with several decanters and glasses of different sizes and shapes. After filling one of the larger tumblers to the brim with the contents of Thomas's wedding present, Quinn shed his outer garments and settled himself comfortably in a large upholstered wing chair pulled up near a warm, crackling fire.

Noelle huddled, forgotten, across the room. She watched him. The snowy white of his shirt and cravat contrasted sharply with the ebony of his hair, his velvet waistcoat, and his gleaming leather boots. The dark eyes that stared into the flames were tortured. He drank steadily. What devils haunted this man who was now her husband?

A sharp knock at the door shattered the silence of the room. With pantherlike grace, he rose from the chair and opened it to admit two work-weary maids carrying steaming buckets of hot water. With practiced efficiency, they set up a large hip bath on the hearth. Darting curious looks at the unlikely couple, they left the room reluctantly, their giggles clearly audible as they disappeared down the hallway.

Quinn locked the door behind them. With a calculating look at his unwilling bride, he placed the key atop a mahogany armoire.

Noelle's eyes traveled to the bath steaming in its shiny copper tub. How long she had dreamed of luxury such as this: immersing herself in the warm water, scouring the grime of poverty from her skin with scented soap, wrapping herself in a fluffy white towel. But not here; not like this.

"Take off your clothes." He stood next to her, not bothering to conceal his distaste for her appearance.

She realized he had no intention of leaving the room. Involuntarily her eyes went to the most imposing piece of furniture in the chamber, the large bed already turned down for the night. Desperation giving her courage, Noelle seethed at him.

"Go to 'ell, you bastard. I'm not taking any more from you!" Her eyes flashed angrily. "Send me to Australia. I'd rather take my chances there than 'ere with you."

Ruthlessly he grabbed her slender shoulders, his voice a snarl. "Listen to me; I'm only going to say this once. For reasons your pitiful little mind can't even begin to understand, I've married you, and I'm going to make sure this marriage can't be annulled. As much as you revolt me, I'm going to consummate it. But first you're going to get into that tub and wash before your filthy body completely unmans me."

"I will not! Get your 'ands off me!" She beat her fists against his massive chest.

"All right. If this is the way you want it . . ." He grabbed the low neck of her tawdry emerald gown and pulled violently, sending the buttons flying throughout the room. She clutched at the dress, but not before the material had fallen from her shoulders, exposing her naked body to the waist. Quinn's eyes widened perceptibly as he saw her young, swelling breasts. Lovely rounded globes tipped in coral, they thrust proudly from her thin body.

"You are full of surprises, aren't you?"

Desperately she clutched at her torn dress, pulling the material back over her breasts.

"Don't play the coy virgin with me." He jerked the dress from her body, taking the rest of her chemise and her single bedraggled petticoat with it.

As she stood naked before his open scrutiny, the torn garments in a pool around her ankles, her pride deserted her. "Please don't do this to me," she begged, her voice shaking with fear. "I'm not what you think. Let me go."

His voice was low and determined. "Get into the bath."

His order was meant to be obeyed. At least the bath would hide her from his assessing eyes. She turned her back on him, and, with what little dignity she could muster, walked to the bath and slid into its soothing warmth.

Quinn removed his velvet waistcoat and untied his cravat. After refilling his glass, he settled himself in the wing chair by the fire, his long legs stretched casually before him. He watched her through impersonal eyes as he unbuttoned his shirt. Hanging from a thin leather thong, a small disk of beaten silver rested against his bronzed chest.

She was scrubbing roughly, her fingers digging into her scalp as she shampooed her short carrot thatch. Meticulously washing each part of herself, she kept as much of her body as possible hidden under the water. When she was done, she began again more slowly, trying to steal precious minutes.

As Quinn watched her bathe he felt no heat in his blood, no tightening in his loins. If anything, the emaciated features that the rough scrubbing revealed were even more unattractive now than when they had been hidden under the garish cosmetics.

He drained his glass and poured another. Alcohol had never before prevented him from performing; perhaps it would fog his brain enough so he could carry through this distasteful task. He rose from the chair and turned down the room's one lamp. Now only the fire provided light. The silver disk on his chest glittered orange like a malevolent eye. He walked toward the tub and picked up the towel, tossing it where she could not reach it.

"Get up."

She looked up at him, her eyes mutely pleading, her lips slightly parted. Frozen with fear, she could not move.

He was beside her in one long stride, pulling her out of the tub. Abruptly he released her and stepped back, taking in the generous spheres of her breasts as they glistened golden in the fire's flames. His eyes dropped to the curly triangle between her legs. Finally he felt himself hardening, and he quickly shed his clothes. Not willing to risk losing his desire, he kept his eyes away from her face and on her nude body, its thinness mercifully obscured by the room's dim light.

Noelle's heart thumped painfully at the sight of him naked in front of her. His broad chest and arms were well-muscled, his flanks narrow. Against her will, her eyes fastened on his manhood, jutting enormous and threatening from the curly black hair beneath his flat stomach. Her heart pounded as the awful memories came flooding back. Like a cornered animal, she backed away from him, her fear hanging tangibly in the room.

But he was past noticing. Fueled by the liquor he had been steadily consuming since early evening, his lust was single-minded. He stalked her slowly, his eyes on the twin globes of her breasts. She backed into a wall and then could go no farther.

Fingers like steel bit into her arms as he pulled her to the bed and lowered his body onto hers. She struggled wildly, finding a strength she did not know she possessed. But it was futile. Easily capturing both her fragile wrists in one of his powerful hands, he pinned them to the bed above her head, and then he cupped one round breast, running his thumb back and forth over the tip. Noelle's teeth bit into her bottom lip, drawing blood; at that moment she would have welcomed death. However, her humiliation was just beginning.

With one powerful knee, he forced her legs apart, exposing her soft, virginal petals to his scrutiny. But it was no tender lover who gazed down on her. It was a man driven by devils and obsessed with some mysterious revenge. She felt his hardness press against her opening. He thrust himself inside her, ripping her maiden's veil as she cried out.

"Good Christ!" he murmured hoarsely.

But it was too late. Passion overrode his reason. He thrust more and more deeply until he exploded within her.

Chapter Three

The smells were what finally awakened her—they assaulted her senses. The hand near her face was perfumed with honeysuckle from the soap she had used; the crisp aroma of starched sheets mingled with a woodsy tang from the smoldering ashes of the previous night's fire. There was something else, too: a faint masculine scent of leather and tobacco.

Noelle's eyes snapped open. She was alone. The memories of the previous night thundered over her. Resting a thin, bruised arm across her eyes, she attempted to ward them off; however, even that small movement made her wince with pain, and so she lay motionless, staring at the ceiling.

All of Noelle's years of desperate poverty had not been able to defeat her. Peddlers, whores, thieves, ragged street urchins, they all called her "Highness," in part to bait her, since she was different from them, but also with grudging respect for her self-sufficiency. She knew instinctively that that was behind her now. In one night the American had conquered her. He had not only violated her body, he had violated her spirit. He was wild, uncivilized. None of her experiences had prepared her for anyone like him, and she found herself with no resources to use against him.

Tears trickled from the corners of her eyes. Harshly she brushed them away and slowly raised herself from the great bed, cropped ends of carrot hair sticking to her damp cheeks. Mechanically she pulled the covers up over the bed, hiding the small bloodstain that marred the white sheet. She walked painfully to the mahogany washstand and surveyed herself with detachment in its oval mirror.

She looked like a corpse. The bruises on her arms stood out vividly against her unhealthily waxen skin. Her orange hair, although clean, was matted in frizzled clumps about her head. She ran her fingers through it, ignoring the carved tortoiseshell brushes that had been tossed carelessly on the washstand's top. Finally her eyes fastened on the insides of her thighs, stained with his spilled seed, the physical evidence of the American's violation of her body. With trembling hands, she grabbed the white china water pitcher and emptied its contents into the matching bowl. The tepid water splashed over the mahogany surface and ran off onto the floor. She ignored it, absorbed in a brutal scrubbing of her painfully thin body. Her clothing had disappeared, so she wrapped her nakedness with the large, soft bath towel unused from the night before.

Just as she finished there was a light tapping on the door, followed by a click. The door swung open, admitting a buxom little dumpling of a woman carrying a heavy tray. Fading ginger curls sprinkled with gray peeked from under an oversized mobcap. The mouth-watering aroma of warm bread and hot chocolate accompanied her into the room.

"How d'ya do there, missy?" she chirped with a crisp Irish brogue. "It's such a fine mornin' for a change." Her bright blue eyes darted around the room. "Oh, ya haven't even opened the curtains. Here, let me do it for ya." Setting the tray down, she bustled to the windows. "I've been given me orders to get you fed and ready to leave with that handsome Mr. Copeland."

Noelle drew in her breath audibly. The woman looked at her more closely, taking in the dark bruises on her arms and her woebegone expression. What was a man like Mr. Copeland doing with a poor creature like this? Inexplicably she felt her sympathies rise for the pathetic young girl and decided to do her best to cheer her up.

"Me name's Brigid O'Shea. Now, sit right here and eat, missy, while I tidy up."

Noelle felt some of her tension slip away as she viewed with wonder the tempting array of food put before her. There was a wicker basket heaped with warm buns and a bowl of porridge topped with spoonfuls of golden honey. A flowered pitcher was filled to the brim with cream. There was a mound of butter and a steaming mug of hot chocolate, foamy on the top. She hadn't eaten since hours before her fateful meeting with the American, and that had been poor fare, a withered apple and a slice of stale bread. She began gulping great mouthfuls of food as though she were afraid it would be snatched from her.

"My, my, dearie, y'are hungry, ain't ya?"

Embarrassed, Noelle began to eat more slowly, savoring each bite.

"I used ta eat like a bird meself when I was younger." Brigid chuckled to herself, indicating her well-padded figure. "To look at me now, you'd never believe it, would ya? Oh, the way the men looked at me, all waitin' for a chance to spend some time with me. It was flatterin', but it wasn't easy, mind ya. Most of them was lookin' for nothin' more than a little fun, if ya take my meanin'."

The kindly woman noticed the tight, stricken look that crossed Noelle's features. Could she possibly be dim-witted, unaware of what a wealthy and powerful protector she had? Brigid began to strip the bed efficiently.

" 'Course they weren't nothin' compared to your rich Mr. Copeland. Aye! To be young again. I'd give up all me fond memories just to spend a night with that handsome man."

Noelle groaned almost imperceptibly just as Brigid threw off the last cover and revealed the stained sheet. The plump Irishwoman eyed the drops of blood with surprise. Aye, so that's how it was, she thought, and here I was thinkin' she was a common whore, may the saints forgive me.

She knelt down beside Noelle, who was sitting vacant-eyed in her chair, and clasped the girl's thin hands in her own plump ones. "Had a bad time of it, did ya?"

Noelle looked into the friendly blue eyes and nodded dumbly. "It was horrible." Suddenly she straightened in her chair and clutched her new friend's hands tightly. "Please, Brigid, help me get away before he gets back. Just get me some clothes to put on and show me the back way out."

Brigid disengaged her hands from Noelle's grasp and began stroking her abused orange hair gently. "What on earth could ya be thinkin' of," she scolded. "Use your head, girl. He's not one to cross. He'd find you in no time if he wanted to, and then you'd be worse off than y'are right now."

"It isn't possible for me to be any worse off than I am now!" Noelle exclaimed.

"Now, calm yourself, dearie, and listen to me." Brigid crossed to a bundle she had dropped when she entered the room.

Unwrapping it, she gingerly pulled out a petticoat, the torn dress, and a small sewing kit. "Mr. Copeland gave orders you're to be sewn back in this dress."

Noelle opened her mouth to protest.

"Would you rather him be walkin' in on you like this with nothin' but that towel wrapped around yer naked body?" Brigid clucked in exasperation. "Though why he should want you sewn into this filthy rag is more than I can say." She pulled away the towel and helped Noelle into the petticoat, then draped the distasteful garment over Noelle's body. She began pinning and stitching. "Yer all bones, child. Look at yer ribs! Though it has to be said that you've a fine bosom."

Noelle turned obediently as Brigid stitched. She felt warmed by her motherly concern; it had been so long since anyone had cared about her or fussed over her. Brigid finally finished and stepped back to observe her handiwork.

Unexpectedly the door banged open and Quinn strode into the room. Noelle whirled around in her chair. He was dressed impeccably in a pearl-gray morning coat with matching trousers. His handsome face was drawn and tired, its harsh planes strongly etched. He regarded her dispassionately, then turned to Brigid.

"Did you feed her?"

"Aye, that I did, sir." Brigid gestured toward the breakfast tray. Only two buns and a bit of porridge were left on it. "Half starved, she was," she sniffed, shooting Quinn a disapproving scowl.

Quinn grinned back at her good-naturedly. "I'll feed her more often. In the meantime, take this with you when you go." He nodded toward the tray, dismissing her.

Noelle watched him. Once again he was acting as though she weren't in the room. The turbulent emotions she had felt the night before were gone. Instead, she was filled with an icy hatred so intense, it consumed her.

"Just a minute." Her voice was cold and steady. She walked purposefully over to Quinn and held out her hand. "I want a guinea."

He raised one dark eyebrow questioningly, but then, with a disinterested shrug, placed a shiny guinea in her hand.

Noelle took it to Brigid and pressed it on her. "Here, take this. I was in need of a friend."

"Why, thank you, miss."

Two could play the game of humiliation. "It's 'missus.' I'm Noelle Copeland, Mrs. Quinn Copeland."

The Irishwoman's apple cheeks paled at Noelle's disclosure. A hundred questions sprang to her lips only to remain unasked. For once the loquacious Brigid was without words.

"Y-yes, ma'am. Thank—thank ya, ma'am." She bobbed an awkward curtsy, her mobcap flopping comically on her curls, and fled from the chamber, closing the door behind her.

Noelle squared her small shoulders and turned to face the American.

Pantherlike, he crossed the room toward her, never taking his eyes from hers. "If you think you can humiliate me, you're wrong. However, you can provoke me, and that would be unwise. You are to flaunt this marriage to no one without my permission, do you understand?"

With every inch of her being, Noelle yearned to slap his arrogant face, to fling herself at him and claw out those unfeeling eyes. But she hadn't the courage, and she hated herself for her cowardice.

"You should have told me, you know." Incredibly she saw pity etched across his chiseled features. "I wouldn't have been so rough. It's not my habit to ruin virgins."

"And if I told you, would you 'ave believed me?" She spoke bitterly, knowing the answer even before the question had passed her pale lips. "Of course you wouldn't 'ave . . . so you just take yer pity and shove it up yer arse."

Ignoring her, he withdrew a small white jar from the pocket of his coat and unscrewed the lid to reveal scarlet rouge. Dipping his finger in the pot, he slashed it across her cheeks and smeared it over her lips.

He began to chuckle infuriatingly. "There, now you look like the girl I married."

Chapter Four

The late morning sun shone brightly on the gleaming white door and the ornate lion's head knocker that adorned it. Lifting it, Quinn rapped sharply. Noelle was overawed as she gazed at the brick exterior of the stately London town house that graced fashionable Northridge Square. The door opened, revealing a thin, elderly man dressed in spotless livery. His sparse white eyebrows lifted almost imperceptibly at the improbable pair on the doorstep.

"Good morning, Tomkins," Quinn said, ushering Noelle inside.

She was entranced. Her eyes drank in the splendor of the foyer with its glossy black marble floor. Sunlight streamed in through two tall windows and splashed the polished brass wall sconces and the graceful daffodil-yellow settee that rested along one ivory wall.

"Good morning, Mr. Copeland," Tomkins said stiffly.

"Is my father in?"

"In the library, sir." The butler hesitated briefly, then glanced significantly at Noelle. "Do you wish me to announce you?"

"No, I think I'll surprise him." Quinn grinned.

Tomkins inclined his head slightly. "Very well, sir." His back rigid with disapproval, he disappeared noiselessly down the hallway.

Quinn led Noelle into a small anteroom. "Wait for me here. I'll be back shortly." He pulled a key from the inside of the door. "You know it wouldn't be any use to try to escape, don't you? This time I won't be stupid enough to leave the key in the other side of the door."

"You don't really think a locked door would keep me 'ere if I made up my mind to leave, do you, Quinn?" she sneered, using his first name deliberately, spitting it out of her mouth as if it were venom.

He ignored her bravado. "You mean you're not going to try to escape the minute my back is turned? Forgive me if I don't believe you, but honesty is not one of your more sterling qualities. You have no one but yourself to blame for last night. You weren't even an honest whore, were you?"

"Honesty," she said flatly. "What do you know about honesty? More money than you can spend. Never 'ad to worry about a place to sleep fer the night or an empty stomach. It's easy fer you to be able to talk about honesty. You're rich enough to afford it."

"You shouldn't have been so quick to judge me. I might have surprised you."

He closed the door, turned the key in the lock, and headed for the library, where the confrontation he had been anticipating for so long waited for him.

Simon Copeland sat at the massive desk, a large ledger bound in tan calf open in front of him. However, he wasn't really concentrating on the rows of figures that stretched in neat columns down the page. Instead, he was wondering how the shipyard in Cape Crosse was operating in his absence. Once again he was grateful that he had been wise enough twenty-four years ago to choose that small Georgia town on Providence Sound as the location of Copeland and Peale's American shipyard.

He remembered how the older and more experienced shipbuilders had scoffed at him. They warned him that a location thirty-five miles south of Savannah was too isolated, that he would have to depend on slaves because skilled labor would be impossible to come by. But Simon had no intention of building a shipyard on human misery. Instead, he traveled to New York and Boston, where he scoured the shipyards owned by some of the same men who had laughed at him.

There, Simon found freed slaves and experienced craftsmen, many of them immigrants from the shipyards of Scotland and Holland, family men who were disillusioned with the crowded conditions of cities and wanted something better for their children. Simon told them about Cape Crosse with its schoolhouse and three churches. He told them of the new white frame houses that were sitting empty, waiting for families to fill them. And, since they loved ships, he also told them of the kinds of vessels he and Benjamin Peale planned to build. Simon Copeland found his workers.

He remembered how delighted Ben had been at his first sight of Cape Crosse. Damn, he missed him! Simon's fingers fondly stroked the carved walnut as he thought of his former partner sitting at this same desk. Simon was a meticulous man, but he smiled as he recalled Ben's chaotic work habits: rumpled papers scattered haphazardly across the polished top, books strewn about this same room, contracts representing hundreds of pounds stuffed into an empty ale mug on the mantel. Perhaps it was just as well that he and Ben had had an ocean separating them; it was probably the secret of their successful partnership. Since the early years, they had seldom seen each other. Still, it had pleased Simon as he sat in his orderly office in Cape Crosse to think of Benjamin here, running the British branch of the company amidst the cheery chaos that always surrounded him.

Since Ben had died eight months ago, Simon had increasingly come to realize how much he had relied on his partner's good sense. It wasn't happenstance that Simon had purchased the Peales' Northridge Square town house. Benjamin's widow, Constance, who now owned half the company, had decided to remain at her country estate in Sussex during her year of deep mourning. Since she only planned to visit London infrequently as her business affairs dictated, she had sold the elegant Northridge Square home to Simon and purchased a smaller house nearby. He had been here four months now, and it probably would be twice that long before he could return to Cape Crosse. Somehow it had comforted Simon to be here among Benjamin's things as he sorted out the affairs of the English shipyard.

If only he could turn the Cape Crosse yard over to Quinn and stay in England himself. Somehow he had hoped . . .

He frowned, his dark brows almost meeting in the middle. Damnation! He was going to have to do something about his son. Almost twenty-eight and still as wild as he'd been as a boy.

Quinn knew all there was to know about building ships; he understood the intricacies of running Copeland and Peale. How could he be so impractical with all his talk of experimentation? He wanted to sink thousands of dollars into the development of a totally new hull shape. Copeland and Peale was a conservative shipbuilder, not some shoddy organization that would fall in with any foolhardy scheme.

Perhaps it had been a mistake to summon Quinn from Cape

Crosse three months before. His son had now managed to swing Constance over to his side. That could present a problem, since she still controlled half the company. Why isn't Quinn like other men's sons, Simon thought bitterly—obedient, respectful of his father?

His thoughts were interrupted as the study door flew open and the subject of his ruminations strode in. At first glance the resemblance between the two men was striking; however, a closer scrutiny revealed that the likeness was more of manner than physical appearance.

At fifty, Simon's dark hair was threaded with silver, but he was still a handsome man, broad-shouldered and muscular with biting blue eyes. Quinn was the larger and darker of the two. His cheekbones were higher and more defined, but the two men had the same strong brow and bold nose.

"Don't you ever knock?" Simon grumbled.

Quinn lit a thin cheroot and crossed to the fireplace. "There's no need for us to stand on ceremony, is there, Simon?" He leaned gracefully against the marble mantel and crossed one booted ankle over the other.

"So"—Simon regarded his tall, handsome son critically—"the prodigal son returns. Don't you think it was a bit extravagant to take private rooms for yourself when you could have stayed here?"

This was an old argument between them. Over the years Quinn had prudently invested his wages. He had long been financially independent of his father, a fact that galled Simon.

"It's my money, Simon, as you well know. Besides, don't you think that would be rather hypocritical, considering all of our differences?"

"Our differences, as you call them, are of your making, not mine," the older man barked angrily.

"Our differences, Simon, started before I was old enough to cause them."

Simon gripped the edge of the desk, his knuckles turning white, and glared at his son. Their eyes locked in silent combat, punctuated only by the ticking of the gilded clock on the mantel. Abruptly Simon slumped back in his chair, impatiently running his fingers through his black hair.

"If I had known you were coming, I would have made

arrangements for Constance to be here," he said gruffly. "I know how you enjoy her company."

At the thought of Constance, Quinn relaxed. He crossed to a leather chair angled near the walnut desk. "The fair Constance. Now, there's a woman!" He settled himself comfortably in the chair and looked significantly at his father. "She's bright, vibrant."

"Bright? How can you say that? She's the most featherbrained woman I've ever met, and she insists on meddling in company affairs."

Quinn regarded his father evenly. "She's half owner of Copeland and Peale now, as well as being an admirable woman. Don't be so quick to dismiss her opinions. She may be flighty, but she's not stupid."

"She's a meddler and knows nothing of the business!" Simon exclaimed, rising from his chair and stalking across the room.

"She was married to your partner for twenty-one years," Quinn reminded him.

"Yes, and Ben paid too much attention to her crazy ideas."

"Which crazy ideas?" Quinn asked coolly. "Building a totally new hull?" He walked to the fireplace and flicked the ash from his cheroot onto the grate. "You're a fool, Simon. You know the rumors about the work at Smith and Damon in New York."

"A fool, am I!" Simon shot back. "Damn it, Quinn, we've been through this a hundred times. A ship without her breadth well forward in the beam will founder. A shipbuilder doesn't go against the natural order of things, and you only have to look at nature to see the error of your concept. There's hardly a species of fish that isn't largest near the head, forward of its center."

"Fish are fish, Simon, and ships are ships. Fish exist in only one element, the sea. And at the depths they swim, the sea is calm. Ships must contend with two elements, wind and sea, and they're both unpredictable. You're so wrong, Simon," Quinn said, his eyes glittering harshly, "but then you always have believed in your own infallibility."

Simon looked at his son sadly, then walked over to the desk and settled himself again in the chair. He spoke softly. "Can't we stop this endless bickering?"

Quinn's smile was chilling; it never reached his eyes. "As a matter of fact, that's why I'm here. I've done something for you, something you've been asking me to do for a long time."

Simon stared at Quinn quizzically, not missing the grim line of his son's jaw. "Oh?"

"Yes, I've taken your advice. Wait here. I have a surprise for you."

Quinn left the room hastily and returned moments later with an apprehensive Noelle in tow. Simon gazed incredulously at the pitifully wasted creature decked out in scarlet rouge and a dirty gown. It was impossible! He had brought a vulgar trollop into his father's house.

Simon's voice was deadly. "What is the meaning of this?"

Eyes gleaming triumphantly, Quinn replied, "I'd like you to meet my wife. We were married last night."

The older man was speechless, his face a mask of astonishment as he took in the outrageous carrot thatch.

"The ceremony was unorthodox, but definitely legal." Quinn watched his father closely, savoring each moment of his revenge. "Tom Sully was the witness."

Outraged, Simon leaped from his chair, his jaw tightly clenched. "If this is your idea of a joke—"

"Oh, it's no joke," Quinn interrupted smoothly. "Remember, Simon, you were the one who wanted me to marry. You wanted me to settle down, become respectable . . . be just as conservative and stodgy as you are." His voice rose angrily. "Though why in hell you, of all people, have turned into a champion of marriage is more than I can fathom." He started to say more, to inflict another small jab of wound-opening memory, knowing even a light touch could make it fester, but he thought better of it, contenting himself with saying, "You were the one who wanted me to take a bride. Well, I did, and now you can have her. I hope you'll both be very happy."

He turned on his heels and walked to the door. As he reached out to grab the knob, he paused and turned back to face his father. "By the way, it took a great deal of persuasion to convince this lovely lady to marry me. She's accustomed to being paid for her services." Reaching into his pocket, he withdrew a fat envelope and tossed it toward Simon. It flew through the air and landed with a slap on the desk top.

"Make sure she gets this."

Noelle could listen no longer. She went mad, leaping toward him with hands outstretched like claws and shrieking loudly, "You son of a bitch! I hate you! The fires of hell are too good for you, you friggin' bastard!"

Extricating himself from her flying fists, Quinn's face broke into a wide grin at her tirade. "Charming, isn't she?"

The door slammed behind him.

Chapter Five

Without moving, Simon stared at the closed door. His face was gray and drawn, but he felt nothing—no anger or frustration or hurt or humiliation or any of the other myriad of emotions that would soon bombard him. He had been stricken a blow so unexpected, so devastating, that he was stunned; this was the tangible evidence of just how great his son's hatred was. Another man might have cried or prayed or screamed out, but Simon did none of these things because he did not know how. Too many years had passed since he had felt any deep sentiments.

Then the pain began.

Memories he had successfully blocked from his mind came rushing back: holding his son close, tossing him in the air, running with him. He remembered how the small child had haunted the Cape Crosse shipyard, sometimes sitting quietly and watching the carpenters as they worked but more frequently bombarding them with questions.

And then, the bitter years, watching the naked hatred in the same eyes that had smiled at him. He had been unable to confront his guilt because the boy was too great a reminder of the disaster Simon had made of his personal life, too great a reminder of the one other person they had both loved so deeply. For the first time in years Simon Copeland comprehended the depth of love he felt for his son.

Now he looked over at the woman who was the instrument of his son's revenge. She stood across the room from him, staring out the window. The glare from the late morning sun obscured her features, but she seemed quiet and calm. Her composure angered him. This slut was his son's wife! Could she really have been as reluctant as she had seemed?

He opened the envelope Quinn had tossed down so nonchalantly and pulled out a fat bundle of pound notes. She was certainly being well paid for her part in this charade. Had she somehow been responsible for what had happened? Simon thought of his strong-willed son and discarded the idea. No one could force Quinn into anything; Simon had firsthand knowledge of that. No, this girl was merely a catalyst, a pawn in Quinn's game of revenge.

A piece of stationery dropped out of the envelope. Simon opened it to find Quinn's bold handwriting glaring accusingly at him:

March 28, 1835

I hereby resign from my association with Copeland and Peale and renounce all claims I have on that company.

Quinn Christopher Copeland
London, England

Simon stared at the short letter in stunned disbelief and then reread it. Its terseness and impersonal tone revealed more than the words themselves. He knew with an unshakable certainty that Quinn was absolving himself not only of his association with the company, but also of any association with his father. He was walking out of Simon's life as he had done once before. Except this time he was leaving something behind.

Simon looked at Noelle and noticed that her chest was trembling slightly. She had turned so that the glare from the window no longer fell directly on her face, and Simon saw the tears coursing down her cheeks. Why, she was not much more than a child! She seemed so defenseless, her grief all the more pitiful because it was silent.

His logical mind took over, and he stuffed the pound notes back into the envelope. She was undoubtedly upset about her earlier angry outburst and afraid that she would now not be paid. His voice was calm but cold.

"There's really no need for you to cry. Here is the money you were promised. I suggest you use it wisely. This is a God-given opportunity for you to better yourself, to improve your station in life." Even to himself, he sounded pompous.

The girl regarded him directly, as though she were assessing him. She made no attempt to conceal her tears, nor did she move to take the envelope he proffered. He felt vaguely uncomfortable, as though she had looked inside him and found him lacking. Placing the envelope on the edge of the desk nearest her, he stood.

"Come now, miss, it's your money. Take it and leave. I'll have my butler show you out."

He crossed to the tapestry bellpull in the corner, but before he could touch it, her voice hissed at him. It was laden with contempt, all traces of the accent of the street erased.

"I don't want that money. I don't want anything from you or your son."

Simon's expression betrayed his surprise.

"You weren't expecting me to refuse, were you? You're both alike, the two of you." Once again the tears spilled over her lashes. "It doesn't even occur to you that there might be a human being with feelings standing in front of you. It doesn't occur to you that things aren't always what they seem. Keep your money. I don't need it."

With those words, she straightened her shoulders and walked proudly toward the library door.

Simon watched the girl's straight back as she crossed the room. Her honesty and dignity moved him, her diction puzzled him; he felt a strange reluctance to let her go. As she reached the door his voice rang out, abrupt and commanding.

"Stay right there. I want to talk to you."

She ignored him; her hand stretched out for the knob.

"Please." The word was out before Simon knew it.

She turned to him. For the first time he could see a questioning in her eyes, an unsureness.

"Please," he repeated, crossing to her, "I apologize for my rudeness. I would appreciate it if you would stay for a few moments and talk with me."

Noelle hesitated briefly and then nodded her consent.

"Please sit down. Over here by the fire so we can be comfortable." He escorted her to a thickly cushioned sofa. "Tea?"

She paused a moment and then said, "Yes, thank you." Sitting gracefully, her back straight, she eyed him warily. He reminded her of his son. They had the same arrogant profile.

Simon strode to the bellpull, gave a firm yank, and returned to Noelle, settling himself in a chair opposite her. He took a moment to study her more closely. It was hard to imagine, but perhaps, with proper food and decent clothing, she might look less absurd.

"I didn't hear your name," he began tentatively.

"My name is Noelle Dorian." She spoke softly but watched him intently as though his reaction were a test of some kind.

"Pretty." For the first time, he saw a flicker of a smile cross her face. "Were your parents French?"

"No. My mother was English, but she loved everything French. She died seven years ago."

"Seven years ago! You couldn't have been much more than a baby. What about your father? Is he still living?"

"I expect so. At least, if all Daisy's stories were true."

"Daisy?"

"My mother. She was an actress when she was young. She used to tell me how my father was rich and handsome, one of the nobility." Suddenly Noelle was embarrassed. Why was she telling him all this? "But then, you don't want to hear me go on. Besides, Daisy wasn't above telling a few clankers. It probably wasn't true at all."

Simon wondered. Was it really so unlikely that a girl like this could have been fathered by an aristocrat? There was a certain dignity about her.

"Who took care of you after your mother's death?"

She looked genuinely bewildered. "Why, I took care of myself. Who else would?"

"But you were only a child."

"I wasn't all that young. I was ten."

"You rang for me, sir?" The butler's voice startled Noelle. She had not heard him enter.

"Yes, Tomkins. The young lady would like some tea. Serve it in here." Simon dismissed him and turned back to Noelle, as if there had been no interruption.

"So you're seventeen now."

"Almost eighteen."

"And you've been on your own since you were ten?" He shook his head in puzzlement and spoke almost to himself. "The English are a truly incredible people. They believe they are the only ones fit to govern the rest of the world, but they can't even tend to the injustices on their own doorstep."

"Here, now," Noelle cried, lifting her small chin. "Don't you say anything bad about the English, especially since you're an American."

"Oh, and what's wrong with being an American?" Simon was amused by her patriotic indignation.

"Why, they're savages," she sniffed haughtily. "Walking around practically naked with paint smeared all over their faces."

Simon chuckled. "Noelle, I think you picked an unfortunate example."

"What do you mean by that?" she questioned suspiciously.

Simon did not respond. Instead, he reached out and gently stroked her hollow cheek, showing her his scarlet-stained fingers. Then his eyes traveled briefly to her décolletage. "Practically naked with paint smeared all over their faces?"

Noelle looked in his eyes and saw them twinkling humorously. An angry retort sprang to her lips, but something in his face stopped her. Just as she had earlier judged him, she saw that he was now waiting for her reaction, testing her. He had made a joke at her expense, but she sensed instinctively that he was not mocking her. Her anger left her as abruptly as it had come, and she suddenly laughed, producing a merry tinkling sound that delighted Simon.

The American businessman and the English pickpocket smiled companionably at each other for several moments before Noelle realized she had carelessly let down her guard. Chiding herself, she quickly dropped her gaze and studied a ragged seam that formed an angry V in the skirt of her garment.

The silence lengthened, but she was determined she would not be the one to break it.

"Would you tell me how you've managed since you were ten?" Simon yearned to ask her how long she had been prostituting herself but couldn't think how to frame the words and did not want to challenge her stubborn pride.

"For the first few years I was a mudlark."

"Mudlark? What in God's name is that?"

"You don't know what a mudlark is?" Noelle was astonished that a man of Simon's wealth and station should be so ignorant.

"No, I'm afraid not." Simon smiled. "There are some gaps in my education. Perhaps you'd be so kind as to fill in this one."

"Why, the mudlarks go to the riverbanks and gather pieces of coal to sell in the streets. I was the only girl mudlark in London," Noelle boasted.

Simon looked suitably impressed. "And how did you accomplish that remarkable feat?"

Hesitantly Noelle began to tell Simon of her early days. He listened intently, totally absorbed in her narrative. Before she knew it, she was speaking of her times with Sweeney Pope and of his tragic death. Although she hardly spoke of Daisy, from the few remarks she did make, Simon was able to obtain a fairly accurate picture of her relationship with her mother. He was most interested to learn that Daisy had been a demimonde, not an old street crone as he had first imagined, for the germ of an idea was beginning to take root in his mind.

"When I was twelve, I knew I couldn't pass as a boy much longer, so I had to find another trade."

Simon leaned slightly forward in his chair. There was a tenseness about his handsome mouth; he found himself unexpectedly reluctant to hear what he knew she was going to tell him. It suddenly mattered to him very much that this spirited young girl was supporting herself as a prostitute. But the story Simon heard was not the one he expected.

Instead, Noelle told him how she had become a pickpocket, describing the old coat she had hung above her head in the tiny corner where she slept. She spoke of her hours of practice while the others who shared her cramped quarters were asleep—pulling a handkerchief out of various pockets, trying not to move the coat. For weeks she had repeated the movements until she was finally satisfied. Then she had substituted a smaller piece of cloth. Finally a stone that lay deeper in the pocket.

Noelle's forehead puckered as she remembered the months of practice. "That was a long time ago," she said, her tone dry. "Since then I've established a reputation for myself." Looking him squarely in the eye, she challenged, "Some say I'm the best pickpocket in Soho."

Simon swallowed hard at this. She seemed to have no conscience, no sense of having done anything wrong. My God, was she as proud of being a prostitute as she was of her times as a pickpocket?

Noelle defied his silent censure. "I didn't have any other choice, you know. It was picking pockets or being a whore, and nothing could ever make me be a whore." A shadow crossed her face. "Nothing, that is, until your son came along."

"My son!" Simon exclaimed. "I'm sorry, but I don't think I understand what you just told me." His eyes took in her costume. "Are you saying, then, that you are not a . . . a prostitute?"

"Mr. Copeland," she said softly, "until last night, I was a virgin. I only dress like this to distract the men so I can pick their pockets."

Simon was incredulous. What had Quinn done to this child? Although he barely knew her, he did not doubt her, for he knew his son too well. Somehow she had become entangled in Quinn's net of revenge, an unwilling victim who had been deeply injured.

He got up from his chair and settled himself beside her on the sofa. "Tell me what happened, Noelle."

Noelle looked into his handsome face. She did not want his pity, but he deserved to know what kind of man his son was.

She told her story ferociously, as if the telling alone would ease her anguish; it poured from her. As she repeated the conversation she had overheard between Thomas and Quinn, Simon's face set into hard, chiseled planes, and she was once again struck by the resemblance between father and son, especially as she saw a ruthlessness in the older man's face that had been absent before.

When Noelle described pulling a knife on his son, Simon felt a brief moment of regret that she had not found her mark. My God, he'd like to kill Quinn himself for this! Noelle had a good memory and could accurately repeat most of Quinn's discussion with Thomas about marrying her. Simon appreciated what Noelle did not really understand—the stunning perfection of Quinn's revenge.

Was it so wrong for a man to take pride in his name? Simon wondered. To want that name to be respected? What was so absurd about asking Quinn to marry a woman of grace and breeding who would bear proud sons to carry on the Copeland name? God damn it! Quinn had made Simon's honest aspirations seem foolish and pretentious.

The idea that had been only the faintest impulse before began to take shape in his mind. If this was the kind of game Quinn was going to play, he would soon find out that he had badly underestimated his opponent.

Noelle's voice faltered as she began to speak of her arrival at Quinn's lodgings.

"You don't have to tell me about this if it's too painful." Simon spoke more gruffly than he had intended, but he did not want to hear any more.

"I have to tell you. You're his father." Noelle looked at him levelly, but not accusingly. "Whatever happened between the two of you has spilled over and poisoned me."

Again, her voice faltered, catching in her throat, but she was going to tell him, make him understand. She would speak about this ugliness she had kept hidden for so long. Only then could he really understand what had happened to her last night. She clenched her fists and dug her torn fingernails into her palms.

"After a while, Daisy's mind . . . She wasn't right in her head. She'd bring men back to our room. Lie with them. And they'd hurt her. They'd hit her and . . . and do things to her. She'd sometimes beg and cry. Other times, she wouldn't even make a sound, just lie there. I knew then that I'd never let a man touch me. That's why I carried my knife." Her eyes bored into Simon's. "I want you to know that I would have killed him and laughed when he died."

Simon made no visible reaction to her savage pronouncement. "Go on," he said. Now he wanted to hear it all, know the truth of what his son had done. He wanted to hear the worst so he could justify the revenge he knew he was going to take.

Noelle would not meet his eyes. She stared past him and continued her story. "He ripped off my clothes and told me to take a bath. I've dreamed of a bath like that as long as I can remember. Hot water with the steam coming up from it, soap that smelled so good, you almost wanted to taste it." She laughed, but there was no merriment in the sound.

"I was unlucky enough to have my dream come true. I had my bath all right, but with him sitting there, watching me with eyes like the devil. He had his legs stretched out in front of him and was sipping his brandy as though he didn't have a care in the world. Just watching me as if I weren't even a real person, as though I had no feelings.

"Then he got up and turned out the light. He picked up the towel, threw it across the room out of my reach, and pulled me out of the tub. I tried to back away from him, to tell him I wasn't what he thought, but he wouldn't listen. I fought him, but he held my hands, pushed me onto the bed. Then he was all over me, ripping me apart." Her eyes were hard and bitter as she turned to face Simon. "Mr. Copeland, I know now that I'll die before I ever let any man touch me like that again."

Now it was Simon who would not look at her. He stood and walked to the book cases that stretched the width of the library. Running his index finger down the spine of one of the leather-bound volumes, he finally spoke, his voice filled with emotion.

"Noelle, what happened with you and my son was ugly and twisted. It was an animal coupling, the act of a stallion mounting an unwilling mare only by virtue of his superior strength. But lovemaking between a man and a woman does not have to be like that. It can be beautiful and full of tenderness."

He turned toward her, but he no longer saw her; another face swam before him. He saw warm dark eyes and hair like rippling black silk. "Some will say that only men enjoy the act of love." His voice rose with the depth of his conviction. "But that's a lie. I have seen such joy on the face of a woman that I knew it shone from her heart. It was magical, something to be treasured forever."

Simon had revealed himself much more fully than he had intended, but it was all for nothing. He saw by Noelle's closed expression that it was useless to try to explain further. Her bitterness formed an unbreachable wall that encircled her. Once again he became businesslike as he crossed to her, his hands clasped behind his back.

"I will make no excuses for what my son did; it was unforgivable. It is inadequate to tell you that I'm sorry for what has happened, but I am. And I promise you, Noelle, that I am somehow going to make it up to you."

The door opened slowly and Tomkins entered. Refusing to acknowledge Noelle's presence by so much as a glance, he majestically placed a silver tray bearing a matching tea service on a small table near Simon and announced, "Mrs. Peale has just arrived, sir. I asked her to wait in the anteroom; however . . ."

"Oh, Tomkins, you old fusspot, there's no need to announce me."

The inimitable Constance Peale, as fresh as a breeze after a morning rain, floated into the library with a swish of ruffles and black silk. Although the appropriate color, her dress could only be categorized as proper mourning attire by the broadest definition. Its revealing décolletage was covered with the sheerest film of black gauze. The overbodice was gathered at the base of her slim neck into layers of lacy ruff.

Her hair was bright auburn with many curls and ribbons. There were several malicious gossips who hinted that a woman of forty-five could not possibly have hair that particular shade of red without resorting to henna. It was a mark of Constance's popularity that the gossips found few willing to listen.

In point of fact, she was not really a beautiful woman at all. Her features were pleasant, but certainly not distinguished. Instead, it was the animation of her personality, her charm and vitality, that had been known to quicken the heartbeats of gentlemen many years her junior.

Despite the frivolity of her mourning attire, Constance's grief for her dead husband was deep and heartfelt. She had loved him since she was little more than a child, and his passing had left a painful void in her life. She hid her sorrow well, however, and few comprehended the depth of her suffering.

"Simon, my dear." Her voice was low and melodic. "It really is dreadful to descend on you like this, but I needed—" She faltered momentarily at the sight of Noelle, and then her green eyes began to twinkle with amusement. "I had no idea you were entertaining, Simon." Tipping her elegant head slightly to the side, she regarded him with exaggerated innocence. "I do hope my untimely arrival has not interrupted anything."

Smothering his irritation, Simon kissed her perfunctorily on the cheek. "You're always welcome, Connie." He could not resist using the nickname that he knew she detested. Drat the woman! Why did she have to appear now?

Just then, the last piece of the puzzle he had been trying to fit together in his mind fell into place, and he knew what he had to do.

"Let's go to the drawing room, where you can be more comfortable, Connie. We can finish our business there. Tomkins, please pour tea for the young lady. Noelle, if you'll excuse me."

Not waiting for Constance to protest, Simon hustled her from the library and led her to the drawing room. He was thinking furiously as he walked, weighing his options. His chances of pulling it off were so slim as to be almost nonexistent, but still, what other choice did he have?

When they arrived in the drawing room, which had been gracefully decorated à la chinoise, Constance disengaged Simon's hand from her arm.

"Simon, do stop pushing me so. I have long known you were a most vexatious man, but until now I never suspected you lacked the niceties of polite behavior. Much more of this and I shall have the vapors!" She sank eloquently onto a small lacquered chair, her hand resting gracefully over her heart.

"The vapors!" Simon's handsome face split with laughter. "Connie, you wouldn't know how to have the vapors if you tried."

"Of course I would. It's all a matter of holding one's breath. Now, do stop calling me that ridiculous name—you know I detest it—and tell me what is happening here. Really, Simon, I know men have their animal needs, but that child is frightfully ugly. Besides," she sniffed daintily, "I have always imagined you satisfied your baser cravings among the ladies of the demimonde, not with a common tart."

"My baser cravings, as you call them, Constance, are none of your concern. However, I will tell you that I have never been so desperate that I had to resort to an alliance with a streetwalker."

As much as Constance would have enjoyed pursuing this topic in greater depth, her curiosity about Simon's visitor overcame her. "Then who on earth is that person, and what is she doing here?"

"That person, Connie, is Quinn's wife," Simon said quietly.

"His wife!" All the ribbons in her auburn curls jerked at once. "You can't be serious!"

"I'm quite serious. They were married last night."

"But why? Quinn could marry any woman he chooses. He has everything. He is handsome, wealthy. He can be charming when it suits him. Why on earth? Surely he did not fall in love with her!"

"Don't be ridiculous. He'd never seen her until last night."

"Then why?"

"Revenge, Connie." Simon smiled wryly. "Like an avenging angel, he has smitten me."

"Do spare me your metaphors and explain yourself in a forthright manner, Simon. But first, please pour me a small glass of sherry. I daresay I'm going to need it." With this, she settled herself comfortably, crossed her dainty ankles, and listened intently as Simon told Noelle's story.

Quinn had made several passing references to Constance about Simon's preoccupation with having him marry well. At the time, she had paid little attention; conflicts between Simon and Quinn were so frequent that she had become inured to them. Now, as Simon spoke, she realized how seriously she had misjudged both Simon's persistence and Quinn's resentment. She loved that tiresome boy so. How could he have behaved like such a barbarian? Ever since Benjamin and she had cared for him when he was thirteen and Simon had sent him to school in England, he had held a special place in her heart.

"He took her," Simon said as he finished his story. "Brutally and without compassion."

Constance felt tears of pity for the bedraggled little pickpocket and for Quinn come to her green eyes. "Oh, Simon, he would never have behaved so if he hadn't mistaken her for a prostitute."

"Don't delude yourself. You know he's always been stubborn and high-handed."

Constance thought of another Copeland man who possessed the same characteristics but wisely kept the observation to herself.

"There is no denying the fact that he has a wildness in his nature that he does not always keep in check," Simon continued. "Of course, I doubt that he would have forced himself on her if he hadn't been drunk and mistaken her for a prostitute. But it's still no excuse for what he did. Besides, he certainly wasn't drunk when he delivered her here this morning, along with his resignation from Copeland and Peale."

"His resignation? Oh, Simon, no."

Constance's distress was justified, and they both knew it. Quinn's knowledge of ships was encyclopedic. He had a kinship with the raw materials of the industry, the wood and metal; an innate understanding of their strengths and limitations. He never attempted to force a new concept on the materials. Instead, he began with the materials and let the concept grow from them. It was Constance's belief that Quinn's creative imagination combined with Simon's keen business sense could have made Copeland and Peale invulnerable. Now all that was lost.

"He will not find it as easy as he thinks to turn his back on Copeland and Peale," Simon insisted.

"Where is Quinn now?" Constance asked, more calmly than she felt.

"I have no idea. But he'll turn up eventually, just like a bad penny."

Constance saw the trenchant pain in Simon's eyes and knew intuitively that his bitterness was directed as much at himself as at the son he couldn't understand.

"And when he does reappear, I plan to have a little surprise waiting for him."

Constance frowned. "What kind of surprise?"

It was then that Simon unveiled the desperate plan that had formed itself almost unconsciously in his mind. "When he returns, he'll have a true Copeland bride waiting for him, ready to take her place in the Copeland family."

"What on earth are you talking about?" Constance asked, abruptly setting down her glass on a small enameled end table.

"I am talking about the malnourished child in the library. Quinn has seen to it that I cannot have his marriage annulled. She's his legal wife. Therefore, she'll have to become worthy of the name Copeland."

Looking at him in astonishment, Constance began to laugh. Simon drew his brows together and glowered at her. Although she tried valiantly to suppress her merriment, she was not wholly successful.

"Oh, posh, Simon, don't fly into a temper. It was unkind of me to laugh, and I do apologize, but really, it's too absurd. I begin to fear that you are in your dotage."

In his dotage, was he? Simon could feel his temper rise. Damnation but she was an exasperating woman! Since the first time they had met when she was a beautiful bride many years younger than her husband, they had been at odds. As the years passed they saw each other only infrequently, but no matter how seldom they met, the sparks continued to fly.

Watching the two of them spar, Benjamin had once smiled fondly at his partner and said, "Simon, *you* should have married her. Perhaps you could have tamed her, for I gave up long ago."

Simon had shuddered inwardly. There was no denying the fact that Constance was a damned attractive woman, but he preferred women who were more serious, women who were respectful of the opinions of men far more knowledgeable than they. Now he must take pains not to antagonize her. With an effort, he smiled stiffly.

"Why is it so absurd, Constance? You forget that I have spent some time with her. The girl has a natural intelligence that even her shabbiness can't hide. Remember that her father was a member of the nobility."

"Really, Simon," Constance cried in exasperation. "You don't know that for certain."

"You only have to watch her closely to know it's true," he exclaimed as he began to pace about the room, trying to convince himself as he convinced her. "She carries herself proudly. She has dignity, intelligence. All of these things speak of good blood. She only needs some polishing to bring it out."

"Polishing!" Constance began to feel faintly alarmed; Simon was in earnest. As infuriating as he could be, she did not want to see him made to look ridiculous.

Rising from her chair, she crossed to him in a swish of ebony silk and placed her hand on his arm. She regarded him levelly, her voice grave. "Not only does she lack any semblance of beauty, but she is undoubtedly woefully ignorant. Why, I doubt that she can even read."

Simon regarded her stonily. "It doesn't matter."

Constance opened her mouth to respond, but Simon would have none of it. "All of that can be easily remedied, Constance. A tutor can be engaged to teach her how to read and instruct her in the rudiments of geography and history."

Indignantly Constance remonstrated. "In faith, Simon, it will take a bit more than teaching her the location of the Baltic Sea and the date of the Battle of Hastings to make her acceptable to society. And if something could be done about her unfortunate appearance, which I heartily doubt, she would still have to be taught to speak properly."

"She speaks beautifully," Simon interrupted. "Much better than would be expected."

"Regardless, Simon, I'm sure her diction would never pass in the drawing room. She needs to know how to manage a household, play the piano, do needlework, dance a quadrille." She ticked off each item on her fingers. "It quite staggers the mind. Even you, Simon, must own that you'd be hard pressed to find a tutor capable of teaching all that. Young women learn so many of these things unconsciously as they watch their mothers."

"Exactly!" Simon exploded triumphantly. Gently placing his hands on her upper arms, he looked down on her small form. "Those are the things only a woman of grace and breeding can teach, a woman such as yourself, Constance."

The spirited widow studied him for several moments as she absorbed his intention and finally declared, "No, Simon, I will not hear of it." She took several steps away and turned her back to him. "I have sometimes found it necessary to disagree with you on business matters, but I have never thought you lacking in common sense. I now begin to wonder."

Constance's voice was adamant, but if the truth be known, her mind was not yet closed on the matter. Although she would barely admit it even to herself, she was a lonely woman. The last few years, during which she had contended with Benjamin's failing health, had been difficult ones for her. Despite her frivolity, she was still an undeniably sensuous woman, and the celibacy that had become her lot was unnatural to her. Her body had begun to rebel; she ached to be held and caressed. She had even thought of taking a lover, but somehow the idea was repugnant to her, for she knew a casual coupling would not still the longings she felt. Of late, it had become more and more difficult for her to sleep. Perhaps if she had something to fill her days and occupy her mind, her nights would once again be peaceful.

She made her voice deliberately casual. "Simon, I must own I am curious. Just what is your plan, and how did you intend to include me?"

Simon wished Constance's back were not turned to him so he could see her face. What was she up to? Casually he walked to the settee opposite her and settled himself, carefully watching her face as he spoke.

"I would like you to take her home with you to Sussex. See to it that she has proper clothing and nourishment, and begin to instruct her in deportment. When you think the time is right, hire a qualified tutor for her academic instruction. I know it will take some time, but I have every confidence that within a year she can be transformed into a socially acceptable young woman."

"A year! Oh, Simon, I fear you overestimate her intelligence and my abilities." Constance was thoughtful for several moments, and Simon did not attempt to rush her. She walked almost aimlessly about the room, stopping once to straighten a vase. Finally she sat next to Simon on the settee.

"Let's assume for a moment that this improbable scheme of yours is successful and you actually manage to make her presentable. What then?"

"I intend to have her presented to society."

Constance's eyes widened. "You intend to present her as his wife?"

"No, of course not. She'll be my . . . my niece. No, that won't do. I don't want her to be a blood relative." He thought for a moment, then snapped his fingers. "I have it. We'll say that my brother married a young widow with a small child. She is that child."

"It's absurd, Simon," Constance argued. "You don't even have a brother. You have no assurance you can find Quinn. And, if you do, how do you then propose to convince him to assume his position as a husband?"

"Oh, I'll find him, rest assured of that." The determined set of his jaw told Constance that he would have no scruples at all about using force against Quinn. "As for convincing him—keep in mind, Constance, that it is one thing to abandon a child of the street with no family or protection; it is quite another to abandon a woman of breeding and grace who has been recognized by society. Quinn is a rogue, but even he wouldn't go that far. The two will meet and then I'll arrange for them to simply disappear from sight for several days. The news will leak out that they have eloped—a case of love at first sight. I, of course, will be properly outraged over their scandalous behavior. Everyone will sympathize with me, cluck their tongues, and be secretly delighted to find a couple so much in love they could not wait to be married properly. Within a month the scandal will be forgotten, and Quinn's bachelor existence will be a thing of the past."

"I don't like it, Simon," Constance declared. "Meddling in other people's lives is a dangerous pastime."

"It's the only way," Simon replied, firmly repressing his own doubts. "Quinn's wildness has gone unchecked for too long. He'll destroy himself." Simon was not above taking advantage of Constance's soft heart, and he did so now without a qualm.

"Constance, as a father who loves his son, I need your help. If you have any feeling at all for Quinn, remember that this may be his last chance."

Constance was not fooled by Simon's attempt at playing on her sympathies, but she did not call him to task for it. Instead, she asked the question that was now uppermost in her mind.

"What of the girl, Simon? From all you have said about her, she seems a most independent sort. Perhaps she won't go along with your scheme."

Simon had some doubts about this himself, but it wouldn't do to show weakness now. "Nonsense, Constance. It will be an opportunity the likes of which she has never dreamed possible." He paused, and his blue eyes narrowed slightly. "Besides, if she does protest, I believe I will be able to persuade her."

Constance looked at him keenly; he was holding back. "Simon, you are an unprincipled wretch. Not an hour ago you vowed to that child that you would protect her, and here you are single-mindedly plotting to reunite her with a man she obviously detests."

"Really, Constance, a year of luxury can't help but change her attitude. She'll regain her health and discover the advantages there are to being a Copeland. Do you seriously believe that she will turn her back on Quinn once she has been exposed to our way of life and sees how marriage will benefit her? Of course not."

He took Constance's hands in his and there was no subterfuge in his voice as he implored, "I know I can make this work. Please help me, Constance. Other than keeping Copeland and Peale secure in our two families, there's not much else in it for you. I know that. But you will have my perpetual gratitude. Please, will you help me?"

Her old antagonist was asking for help, and she had to admit that, for one so self-sufficient, he certainly did it splendidly. Raising her hands in a gesture of surrender, she smiled.

"In truth, Simon, you've worn me down, although I am undoubtedly a peagoose to have fallen in with you."

Simon slapped the palms of his hands together and laughed jubilantly.

Wagging a finger at him, Constance continued, "Do not for a moment think I am such a ninny as to enter into this May game of yours without issuing several provisos with which I expect your full compliance." Her voice was crisp and efficient, at odds with the fluttering ribbons and lace that bedecked her. "Financially, you are to be responsible for any and all expenses incurred during her stay. I will be the sole judge of the necessities of her wardrobe, and, I warn you, Simon, there will be no skimping."

"Agreed." Simon grinned as he triumphantly paced the perimeter of the Aubusson carpet.

"Simon, do stop moving about! This situation is difficult enough without forcing me to address the back of your head.

"I have one further condition. You are not to interfere with any of my methods. I will proceed in my own way and will brook no intervention from you. Is that understood?"

"Yes, yes." More like a boy of nineteen than a mature man of fifty, Simon pulled Constance up from her chair and enveloped her in an effusive hug.

His tiny business partner found herself clasped against his chest, the woolen of his morning coat pressing her cheek. Involuntarily her hands moved to his back, and she closed her eyes, drinking in the joy of once again having a man's arms encircle her. She breathed in the scent of him as her hands tentatively touched the muscles of his back. She wanted to feel his skin without the encumbrance of clothing, run her hands down his naked body, to . . .

Her eyes flew open. Really! What on earth was she thinking of! Hurriedly she extricated herself, snapping at him angrily, "Simon, I fear you have lost your sense. You will crush me, you wretched man."

Simon grinned at her, too overjoyed by her acquiescence to take umbrage with her scolding. "I apologize, Connie. I forgot myself."

Noelle sucked on her index finger to wet it and then dipped it experimentally into the sugar bowl. She licked off the crystals, savoring their sweetness, and ignoring a snowy napkin that lay carefully folded next to the silver pot, wiped her damp finger on the skirt of her dress.

During the absence of Simon and Constance, Noelle had finished two cups of tea, each of which she had fortified with several heaping teaspoons of sugar, and had devoured every crumb of a pair of buttery scones. Despite her large breakfast, she had eaten as if each bite were her last, but she could not seem to help herself.

At the same time she was licking her finger, her greedy eyes were consuming the elegant room. If Simon could have read Noelle's thoughts, he would have been delighted, because she was unconsciously proving that his instincts were right. She knew she looked cheap and out of place in the midst of such elegance, but she did not feel out of place. This gracious room, so foreign to her existence, felt more comfortable to her than any place she had ever been in her life. She loved the way the draperies looped above the windows, the warm colors of the carpet, the symmetry of the two chairs that flanked the library door. Her eyes approved the plasterwork of the ceiling and caressed a porcelain vase that was filled with early daffodils.

She yearned to touch it, feel the fine glass with her fingers, but she did not go near the beautiful vase, afraid that Simon Copeland would enter the room and see her coveting it. And why do you care what he thinks? she scoffed at herself, biting nervously on her thumbnail. Why was she still here anyway? The door was unlocked; there was nothing holding her.

But Noelle knew she wasn't ready to leave just yet. There was something about Simon Copeland that had stirred a deep, responsive chord inside her. She thought of his face, so like his son's, but somehow softened. And this woman, Constance. Who was she? What did she have to do with all this?

As if Noelle had conjured her, Constance entered the room, shuddering inwardly as she took a closer look at her new charge. She paused inside the door to wait for Simon, who followed almost immediately. Noelle was instantly struck by the handsome picture they presented: Simon Copeland, so tall and powerfully masculine, and Constance Peale, tiny and feminine.

"Noelle, I want you to meet Mrs. Peale, widow of my business partner. Constance, my daughter-in-law, Noelle."

Daughter-in-law! Noelle was incredulous. Simon was openly acknowledging the relationship between them to this sophisticated woman. Her eyes flew to his questioningly, but he merely quirked a dark eyebrow at her in what she could only read as a challenge.

Lifting her chin, she rose gracefully from her chair and met Constance's assessing gaze levelly. She would show him!

A spark of admiration flashed in the eyes of the older woman. Simon had been right. There was an air about this girl that transcended her ridiculous appearance. Her voice was soft and warm as she approached Noelle.

"I am delighted to make your acquaintance, my dear. Simon is quite taken with you, and I can surely see why."

Was this woman making fun of her? Noelle wondered. What was behind her honeyed words? She was out of her natural element among these people. On the streets, she knew her enemies. But here, an enemy could hide behind a polite smile. Well, she would play by their rules, she thought, as she returned Constance's smile with one of her own, but she would be on her guard.

"Noelle, I have asked Constance to join us so we may talk about your future."

Noelle felt her face burn. "You told her about me?" she burst out angrily.

Attempting to forestall the attack that he knew was coming, Simon pushed Noelle gently down on the settee, his eyes boring into hers. "Listen to me, Noelle. What happened to you is not your shame; it is Quinn's. Constance has been a friend for years. There was no way I could keep this from her, nor did I want to because I think she can help you."

Noelle lifted her small chin defiantly. "I don't need help from no—anybody."

"But you do, you know." Simon spoke softly and regarded her so kindly that Noelle felt some of her anger at his betrayal dissolve. "You have been through a great deal since last night. You need some time to rest. I could never forgive myself, my dear, if anything happened to you now while you're so upset. You also need some time to think about what you're going to do with your life. You don't have to go back to the streets again, you know."

Simon could see that his words were having an effect on Noelle. Suppressing the urgency he felt rising within, he kept his voice smooth and even. "Mrs. Peale has invited you to stay with her at her estate in Sussex. Since she is still in mourning for her husband, her life is quiet, and you'll be able to get the rest you must have."

Noelle set her jaw stubbornly. "You have no right making arrangements for me. I've taken care of myself this long without anyone's help. I don't need charity from either of you."

"I would hardly call it charity, Noelle," Simon protested.

"And just what would you call it?" she retorted. "Or does Mrs. Peale make it a habit of inviting pickpockets to stay with her?"

"I really don't think—" Simon began, but Noelle interrupted him angrily.

"I can see her now, introducing me to one of her grand friends." With uncanny accuracy Noelle imitated the voice of a society matron. "Millicent, I'd like you to meet my house guest. Quite an interesting girl. Hooks watches, you know."

This last was too much for Constance, who had been watching the sparring between Noelle and Simon with great interest. Her silvery laughter rang out.

"Oh, dear, Simon, she does have you there. I fear you've met your match."

"Do be quiet, Connie," Simon snapped. Damn the woman! If she wasn't going to be helpful, she could at least keep her mouth shut. He calculated his next move.

"It seems you still don't grasp your circumstances," he said harshly.

"What do you mean by that?"

"You may be carrying Quinn's child, you know."

Noelle felt as though she had been slapped. A tremor shot through her thin body.

Simon moved in quickly. "I see you hadn't thought of that. Well, perhaps it's time you did." His voice was wintry as he began his attack. "Do you want your child raised as you were? Grubbing about in the mud for a lump of coal?" He drew his lips into a sneer. "How old will the child be before you hang up a coat and train him to be a pickpocket?"

Noelle's face drained of all color, but Simon did not ease his assault. "Of course, it won't be so bad if you have a boy. It's easier for boys to survive. But what if it's a girl? Perhaps she won't be as lucky as you've been. I understand there are noblemen who are convinced that deflowering a virgin will cure them of the French pox. They're willing to pay as much as a hundred pounds for one. Do you want that to happen to a child of yours?"

"Stop it!" Noelle screamed. "Stop it!" She buried her head in her hands, trying to collect herself. She had thought her nightmare was over, but now she saw that fate was not going to release its hold on her so easily.

Constance sprang angrily from her chair. "That's quite enough, Simon. You are being cruel, and I won't have it."

A biting retort died on Simon's lips, and he turned away.

Noelle felt herself enveloped in fragrant black silk. Constance's voice was calm and soothing. "You must understand, Noelle, that Simon is used to having his own way in all things. He is a businessman, and businessmen are afraid to speak from their hearts. Simon does not want to lose you now. Although he would never admit it, he admires fiery spirits. And, Noelle, he has a right to know if you are carrying his grandchild."

For a moment Constance felt a stab of guilt. In her own way, she knew she was manipulating the child just as much as Simon had been.

Slowly Noelle raised her face to Constance, hating the benevolence she saw there, hating the circumstances that were inexorably bending her proud spirit to the protection of these two people. "I don't seem to have much choice, do I?" she said bitterly.

They had won; she was going to have to do as they suggested until she discovered if she was going to have a child. But if they expected her to be fawning in her gratitude, they were due for a rude surprise.

"If I do as you say, I want your promise that you will tell no one that I am married to Mr. Copeland's son."

Constance nodded her assent.

"Also, I will only stay until I know if I am going to have a child, then you will immediately return me to London."

Constance forestalled the protest she could see Simon preparing to voice. "Fair enough, my dear. Now, let's find something a bit more suitable for you to wear." Turning to Simon, Constance said, "I wish to leave within the hour. Will you see that I have fresh horses?"

Nodding his assent, Simon left the room quickly, well satisfied with the turn of events.

The two women regarded each other levelly for several moments. Finally Constance spoke with some satisfaction. "I think we shall get along together very well, don't you?"

But Noelle did not respond. Somehow she knew it was not going to be quite that easy. Nothing in life came free of charge; sooner or later she would be expected to pay the price. What it would be she did not know, but of its inevitability she was certain.

PART TWO

Dorian Pope
Sussex

London's streets were now behind them; the last afternoon sun shone on tidy fields and small cottages, fresh and clean after the smoke and dirt of the city. The two other occupants of the carriage had each settled into the trip in their own fashion. Letty, Constance's abigail, a homely young woman with a florid complexion, had fallen asleep, her mouth open slightly and her plump bosom rising and falling rhythmically. Constance was staring vacantly out of the window, absorbed in her own thoughts, tiny lines of tension evident at the corners of her soft mouth.

Noelle looked hideously unattractive and out of place as she sat in the Peale carriage with a small bundle resting on her lap. Before she had left the house on Northridge Square, she had been led to a small room off the kitchen, where she had scrubbed the last vestiges of crimson from her hollow cheeks and unsuccessfully attempted tidying her hair, only managing to tame the most unruly of the tufts. She ran her finger under the collar of the dress she now wore, a shapeless garment of brown merino that Letty had apparently secured from one of the maids. It itched abominably at the neck.

Noelle did not miss Constance's inquisitive gaze as she set her bundle on the floor of the carriage, but she had no intention of enlightening the woman about its contents. Her curiosity was understandable, since Noelle had abruptly rejected Constance's offer to stop at her lodgings on their way out of London so she could collect her belongings. But Noelle had shuddered at the thought of exposing her room to this sophisticated woman, imagining the revulsion that would stamp itself on those fine features when they first observed the squalor of the tenement.

Noelle realized there was really nothing she wished to take with her. Her possessions were painful mementos: a few of Daisy's old playbills, now yellow and brittle with age; a piece of blue glass Sweeney had fished from the river for her; a length of mauve ribbon she had worn as a child; a stub of candle; some tattered garments. When Noelle did not return, the other occupants of the dwelling would descend on the unoccupied room like cockroaches and carry off everything.

They were welcome to it, Noelle thought bitterly. She had everything she needed with her.

The smallest object in the bundle at her ankles was the gold wedding ring that had been pushed on her finger. Noelle had thrust it deeply into the pocket of the emerald dress when she had changed her clothes. But it was the dress itself, that much-abused piece of tawdry finery, that took up the bulk of the bundle. It would serve as a constant reminder of everything she had endured.

She vowed she would not destroy the dress until she had wreaked vengeance on the one who had humiliated her. She refused to listen to the realist in her that warned it would not be a simple task to revenge herself on Quinn Copeland. No matter how difficult, she would bring him to his knees, make him beg as she had begged, see him degraded. There could be no life for her until then.

One last object was concealed in the bundle—a sturdy knife with a short blade and a pale bone handle. When Letty had led Noelle through the kitchen, the girl's sharp eyes had spotted it lying on the corner of the table next to a pile of scrubbed potatoes. With lightning deftness, she had plucked the knife from the table and secreted it in the folds of her skirt.

If she had thought of it, she would not have found it at all ironic that she could steal the knife without a qualm but that her pride would not allow her to keep the money that had been given to her. The money would make her a whore; the knife was merely a replacement for what had been taken from her. The thought of the tempered steel blade nestled securely within the emerald dress was like a tiny, glowing ember warming her and bolstering her courage.

The sun burned low on the horizon, blazing in final defiance before succumbing to the force of nature that would remove this part of England from its influence. Noelle closed her eyes against the glare. She felt drained, ill, emptied of herself. The carriage swayed easily, its wheels whispering rhythmically. Her last conscious image before she slipped into an uneasy sleep was of a lean face with black, bitter eyes and a hard mouth locked in a mocking sneer.

"Time to wake, ma'am."

Noelle's eyes flicked open just enough to see the taciturn Letty lumber into the room.

Speaking as if each word were an effort, she muttered, "Mrs. Peale would like you in her sitting room when you've done with breakfast." Letty's ponderous movements seemed in keeping with her large, bovine eyes, blunt features, and ruddy complexion. She set a small breakfast tray on a marble-topped table near the front of the sunlit room.

It was the unfamiliar aroma of fresh croissants mingling invitingly with the delicate, rich scent of chocolate that finally forced Noelle to lift her head from the soft pillow. Of her arrival the previous night, she could recall little beyond being led upstairs and helped into a nightgown, and so she was totally unprepared for the beauty of the room in which she found herself.

The wall behind the bed supported a graceful curve of mahogany. Sprigged blue silk draperies were hung from this wooden crown. The draperies were bound twice on each side by tasseled golden cords producing curved puffs that were looped against the wall. A dressing table was covered with the same sprigged fabric. Three windows, draped in a paler shade of blue, ran symmetrically across the front of the room. Alabaster white walls were accented by moldings painted the same blue as the draperies.

Rising stiffly, she stood for a moment next to the bed, taking in the room's furnishings. There was a mirror with a gilded frame, a bureau, a delicate chair with a small curved back, two alabaster candlesticks, and a lamp with a blue globe. It was finer than anything she had ever imagined.

As she surveyed the room she waited for Letty to leave so she could dress, but the servant was taking her time, straightening the bedcovers with mathematical precision. Noelle wondered if it were the custom of the gentry to permit servants to remain in the room while members of the household dressed. If so, it seemed a stupid custom. Even a pickpocket from Soho knew that privacy was just as important as food.

As the maid seemed to have no intention of leaving, Noelle

decided to take advantage of the privacy of a small curtained alcove off the side of the room. She stepped inside, drawing the drapery behind her.

What a contrast the tiny room was to the crude sanitary facilities to which she was accustomed! There was a washstand, an assortment of elegant bottles holding a variety of sweet-smelling toiletries, embroidered linens, and an enormous chamber pot embellished with a full-length ceremonial portrait of the late George III. For the first time since she had awakened, her spirits lifted, and a soft giggle escaped as she contemplated relieving herself in the presence of His Majesty. The ways of the gentry were certainly strange.

She had just finished tidying herself when the curtain of the bathing alcove was drawn back to reveal the silent Letty, ugly brown dress in one hand, petticoats in another. Noelle spun about, indignant at this further invasion of her privacy.

The maid stood awkwardly, her expression stoic. It was difficult for Noelle to understand how such an ungainly woman could serve as abigail to one as elegant as Constance Peale. What she could not know was how well-suited mistress and maid were. Although slow, Letty was painstaking in her care of her employer's person and wardrobe. In turn, Constance was sensitive to Letty's awkwardness and provided her with a quiet refuge.

Noelle, however, knew none of this. Letty was merely another forbidding guardian of this strange land that had been thrust upon her. "What do you want?"

Noelle's sharp tone did not alter Letty's expression. "Help you dress," she mumbled.

"I can dress myself very well, thank you," Noelle retorted, taking the brown dress from Letty and snapping the draperies back into place.

She donned the fresh undergarments and settled the dress over her head, then slipped out of the bathing alcove to find Letty standing patiently beside the breakfast tray, her eyes downcast.

Noelle felt a quick flash of remorse for having spoken so impolitely to the woman. She was obviously doing her job as she had been trained. In an effort to make amends, she gestured toward the breakfast tray.

"It all smells so good, but there's more here than I can eat. Would you like some?"

The bovine eyes flickered with surprise, and the stolid mouth, while it did not go so far as to smile, softened. "I already ate."

Her conscience eased, Noelle settled herself in front of the breakfast tray and nibbled a flaky croissant.

"Thank you, ma'am, for the offer."

Noelle looked up to find the abigail's face flushed at the effort of making conversation. "You're welcome."

Letty turned to leave the room and then paused. "The mistress's sitting room is across the hall when you're ready to see her, Mrs. Copeland."

Mrs. Copeland!

Fury choked Noelle. She set down the croissant, her appetite lost. Letty had been told her identity! Constance had promised to keep it a secret, but not even a day had passed before she had broken their agreement. Gentry! Just because they had money, they thought they could trample over those who didn't. Well, she would show them! She was not going to be pushed about by anyone again.

Shoving herself back from the table, Noelle rushed from the halcyon room to confront her hostess. The sound of voices within led her to the proper door. She had just raised her fist to bang on the door when she heard an indignant exclamation.

"It's a disgrace; that's what it is, ma'am. Mr. Quinn marrying a common harlot and her livin' right here with us."

In the sitting room, unaware that they were being overheard, Constance was engaged in a painful interview with Violet Finch, her housekeeper and cook. Mrs. Finch, one of the few cooks in England who had totally mastered French cuisine, had been Constance's prize employee for eleven years. Her kitchen had helped make the Peale dinner parties legendary with offerings such as a ratatouille that breathed of the shores of Provence, *coq au vin* lightly touched with thyme, airy fish soufflés, rich brioches, and *bombe glacée* garnished with a delicate web of spun sugar.

However, as Constance had long ago discovered, having Mrs. Finch in her employ was a mixed blessing, for she had a strong sense of the way things should be and was indignant when others saw differently. For over a decade, Constance had been soothing her cook's ruffled feathers, for she had no intention of losing the irreplaceable services of Violet Finch.

"A harlot! Come now, Mrs. Finch, where on earth did you hear that?"

As if I didn't know, thought Constance, imagining the interrogation poor Letty had suffered at the hands of Mrs. Finch. She should have warned her last night to keep silent. Not that it would have been much use. Mrs. Finch's methods would have done the Spanish Inquisition proud.

"I got it from Letty, ma'am." The cook pursed her thin lips sanctimoniously. "As you well know, I consider it my Christian duty to watch over the girl and see that she doesn't fall into bad ways. I must admit, Mrs. Peale, I was that surprised last night when you told me the . . . person . . . was to be your guest. Dressed as she was, I'd taken her for a new maid. And then, when Letty told me how she'd had her face all painted and been wearin' a harlot's dress that left her bosom to no one's imagination . . . I don't want to upset you, ma'am, but I felt my heart palpitations comin' on again."

Curse you and your heart palpitations! Constance wanted to shriek. What a muddle this was turning into.

"Now, now, my dear Mrs. Finch, it is most unlike you to judge someone by such thin evidence. I am not at liberty to divulge the circumstances behind Mr. Copeland's marriage, but I can assure you that Mrs. Copeland is not, nor has she ever been, a harlot." Constance managed to look deeply offended.

Somewhat subdued, but certainly not satisfied, Mrs. Finch protested, "But the way she was dressed? And what about that hair?"

Constance delicately pressed her hand to the base of her throat. "Come now, Mrs. Finch, surely you would not have me break a solemn oath!" She appeared to think for a moment. "Perhaps it is just as well this has come up after all, for now I can approach you openly. As you can imagine, I am in dire need of a confidante, a woman of discretion and great Christian charity. Yes, Mrs. Finch, I see that I have no choice but to cast myself on your tender mercies."

The cook's plump face beamed with pleasure. "Mrs. Peale, you know you may depend on me. It's difficult for you, bein' a woman alone without the counsel of a husband. Ever since the death of Mr. Peale, God rest his soul, I've been sayin' to myself—"

"Quite so," Constance interrupted smoothly. "As you have

realized, the new Mrs. Copeland is not a woman of, shall we say, the breeding one would expect of a Copeland bride. She is, alas, a poor, defenseless creature, too ignorant to deal with even the simplest demands made upon her." Forgive me, Noelle, Constance thought ruefully, but Violet Finch's cooking is my Achilles' heel.

"It is useless for me to pretend that she will be anything but a great burden to us." At this pronouncement, Mrs. Finch, her eyes sparkling with satisfaction, gave a great sigh. "However, I hope I know my duty when I see it. When Mr. Simon Copeland pleaded with me to take her in . . . well, what else could I do?" Shrugging her shoulders pitifully, Constance Peale was a portrait of helplessness.

"You did right," the cook pronounced, her lips set in a determined line. "Now, you just stop fretting, ma'am, and leave everything to me. The staff will treat the poor creature well, or they'll have to answer to Violet Finch."

Noelle, her cheeks burning with humiliation, fled back to her bedroom and had barely shut the door before she heard Mrs. Finch's footsteps disappearing self-righteously down the hallway.

As she sank down in front of the dressing table she caught sight of her reflection in the gilded mirror. Dressed as she was, with her crudely dyed hair, skin so unhealthily pale it seemed almost waxen, and great sunken eyes, she appeared exactly as they had characterized her, an object of charity. "Poor defenseless creature." "Ignorant." "Great burden." The words stung like a slap. On the streets they had called her "Highness"; she had been respected, even feared by some.

Leaping up from the dressing table, she vowed that they were not going to do this to her. She would not be sniveled over with talk of Christian charity. They could all go to hell; she was going back to London!

In her exhaustion of the night before, she had thrown her bundle under the bed. Now she retrieved it and tossed it on top of the bedcovers. Her fingers fumbled at the buttons on the bodice of the brown merino. She would not take this charity dress with her; she would rather walk to London in the hated emerald gown. Cursing herself under her breath for her stupidity in ever having agreed to leave London, she peeled the brown dress off and, standing in her undergarments, began unwrapping her bundle. Angry tears coursed down her cheeks as she pulled out the gown, but she paid them no heed. She was not taking anyone's charity!

Unbidden, Simon Copeland's words began assaulting her. "Will you hang up a coat and train him to be a pickpocket?" he had sneered. "Deflowering a virgin will cure them of the French pox."

"No," she sobbed aloud, but his words continued echoing in her mind.

"What if it's a girl? What if it's a girl? A girl . . . a girl . . ."

With a strangled cry, Noelle threw the emerald dress down on the bed. "God damn them!"

She was trapped. No matter how much she suffered, she could not risk leaving here until she knew if she was carrying a child. Her dreams were already haunted by the starving children she saw every day, their bellies swollen with hunger, their faces empty and hopeless. Forfeiting her pride was a small price to pay to insure that a child of her body would never be among them.

She consoled herself with the reminder that, if she were not pregnant, it would only be a matter of weeks before she could leave this luxurious prison.

And if she were? Her stomach knotted at the thought. If she were pregnant, she would be forced to accept their charity until the birth. It would be a bitter sacrifice, but when she had delivered, she could leave the baby to the protection of these wealthy people, knowing it would be well cared for. Then she would be able to return to the freedom of her old life.

Her shoulders slumped in defeat as she pulled the brown dress back on. It sickened her that she was going to be forced to accept Constance Peale's smug charity. At least no one would ever know that she had overheard the women's conversation; that much of her pride she could salvage.

As she angrily stuffed the green gown back into the worn sack, her hand skimmed against the knife she had stolen from Simon's kitchen. Thoughtfully she lifted it out and set it on the bedcovers. She would have at least one friend while she was in this house! Tearing a ragged strip from her chemise, she strapped the weapon to her calf, then reluctantly faced the door, determined to go through with her interview. "I'm going to make that woman wish she hadn't been so quick to do her Christian duty," Noelle pledged as she took a deep breath and once again crossed the hallway.

She attacked Constance's door with three ferocious knocks.

"Come in," her hostess's voice rang out.

Constance's sitting room and adjoining bedroom were delicate pink and green confections. Benjamin himself had purchased the hand-painted wallpaper in Canton as an anniversary gift for his wife. From the top of the painted wainscoting to the ceiling, a filigree of pale green bamboo climbed the walls. Tiny figures dressed in shell pink robes and carrying gossamer parasols adorned the paper at eye level. There were lacquered chests, Chinese vases, and porcelain figures. The same pink of the wallpaper figures was repeated in the silk bed hanging and the Chippendale chaise on which Constance reclined.

She wore a lime-green froth of ribbons and deep lace that rustled softly as she set aside some papers she had been studying.

"Noelle, my child, I'm delighted to see you. I trust you slept well." Her nose wrinkled becomingly as she smiled warmly at her guest, carefully concealing the distress that overcame her each time she caught sight of the starved, pinched face.

"I slept well," Noelle responded stiffly.

"Do sit down, my dear. I have so much to discuss with you." A large pearl ring set in gold flashed on Constance's hand as she indicated a chair next to her chaise.

Noelle sat rigidly, not permitting her back to touch the chair.

"You do look better after your rest last night."

What a liar she is, Noelle thought scornfully. Does she think I haven't looked in the mirror?

"We live simply here, you know," Constance continued brightly, "so you needn't worry about hordes of people descending on us. So tiring, I think, to be forced to maintain a conversation with someone who is a total stranger."

Constance paused, obviously expecting some response from her guest, but Noelle retained her stony silence. There was a tiny narrowing at the corners of Constance's eyes, but then she continued with her monologue, her manner as charming as it had been when Noelle first entered the room. "Let me acquaint you with our routine so that you'll be comfortable here. Breakfast is served in your room whenever you call for it. Lunch is at one and dinner at seven. We have both in the dining room. Tea is at four. I want you to rest and enjoy yourself while you're visiting, my dear. Feel free to explore the house and the gardens. They are lovely now as the buds just begin to unfold."

Noelle could stand Constance's hypocrisy no longer. "You broke our agreement," she declared flatly.

"Oh?" Constance regarded Noelle with an expression that was faintly quizzical, but otherwise she seemed totally unruffled by the accusation.

Noelle's enormous eyes were hard and angry from the hurt that ached inside her. More than anything she wanted to lash out at this woman, to challenge her. You had no right to talk about me as you did! I don't need your charity. I can take care of myself.

But the words remained unspoken. Instead, she glared coldly at Constance. "You told Letty who I am. She called me 'Mrs. Copeland' when she brought my breakfast tray this morning. We had an agreement, and you have broken it."

Constance regarded Noelle calmly. "I did not tell Letty who you are. She must have overheard part of our conversation in the library."

Uncertain whether or not Constance was telling the truth, Noelle pressed her attack. "Nevertheless, you promised me that no one would know I am his wife. Now everyone will know."

"No, they won't, Noelle."

"And just how are you going to manage that?" Her tone was venomous. Noelle thought she saw hurt reflected in Constance's eyes, and for an instant she was confused. Don't be a fool, she scolded herself. This woman is as gifted an actress as any on the London stage. She has no real feelings.

As if confirming Noelle's opinion, Constance dropped her eyes and calmly retied a ribbon that had come undone at the front of her robe. When she spoke, it was dispassionately.

"Only Letty and Mrs. Finch, the woman who serves as my housekeeper and cook, know who you are, and even they do not know of your past. They have both been with me for some time and are completely trustworthy. I will instruct Mrs. Finch as to how I want your presence explained to the rest of the staff. You may be assured that within forty-eight hours, the story I have fabricated will have been discussed in every household throughout the countryside."

"What kind of story?" Noelle asked suspiciously.

"You are to be Simon's niece, Noelle Dorian," Constance began.

Noelle interrupted abruptly. "No, I don't want anyone to know my real name."

"Very well. Perhaps you could use Dorian for your first name, then. It has a rather aristocratic ring, I think. It will also be easier for you to answer to a familiar name."

Constance took Noelle's silence for consent. "Now, for a last name . . ." She tapped the side of her chin with a slim finger as she considered the possibilities.

"Pope. Dorian Pope." It was a statement, not a request.

Constance smiled responsively. "Perfect, absolutely perfect. How did you ever think of it?"

"It's the name of someone I once knew."

Constance wisely refrained from asking any questions, although her curiosity was piqued. "All right. You are Simon's niece, Dorian Pope, the stepchild of his brother. Actually, Simon has no brother, but, then, no one in London knows that." Rising from her chaise, she walked about the room as she narrated the story, gesturing gracefully with her hands.

"You were born in India. When you were small, your father was killed in a border skirmish. Later, Simon's brother, who was an engineer in the East India Company, married your mother. You lived in India all of your life until only a few months ago, when your stepfather and then your mother died in a cholera epidemic. You were also stricken and came close to dying.

"Simon has asked me to keep you here so you can recover from your illness and the tragic loss of your beloved parents in a peaceful atmosphere. You, of course, must have total rest and quiet; therefore, it is quite impossible for you to receive." Constance smiled. "I think that's a nice touch, don't you?"

Noelle had only the vaguest idea where India was and no idea at all what it meant to "receive," but she had no intention of letting Constance discover her ignorance. Instead, she spoke sarcastically. "And we shall all live happily ever after, I suppose."

The smile disappeared from Constance's face, and all the warmth left her voice. "That, Noelle, will depend upon you."

Chapter Seven

Considering Constance's comfortable station in life, her house, built in the style of Queen Anne, was rather simple, a neat rectangle without wings or courtyards. It was constructed of creamy white stone that changed color according to the weather and the time of day. Sometimes it assumed a rosy hue; at sunset it glowed golden. There was a dark brown doorway in the center ornamented only by a simple pediment carved from the same stone as the rest of the house. Three tall windows stood on each side of the door. The second floor had seven windows, the center one somewhat larger than its mates. Magnolias had been trained to cover much of the right side of the house, their waxy emerald leaves curling around the window frames. On the left side of the house yellow climbing roses clung to the stone, a few even attaching themselves to the windowsill of Noelle's second-story bedroom.

Inside, the unhappy girl restlessly paced the room, her steps muffled by the thick carpeting. The cool blue and white of the walls and the calm elegance of the furnishings stood in decided contrast to the unrest of her young spirit.

Her encounter with Constance Peale disturbed her far more than had her frequent, often violent confrontations on the street. Noelle's method was to spot the enemy and attack face on. But this woman was from outside her experience, and she sensed that the methods of the street would not work in this new world.

Finely honed instinct nagged at her. How could the woman present such a convincing display of friendship and sincerity when it was all false? If there were only some way she could strip it all away.

A sound coming from the front of the house drew her to the window. Peering out from behind the sprigged blue silk draperies, she spotted Constance being assisted into an elegant dark green carriage. This was her chance to explore without risking another unwelcome encounter with her hostess.

She began in the drawing room, at first studying the rich composition of ivory and gold as if it were a key that would unlock the mystery of its owner. But her compelling sense of beauty, starved for so long, overpowered her reason, and she fell captive to the artistry and quiet elegance around her.

She moved from room to room, running her hands along the soft nap of velvet draperies, gingerly stroking a china figurine, scrutinizing the elaborate plasterwork of the many fireplaces. She loved the graceful sweep of the stairway as it curved down into the center hallway and could even admire the full-length portrait of Constance as a young woman that hung on the landing. The hard, aching knot inside her eased.

She was preparing to walk into the gardens that lay at the rear of the house when the great clock in the foyer struck one. As if the toll were a signal, a young maid with a pitted complexion and sulky eyes materialized from the back hallway that Noelle correctly concluded led to the basement kitchen.

"My name is Molly, Miss Pope. I'm the downstairs maid."

So, Noelle mused, as she heard herself addressed by her assumed name for the first time, at least in this, Constance has kept her word.

"The mistress will not be back in time for lunch," the maid went on, not bothering to hide her scorn for a house guest who looked so vulgar. "Will you be eating in the dining room or would you prefer a tray in your bedroom?"

Noelle did not hesitate. "In my room, please." She had already peeked in at the resplendent dining room and even her indomitable spirit flagged at the thought of eating a meal alone in such formidable surroundings.

Not bothering to respond, the maid disappeared back down the hallway.

Noelle returned to her room and discovered that a plain, dark blue muslin dress had been placed on her bed. She fingered the material; it was soft from many washings. The fact that the dress was not a new garment convinced her that she could accept it.

Shedding the uncomfortable brown merino, she slipped the dark blue dress over her head. It hung on her emaciated frame, the hem barely reaching her ankles. She used the belt to gather the loose folds closer to her body and looked at the result in the mirror.

Having no vanity about her appearance, it did not bother her that this dress was as unflattering as the garment it had replaced. She was merely grateful that it did not itch. Still, she sighed at the contrast between the ornate gilded frame of the mirror and the pitifully unattractive reflection it enclosed.

Quickly she turned her attention to her luncheon tray. She was astonished by the amount of food: generous servings of poached salmon, roast beef, potatoes, fresh bread, and a fragrant vegetable that Letty later told her was called asparagus. She ate every bite and then lay down on her bed, the unaccustomed fullness in her stomach and the weakened condition of her own body quickly putting her to sleep. She awakened feeling more rested than she could remember, and with a somewhat lighter step, headed for the gardens. On the way she noticed an imposing set of double doors leading off the back of the center hallway. Curious, she pushed on the knob and stepped inside. What she saw erased all thoughts of the garden from her mind.

Quickly she closed the door behind her and then stood as if rooted to the spot. It was the Peale library, a stately room of oak and leather with high ceilings that dwarfed her. Light streamed in from one end falling on the heavy, highly polished furniture and highlighting a massive portrait that dominated the room. From the dress of the man, Noelle deduced that it was a likeness of Benjamin Peale. He was no longer young when the artist had captured him, but still a handsome man with thick white hair parted on the side and heavy eyebrows that almost met in the middle.

All of these books must have been his, Noelle concluded, awestruck, as she transferred her gaze from the portrait to the towering shelves that lined the walls. Her feet finally freed themselves from the floor, and she forgot everything except the wealth she had so unexpectedly discovered.

The clock struck, and, with it, the library door opened and Molly appeared.

"I've been looking for you half the afternoon," she declared, irritated at the orders she had received from Mrs. Finch to treat the cheap-looking upstart with the utmost civility. "The mistress wants you to know that dinner is at seven o'clock in the dining room. And she doesn't like people to be late."

Noelle looked up from the slim volume she had been perusing. Here was an enemy she could understand. Rising from the chair, she advanced, her height giving her several inches advantage over the wiry girl. She bit out each word precisely. "Tell me, Molly, since you're such an expert on what the mistress likes and doesn't like, how does she feel about nasty little maids who don't know their place?"

The maid's eyes widened at the unexpected assault. "Excuse me, miss." Only taking time to bob a respectful curtsy, she fled.

At exactly seven o'clock Noelle entered the dining room. Constance stood at the end of the room, framed by the mantel and carved sides of the fireplace. She wore a black gown shot with silver threads, an enormous spray of diamond lilacs at her throat.

The dining room, which Noelle had glimpsed earlier, was in the same rich ivory and gold as the drawing room. There were two sideboards against the wall and four shield-back chairs that were mates to the eight already around the oval table. Two places had been laid, one at the head of the table and another to the immediate right. As Constance seated herself, she indicated the other place.

"I apologize for not being here to lunch with you, Dorian, but I received a message that an old friend had been taken ill." In deference to the maid standing at the sideboard, she addressed Noelle according to their agreement. "Just a trace of indigestion, as it turned out, but she is rather frail, and I could not be satisfied until I saw for myself that she was all right. I trust your lunch was satisfactory?"

"It was excellent, thank you," Noelle answered coolly.

Thin porcelain bowls filled with Mrs. Finch's prize bouillabaisse were set before them. Noelle watched as Constance carefully chose the largest of the spoons before her and gracefully dipped it into the bowl. Noiselessly she sipped the soup from the side of the silver spoon and then returned it to the bowl. Noelle continued to watch this procedure until Constance had consumed almost half of her soup. Her motions were so deliberate that Noelle rapidly concluded she was being subtly instructed in proper table manners. She did not see a hostess trying to make a guest comfortable; instead, the fateful conversation she had overheard that morning tormented her: ". . . *the new Mrs. Copeland, not a woman of the breeding one would expect of a Copeland bride.*"

Angrily resting both her elbows on the polished surface of the table, Noelle took her bowl in both hands, raised it to her lips, and noisily filled her mouth with its delicious contents.

Constance's eyebrows shot up. For a moment Noelle thought she had managed to pierce her hostess's armor as she saw the green sparks glittering in her eyes, but the moment passed, and Constance gestured wordlessly to the maid to remove the bowls.

The next course was set before the silent combatants.

Throughout the rest of the meal Noelle carefully observed Constance and then did as close to the opposite as possible. If Constance chose a fork, Noelle used a spoon. When Constance carved her quail with a knife, Noelle tore hers apart with her fingers. She slurped from her water glass, carefully mashed her peas into the potatoes, and, finally, cleaned her hands by sucking each finger noisily.

Two strawberry tarts garnished with generous dollops of whipped cream were set before them. Constance began to pick up her fork and then, eyeing Noelle, deliberately replaced the instrument on the table and folded her hands in her lap. Noelle studied her hostess and then the juicy pastry. Pushing herself back from the table, she picked up the dripping tart in her fingers and walked toward the dining room doors.

"Nice meal," she tossed back over her shoulder, deeply regretting that she had never mastered the art of belching at will.

After a deep, dreamless sleep and breakfast in her room the next morning, Noelle headed for the library. She chose three volumes from the shelf and took them out into the sunny garden. The garden was enclosed by the house on one side and a wall of golden-brown brick on the other two sides. Its open end afforded a breathtaking vista of hills and valleys still enshrouded with morning mists. Clumps of alder and beech rose from ground newly green with spring grass. Noelle breathed in the fragrant Sussex air and settled herself on one of two stone benches that surrounded a small fountain topped by a spouting cupid. The chill of the stone soon seeped through her petticoats, but she did not notice. She was lost in the mystery of the books.

When it was time for lunch, Noelle prepared herself for another battle of wits with her hostess. Walking into the dining room, she saw several changes had been made.

Again, two places had been laid, but instead of locating the second place to the immediate right of the hostess as before, it had been moved to the foot of the table. Dominating the center of the table was an elaborate silver epergne. It stood perhaps six hands tall, its slender branches supporting, at various heights, silver baskets and shell-like dishes. Above the branches was a double-tiered pagoda hung with five silver filigree bells, each over two inches in diameter at its base. Designed to hold relishes and condiments, the enormous piece was curiously empty.

As Noelle sat in her new place at the foot of the table, she felt her first glimmer of respect for her hostess. The enormous silver piece entirely hid Constance from her view and she, in turn, was hidden from Constance's.

Chapter Eight

Two days later, Constance snipped a miniature peach-colored rosebud from one of the bushes she cultivated with much care in her small greenhouse. She held it up to the filtered sunlight and gazed at it thoughtfully as she puzzled over the problem foremost in her mind. I can take a cutting and help it develop into a thing of beauty, she mused. A little knowledge, some care, and a bit of luck. That's all it needs. But not Noelle. Since she has been here she has shown herself unwilling to accept even the slightest kindness. She bristles when I come near and defies me every way she can. Why? For three days Constance had been asking herself this question, and she was still no closer to an answer.

Placing the tender bud on top of its sisters in a wicker basket, she smiled grimly to herself as she thought of their twice daily mealtime duels. Just today, Noelle had managed to consume an entire lobster stew without once touching fork or spoon. She infuriates me so, I'd like to strangle her, yet I can't remember when I've met a person I admire as much as that girl. She has such fierce determination, such pride. If there were only some way I could pierce her hostility.

Sighing, she picked up the rose-filled basket and walked into her house. It seemed the only thing she'd done right was to put out that ugly old blue dress so Noelle could have a change of clothing. If she could just order some pretty things for her and a few caps to cover that absurd hair, but as she had several times before, Constance abruptly dismissed the thought. Noelle was definitely not a doll to be costumed.

I'm afraid Simon is destined to be bitterly disappointed, she told herself. He'll never be able to convince her to stay here with me.

As she passed the library door she saw that it had been left ajar. Curious, she peeked in.

Noelle, looking very small in the lofty paneled room, was running her hand along one of the shelves. Finally she extracted a dark green leather-bound tome and took it to the library table, where she set it on the tooled leather top. She has spent more time in there these last few days, Constance thought, than she has anywhere else in this house. And every time I look in, she seems to have a different book in her hands.

Constance pasted a bright smile on her lips and entered the room. "Hello, Noelle, aren't these lovely?" She held out the peach roses for Noelle's scrutiny.

"Yes," Noelle responded coldly, not bothering to pick up her head to look.

Suddenly Constance felt a great resentment rising within her. She was tired of being rebuffed, tired of Noelle's perpetual rudeness.

"I said, aren't these lovely?" Although her voice was quiet, the tones were icy and commanding.

Startled, Noelle lifted her head to find Constance's green eyes, usually so warm, scrutinizing her angrily. Noelle looked at the rose Constance held extended in her hand. "It's a beautiful rose," she said flatly.

Encouraged that the girl had responded at all, Constance pressed on. "I have noticed, Noelle, that you are spending a great deal of time in the library. I would like to see what you are reading." Imperiously she held out her hand for the book that lay in Noelle's lap.

Noelle's interest was piqued by her hostess's newfound aggressiveness. "If you wish," she answered with seeming indifference.

Constance concealed the tiny stab of triumph she felt as she took the book and then barely hid her surprise when she saw what Noelle had been perusing. It was a work by Schiller, an author much admired by English readers. The book had been a gift from one of Simon's Prussian clients and was written entirely in German. "Do you often read Goethe?" Constance asked carefully.

"No, I don't," Noelle answered as she took the book back from Constance and returned it to the shelf. Deciding the encounter had lasted long enough, she turned and left the room.

Her roses temporarily forgotten, Constance stared thoughtfully at the empty doorway. Finally she picked up the wicker basket, a tiny smile playing at the corners of her mouth. This had proven to be a most informative encounter, most informative, indeed. Perhaps something could be made of all this yet.

Constance had almost finished her consommé when Noelle made her entrance for supper ten minutes late. For once Noelle was not being deliberately rude. It seemed the more of Constance's food she ate, the more her body wanted to rest. This time she had slept away the whole afternoon.

She immediately noticed that Constance had again made changes in the dining room. The silver epergne was gone. In its place was a simple blue glass vase that held the peach rosebuds Constance had shown her in the library that afternoon. But it was the second change that made Noelle uneasy: Her place had once again been set directly to the right of her hostess.

She darted a curious glance at Constance and then took her chair and studied the soup. She could almost hear Constance's silent command, *"Use your spoon. Use your spoon."*

Noelle picked up the shallow bowl in her hands and defiantly drained the savory contents.

Constance gave no visible sign that she had noticed Noelle's behavior. Instead, she spoke impersonally, her tone more formal than it had been in the past.

"I'm pleased you have been using the library. It used to be my favorite room, but now"—she shrugged her shoulders philosophically—"it reminds me too much of my late husband, as he was before his illness. He spent so much time in that room. Now I much prefer reading in my sitting room."

Constance nodded to a chastened Molly, standing silently in the corner of the room. The girl removed the bowls and set a fluffy omelette *aux fines herbes* in front of each of the two women. The savory aroma of dill and parsley filled the air. Silently Constance took several small bites of the omelette and then continued her monologue as if she had expected no response from Noelle.

"I find it most relaxing in the evening to read before I retire. Of course, it's not without risks. I was so enjoying myself last night that I just couldn't bear to turn out the light. Alas, it was past two o'clock before I was done, and I suffered a beastly headache all morning as a result. Faith, it was worth every minute. I can't think when this past year I've been so entertained."

Noelle was faced with a dilemma, and a small frown etched two verticle lines between her eyebrows. Finally she raised her head and, in a tone so casual that she hoped her question would seem inconsequential, asked, "What were you reading?"

Constance watched Molly fill her tulip-shaped crystal goblet with a delicate sauterne and then took a small sip before she responded. "Molière's *Le Malade Imaginaire—The Imaginary Invalid*. In truth, it was not new to me. I had seen it performed at the Royal Olympic Theatre a number of years ago."

Again Noelle kept her manner offhand, as if she were merely being polite. "I don't believe I've ever read Molière. Do you read many plays?" She thrust an overly large bite of omelette into her mouth.

"A great many recently," Constance responded casually. "I miss attending the theater. For the past few months I've principally been reading comedies: Shakespeare, Goldsmith, Sheridan, Molière."

"Molière. His name sounds French," Noelle muttered.

Constance took a bite of the fragrant omelette and nodded. "He is undoubtedly the greatest playwright France has ever produced. Oh, some will extol the tragedians: Racine, Corneille, Voltaire. But for my taste, Molière tells us more about the human spirit than all of them. Of course, we are very lucky to have his plays. It is really only by chance that Molière was in a position to write as he finally did."

"What do you mean?" Noelle could not entirely conceal her curiosity.

Constance touched her napkin to the corners of her mouth. "For most of his creative life, Molière had been touring the French provinces as an actor. He and his fellow actors performed tragedies, intrigues, and an occasional farce. Finally Molière began to write for the company himself. He wrote comedies that became very popular. Eventually he was invited to perform before Louis XIV. Alas, Molière made a mistake that was to prove almost fatal to his company. Instead of choosing the farces that his company did so well, he selected a tragedy for them to perform."

Constance took another sip of wine and consumed the last bit of her omelette. Noelle had stopped eating, so totally lost was she in the narrative.

"The performance was a disaster, of course," she continued. "The audience was bored. They shifted in their seats, coughed.

Before the play was over, Molière knew he had failed to win the King's interest. But he took a bold step.

"As soon as the performance was ended, he stepped forward and addressed the King. He asked permission to perform one of his comedies that had been accepted so well in the provinces. Permission was granted and, needless to say, everyone was enchanted with the performance. Molière's success in Paris was assured."

"It's just like a fairy story." Noelle was barely aware she had spoken her thought aloud. "He must have been a courageous man to speak up as he did."

"I'm sure he was," Constance responded. "His later life bears testimony to that. Even with the King's patronage, the way was not always easy for him. In his best plays, he pokes fun at the rich and powerful as well as their sacred institutions. Several of his plays were declared immoral. One was even condemned as a sacrilege, and Catholics were warned they would be excommunicated if they attended. Of course, greatness like Molière's can never be repressed. I've always thought his death was so appropriate."

"What do you mean?"

Constance gestured to the maid to remove their plates and leave the room. "Molière was not a well man; he was plagued with consumption when he wrote *The Imaginary Invalid*. It is the story of Argan, a man who is always imagining himself the victim of some terrible disease. Molière died only a few hours after appearing as Argan. The poor man; he was completely at the mercy of his doctors for years. They were just as pompous and condescending then as they are now. He satirizes them most cleverly." A faint look of surprise crossed Constance's face. "But why am I telling you all this? You can read it for yourself. I'll give you my copy this evening."

Noelle felt as though she had been dashed in the face with cold water. She opened her mouth to reject Constance's offer, but no words came out. In a blinding flash she recognized too late that she had underestimated her opponent. She was the victim of a neatly set trap.

Constance had recognized the truth.

"You can't read, can you, Noelle? You've sat in that library with books open in front of you for four days, but you can't read a word."

The words were taunting, but Constance's manner was not. She spoke matter-of-factly. There was no pity on her face, no compassion, only a faintly quizzical expression.

Noelle lifted her small chin. "And what if I can't? Most people don't know how to read."

"But you're not most people, are you, Noelle? Beneath that rude manner of yours is a keen mind. Beginning tomorrow, I shall teach you to read. I want you in the library precisely at nine. If you are one minute late, I won't wait for you. Is that understood?"

"Why are you doing this for me?"

Constance opened her mouth to respond and then seemed to think better of it. Finally she shrugged and said, "I've been bored lately."

Moonlight splashed over the bed, touching the face of its occupant before spilling onto the blue French carpet. It was no use; she was too restless to sleep. Throwing the covers back, Noelle slipped from the bed and went to the window.

The trim grounds, washed in silver light, stretched in front of her before disappearing into a grove of budding elms. Softly she slid the window open and then knelt on the floor in front of it, resting her arms on the sill.

The spring air was chill; it smelled green, like the season. It was a silly fancy, and she smiled as she lay her cheek in the crook of her arm. The night was so clear that the stars seemed to be suspended just above her head on invisible cords. It was as though the heavens had been cracked open to admit her.

Was that what was happening? Was Constance Peale going to be the one to crack the heavens open for her?

She'd dreamed of being able to read for as long as she could remember, sensing that there was a world waiting to be unlocked if she only had the proper key. Even as a child her mind had been active, restless, ready to devour any new scrap of information that was put in its path. She craved more but was unable to satisfy her gnawing hunger because there was no one to teach her. Daisy herself could not read. As with many actresses of the time, she learned her parts with the aid of a reader, a person whose profession it was to recite an actor's lines until the part was memorized.

Noelle remembered a humid summer evening shortly after she was eleven. She was walking near the docks, trying to sell some battered walnuts, when she spied a grizzled old sailor sitting on a pile of rope, a tattered book open in his lap. Her curiosity driving her closer, she could see his lips moving soundlessly as he pored over the page in front of him. When he finally looked up and saw her staring at him, he offered to show her his book.

She could still remember his grimy finger with the misshapen knuckle pointing out letters to her; the excitement shooting through her when he offered to teach her more.

She also remembered her revulsion when his gnarled hand slipped under her skirt and moved upward along the inside of her calf. He drew back quickly enough when the point of her knife pressed against his throat. She never saw him again and, after that, she gave up her search for a teacher. Nothing came free, and she had no money to pay anyone.

Now all that had changed. The woman she had named her enemy seemed about to become her teacher. Reluctantly she acknowledged a growing respect for Constance. But Noelle's pride would not permit her to accept Constance's gift without giving something in exchange. Since she had no money, the payment could only be a token and it was obvious to Noelle exactly what that token must be. She must extend at least some measure of courtesy to Constance. No more dinner-table mischief or open rudeness. In the short time she had left in this house, she would do her best to forget the conversation she had overheard. She would check her insolence.

The short time she had left . . . Could she learn to read so quickly? She must. A chance such as this would never again present itself.

Being able to read was going to make all the difference for her. She would never have to go back to her life on the streets. No more living with the fear of being caught and imprisoned. No more hair dyes and rouge. Perhaps she could find work in a shop. Anything would be possible.

But what made her think her remaining time here would be short? If only she knew the day her monthly flow should begin, but she had always been so irregular—sometimes going three weeks, sometimes two months—that she had long ago abandoned marking the time.

A baby. She shivered as a raw gust of air penetrated her cotton nightdress. Could fate be so cruel?

Her mind rebelliously shut out the possibility. Pulling her head back into the room, she slid the window closed and padded across the carpet to her bed.

Images of small children with hungry eyes and empty bellies plagued her as she slipped between the fragrant sheets. Now there was no one to take care of the little group of urchins she had been feeding with her own pennies, the pennies she could ill afford to spare.

Laying her head back on the soft pillow, she sighed, doubting whether she would ever be able to save her money, even if she did get a job in a shop. At the first sight of a hungry face, her purse strings would always open. Still, what was the use of a new dress or a pretty bonnet when the money could be put to better use buying cups of hot eel soup and loaves of bread?

Outside a night owl called to its mate, but the young girl in the elegant blue bedroom did not hear. She had finally fallen into a troubled sleep haunted by nightmare images.

She was lying in front of a fireplace, the heat from the flames searing her naked skin. Her arms had been shackled above her head, her legs spread and pinioned. Simon and Constance, dressed in evening attire, were sipping sherry from crystal soup bowls and watching her, while starving children huddled in the corners of the room. Occasionally Constance would walk toward her, poke at her body with an elegantly slippered foot, and shake her head sadly.

"Poor creature. What a pity; she's not done yet. Ah, well, soon she'll be ready."

Then they were all gone, and Quinn was with her, his figure enveloped in a black cape. "You should have told me you couldn't read. Now I'm going to have to punish you for your stupidity."

His face, a mask of unleashed savagery, loomed over her, coming closer and closer until his blazing eyes seemed to be cutting into her soul. Pulling her naked limbs from the shackles, he raged at her.

"Hang by the neck until dead!"

Then they were all around her, even the children, circling and shrieking, "Hang her! Hang her! Hang her!"

Letty's knock awakened Noelle. What a horrible nightmare! She pressed the heels of her hands into her eyes, shutting out the daylight.

"Come in."

"Morning, Miss Pope," Letty murmured. "Do you want your tray on the table, or would you rather eat in bed?"

Noelle struggled into a sitting position. "On the table," she muttered. She felt awful; the smell of the warm rolls, instead of whetting her seemingly unappeasable appetite, was making her stomach churn. "Take it away, Letty," she croaked. "I've changed my mind." As an afterthought, she added, "Leave the tea."

"Yes, miss." Letty darted a curious glance at Noelle and then removed the tray from the room.

Noelle fell back on the pillow and took several deep gulps of air. That awful nightmare—it had actually made her ill. Lifting her head slightly, she peered at the small clock on her nightstand. It was after eight-thirty; she had to hurry to be in the library by nine o'clock. Perhaps the tea would help settle her stomach.

She drank it hot and strong and did seem to feel better for it. After stepping out of her nightgown, she washed and brushed her hair, tucking the frizzled strands behind her ears. The navy blue dress was being laundered that day so she resigned herself to an itching neck and stepped into the brown merino. Barely glancing at her image in the mirror, Noelle sped from the room, almost colliding with Constance in the hallway.

Constance's green eyes regarded her reproachfully. "I'm happy to see you are prompt, Noelle. However, a bit less haste would be more seemly."

"Yes, Mrs. Peale," Noelle said, smiling sweetly and then smothering a giggle at the sight of Constance's suspiciously lifted eyebrows.

Constance proved to be an excellent, if demanding, instructor. Since Noelle already recognized the letters of the alphabet, Constance began teaching her the sound each letter made. Noelle's quick mind absorbed all the information Constance gave her, and by the end of the morning she could slowly read down the columns of words Constance had printed out for her.

"Hat, cat, fat, pat, rat, sat, tat, bat . . . had, bad, lad, mad, pad, sad." Slowly she sounded out each word.

Finally Constance pushed herself back from the library table, where they were seated, and consulted a gold watch pinned to the bodice of her gray cashmere dress. "I think that's enough for today. Tomorrow we will begin work on the sounds that are produced when letters are combined."

Noelle looked up, her mind full of its new discoveries. How tantalizing it was . . . the way letters became sounds and sounds fit together to form words. "How long do you think it will be before I can read something by myself?"

"That's difficult to say, Noelle. You're my first pupil, so I really have no experience to draw upon. I do know we still have much to do. However, you learn very quickly and are certainly most conscientious about applying yourself." Constance paused thoughtfully for a moment. "I believe I know just the thing."

She walked to the library shelves, where she climbed up on a small stool and pulled a book from a shelf above her head. "This is Daniel Defoe's *Robinson Crusoe*," she said, handing a worn volume to Noelle. "As you can see, it's a bit the worse for wear; it was one of Benjamin's favorites."

As Noelle studied the first page Constance remembered another one who had loved it. She could see him now, perched on a branch of the tall elm that stood near the back of the house, an unruly lock of black hair tumbling over his brow, this same book open in his lap. Her inability to have a child of her own had been like a knife in her heart that summer as she had watched him running and climbing, building a raft. Life was so ironic! Here she was sitting with his wife, and she didn't dare share the memory.

Noelle sighed. "I can't imagine ever being able to read this."

"Of course you will," Constance responded briskly. "Put the book next to your bed. Every night before you go to sleep, open it and try to read from it. One night you will surprise yourself."

The clock in the hallway chimed. "I have some matters I must attend to before lunch," Constance said. "This afternoon I would like you to practice what you have learned this morning, but only after you have a nap and then a long walk. Exercise is as invigorating to the mind as it is to the body." Constance swept from the library, leaving the fragrance of violets in her wake.

The next few weeks quickly settled into an established routine. Noelle ate a sizeable breakfast, and then the two women worked together in the library most of the morning. Constance was an exacting taskmaster, even modifying Noelle's pronunciation if it rang too harshly to her sensitive ear. Declaring it was not enough for Noelle to be able to read, she soon decreed that her pupil must also write.

"But I won't be here nearly long enough to learn that," Noelle argued. In fact, she was not as certain of that as she seemed. There was still no sign of her monthly time and a heavy band of fear was settling itself around her.

"Nevertheless, you will begin," Constance insisted stubbornly. "You must first learn to print the alphabet in upper and lower case. After you have mastered that, you will begin practicing the letters in script."

Noelle complied with Constance's dictate; however, the task proved maddening for her. The recalcitrant letters stubbornly refused to stay in an orderly row. They clumped together or developed spidery blots at their ends. Her final product was so different from Constance's flawless model that she invariably crumpled it into an angry ball and flung it into the basket.

At meals, the two women remained polite but distant with each other, their conversation strained and desultory. The silver epergne had permanently disappeared from the center of the table, but Noelle found herself sometimes wishing it were back, for she soon determined it was not as easy to eat properly as she had at first thought, especially when she was always so hungry.

There were so many rules. She was also unaccustomed to using a fork. A spoon was the utensil she had grown up with and she had felt lucky to have that, since the others she knew relied on their fingers. It did secretly amuse her to discover that she had somewhat better luck wielding her knife. It, at least, felt familiar in her hand.

Each day after her nap, Noelle began taking long walks, venturing farther into the countryside surrounding the estate. She feasted on all that met her eyes, a world clean and pure, unmarred by muddy potholes formed from sunken cobblestones or filthy, open sewers. She found a nest of violets cradled by the roots of a sycamore; moss, tender and new, near a brook. One day she walked far out into the hills, reveling in the joy of being totally alone.

She met Boggin, the old, wrinkled gardener. He liked to identify the plants in his herb garden for her or talk of flowers that were just beginning to bloom. He named the trees that surrounded the house, often repeating himself, sometimes lapsing into silence in the middle of the conversation. But Noelle didn't mind; she felt comfortable with him.

When Noelle returned from her walks, she would enter the house through the kitchen as a precaution against encountering any of an increasing number of neighbors who were making their way to the Peale doorstep. As Constance had predicted, the story of her unusual guest had spread rapidly throughout the countryside, and rivalry was growing by the day to be the first to catch a glimpse of the young Englishwoman who had been raised in India. Despite the announcement that her guest was convalescing and would not be strong enough to have visitors for some time, Constance's callers continued to arrive on one pretext or another.

So, during the late afternoon when they were most likely to appear, Noelle made it a habit to secrete herself in the library, where a maid would bring her milk and a generous stack of tiny watercress sandwiches. Sometimes she would practice printing her letters, but more frequently she would continue browsing through the books that fascinated her.

In the evenings Noelle would excuse herself from the dinner table and retire to her bedroom and *Robinson Crusoe*. She now recognized many of the shorter words; however, the longer ones continued to befuddle her. She would sound them out laboriously, but by the time she was done with a sentence, she would realize she had concentrated so hard on reading the individual words that she had lost all sense of the meaning. So she would start again. "I was born in the year 1632, in the city of York . . ."

One evening as she lay propped up in her bed, *Robinson Crusoe* open in her lap, there was a soft rap at her door. It was Letty.

"I'm here to brush your hair, miss," she murmured, staring at the toes of her shoes.

Noelle was startled. "Why would you want to brush my hair, Letty?"

"Mrs. Peale told me I'm to brush it every night," she answered stolidly.

"Well, you can just tell Mrs. Peale I'll brush my own hair." Noelle was indignant; she had been as cooperative as she could manage since Constance had agreed to teach her, but this was too much. She wasn't about to be combed and brushed like a trained lapdog.

For the first time since she'd entered the bedroom, Letty's bovine eyes rose to meet Noelle's. "I couldn't do that, miss," she said impassively.

"Why on earth not?"

Letty seemed to be confused by the question as if the very thought of going against Constance Peale's will were so foreign to her as to be incomprehensible. Finally she clumped to the dressing table, where she picked up Noelle's hairbrush and stood waiting patiently.

Noelle sighed with exasperation. "Please tell Mrs. Peale that I do not require your services."

But Letty was not to be deterred. She anchored her bulky form into the French carpet, a marble Nike armed with a hairbrush. "Mrs. Peale said I'm to brush your hair every night," she repeated phlegmatically.

Winning an argument with a block of wood would be easier than swaying Letty from her purpose. Noelle cursed softly under her breath as she seated herself in front of the gilded mirror.

Letty set to work. She began slowly, pulling the brush carefully from Noelle's scalp to the cropped ends of her hair. Gradually she became more forceful, brushing until Noelle's scalp tingled. Finally she stopped and pulled a small pair of silver scissors from her pocket. With practiced efficiency, she snipped away at the damaged hair.

Noelle sighed as she studied her reflection. True, her hair no longer looked like such an unruly thatch; there was even a faint suggestion of curl to the now even ends. But the cutting, so far, could not change the ugly carrot color she was coming to detest more each day in this house, which held far too many mirrors.

These days would have been ones of peace and contentment for Noelle had it not been for her nightmares and the ever-increasing likelihood that she was pregnant. Her relationship with Constance settled into one of polite formality. They were together at lessons and at meals; otherwise they avoided each other.

Noelle came to love the beautiful house more and more as each day passed. She would wander through the rooms, admiring the graceful proportions of the furnishings or running her hands over a smooth curve of polished wood. Picking up a piece of crystal, she would feel its weight, then hold it up to a window and watch the sunlight fractured into rainbows.

Her old life began to take on a sense of unreality, and she had to remind herself more and more frequently that her presence in the white stone house was the dream.

Chapter Nine

It was six weeks to the day since she had arrived in Sussex. Noelle had awakened to find that her body had not accepted the bitter seed that had been forced upon it. Jubilantly she had danced a circle about the blue bedroom, finally catching one of the bedposts in her hand and swinging herself out in a gay arc.

Now, as she fastened her petticoats around her waist, she tried to absorb the realization that she was finally free; her nightmare was over. She could return to an existence she understood, a place where she was respected.

Plopping herself down on the floor, she brought her knees up under her chin and contemplated going back to her old life. Her bare toes dug into the carpet; absentmindedly she reached out her hand to stroke the soft pile. Such a pretty room; the blue and white, so calm and clean. She was going to miss this bedroom.

Snatching her hand from the carpeting, Noelle uttered a particularly foul expletive and pushed herself from the floor. She tried to recapture her earlier happiness as she finished dressing, but she could not. The relief at not being pregnant was still there, but with it was a sadness at the thought of leaving this beautiful house. She realized too late how much better off she would be if she had never lived here. How squalid and desperate her old life seemed in comparison.

She draped a dun-colored shawl around her shoulders, picked up her copy of *Robinson Crusoe*, and decided to sit in the garden until it was time for her lessons. She needed a chance to sort out her thoughts.

A hint of chill still hung in the morning air as she let herself out of the house. She gazed around her at the brick wall covered with fragrant honeysuckle, the fountain with its stone cupid, and finally, inevitably, admitted to herself that she did not want to leave. She had become ensnared by this house and the existence it represented. It was as if she had permitted a net to be thrown about her the night she arrived. It had seemed inconsequential, a delicate thing, fragile, easy to throw off. Now, when it was too late, she had discovered that she couldn't rid herself of it so simply; its gossamer strands were intricately woven and strong beyond their appearance.

She sat on the edge of the fountain, dipping her hand into the frigid water as she tried to understand the changes that had come over her in the past weeks. She remembered the carriage ride that had brought her here and the solemn vow she had made to revenge herself against Quinn Copeland. What of that vow now? Had she become so softened by her new life that she had forgotten it? Was this what luxury had done to her—blunted the edges of her will, made her soft and vulnerable, incapable of grappling with the unlovely?

No! Every fiber of her shrieked denial. Perhaps she was more vulnerable now, but her hatred for Quinn Copeland still burned as strongly today as it had the night she was violated. Even though she was no closer to avenging herself than she had been that night, she knew, with a chilling certainty, that the day would come when she would make good her promise.

Feeling somewhat better, she rose from the side of the fountain and began wandering about the garden, enjoying it for what might be the last time. The earth smelled rich and fecund as it began to warm to the day, and she turned her face up to the sun.

"Oh, there you are." Constance swept into the garden. "Since it is so pleasant this morning, let's treat ourselves and have our lesson here. Goodness knows, we should enjoy it now, for it will almost certainly be raining before the day is over."

Sitting down upon the stone bench, she held out several sheets of paper to Noelle. "Why don't you begin with the list on top? You've learned so quickly, I see no reason to keep reviewing the simpler words."

Noelle looked at the papers in Constance's outstretched hand, but instead of taking them, she walked to the fountain and bent over to pick up her copy of *Robinson Crusoe* from where she had laid it on the gravel.

"If you don't mind, Mrs. Peale, I would like to read this instead."

Constance quirked her head slightly. "So," she said quietly, "it has happened."

Noelle smiled, and with her back proudly straight, settled herself beside Constance. She opened the worn volume and began to read hesitantly.

> I was born in the year 1632, in the city of York, of a good family, though not of that country, my father being a foreigner of Bremen, who settled first at Hull. . . .

As she went on she gained confidence, and the words came more easily. Sometimes she stumbled; occasionally she held onto a vowel longer than she should or dropped a consonant; but by the end of the first chapter it was obvious that Noelle could read.

When she was done, she raised her eyes to meet those of her teacher. Constance was looking at her with unveiled pride, a wide smile on her face. "Noelle, you are an amazing young woman. You should be very proud."

"And you as well, Constance."

Noelle jumped at the intruding voice and spun around to see Simon Copeland stepping out of the deep shadows next to the house. He walked toward them with an easy stride, a commanding figure in a well-fitting dark brown coat with buff trousers and a mustard waistcoat.

"Simon!" Constance exclaimed as she sprung up from her seat. "You didn't tell me you were coming." Two faint pink spots caught on her cheekbones.

"I was nearby," he said, his American accent sounding out of place in the English garden. "Spent the night with Lloyd Graham over at Hightowers and thought I'd drop by to see how you both were faring before I returned to London. I see you've been faring very well."

Slowly his eyes took in the changes that rest and good food had brought to Noelle's appearance. Her body still looked painfully thin, especially in the hideous oversize dress she was wearing, but her face had lost its pinched, starved look.

"I apologize for not telling you I was coming, but my trip was last minute. I didn't have time to send you word. Actually, I was looking forward to surprising you."

Once more his gaze turned to Noelle. "But it seems as though I was destined to be the one surprised. So, you can read now."

"Mrs. Peale has been kind enough to teach me." She kept her tones even and clear as Constance had instructed.

Simon gave his business partner an admiring grin. "You really are a paragon, Connie. Is there anything you don't do well?"

Constance answered tartly. "I'm not the paragon, Simon. *I* already knew how to read. It is Noelle who is to be admired. She is a remarkably determined young woman."

"So I see. Well, Noelle, now that you have learned to read, what is next? Painting? Music?" Then, eyeing her dress distastefully, he added, "Fashion?"

Resignedly Noelle rose from her seat and faced them both. "Nothing is next. I am going back to London."

Simon's words went unheard in the force of Constance's protest. "But, Noelle, I thought we agreed."

"Yes, we did. And I have kept my part of the agreement," she responded flatly, keeping her warring emotions well in check.

Suddenly, understanding dawned on Constance's face. "You have discovered you are not carrying a child."

Noelle nodded her head, not trusting herself to speak. She would never let either of them see how the decision to leave tore at her.

"When did you find out?"

"This morning."

Even in her misery, Noelle had to suppress a smile as she saw Simon redden at the intimacy of the discussion and turn his eyes to the ground.

"And so, you chose today to read to me from *Robinson Crusoe* because you believed this was to be your last lesson."

"Not 'believed,' Mrs. Peale. It *was* my last lesson."

"Ridiculous!" Simon erupted. "There is no reason that your lessons can't continue. I want you to stay right here."

"No," Noelle exclaimed more harshly than she had intended. "I agreed to stay until I knew if I was carrying a child. Well, now I know I'm not, and that's that."

Constance's eyebrows rose at the emotion in Noelle's tone. "You are welcome to stay as long as you like."

"No!" Gathering up her shawl, she faced Simon. "Mr. Copeland, I would like to leave this afternoon if that is possible. Will you please honor our agreement and see that I am returned to London?"

She turned her back on the two and had begun to stride purposefully toward the house when Simon's hand caught her shoulder, and she was turned to face his anger.

"Dammit, Noelle, you're not going one step further until I hear what this is all about. What in the name of God is so special about your sordid little life in London that you're willing to give up all of this?"

Furious at his touch and at herself for wanting so much to abandon her pride and agree to stay, Noelle shook herself from his grasp and raged at him. "It's none of your business why I want to go back to my sordid little life. It's my life, and it has nothing to do with you—or with you." She stabbed her finger toward Constance.

Simon turned his anger on Constance. "What the hell is she talking about?"

For a moment Constance was speechless. First Noelle shaking her finger at her, now Simon shouting. It was all too much! Her voice was tight with fury as she vented the indignation she had been suppressing for so long at Noelle.

"Why, you disagreeable little chit! How dare you speak so rudely. It will be a pleasure to have you out of my house. From the moment you arrived here, you have been insufferable, rebuffing every friendly overture I have made with insolence and hostility. And all without the slightest provocation from me."

"Oh, I've had plenty of provocation. Why can't you be honest enough to admit it?" And then the words she had never intended to utter burst from her. "You breeze through this house so sure of yourself. Your money, your upbringing, your education—they're all just the way they're supposed to be. It really is too much for you to be expected to take a pickpocket into your home, isn't it? Oh, but I forget, a woman of background must take pity on those less fortunate." Emotion choked off any more of what she would have said.

There was something so agonizing in her face that Constance felt her own anger abating and began to speak more calmly. "Noelle, you are mistaken. Oh, I have often thought what a shame it was that you did not have the advantages you so obviously should have had. But pity? No one could pity you. You are an intelligent young woman with a strong character, and I happen to hold those traits in much higher regard than I do upbringing and family background. I am not such an elitist as you seem to think."

Refusing to listen to the part of her that said that Constance was speaking from her heart, Noelle chose to interpret her words as patronizing. "Elitist!" Her voice was filled with scorn. "What big words you hurl at the stupid little pickpocket. The poor, ignorant creature; so defenseless; such a burden." She glared venomously at Constance. "Well, you did your duty. You practiced your friggin' Christian charity so now your precious conscience can rest easy!"

"That's enough!" Simon's voice cut through the fragrant morning air of the garden like the crack of a whip. "I will not have you abuse Constance any longer."

Impatiently he thrust a hand through his thick, dark hair. What happened between these two strong-willed women to upset all his plans?

"You don't have to defend me, Simon. Now, if you will excuse me."

Without so much as a glance in Noelle's direction, Constance walked toward the house, her tiny embroidered slippers making a soft, crunching sound on the gravel path. A robin, peacefully sunning himself near the house, flew up in alarm as the door of the house shut behind her.

Suddenly Noelle was overcome with shame. She had transferred her own pain at leaving into anger at Constance. Regardless of her motives, Constance had given her the most precious gift she had ever received, and Noelle was deeply in her debt.

"Mrs. Peale!" Gathering up her skirts, she ran toward the house. Roundly cursing both of them, Simon followed.

Constance had just reached the base of the staircase when Noelle caught up with her. "Mrs. Peale, I'm sorry. I should never have said what I did. I owe you so much that I can never repay, and I am deeply grateful."

Slowly Constance turned, knowing what it had cost Noelle's pride to admit she was wrong. "I accept your apology." She smiled faintly. "Now, you must tell me why you have been so antagonistic to me. There is a reason, isn't there?"

Holding his breath, Simon watched as Noelle slowly nodded her head and then paused to collect her thoughts. Finally she said, "I overheard you talking with Mrs. Finch about me on my first morning here."

"Mrs. Finch? What on earth . . . ?"

Slowly comprehension dawned on Constance's face and, with it, consternation. Mrs. Finch's accusations . . . her own attempt to placate the woman's injured dignity . . .

"Oh, my dear," she cried, resting her hand on Noelle's arm. "What a muddle. No wonder you have resented me so."

"I've been waiting patiently, hoping that, if I kept silent long enough, I'd be able to discover what the devil is going on," Simon interjected. "Neither of you, however, seems to want to tell me. Now, by God, I'll have some answers." His eyes were the color of pewter as he advanced on the women.

"Don't growl so, Simon. The whole thing is a frightful misunderstanding. Now, let's go into the drawing room, where we can unravel all this privately."

She swept the two of them ahead of her into the magnificent gold and ivory room and then, closing the doors firmly, began.

"The morning after Noelle's arrival, Violet Finch came to me all in a flutter because she had heard from Letty how Noelle was dressed in London and had concluded that I was sheltering a harlot. Simon, you know what a sanctimonious snob she has always been. You also know she is probably the best cook in England and that, at one time or another, practically every member of the *ton* has tried to steal her from me.

"When Benjamin was alive, I didn't worry about losing her. She was totally devoted to him, which, I might add, frequently caused him a great deal of distress." She smiled softly at the memory.

"Will you get on with it?" Simon barked impatiently.

Constance looked at him reproachfully but continued her story. "Since Benjamin's death, several ladies of quality have resumed their pursuit of my cook—among them, the Duchess of Allsworth, who is a frightful old curmudgeon and, in my opinion, the worst of the lot. To top it, she will insist on wearing puce."

Simon cleared his throat in a manner that Constance could only interpret as ominous.

"At any rate," she hastened, "I have no intention of losing her to anyone, so, when Mrs. Finch was so outraged at Noelle's presence in the house, I thought it only sensible to play on her sympathies.

"After assuring her that Noelle was not a harlot, I proceeded to

'cast myself on her tender mercies,' as I believe I put it."
Constance smiled. "She rather liked that. I then painted Noelle as
poor and ignorant—a person with no advantages. This, of course,
is what Noelle overheard. I led Mrs. Finch to the conclusion that
she and I, as women of good conscience, could do nothing else but
clasp her to our bosoms, so to speak, in the spirit of charity."

Turning to Noelle, she was suddenly serious. She cared deeply
about this child and regretted inflicting such pain. "I'm sorry, my
dear. It was certainly a less than noble thing to do, but I confess a
dreadful weakness for properly prepared food. If the truth be
known, I attached no importance to the encounter at all. If I had, I
would certainly have discussed it with you."

Noelle knew that Constance spoke the truth. Her own prejudices
against the privileged classes had been her greatest enemy, not this
woman.

"I'm so ashamed," she murmured. "You should have thrown me
out weeks ago."

Constance laughed in relief. "Not for the world! For the first
time in months I haven't awakened in the morning trying to decide
how to fill the hours until bedtime. Just wondering what trick
you'd pull at the dinner table was enough to keep me amused for
half a day."

Noelle looked at the older woman in amazement. "How can you
smile about it? What I did was horrible."

"Absolutely," Constance agreed cheerfully, her green eyes
dancing. "Several times I would have happily strangled you. Why,
the first time you picked up your soup bowl and drank from it, I
feared I should have a spasm."

At the sight of Constance's features alight with amusement,
Noelle's admiration for her blossomed into full flower. "You are a
remarkable woman, Mrs. Peale. I've greatly misjudged you."

Constance waved a hand in elegant dismissal. "I'll hear no more
of it. We were both in the wrong. Now, I don't know about either
of you, but I am in dire need of a cup of tea."

She rang a small silver bell, then settled herself on the settee,
pulling Noelle down beside her. "Now, tell me, Noelle, what
would you like to read after you've finished *Robinson Crusoe*?"

Although Noelle knew how unlikely it was that she would have
access to the books she yearned to discover, she pondered
Constance's question seriously. "Molière's plays, I think."

The two women were soon engrossed in conversation. The arrival of the maid compelled them to slow down, but when their cups were filled, they began anew, Noelle bombarding Constance with questions about the books in Benjamin's library and Constance dancing from one answer to the next.

Simon stood forgotten in the corner of the room. Although it was still morning, he poured himself a large brandy and sat down to wait them out, studying the two women as he lit his pipe. Constance's elaborate auburn curls rested near Noelle's shorn locks. So tall and proud, she reminded him of a young lioness. Perhaps, just perhaps, his gamble would pay off. If only she weren't so unattractive, for she certainly had the spirit to ensnare his wild son.

Caution, Simon, he warned himself. She still has to be convinced to stay. His pipe had gone out. He relighted it, the smoke clouding around his handsome head as he spoke. "Noelle, your stiff-necked pride almost ruined your chance for a good life. Are you going to let it happen again?"

Although Noelle had been absorbed in her conversation with Constance, she knew instantly what he meant. "Mr. Copeland, I can't take charity from either of you. You must understand that all I've really ever had is my pride."

"Rubbish! How can it be charity? In the past weeks I have interviewed that fool, Tom Sully, as well as consulted with several barristers. There is nothing I can do to terminate your marriage." Unvoiced was the knowledge that there was nothing he would do, even if he could. "Whether you like it or not, you are legally married to my son, so it can hardly be called charity."

Noelle shook her head stubbornly. "I have taken care of myself since I was ten, and I will keep on." She tried to make them understand. "When you don't have food or clothing or even a clean body, other things become important, like courage, pride."

"You talk of pride," Simon countered, advancing on her. "What of mine? Am I not permitted to care for my own son's wife?"

This was an argument Noelle understood. There was no way a man like Simon Copeland could back away from what he perceived as his responsibility. His pride was as fierce as hers.

Rising from her place beside Constance, she lifted her chin with determination. "There is something you should know, Mr. Copeland. My feelings toward your son have not changed. If anything, they are even stronger. I hate him, and I am going to make him pay for what he did to me. I don't know how I'm going to do it, but I will make him pay."

"Fair warning," Simon said easily, "but it does not change my mind in the least. You are my responsibility now, and I will provide for you." He began closing the distance between them.

Impulsively Noelle darted a quick hand under the hem of her skirt and pulled out the knife, pointing its blade within inches of Simon's chest. Behind her, Constance gasped in alarm. Simon's face paled.

"This is the kind of woman I am, Mr. Copeland. The kind of woman you want Mrs. Peale to take into her home. I've been wearing this on my body since I arrived. I stole it from your kitchen because your son took mine. It didn't bother me a bit to steal your knife. I felt it was due me." She lowered the weapon to her side. "But what you're offering, I didn't earn, and I don't take what I haven't earned."

"All right, then! You can God damn well earn it," Simon roared, his face a mask of fury. "You will stay here with Mrs. Peale for a year. More, if need be. Then you will take your place in London as my niece and my hostess. I will pay you a generous salary, but out of that, you must give Mrs. Peale a monthly sum to cover your expenses with her. You must also pay for your own clothing, and, I warn you, I expect you to dress as well as any woman in London. By the end of one year you must be well versed in literature, history, and current events. You must know how to dress, pour tea, and engage in polite conversation. And, by God, if you can't do all of those things by the time the year is up, I'll throw you back on the streets and have every constable in London watching you, waiting for you to dip your hands into a pocket! Now, does that satisfy your damnable pride?"

The room fell silent as the two glared at each other. Constance held her breath. Noelle looked so enraged that Constance waited with horror-stricken certainty for the moment when the girl would again raise the knife that was clenched at her side.

There was the muffled sound of a pot banging from far below in the kitchen . . . a branch brushing against the window pane , . . then Noelle threw back her head and laughed so merrily that Constance closed her eyes and released a long sigh.

"It satisfies my pride very well indeed, Mr. Copeland. I am delighted to accept your offer."

Turning her back on Simon, she walked over to Constance and sank down on the settee beside her. "Will you have me for a year, Mrs. Peale, and continue to teach me?"

"I shall be delighted, my dear." Constance reached out a gentle hand and tenderly brushed away a strand of hair that had fallen across Noelle's thin face. "Provided, of course, that you call me Constance and stop wearing that villainous weapon on your body. I vow, Noelle, you shortened my life by at least a year when you pointed it at Simon." Constance shuddered at the memory.

Noelle grinned mischievously. "A most sensible suggestion. You know how bad-tempered I become when you nag at me about my printing. I might forget myself and pull it on you."

Constance's expression of disapproval was somewhat marred by the twinkling in her green eyes. "I will excuse you now to go to your room and put it away. Otherwise, I shan't be able to eat a bite of dinner, and Mrs. Finch has prepared a walnut cake."

Noelle nodded and, with a smile for both of them, tripped from the room.

Simon slammed a triumphant fist into the palm of his hand. "What a wife she's going to make for Quinn! Hire a tutor for her right away. And see that your dressmaker comes soon, Connie. I don't want Noelle in those rags any longer. Soft colors, I think, and not too many flounces. She doesn't need them. And, for God's sakes, do something about that hair!"

Constance shot up from her seat. "You are overstepping yourself, Simon. Do not dictate to me. When I agreed to take Noelle, it was with the clear understanding that you would not interfere."

"Interfere? Is that what you call it?"

There was such outraged innocence on his face that Constance would have been amused if she had not been so annoyed with his overbearing manner. "You were to give me a free hand," she reminded him coldly, "and not interfere with my decisions. Yet here you are dictating her wardrobe, her tutoring . . ."

"Dammit, Constance!"

"And you watch that vulgar tongue of yours in my presence," she snapped.

"So I'm vulgar, am I?"

With all their old hostilities biting at him, he stormed across the room toward her. For a brief moment she thought he was going to topple her, but he stopped just inches away.

"The way I see it, you're damned lucky I showed up when I did. We could have lost her after that fool thing you did with Finch. You know, after seeing you with her, I'm beginning to wonder just where your loyalties do lie. I asked you to keep Noelle here so that she and Quinn could be reunited one day, but from what I've just seen, I wonder if Noelle doesn't come first in your loyalties, with Quinn a poor second. Or maybe you just want her here to relieve your boredom."

"That's not true, and you know it. Nothing would make me happier than to see Quinn and Noelle together, but I don't want to have it happen on your terms, without her knowledge. She is a human being and deserves to have a choice."

"Are you saying you are going to go back on your word and tell her my plan?" His voice was low and threatening. "Because if that is what you mean to do, you're going to have that girl's future on your conscience for the rest of your life. Do you think she would stay here for one moment under those circumstances?"

Constance felt some of her anger begin to drain away. Wearily she dropped into the small chair next to the window.

"No." She shook her head. "Of course she wouldn't stay."

The room became very quiet. Something stirred inside Simon. She looked so fragile and unhappy, not at all like the self-sufficient woman he was used to seeing. Suddenly he felt like an overbearing bully.

"What do you plan to do, Constance?" he finally asked softly. "The deck is stacked, and it's all in your favor. It looks like it's your game."

Then he went to her and gently put his hand under her chin. Tilting it up, he looked at her almost tenderly. "Don't back out on me now, Connie."

Constance felt a tremor pass through her body. His lips were so close. Would they taste sweet? Her body filled with a longing for a more intimate touch. It yearned to mold naked to his, pliable and yielding. She envisioned him caressing her, burying his lips at her throat, moving them down to her breasts. The frenzy of his touch as she opened herself . . .

"Connie, are you all right?"

She plummeted back to reality to see the concern on his face. Sweet Christ! What was happening to her?

"Of course I am." Angrily she slapped his hand away and pushed herself past him toward the door. "I don't want Noelle to know there is anything wrong, so I will expect you to dine with us at one o'clock, but I want you out of this house immediately afterward. I will let you know what I plan to do before you leave."

As she put her hand on the knob his voice taunted, "You're a cold fish, Connie."

In her room, Noelle stowed the knife under some petticoats in her bureau. As she shut the drawer her thoughts were spinning, a jumble of ideas, feelings, misgivings. It had been an extraordinary morning.

Tossing herself down on her bed, she rested her elbow atop the smooth mahogany cylinder that made up the headboard and tried to imagine what the next year would bring. Doubts plagued her. Was she going to be able to learn all Simon expected of her in so short a time? Although she did not take his threat to toss her back on the streets seriously, she still knew she could not allow herself to fail. She would earn every farthing of the salary he was going to pay her. If she were to become his hostess, she would be the best hostess in London!

For the first time since the night she had been violated, her dream of revenge seemed more than a shadowy specter. The odds had abruptly shifted, and a ragged little pickpocket setting herself against a rich and powerful man no longer seemed such a patent absurdity.

Except it wasn't really the little pickpocket who would even the score! Instead, it would be a sophisticated, educated woman made deadly by possessing the same knowledge that had enabled the pickpocket to survive for so long on London's brutal streets!

She jumped up from her bed. It was nearly time to dine, and her dress was hopelessly crumpled. She certainly couldn't appear in the dining room like this.

The hallway clock chimed one as, her face washed and her hair combed, she reached the bottom of the stairs. Constance was speaking to Simon outside the dining room doors. ". . . for me, I'm not pleased about it, but I see no other way."

Noelle noticed that Simon was stiff.

"You won't regret it, Connie. I promise you that."

"Don't make promises over which you have no control, Simon."

She seemed about to say more, but then she caught sight of Noelle. "Hello, dear. Mrs. Finch has really outdone herself this afternoon." Linking her arm in Noelle's, she began a stream of conversation so amusing that Noelle soon forgot the puzzling exchange she had overheard.

Chapter Ten

Constance did not immediately call in her dressmaker. Instead, she quietly purchased some lacy caps and several simple cotton frocks to replace the unattractive dresses Noelle had been wearing. With each new day Constance could detect marked changes in Noelle's features, and now she intended to give the girl's frail body a chance to heal itself before she properly outfitted her.

The time passed pleasantly. They continued to have their lessons in the morning; in the afternoons, Noelle napped and walked. Throughout the day she consumed generous quantities of the nourishing food Mrs. Finch thrust upon her, eating with such relish that the cook soon forgot she had ever been opposed to the young girl's presence in the house.

Noelle and Constance spent each evening relaxing after dinner over thimbles of sherry. Constance told Noelle about her girlhood, her education, and even the loneliness she felt after her husband's death, and Noelle spoke about her mother. She could not tell it all —it was buried too deeply—but she sensed Constance understood much of what was left unsaid.

Every evening Letty came to her room and brushed her hair. The lamplight began to pick up warm, golden-brown strands growing from the healthy scalp. With repeated washings, and the help of Letty's silver scissors, the bright carrot hues were becoming less and less noticeable.

Noelle's eighteenth birthday came and went. She received a beautifully bound copy of Jane Austen's *Pride and Prejudice* from Constance and, from Simon, a gold locket with a note expressing his regrets at not being able to be with her.

The days grew warmer, and Noelle found herself napping less frequently as her body gained strength. One warm June afternoon she was in the garden enjoying her new book when Constance came out to join her, a shawl dangling from her ringed fingers.

"Put this around your shoulders, dear. I don't want you to get chilled."

Noelle took the shawl and looked fondly at Constance. "You spoil me, you know."

"Posh! I enjoy taking care of you." She reached out her hand and lightly stroked Noelle's cheek. "Have you looked at yourself lately in the mirror?"

"I don't like mirrors very much."

"Perhaps you should give them another chance." Constance smiled cryptically.

That night, Constance's curious statement came back to Noelle as she was preparing for bed. Inpulsively she stepped over to the mirror she had been so studiously avoiding.

It was as if she saw a stranger.

First to catch her attention were her eyes. No longer dimmed by poverty, no longer obliterated by great purple shadows, they almost leapt from her face—beautiful, bright, tawny as sparkling topazes in her clear, smooth skin. She lifted her hand in wonderment and gently slid the tip of her finger along the dainty curve of her jaw. She tilted her head to the side and stroked her cheek and the smooth expanse of her forehead. Her face was still thin, but now it was the thinness of bone structure, not of poverty. Yes, there were still a few pale mauve shadows. In places, the skin seemed stretched too tightly. But, dear God, the difference! Delicately carved, finely molded, the face in the mirror stood, incredibly, on the threshold of great beauty.

Her eyes flew to her hair. It curled in a shiny nimbus around her head, only the ends having retained any trace of the orange dye; the rest was a rich golden brown as warm as spilled honey. It was as if another had taken her place in front of the mirror.

With trembling fingers she unfastened her petticoats and then shed the thin camisole beneath so that she stood naked. Here, the steel jaws of poverty were giving up their hold more reluctantly, but the improvement was still amazing.

Her long legs were more shapely, the muscles beginning to define themselves. Although her rib cage was visible, each rib no longer stood out so rigidly, nor did her hip bones protrude at such sharp angles. She doubted that she would ever develop the fashionably dimpled buttocks and rounded stomach that so delighted painters and sculptors, but at least she looked healthy. Then she scrutinized her breasts. High and full, they stood out proudly from her body, the nipples blushed with coral.

Intensely she studied her reflection, searching for the truth of it, unclouded by her preconceptions. Her old self was gone. No one seeing her now would ever recognize this finely made sylphid as the shabby Soho pickpocket. The breathless promise of the mirror's reflection stunned her.

The breathless promise of the mirror's reflection stunned her.

Several weeks later, Scheherazade herself would not have felt out of place had she wandered into Constance's sitting room, for it looked like something from *The Arabian Nights*. Filmy gauzes and exotic silks lay next to gay muslins and taffetas that gleamed like precious jewels. Bolts of every stylish fabric of the day were strewn haphazardly about the room. Some lay in stacks; others were unrolled with great lengths draped across furniture, carpets and, in the case of a vibrant cherry satin, the arm of Madame Renée LaBlanc.

"*C'est parfait*, Madame Peale. With those beautiful eyes, it will be *magnifique, non*?"

"No." Constance shook her head. "Absolutely not. The color is much too vibrant; she has not yet come out." Despite Constance's tendency toward the ruffled and beribboned for herself, her taste was excellent, and she had an unerring instinct for the fabric and cuts that would be most flattering on Noelle.

"Ah, but of course, one forgets. *Elle est tout sophistiqué*, just like her charming curls. The old hairstyle of the Empire looks so fresh and modern on her." The dressmaker picked up another bolt. "Now this, perhaps, would be better."

Clad only in her chemise, Noelle stood on a small stool in the center of the room, thankful that the remainder of her carrot hair had fallen victim to Letty's scissors only the night before, leaving a short cap of curls. She was content to be a bystander as Constance and Madame LaBlanc discussed her. Since early morning she had been poked, prodded, and scrutinized from every direction. The garrulous little Frenchwoman's measuring tape had not missed a single curve of her blossoming figure.

Noelle's eyes wandered to the window, where raindrops were drilling against the panes. She was not going to be able to take a walk again today, the second day in a row. Still, there was something so agreeable about being inside on such a dreary day. So much better than haunting the wet, stinking alleys off Bow Street or Charing Cross Road.

As Noelle mused, Madame LaBlanc issued orders to her two assistants, sending them scurrying in a torrent of French and then countermanding her original instructions with conflicting ones. *"Estelle, tu cagnarde, arrange cette chambre. Mariette, apporte-moi la soie verte. Celle-la. Non, tu imbécile, pas la verte, la blanche."*

Madame LaBlanc handed Constance a small bolt of creamy silk. "Madame Peale, I must insist. Only this shade for Mademoiselle Pope's ball gown."

Constance unrolled the fabric and then held it out for Noelle to touch. "Do you like it?"

"It's beautiful." The delicate silk slipped through her fingers like raindrops. "I can't believe it's for me."

"Madame LaBlanc is correct, it will be perfect. Now, I think a rounded neckline, not very low . . ."

"Ah, but Madame Peale," the Frenchwoman interrupted as she began draping the creamy silk over Noelle's body. *"A décolleté,* perhaps a little off the shoulder, *c'est à la mode.* She is young, *très belle.* To show off a little is not too bad, eh?"

Constance threw up her hands in mock exasperation. "In truth, I don't know why I attempt to argue with you. Very well, I agree to the lower neckline but only if it is edged with a ruffle of the wide lace you showed me earlier. It will give a softness."

"Madame's taste is faultless, as usual." The submissive manner in which the dressmaker lowered her head did not fool either Constance or Noelle, and they exchanged a smile.

"Now, for the rest of the gown . . ." Constance began, only to be interrupted again.

"I'm sure madame will agree that the sleeve *à la folle* is too extreme." With an expressive lift of her eyebrows, Madame LaBlanc contemptuously dismissed the current fashion of grossly oversized sleeves. "I am certain you will prefer the balloon sleeve with a wide cuff in the same lace as the neck ruffle, *non?"*

For the rest of the day and much of the next, the discussions continued. Finally Madame LaBlanc and her assistants sealed themselves in the sewing room. But for Noelle, this was only the beginning.

Merchants arrived brandishing kid gloves and slippers with tiny bows. Shawls and reticules were purchased.

After several days, a simple cotton frock emerged from the sewing room, then another. Noelle slipped them on and pirouetted gaily in front of her mirror. A bolt of fine lawn was transformed into delicate chemises and petticoats. There was a beautiful morning gown, then an afternoon ensemble with a pleated bodice and tiny shoulder cape.

The days passed. A note arrived from Simon with a draft covering the first four months of her salary. The amount was staggering until, with Constance's assistance, she calculated the cost of the purchases that had been made on her behalf and, over the protests of her hostess, deducted a separate amount to pay her living expenses. She set aside the little that was left. Somehow she would have to get this money to the children. Otherwise she would find no pleasure in her new clothes.

The creamy silk ball gown was finished and hung carefully away in her closet. A gay sprigged muslin appeared. Noelle moved through her days as if in a dream.

The tutor Constance had hired appeared. The day of her first formal lesson she arrived in the library to find him standing at loose-limbed attention in the center of the room. Tall and spindly, he had thinning sandy hair and rimless glasses that kept slipping down his bony nose.

His adam's apple bobbed up and down in his cadaverous neck as he observed his new student. She stood before him in a lavender muslin frock. There was a delicate ruffle of deep violet at her throat and twin bands of the same color encircling the wide hem. A grosgrain belt emphasized her tiny waist. He took in the wide topaz eyes, the tawny cap of curls that barely brushed her ears. Oh, dear, he'd never imagined . . .

With shaking hands, he began searching the pockets of his ill-fitting jacket until he finally pulled out a much-abused scrap of paper. With his index finger, he shoved his glasses back on the bridge of his nose and consulted the paper.

"I'm looking for Miss Pope." His voice cracked like a pubescent choirboy's. Mortified, he tried again, but with little improvement. "I'm looking for Miss Dorian Pope."

Noelle suppressed a smile. "I'm Dorian Pope."

"Well, if you are M–M–Miss Pope, I think it is only l–l–logical to conclude that I am to be your new tu–tutor. That is to say . . . I'm Percy Hollingsworth, instructor in history, geography, government, and ma–ma–mathematics."

Remembering Constance's instructions from the day before, Noelle glided toward him, her hand outstretched. "I am delighted to meet you, Mr. Hollingsworth," she carefully articulated.

Crimson crept up from his collar; he stepped backward. Recovering, he braced himself and took her hand only to feel his knees turn dangerously weak at the touch of her warm flesh.

Noelle's amusement was tempered with curiosity. Was it this easy to make a man behave like a fool? It was a new idea—an intriguing one.

Percy Hollingsworth proved to be an able, if somewhat unorthodox, instructor. Although he had had every intention of proceeding with Noelle's instruction in an orderly and sequential manner, she would tease him and torment him so that when the subject was not to her liking he soon abandoned the effort and let his student's natural curiosity and keen mind guide their lessons.

She returned from a walk, her magnificent eyes full of the beauty of a wildflower she had discovered, and the lecture he had planned on ancient Greece was abandoned in favor of perusing *Flora and Fauna of the English Countryside*. When the London newspapers arrived each week, she pored over them—circling, underlining, demanding explanations.

She learned that Benjamin Peale had been with the Duke of Wellington at Quatre-Bras. The next morning she entered the library and presented her tutor with a handful of pebbles, ordering him to reenact the Battle of Waterloo on the library carpet. Constance, seeing the two of them sprawled so informally on the floor as she passed the door, had rushed into the library only to find herself ordered to take charge of Napoleon's main forces.

All in all, Percy Hollingsworth and Noelle were well satisfied with each other, and Constance was delighted with both of them. She was far from delighted, however, when a hastily scrawled note arrived one day from Simon:

My dear Constance,

I have just received word that there has been a fire at the American shipyard. If you will remember, I told you that Quinn had some trouble with a man named Luke Baker before he came to England. Baker may have been involved. At this point, I have no report on the extent of damages, but, regardless, duty dictates that I return home with all possible speed.

It is with regret that I leave my work unfinished here at the London office, but I trust you understand that I have no other recourse.

My warmest regards to Noelle. I have placed £500 in your name in the company account so you can administer her salary until my return.

Simon

Furious at the impersonal tone of the missive, Constance tossed it in the fire.

As the days went by, callers continued to arrive, more and more impatient to catch sight of the mysterious Miss Pope, but Noelle always managed to avoid them. At the first sound of carriage wheels crunching on gravel, she would seal herself in her room with her studies or slip out the back door and into the countryside.

With Christmas came another tutor to instruct her in piano and voice, as well as dance. It was at the latter that she excelled. Her step was light and fanciful, and it was not long before she outgrew her instructor.

Each day, Constance found time to instruct Noelle in the social graces. She learned to pour tea without spilling a drop, play whist, and use a fan. She could also effect a proper introduction and curtsy gracefully.

Noelle decided making polite conversation was, by far, the most difficult of the skills she had to learn until the time came when Constance told her she must be able to embroider. After a week of crooked stitches and tangled threads, Noelle uttered the foulest of oaths and tossed the wretchedly abused piece of fabric into the fire, declaring that she would begin to wear her knife again if she were forced to sew another stitch. Constance hastily surrendered.

Her progress with her studies was remarkable. Although Percy Hollingsworth was not an experienced tutor, even he recognized that she was an extraordinary student with keen insight and an exceptional memory. She spent all her spare time reading— devouring books, one after another.

The modern poets captivated her, and she loved to read their poems aloud to Constance. Her voice was low with a trace of huskiness that was appealing and strangely compelling. "The Prisoner of Chillon," "Endymion," "Kubla Khan"—they all whispered to her of mystery and beauty, and she would lose herself as she read.

She was living in a silken cocoon, and it was only in the darkest core of night that the careful insulation sometimes fell away, and the past crept upon her. When the nightmares plagued her, they were inhabited by the haunted phantasms she had left behind: the children, the withered old hags of the alleys, the poverty, stench —and, sometimes, the face of the man who was her husband.

She spent one February day studying the legend of Agamemnon, the king who sacrificed his daughter, Iphigenia, to the gods, only to be murdered for his deed by his wife, Clytemnestra. When night came, she paced the floor of her bedroom until she was exhausted, knowing that a nightmare lurked on the other side of her consciousness.

Finally she sat at her desk and tried to put into words what churned inside her. She wrote:

> Hatred coils inside my heart;
> Untempered by sunlight, it is wedded to my spirit,
> Waiting like vengeful Clytemnestra for the time
> When, unfettered, it will be set free to play its part.

When she finally fell asleep, it was only to become a victim of the nightmare she had feared. But, instead of the avenging Clytemnestra of her poem, she was Iphigenia, the virgin sacrifice, clutching at the robes of a faceless father, only to be torn away and held aloft over an altar. As her robes were ripped from her body, she felt herself being lowered to the altar. But in her dream it was not cold stone that met her naked flesh. It was a cloying, enveloping softness that sucked her into its depths and held her limbs captive. Helplessly she watched a swarthy figure approach her, his eyes of bitter black pushing her deeper into the suffocating mass. And then he was beside her, spreading gold coins on her body. Across her lips, her nipples, her stomach . . .

"One hundred pounds," he sneered, "one hundred pounds for the virgin."

She jolted awake, sweat drenching her body. The poem she had written was lying on the carpet. Springing from her bed, she tore it into tiny pieces and buried her words in the ashes of the fire.

Chapter Eleven

Watching from her bedroom window, Noelle saw the trim carriage come into view around the curve of the driveway. A sharp gust of April wind, reluctant to abandon the bite of March, threw itself against the rig, making it shudder as it approached the house. Inside the carriage were three people Noelle had never met: Mrs. Sydney Newcombe, her daughter, Margaret, and her son, Robert. Today, more than a year after Noelle had arrived at the white stone house, she was to take her first tentative steps into the world of the fashionable by having tea with Constance and the Newcombes.

"I confess that Mildred Newcombe is not my favorite acquaintance," Constance had said when she issued the invitation, "but she'll do very well for our purposes. She is so taken with her own opinions that she rarely notices anything else. So, if you do make a slip, it will undoubtedly pass her by. I've observed that her daughter is cut from much the same cloth."

Of course, when Constance had extended the invitation, she had not realized that Robert Newcombe, whom she had never met, had arrived from London to visit his mother and would be accompanying her here today. Still, Noelle knew she could not seal herself away forever. A disconsolate Percy Hollingsworth had left last week to take a new post; it was time for her to put to use what she had learned.

From below, she could hear the sounds of the Newcombes alighting from their carriage. To bolster her lagging self-confidence, she mentally catalogued her accomplishments: her table manners were flawless; she could dance exquisitely, play a simple tune on the piano, and speak without her accent or grammar betraying her. It was true that mathematics and needlework had escaped her; however, any well-bred young woman might be expected to have some failings, and thanks to the efforts of Constance and Mr. Hollingsworth, hers were few. She was even becoming proficient at making polite conversation, although it was frustrating to be restricted to such uninspiring topics as the weather or Mrs. Ann Radcliffe's latest melodramatic novel when she would much rather discuss more interesting subjects.

Noelle sighed as she thought of how much more there was for her to learn and wished she were curled up in the library, reading one of the books on the reading list Percy had left instead of standing here trying to get up enough courage to go downstairs. She moved to the mirror and checked her tawny hair. It was just long enough for her to catch up loosely off her neck with a satin ribbon. Wispy escaping curls brushed the nape of her neck and feathered charmingly around her face. Reluctantly she picked up a paisley shawl and draped it around the shoulders of her well-fit bottle-green cashmere dress.

"I'm ready, lions." She smiled ruefully to herself as she slipped out of her room and prepared to step into the arena.

Robert Newcombe was bored. Dash it! He should have never let his mother talk him into coming with her today. Not that Mrs. Peale wasn't a pleasant surprise, but even she wasn't quite enough to make up for that cursed carriage ride, where he'd been captive to the incessant chatter of his mother and sister. Damn! He'd like to jump on a horse and ride to the nearest posting house for a full tankard of ale.

As the door of the drawing room opened, any serious intention Mr. Newcombe might have had of actually fleeing the Peale residence vanished instantly. Entering was a creature so exquisite, he could only stare speechlessly at her slender form.

"Dorian! Come in, my dear, and meet our guests."

The creature smiled charmingly as Mrs. Peale presented her to his mother and sister. Then she was standing in front of him, their eyes nearly level.

"And this is Mrs. Newcombe's son. Mr. Newcombe, my ward, Miss Pope."

The vision extended her hand and bestowed a smile so dazzling that for a moment Mr. Newcombe had difficulty finding his voice. "Delighted, Miss Pope," he finally managed as he took her hand and touched his lips to it.

Margaret Newcombe darted an angry look at her brother. He thought himself to be such a man of the world just because he had come of age and had his own lodgings in London. Well, if he could see himself now, he'd find that he looked like nothing so much as a love-sick calf! Obstinately she placed herself in his path as he tried to maneuver next to Miss Pope on the settee and seated herself there instead. She ignored the furious glare he shot at her and jealously studied the young woman who sat beside her.

Mrs. Newcombe, in the meantime, was proudly displaying a gaudy ruby and diamond bracelet to Noelle. "My husband is such a generous man. He felt it was the least he could do, as I have been so wretchedly plagued with illnesses lately. I tell you, Miss Pope, shortness of breath is well known to be the first sign of consumption. It quite terrifies me."

Observing the florid hue of the woman's complexion, Noelle thought it more likely that she was suffering from too tight lacing of her corset, but she wisely did not voice this opinion.

"Miss Pope, I understand you've lived most of your life in India!" Mr. Newcombe took advantage of the slight lull to inject himself into the conversation.

"Yes, I have. Until my parents' death."

"Such a tragedy." Mrs. Newcombe pursed her lips mournfully. But her son was not about to let her back into the conversation so easily. "Tell me, how did you find India?" he asked.

"Have you ever been to India, Mr. Newcombe?" the beauty inquired innocently.

"No, I have not been so fortunate."

"Well, then, let me tell you all about it." She sent him a shattering smile that left him weak-kneed. He listened, entranced by her perfect features, as she described the air of Kashmir and cruel poverty of Calcutta to him.

Finally Mrs. Newcombe decided she had kept silent long enough. "Tell me, Miss Pope, how do you find England now that you are here?"

"Much as I had expected, Mrs. Newcombe," Noelle replied.

"Ohhh." Mildred Newcombe drew out the single syllable and then gave a tight, offended sniff. She was obviously less than satisfied that one who had lived among the heathen for so long should dismiss His Majesty's realm so lightly.

Noelle looked at her solemnly, aware that her response had displeased the woman. A mischievous elf teased her.

"As a matter of fact, I found it just as I had dreamed it would be —a demi-paradise, a precious stone set in the silver sea. As I first set foot on England's soil, I thought, this blessed plot, this earth, this realm—this England!"

She smiled sweetly at the Newcombes and then folded her hands demurely in her lap.

Constance almost choked on her tea. The little imp! She was quoting *Richard II* at them, and none of them knew it.

Mrs. Newcombe looked slightly bewildered. "Quite so, Miss Pope," she muttered faintly. A hush fell over the drawing room.

Constance jumped into the gap. "Tell me, Mr. Newcombe, are you enjoying your stay in the country?"

"Very much so." He responded with more enthusiasm than he could possibly have mustered a half hour before. "The country is always pleasant, although I am generally partial to life in the city. Have you seen the sights of London yet, Miss Pope?"

Noelle picked up her teacup and took a small sip, then looked at him golden-eyed over the rim of her cup. "What sights would those be, Mr. Newcombe?"

"Why, the Tower of London, Hyde Park, Oxford Street."

"No," she responded. "I have not been so fortunate."

"You must permit me the honor of being your guide when you do visit," he urged. "It is a fine city."

"Fiddlesticks!" Mrs. Newcombe snapped. "Fine city, indeed. I vow, I do not know what you see in the place, Robert. I only pray you shall soon come to your senses and settle down here where you belong."

Margaret watched with satisfaction as her brother's face reddened in embarrassment.

"Why, you know very well what happened to your father only last month when he was in London." Mrs. Newcombe turned to Constance and Noelle, her face stiff with indignation. "The poor man had his pockets emptied while he was strolling through Piccadilly."

Noelle's eyes flew open, and Constance gazed at her uneasily.

Mrs. Newcombe touched a lace handkerchief to the faint beads of moisture that had gathered on her upper lip. "I see you are shocked, Miss Pope, that such a thing could happen in our civilized country. I assure you that it is commonplace in London. The city is filled with peddlers and beggars. I find the worst to be those dirty little guttersnipes that are always scampering about. Thieves, every one of them."

"Guttersnipes?" Noelle purred dangerously. "Do you mean children?"

"Children?" she responded haughtily. "I don't know that I would dignify them with that description. They are barely human,

Miss Pope. Yet they are permitted to run loose. It is a disgrace. Why, any person of good sense can't help but agree that they simply do not belong out in the open where they can taint the rest of us. How much better it would be if they were locked away in orphanages or asylums. Perhaps the prisons could even be used."

"Have you considered the possibility of hanging them?" Noelle interjected, lifting one arched eyebrow.

Even Mildred Newcombe was taken aback. "Why, I hardly think . . ."

"Oh, hush, Mama," Margaret snapped. "Don't you see that Miss Pope is poking fun?"

"Really, Margaret, she's doing no such thing!" Mr. Newcombe exclaimed, sounding more positive than he actually was.

Constance decided things had gone far enough. "You misunderstood her, I'm sure, my dear. Here, let me pour you another cup of tea. Now, Margaret, you must tell me who made your frock. I vow, I can't remember when I've seen so many pink ruffles. Unusual to place them at the waist like that."

Thus distracted, Mrs. Newcombe and her daughter launched into an enthusiastic account of their dressmaker's latest creations while Mr. Newcombe ate four chocolate madeleines and sighed over the tilt of Miss Pope's charming nose.

The hour was finally over. Standing in the doorway next to Noelle, Constance waved to the Newcombes as their carriage pulled away. She had not failed to note the stubborn set of Noelle's jaw and was relieved that the rest of the visit had passed without incident. With the exception of her remark about the children, Noelle had been a model of graciousness. She had obviously smitten Robert and had even managed to draw Margaret into conversation. All in all, it had gone well, and Constance was pleased. Still, she had not been entirely sure of the success of the visit until Mildred Newcombe had put on her bonnet and whispered to Constance how extraordinary she thought it was that one raised in a heathen country could be so charming and well-mannered.

"Miss Pope, you minx, what a delight you were." Constance hugged Noelle affectionately. "Next time, however, I'm going to choose our callers more carefully. Faith, I had forgotten how dreadful Mildred can be."

"Really, Constance, you surprise me." Noelle's expression was mildly reproving. "It's not like you to speak badly of someone who is suffering."

"Suffering? What on earth do you mean? Mildred is hardly suffering."

"Perhaps not now," Noelle said, her eyes bright and guileless, "but she certainly will be. I hope you will see that this is returned to her first thing in the morning. The poor dear won't be able to sleep a wink all night wondering what has happened to it."

Into Constance's hand, Noelle slipped Mildred Newcombe's ruby and diamond bracelet.

Word of the Newcombes' visit spread through the countryside, and the two women found themselves deluged with callers and invitations. Within a fortnight Noelle had consumed countless cups of lukewarm tea and enough currant buns to satisfy even her voracious appetite. She discovered that most of Constance's acquaintances were genial people and making conversation with them, while not particularly inspiring, was also not very difficult. She discovered, too, that the men she met, whether young or old, were drawn to her like moths to a flame. They praised her beauty, her wit, her intelligence, and made themselves willing providers of her slightest whim.

As the weeks passed she began to toy with them, tentatively searching for the limits of her powers. She would flirt outrageously one day, only to ignore her unhappy victim the next. Still, they flocked to her, spellbound by her uncommon beauty.

Constance made the painful decision that Noelle must begin to accept some of the invitations she received from them despite the fact that she was legally a married woman. If it ever became known, the scandal would be ruinous, but Constance felt she had no choice. A young woman as beautiful as Noelle could not remain sequestered from male company without arousing suspicion and dangerous conjecture.

Constance watched as Noelle began to accept invitations and tried to come to terms with the changes in her life. She was well aware of the animosity the young women in the neighborhood were directing at Noelle and, in truth, could not find it in her heart to blame them overmuch. The exquisite Miss Dorian Pope had created a sensation, and they were not at all pleased to see their favorite beaux so distracted.

One morning Noelle found Constance in the greenhouse, arranging cut flowers in a vase of black basalt. "Robert Newcombe is pressing me to attend a picnic with him in two weeks. What do you think?" She handed Constance a white, long-stemmed blossom.

"Not a delphinium, dear. Give me that gladiola."

Noelle placed the proper flower in Constance's gloved hand.

"I don't see why you shouldn't attend. Robert is a sweet boy. Who is to chaperon?"

"George and Emma Simpson are back from their honeymoon and have agreed to accompany us, if you can imagine those two as chaperons." She tossed her comely head disdainfully. "They wouldn't notice if lightning struck in front of their noses. I've never seen anything as silly as the way they ogle each other."

"They're in love, Noelle. You mustn't be so cynical."

"I'm just being realistic, Constance. Besides, I don't really believe in love. It's just a charming invention of the poets."

"Now, there you are wrong, my dear," Constance said, her features hidden from Noelle's view as she turned away to pick up another flower. "It does exist, and it is magical."

The memory of that long-ago day in London when Simon Copeland had said almost those exact words came back to Noelle. Swiftly, she planted a light kiss on Constance's cheek.

"Forgive me; I'm being a cynic. It's just that it can never happen to me."

Constance put the final flower in the vase and then stepped back to examine the finished bouquet. At last she removed her gloves and turned her attention to Noelle, a frown puckering her forehead.

"Noelle, you have been with me for over a year now. Simon should be returning to England next month, and soon you will be leaving to take your place with him in London." She hesitated. "Are you happy with your new life?"

Noelle's eyes widened. "How could I not be? I have more than I ever dreamed possible, and you've been wonderful to me."

"I've loved having you with me, Noelle. You've been like the daughter I never had. But, lately, as I've watched you, I confess I've been concerned."

"About what?"

"I detect a certain—for lack of a better word, I can only call it —callousness in your attitude toward the gentlemen who are so smitten by you. If it were any other girl, I would just assume she was insensitive to the feelings of others. But you are not a shallow person, Noelle. It seems unlike you to behave so. Why? What do you hope to achieve?"

Touched by the deep concern she saw etched on Constance's face, Noelle said, "I have upset you, haven't I? I'm sorry, Constance. I wouldn't hurt you for the world. You're correct, I have been behaving badly."

Noelle framed her words carefully. "It's as if I were an actress and this, my dress rehearsal."

"Your preparation for London?"

"No, Constance, my preparation for Quinn Copeland."

"Quinn?"

"As long as I continue to maintain contact with his father, I realize I'm also making myself accessible to him. I suppose I've been testing my new powers. Finding out what they are and how to use them. If I meet him again, I must be ready."

Constance reached out and put a hand on Noelle's arm. "You cannot know how it distresses me to hear you talk like this. What Quinn did was unforgivable, but you must stop all these foolish thoughts of revenge. Noelle, I have known Quinn since he was a boy. I care deeply about him, but I warn you, he is a dangerous enemy."

"I underestimated him once, Constance. I'll not do it again."

"Noelle, do not attempt to toy with him as you have with the others."

Noelle put a small hand to Constance's worried cheek. "I know you mean well, Constance, but I must live my life in my own way. Please don't worry. I can take care of myself." With a smile that was meant to be reassuring, she left the greenhouse.

Constance shook her head sadly. "That pride of yours, Noelle, is going to be your undoing."

Chapter Twelve

Three mornings later an envelope lay on Constance's breakfast tray beside her cup of chocolate. It was addressed to her in Simon's familiar handwriting. Constance tore it open, her eyes flying over the single page.

> My Dear Constance,
>
> I returned last evening to Northridge Square. There are some pressing matters to which I must give my immediate attention, but I hope to be free to travel to Sussex on Friday next as I am most anxious to see both you and N. If I do not hear from you, I will assume this is satisfactory.
>
> Simon

Constance felt a curious weakness come over her. Her hands trembled slightly as she returned Simon's note to its envelope. It was only excitement, she told herself, for she had never informed Simon about the startling change in Noelle's appearance, preferring to let him see for himself. Now she was anxious for him to meet his beautiful daughter-in-law.

When Noelle discovered Simon was to arrive on the day of the picnic, she prepared to write Mr. Newcombe a note, telling him there had been a change in her plans and that it would be impossible for her to attend. Constance, however, would not hear of it.

"There is no reason at all to cancel your picnic, Noelle. I doubt that Simon will arrive before dusk, and you'll have returned long before then."

Noelle allowed herself to be persuaded, and on the morning of the picnic she even found herself humming a tune softly under her breath as she tied the bright gauze sashes of her straw hat into a bow beneath her chin.

It was a beautiful spring day. Peonies were pushing their shoots through the rich Sussex soil, and a hint of early summer touched the air. Constance watched from the doorway as Robert Newcombe placed Noelle's hamper in the back of his carriage and then helped her up onto the front seat. They waved gaily to her as the carriage sped down the driveway. She watched until they disappeared from view before turning back into the house and mounting the stairs to her sitting room.

With all the recent activity, she had been badly neglecting her household accounts and her correspondence. Today would be a perfect time to put everything in order. First, however, Constance cast off the rather plain blue muslin dress she was wearing and slipped on her new jade silk. Silly, really, to put on a new dress just to work at her desk. Still, it was so nice finally to be able to wear something other than black or gray; why shouldn't she pamper herself?

Concentrating on the stack of papers in front of her proved to be more difficult than Constance cared to admit. It was mid-afternoon, and she was still at her desk when Molly interrupted with the announcement that Mr. Simon Copeland had arrived and was waiting in the drawing room.

Rising too hastily, Constance dismissed the young maid and then rushed to the pier glass to check her appearance. Although she was a bit pale, the jade silk could not have been more flattering. It had been cut low at the neck and fell slightly off her shoulders. Satisfied with the fit of the dress and the appearance of her auburn curls, she pinched color into her cheeks and then descended the stairs.

She stepped into the drawing room to find Simon wandering about, leisurely smoking his pipe. He swept her with an admiring gaze as he caught sight of her.

"Simon, it is so good to see you." She went over to him, her hand extended graciously.

"Why all the formality, Connie?" He grinned as he ignored her outstretched hand and scooped her into a warm embrace. "You look beautiful." Gently pushing her back from him, he smiled down into her green eyes.

Constance was shaken by the depth of her response to his

presence. The past year had dealt too kindly with Simon. His face was as handsome as ever, his body still firm and muscular. There was a touch more gray at his temples, but its effect was dashing rather than aging.

"You're a flatterer, Simon Copeland," she bantered, exhibiting more composure than she felt. "Noelle will be disappointed when she finds she has missed your arrival. In truth, it is my fault. I did not expect you until evening and told her I saw no reason she should stay home from her picnic. The others would have been so disappointed."

Simon's dark brows shot up. "Others? Is it wise for her to go off without you to guide her?"

As she sat in a small gilded chair Constance reminded herself that Simon had not seen Noelle in more than a year. "Noelle does very well."

"Tell me how she is." He settled himself across from her, the slight tension in his upper torso the only evidence of the importance of her response to his question.

"I will let you judge that for yourself, Simon."

Noting the stubborn set to his jaw, she quickly interjected her own question. "What of Quinn? You mentioned nothing about him in your letters. Did you locate him?"

Hard lines etched themselves around Simon's mouth. "My son seems to have disappeared from sight. He's quite good at that, if you remember."

Constance thought of Simon's beautiful wife, whom she had met only once a few short months before her death. "Did you contact his mother's people?"

"He's not with them. Nor with any shipbuilder in America as far as I can determine."

"Simon, what about all of the men he was corresponding with about his hull experiments?"

"I've contacted them, but no one has heard anything." Simon's voice had a final ring to it, as if he were dismissing the subject.

"Did you think to go through his files? Perhaps there are some names you're not aware of."

"I tell you, no one has heard from him. I've been through his files a dozen times, all his notebooks, his letters. No one admits to any knowledge of his whereabouts."

There was a brief silence in the room. As Constance studied

Simon's troubled face comprehension began to grow inside her. She made her question casual, as though she were merely offering polite conversation.

"What did you think of Quinn's work?"

"It's inconclusive." Simon was abrupt.

"I believe Quinn said as much himself." Her rebuke was softened by the sympathetic expression on her face.

Simon sighed resignedly. "All right, Connie. I deserve that. His work is good."

"I see."

"No, it's more than good, and I was too hasty in dismissing it."

"You did what you believed was best, Simon."

He slapped his hand vexatiously against the top of his thigh. "It's his damned arrogance. Brings out the worst in me. I thought he was off on a wild goose chase when he should have been attending to business."

Seeing how troubled he was, Constance shifted the conversation to the fire at Cape Crosse that had precipitated Simon's sudden journey last spring. In his correspondence, he had indicated that a warehouse had been destroyed in the blaze, and that Luke Baker, the man they suspected was responsible, had disappeared without a trace. Now he told Constance of the rebuilding of the warehouse and a dock that had been slightly damaged. They talked of the work in progress at Cape Crosse and a merchant ship launched shortly before he left for England.

But Simon found himself curiously distracted, his mind more occupied with Constance herself than with their conversation. Damn! She had always had an unsettling effect on him. She was so delicate and giddy, such a contrast to the earthy creatures he sought out for his pleasure. Those were the women he was comfortable with, not one who looked as though she would break under a man's weight.

He was lying to himself! He seemed to make a practice of deceiving himself about her. For some reason he wanted to believe that she was cold and unimaginative in bed, but he knew it wasn't true. He had known it for years.

Benjamin Peale had always been a lusty man. In the early days of their friendship, long before his marriage to Constance, he had taken the young Simon under his more experienced wing. Together they had sampled most of the better brothels on the eastern seaboard and also a fair share of the more respectable women, married and unmarried. But after he had wed, Benjamin's philandering abruptly stopped, never to be repeated as far as Simon knew. Yet he always had the unmistakable mark of a man well satisfied.

Something of what he was thinking must have shown itself, for Constance paled, then stopped speaking abruptly, her lips moist and slightly parted. The unconscious sensuality of her face stirred an ember deep inside Simon.

Why had he never noticed the distinct shade of green her eyes were? Like polished jade. And the tiny lines at the corners. Instead of aging her face, they gave it a fascinating animation. She was so tiny and elegant, always perfectly coiffed and dressed. He suddenly wanted to see her rumpled; her auburn hair undone and her clothing in disarray.

He knew then that he wanted her; he had wanted her for years but had refused to admit it to himself out of loyalty to Benjamin Peale. He leaned toward her, and she jumped up as if stung.

"Let me get you some brandy."

As she walked unsteadily across the drawing room to a graceful Sheridan table where several crystal decanters were grouped, she could feel Simon's eyes burning into her neck. Fighting for control, she reached for the brandy, splashing several drops as she poured. Conscious that Simon had risen from his chair behind her, she picked up a decanter of sherry and poured a large glass for herself. Her heart raced wildly. She must not make a fool of herself again! Taking a deep breath, she turned toward him, a glass in each hand.

He was standing next to the fireplace, watching her, one elbow resting on the mantelpiece. Their eyes riveted. Glass extended, she walked toward him slowly, almost hypnotically, unable to drop her gaze from his.

He took his glass from her. Instead of sipping from it, he set it untasted on the mantel, then took her own glass and placed it next to his. Wordlessly, he drew her toward him, his hands strong and forceful as they curved around her bare shoulders. She was conscious of his face coming nearer and nearer, and then his lips claimed hers.

She moaned softly and gave herself to him. His mouth was hard and demanding, his kiss experienced. As her arms reached around his back she ached with the relief of finally being able to embrace him.

And then he was kissing her temples, the soft space at the base of her earlobe, her throat. His hair brushed against her lips, and she parted her mouth, tasting it with the tip of her tongue.

A faint chill touched her as his hands slipped one side of her dress down, exposing her small breast to the air. Tenderly he claimed the softness that had been so long starved for a man's touch, and her flesh was instantly warm and secure. Sensation rolled over her. He gently pushed her back until she rested on the carpet.

She was vaguely aware of the sound of the key turning in the lock as he protected them from a servant's intrusion, and then he was back beside her, freeing her from her dress. Her petticoats, her chemise—his experienced fingers had no difficulty finding the fastenings of her garments.

Soon he was lying naked beside her, tormenting her with his caresses. Finally, when she thought she could bear it no longer, he rolled on top of her, and she opened herself, surrendering unashamedly as he filled her.

Later, as he pulled on his clothing, Simon studied Constance's naked form lying asleep at his feet, her head resting on a small embroidered pillow he had pulled from the settee. He watched as her small breasts rose and fell rhythmically and found that his hands, as if they had a will of their own, yearned to reach out to her and once again stroke the soft contours of her flesh.

"Fool," he chided himself, clenching his fists until the skin stretched white at the knuckles.

In the years since his wife's death, Simon had enjoyed the favors of many women, but today had been different. This woman who had been a thorn in his side since she had first come into his life had filled a bleakly empty part of himself that he had never imagined could be replenished. And he had humiliated her. Taken her on the floor like a common whore.

A deep shame filled him. He had taken cruel advantage of her. She was a passionate woman; he had always sensed that. The unnatural celibacy that Benjamin's illness and death had forced upon her had obviously made her an easy victim of what she would only see as his lust. She would never forgive him for what he had done.

Memories of their lovemaking came back to him. She had been so warm, so receptive. God! How he had wanted her! Why had he not realized earlier what she had come to mean to him so he could have treated her with every respect as she deserved? Now it was too late.

Reluctantly he picked up one of her discarded petticoats and gently covered her. She stirred, murmuring something that was inaudible to him before her lashes opened and her green eyes locked searchingly with his. Simon looked away, unwilling to see the condemnation in her gaze.

His eyes fell on the jade silk dress. Gathering it up with the dainty underthings that lay near it, he wordlessly offered her the garments and then quietly left the room to allow her some privacy while she dressed.

A tear trickled down Constance's face as the door shut behind him. She began hastily donning the garments, trying to shut out the memory of Simon's dreadful silence after their lovemaking. She had repelled him with her wantonness, and she could only blame herself for her lack of control.

Pain, no less real for not being physical, seemed to take possession of her body. If it had been any man other than her business partner, she would never have had to see him again, never had to endure the indignity of facing him.

But that was the point, wasn't it? It could never have been any other man.

She fled to her room.

Some time later, after he had washed and changed from his travel-stained garments into evening dress, Simon once again found himself in the drawing room. He walked to the fireplace and picked up the brandy that still waited for him in a crystal goblet on the mantel. He swirled the amber liquid in the glass, watching it coat the inside before sliding down to pool at the bottom. Constance's untouched glass of sherry condemned him from the mantel.

"Damn!" he exclaimed. Tilting his head back, he drained his glass in a single gulp.

There was a soft rustle, and he looked up to see a young woman of such incredible beauty standing in the doorway that his breath caught in his throat. He remembered Constance telling him that Noelle had gone on a picnic. This must be one of the young women of the party.

She wore a fashionable muslin dress printed with scattered sprigs of gay blue periwinkles. In her hand she trailed a straw bonnet by its bright sashes. But her garb, charming as it was, did not hold his attention, for never had he seen a face so exquisite. It could have been called patrician with its delicately carved bones and small nose had it not been for her incredible eyes, like finely polished topaz. They lent a piquance to the perfect features, an incredible sensuousness that was underscored by the shining tawny gold curls caught up on top of her head and feathering so gracefully in front of her dainty earlobes.

As Simon saw before him the embodiment of all he had wanted for his son, his already depressed spirits plummeted even lower. His plan had been absurd. He had expected too much.

She stood quietly, with the self-assurance of a woman who well knows the effect her beauty has on others and is no longer surprised by it.

Suddenly he realized he was gaping at her like an ill-bred lout. Recovering, he apologized. "Excuse me for staring. I hadn't expected to see anyone other than Mrs. Peale and . . ." He searched for the name Constance had told him Noelle was using. What the devil had . . . ? "And Miss Pope, of course."

He began to walk toward her, and then, when he was halfway across the room, she spoke.

"Hello, Mr. Copeland."

He froze in mid-stride, the color draining from his face. "Noelle?"

A hint of a smile played at the corners of her lips. "I'm Dorian Pope, now."

Never had Simon been so stunned. "I can't believe this," he stammered. "It's incredible! Why, you're . . ." Suddenly he threw back his head and roared with laughter. This was the little pickpocket Quinn had pulled from the gutter! The street urchin he had chosen to marry so he could humiliate his father!

He ran to her and enveloped her in a great bear hug. Then, forgetting in his jubilation all that had happened with Constance such a short time before, he set her aside for a moment and dashed from the room, flying to the bottom of the stairs. "Constance!" he bellowed. "Constance, come here. Hurry!"

He rushed back and caught his daughter-in-law to him again, showering her with questions that he gave her no time to answer. Finally he let her go and stood back to look at her. "I just can't believe the change."

"I hope I'm to take that as a compliment." Smiling, she walked toward the window and tossed her bonnet down on a chair. The sun chose that moment to glide out from behind a cloud and spill its rays through the glass panes, setting tiny golden fires in her curls.

Simon drank in the sight, still unable to believe his good fortune.

When Constance joined them in the drawing room, no trace of the upheaval that raged within her showed itself on her face. Propelled by the discipline of generations of finely bred English gentlewomen, she glided serenely over to Noelle and planted a light kiss on her cheek.

"Did you enjoy yourself, dear?"

"The food was better than the company, Constance. I'm beginning to believe Mrs. Finch is a sorceress."

"Of course she is. Now, run up to your room and change before dinner. There's a grass stain on your hem."

Noelle laughed. "I'm afraid I'm hopelessly rumpled. I don't think I shall ever learn to look as neat as you, Constance. If you'll both excuse me." She paused at the doorway to smile back at them and then disappeared.

As Simon turned toward Constance memory rushed painfully back to him. It was only with difficulty that he could meet her gaze. To his surprise he found no trace of condemnation in the cool green eyes. So, he mused, she is not going to hold what happened against me after all. All right. If she could be that forgiving, he would make certain that she had no cause to regret it. From now on, he would behave with only the utmost respect. Never again would she find cause to censure him.

"Constance, I don't know how I can ever thank you. She's perfect. Absolutely perfect."

"I'm glad you're pleased, Simon," she responded pleasantly. "Now, if you will excuse me, I must see Mrs. Finch about dinner."

Chapter Thirteen

As Noelle rode beside Simon in the open carriage, wind plucked at the wide brim of her bonnet and ruffled the curls that had escaped. Despite the fact that Constance had decided not to accompany them on their trip to Brighton today, Noelle was enjoying herself enormously. Much of her pleasure sprang from yesterday's triumph.

She looked over at Simon handsomely arrayed in a dark brown coat, lemon waistcoat, and brown-striped neckcloth. She could not remember when she had enjoyed herself as much as she had last night at dinner. Simon Copeland was far different from the young men whose presence she had been enduring. Without being fawning, he was attentive, self-assured, and charming. He had complimented both his dinner companions extravagantly and kept them entertained with anecdotes of his early years in Cape Crosse. Then, he and Constance had told Noelle stories of some of Copeland and Peale's most famous ships: the *Episode,* the *Star of Wilmington,* and *Dream Dancer.*

For the first time Noelle noticed a salty tang hanging in the late morning air. She shivered with excitement.

"Are you cold?" Simon asked.

"Not at all, Mr. Copeland."

"Please, Noelle, won't you call me Simon? Now that I've returned, I'm hoping we can have a close relationship. After all, we're both Copelands, and I must say that Noelle Copeland is certainly a credit to our name."

Some of Noelle's pleasure in the morning and in her companion dimmed. There was a smugness about his words, a possessiveness she did not like.

"Noelle Copeland?" She quirked an ironic eyebrow at him.

"Noelle Copeland does not exist, or, if she does, it's only on a piece of paper, not in the flesh."

"Of course, dear." Simon patted the back of her hand and then turned his attention back to the horses.

His gesture of dismissal irritated Noelle, and she pressed, "Simon, I have not lost sight of who I really am, and I don't think you should, either. I'm Noelle Dorian, a London pickpocket who was given an incredible chance by two very generous people to be something more, something better. But remember that beneath these beautiful clothes and this clean face, there is still a London pickpocket."

"You're talking nonsense, Noelle, and you know it." Simon's voice was tight. "It is the pickpocket who doesn't exist. She never really did. You come from good stock, despite the squalor of your upbringing. No, my dear, this is the real Noelle sitting beside me now. The pickpocket was the deception."

Simon was spared Noelle's response as the carriage rounded a curve and the town of Brighton came into view. He drove down to the sea along Ship Street, parking the carriage under a shady tree and letting Noelle take in her first sight of the gray waves and sandy beach. She couldn't seem to tear her eyes away. The sea mesmerized her as she saw freedom of the highest order. When it was time for them to leave, Noelle requested a last view before they set back. Simon helped her down from the carriage, and they strolled along the walk that overlooked the beach, Noelle's ruffled pink parasol protecting her complexion from the sun. Her perfection reminded him of a portrait by Gainsborough.

"You've become a very beautiful woman, Noelle."

A tiny frown gathered near her eyes. "So I've been told."

"You seem less than pleased. Is being beautiful such a horrible burden?"

Noelle was thoughtful. "It has been difficult to adjust to the change. Especially the effect I have on . . . others."

Simon did not miss the tiny hesitation. "Especially the effect you have on men?" His next question seemed casual. "And have any of these young men caught your fancy?"

Noelle's voice was quiet, almost contemptuous. "They are silly boys who have never done an honest day's work in their lives. All they know is riding, hunting, and cards. They are attracted to me only because of my appearance. They look for nothing more."

Simon's eyes as he gazed down upon her were oddly disturbing. "Then you should pity them, for that is their loss."

Noelle stopped and tilted back her parasol, its pink interior forming an enchanting halo behind her head. "I'm not like other women. Intrigues and romances hold no attraction for me."

"You have not met the right man."

"No, Simon. I think all those nights I spent listening to Daisy and those horrible men she brought home have made it impossible for me to feel the same emotions as other women. And, then, after what happened with your son . . ."

"Please, Noelle—" Simon put a hand on her arm.

"I can't pretend that it didn't happen," she insisted, determined to make him realize how serious she was. "Now, something must be done about it. This marriage must be ended. I can never find any peace until I am freed from it. You are an important man, Simon. You can get the best legal advice. Please help me."

Simon turned his eyes to the shoreline, his expression inscrutable. "It's a complicated matter. Women have so few rights, and you know how thorough Quinn was about making this marriage legal."

"There must be a way," Noelle insisted. "What about desertion? Surely I must have some rights. The law cannot be so unjust."

"The law was made by scholarly men anxious to protect the best interests of the family."

Noelle stamped her foot impatiently. "The law was made by men anxious to protect the best interests of men."

"Really, Noelle, you hardly qualify as an expert on jurisprudence. I suggest you let me handle the situation."

"And will you handle it, Simon?" she challenged. "Or do you intend to see that things remain just as they are?"

"That is most unfair. I'll certainly continue making inquiries on your behalf when we reach London."

Although dissatisfied with his response, Noelle realized nothing more could be gained by pushing him further today.

"Very well, Simon. I shall hold you to that."

PART THREE

Dorian Pope
London

Chapter Fourteen

Noelle arrived in London with Constance during the last week of August. A year and a half had passed since the morning Quinn had delivered her to this same house. Now, she was elegantly gowned in apricot velvet. Her shining hair, which fell below her shoulders when she brushed it, was swept up into a flattering arrangement of small braids and soft curls. Even though there was no longer any resemblance between the carrot-thatched pickpocket and the beautiful young woman who stepped so gracefully from the carriage, the house on Northridge Square still overwhelmed her.

Northridge Square was, in fact, not a square at all but a small rectangle with ten houses forming the perimeter, two at each of the shorter ends of the rectangle and three on the longer sides. There was a park in the center with carefully groomed shade trees and a granite pedestal holding a bust of Lord Nelson.

Simon's residence rested in a direct line with the hero of Trafalgar's bronzed gaze. Built of red brick, it was an imposing house, both larger and grander than the one in Sussex. It had high-ceilinged rooms, massive fireplaces, and a set of twin staircases that curved up from each side of the black marble foyer.

One of the first things Noelle did after she was settled was to take out one of the coins she had been so carefully hoarding and slip away from Northridge Square. Tilting her head far enough forward so that the rim of her bonnet obscured her face, she walked rapidly eastward until the homes of the wealthy gave way to poorer dwellings. She had not gone far before she came upon an old costermonger peddling a barrow overflowing with shabby clothing. In rapid succession she bought a black, closely woven shawl, a threadbare cloak, and a pair of worn boots. A quick stop at an apothecary's, then a wigmaker's, and her purchases were complete.

When she returned home, she let herself quietly in through the back garden and stealthily climbed the stairs to her room, where she hid her purchases in the back of her armoire.

Determined to earn the generous salary Simon was paying her, Noelle swallowed her apprehension and set about her new duties as his hostess with all the confidence she could muster. She learned the routine of the household as well as the names of all the servants—from Tomkins, the forbidding butler, and Mrs. Debs, the housekeeper, to Norah, the kitchen maid.

As she explored the house she discovered behind the dining room a small parlor that Constance had rather fancifully decorated some years before in shades of peach and powder blue. There was a set of bookshelves and a sunny bay window with an upholstered window seat, originally bright peach but now faded into softer tones. The room was warm and comfortable, and Noelle immediately appropriated it as her own, adding a small pigeonholed desk.

There Constance showed her how to set up an inventory with the housekeeper, go over menus with the cook, and issue and respond to invitations, all tasks that Noelle immediately detested. To console herself, she hung a fern in the bay window and then added a comfortable pillow so she could curl up and read.

Unfortunately she had little time for literature, as Constance and Simon were both insistent that she begin to be seen socially. It was a mark of Simon's determination to have her accepted by his peers that he reluctantly left his desk several afternoons a week to accompany the women on their rounds. He felt amply rewarded for his sacrifice when he learned that wagers were being laid at several of the most exclusive clubs in London, and Simon Copeland's niece was an odds-on favorite to be the surprise hit of the social season. He was less pleased, however, to observe the collection of young dandies in his drawing room growing by the day.

For her part, Noelle was waiting impatiently for another chance to slip from the house. One chilly afternoon almost a month after her arrival, Simon and Constance were both required at the Copeland and Peale offices to sign a new contract. Taking advantage of the opportunity, Noelle pleaded a headache and informed Tomkins that she was not to be disturbed for the rest of the afternoon.

Locking herself in her room, she took off her crisp muslin dress and fine petticoats and carefully hung them away. From beneath a pile of chemises, she drew out her knife and tied it securely around her calf with the strips of material she had saved. Then she pulled her secret purchases from the bottom of the armoire. With the briefest hesitation, she took out her old emerald gown and slipped it on, shuddering at the terrible memories it brought back.

Her next task took considerably longer. With a pair of silver scissors, she snipped away at the section of fake hair she had purchased at the wigmakers. It was not quite the ugly shade of orange she remembered, but it was close enough. Then using a needle and thread, she sewed the ends of the tufts of hair to the edge nearest the center of the black shawl, settling the shawl around her face several times to adjust the strands. When she was finally satisfied, she tucked her own honey tresses securely out of sight and knotted the shawl under her chin so only the artificial strands of hair protruded, uneven and frizzled. As a final step she pulled on the worn pair of boots and smeared the scarlet rouge that she had purchased from the apothecary across her cheeks and rimmed her eyes in kohl.

Noelle surveyed herself in the mirror. What she saw did not completely satisfy her. She would have to rub some dirt on her face to disguise her healthy complexion; then if the light were dim enough and luck was with her, she could still pass as Highness. Her chances were made better, she knew, by the fact that the one she was going to see was almost blind.

Noelle wrapped only five coins in her handkerchief—too many questions would be asked if she appeared with more—and, throwing the threadbare old cloak over her shoulders, opened her window.

She had chosen a bedroom at the back of the house, although Constance had chided her at the time. "It's such a little room, Noelle. The curtains are old, and it needs repainting. Why not take the pretty yellow room at the front?"

But Noelle had argued that the bedroom in the back would be quieter. After the peace of Sussex, she declared, the front of the house would be too noisy with carriages rattling by all night. Constance pointed out quite logically that Northridge Square was very quiet, and it was not likely there would be many carriages to disturb her sleep, but Noelle remained adamant.

The truth of the matter was that she had spotted a network of sturdy vines growing up around the bedroom's back window. The vines, many as thick as her arms, were shielded from casual view by a dense clump of oaks. She would be able to come and go at will with no one to see her unorthodox stairway.

Opening the window, she slung one slim leg over the sill and caught the toe of her boot in the crook of a vine. Cautiously she tested it. It held her weight. Gingerly easing out the other foot, she began a careful descent.

The vines proved to be as sturdy as they looked, and she was soon on the ground, where she rubbed some dirt on her face and hands and then let herself out the garden gate and into the network of back streets that skirted the prosperous environs of Northridge Square.

Less than two kilometers away in distance, but a universe away in reality, Noelle found herself at the entrance of a fetid alleyway in Soho. The passage was so narrow and the buildings set so closely together that only on the brightest of days did a few feeble rays of sunlight penetrate the dark, mildewed cavern.

As she stepped into the alley the odors of the past attacked her: the smells of decay, hopelessness, and human excreta. There was another odor that caused the bile to rise in her throat, one vilely familiar to the poor. It was the putrification of human flesh, a corpse waiting until the pennies were borrowed or stolen so it could finally be buried. In the cesspools of Soho, Whitechapel, Seven Dials, and Drury Lane the dead were sometimes to be envied; they had escaped the hellish eternity of living.

Noelle pulled the bottom of her shawl across her nose and went on to the end of the alleyway. Peering through what at one time had been a door but was now merely a gaping hole with uneven boards and some crude sacking nailed over it, Noelle looked into the common room that had housed her for many years after Daisy's death.

Filthy straw covered with rags lay in piles along the seeping walls. In two corners of the room were ragged mattresses for the boarders who could afford the extra tuppence a week rent. The room was empty except for a misshapen lump huddled near the apathetic fire.

Noelle gingerly pulled aside the sacking and stepped down into the room. "Bardy?"

"Oos 'at, now?" he called out threateningly.

Dread enveloped her like a shroud as she walked closer to the feeble flicker of the fire. It felt as if she had never escaped.

"It's me, Bardy."

" 'Ighness," the old man cackled. "Blimey! I knowed yer'd be back. There's them that says yer got nabbed, but I tole 'em ya was too peevy a cove fer that. Where yer been?"

She shrugged evasively. "Lots of places, Bardy. I'm up on my luck."

"I'm 'appy fer yer, lass, but the tykes missed yer, they did. With yer gone, there weren't nobody cared 'bout 'em."

"There was you, Bardy."

"Lord love ya, and wot can an old man like me wot's 'alf blind do?"

"You can take this. I'm sorry it's been so long since I could bring you anything." She pressed the coins into his hand. "See that they get what they need. I'll bring more when I can."

He inspected the coins before they disappeared into the ragged folds of his coat. "Yer've got a soft 'eart, 'Ighness. Always did."

"I have to go now, Bardy. I'll be back soon. Buy yourself something, will you? A purple muffler to keep your bones warm."

Noelle heard Bardy's cackle as she slipped hurriedly out of the room and into the alley. She tried to tell herself she was rushing to get back before she was discovered, but she knew she was really fleeing the children. She had to be away before they returned. It had been nearly two years; many of the familiar faces she remembered would be gone, claimed by either death or the law. As for the few remaining, the very fact that they had survived was evidence that they would have changed past recognition. Worse, still, would be the new faces, each one a reminder of the thousands of other abandoned children.

As Noelle sped through the streets of Soho she was surprised to discover that she was crying. Abruptly she dashed away the tears with the back of her hand.

Slowing her steps, she tried to decide what she would do next. She could throw caution to the winds and bring the rest of the money with her on her next trip. There was enough for Bardy to lay in a supply of food and buy clothing and bedding for the children. But she dismissed the idea; it would be dangerous for him to have so much money at once. No, she would just have to bring a few coins with her each time and make more frequent trips, even if it meant traveling at night.

She must also save more of her money. What she had now would only last a few months if the children were to get what they needed. Although Simon insisted she be well dressed, he wouldn't notice if she had five pairs of gloves instead of seven or a refurbished bonnet rather than a new one.

Noelle slipped into the garden at Northridge Square with renewed determination, refusing to admit what she knew—that her mission was ultimately futile, her coins too few, the children too many.

The following week the painters finished in the elegant little dollhouse Constance had purchased near St. James's Square, and she moved in. Although they still saw each other daily, Noelle missed living under the same roof with the woman she had come to depend on for advice and friendship. She consoled herself with the fact that it was now easier for her to slip away and made two more successful trips into Soho. Being able to help the children in however small a way lifted her spirits, so that when Simon announced he would hold a ball in Noelle's honor, she was able to enter into the preparations with a much lighter heart.

Chapter Fifteen

Simon heard a rustle coming from above him and looked up just in time to see Noelle sweep around the curve of the staircase into his view. Her long shining hair was swept up into an artfully arranged composition of soft curls wreathed with fresh ivory rosebuds, archetypes of the silken ones that gathered the hem of her gown into graceful scallops to reveal a filmy underskirt. Only a few honey tendrils had been permitted to escape the charming coif. These fell at her temples and in front of her dainty earlobes, each of which held a single pearl, her only jewelry. Encircling her slim throat was an ivory velvet ribbon fastened at the center with a white rosebud. Beneath the rosebud, the twin mounds of her full breasts swelled, enticingly accented by the lace that edged the bodice of the ball gown. All cream and ivory, she was both virginal and sensual, still the most exquisite woman Simon had ever seen.

For the first time since he had announced to Constance his intention of holding a ball to present Noelle formally, he regretted his decision. She was so breathtakingly beautiful, every man attending would covet her. If she were to fall in love with one of them, he would have no one to blame but himself.

"I thought this was to be a ball, not a funeral. How can you look so solemn, Simon? Is there something about my appearance that displeases you?" She smiled mischievously up at him through thick, dark lashes.

"You little scamp," Simon growled. "You know damned well that you've never looked more beautiful. It seems to me you're trying to weasel a compliment."

"You're absolutely right." Noelle giggled and turned in a graceful pirouette, swirling alabaster against the black marble of the foyer. "Did you ever see anything as exquisite as this gown? It could even make an old stick look beautiful."

Simon's eyes strayed briefly to the lovely breasts rising from their lacy nest. "No one could ever confuse you with a stick."

Disturbed, Constance watched them from the doorway of the ballroom, where she had been surpervising the final preparations. Simon was no more immune to Noelle's beauty than any other man. It seemed that all women were destined to fade into insignificance beside her, especially one to whom he had been as unfailingly polite as herself. She yearned for their old relationship, having him growl at her, call her Connie.

"Constance, you look magnificent!" Noelle cried as she spotted her friend. "Look at her, Simon. There's not another woman in London who could carry off that gown."

Constance was wearing layers of fuchsia silk. The vibrant color of the garment should have clashed with her flaming locks but somehow didn't.

"The two of you together look like dessert." Simon laughed admiringly. "Raspberries and Devonshire cream."

"Faith, Simon, I did not realize you had so poetic a nature."

"You know that every shipbuilder has to be a poet at heart, Constance. How else could he build beautiful ships?"

A knock resounded at the front door, and Simon's guests began to arrive. Noelle stood next to him for almost an hour as he welcomed each one warmly and then presented her. Some she had already met, but most were strangers anxious to judge for themselves if the rumors they had heard of Dorian Pope's beauty were overstated. It was obvious from the open admiration written on the faces of the men that they did not find the gossips had exaggerated. As for the women, those content with their own lives silently wished her well. The others scrutinized her minutely and, unable to find fault, whispered to each other that, for all her beauty, it was a pity she was said to be so high-spirited. Too lively a manner was unbecoming in one so young.

The ballroom was dazzling. Hundreds of crystal prisms suspended from three magnificent chandeliers shone down on the polished floor and gilded moldings of the room. Set in gleaming brass pots, clusters of potted palms rustled gently in the cool October breeze from the open doors, their vivid green fronds challenging the white walls behind. Backless brocade sofas of the

First Empire were placed strategically along the sides of the room, inviting the grandly coiffed and elegantly appareled to lean against their rolled pillows and chat, expound, reminisce in comfort.

As soon as Noelle entered she felt the intoxicating tension of the room. Tonight she was going to dance, laugh, be gay, with no thought of anything but the present. A great burst of joyous laughter escaped her as Simon caught her in his arms and whirled her into the first dance.

The evening sped by. She flew from one set of masculine arms to another. The men, some famous, some talented, some ordinary, all vied for her attention. She smiled enchantingly at each one, laughed at his stories, and forgot him the instant another partner claimed her. Only the patterns of the dance mattered. The blood of kings rushed through her veins. Life was suddenly wonderful.

Simon watched her. She was a temptress, the Lorelei ensnaring with her dancing instead of her singing. Suddenly he found himself wanting to forget she was his son's wife.

He approached her just as Lord Alfred Haverby took her arm to lead her to the floor. "I believe you promised me this dance, Dorian. Did you forget?" asked Simon.

Although Noelle knew she had done no such thing, she excused herself prettily and went to Simon. "Thank you for rescuing me," she whispered as soon as Lord Haverby was out of earshot. "I fear his lordship is in his cups. He reeks of port."

"Purely medicinal. His mother is a nasty old curmudgeon who rules him with an iron fist. She still calls him 'Sonny.'"

Noelle laughed. Then the music started, and she forgot the unfortunate Lord Haverby as she and Simon began to dance. The tune was a spirited polka. With each bar, its speed increased until, finally, the pace was frenzied. She twirled faster and faster, the room and its occupants becoming a blur. Faces sped by, their features indistinguishable. Colors blended one into the other. Each beat pounded louder, faster. She turned, she swirled, she flew. *Lighter. Quicker. Higher.*

The music climaxed with a thundering crescendo, and she and Simon fell, exhausted, into each other's arms. The other dancers began to leave the floor, but Noelle and Simon did not move. Then she thought she felt the faint brush of his lips against her temple. Startled, her eyes flew up, but they never reached his, for, over his shoulder, she saw watching them the face that had haunted her nightmares for so long!

If possible, he was more dangerously handsome than she remembered. His jet-black hair was longer than it had been, casually tousled, a front lock falling carelessly across his forehead. His jaw, square and proud, was hard, masculine. As he surveyed her a lazy speculative grin played at the corners of his mouth, emphasizing the firm planes of his face. But it was the reckless glitter of his eyes that chilled her. Those eyes saw through mere flesh; they could sear the soul. Did they recognize her as the ragged little pickpocket he had married?

As Noelle stiffened in his arms Simon released her and followed the direction of her horrified gaze until his eyes, too, came to rest on his son.

"Quinn," he said softly.

Alone on the ballroom floor, the three of them were caught in a motionless tableau, frozen sculptures entombed in time.

Then, slowly, Quinn started toward them, his carelessly open tailcoat revealing an elegant evening waistcoat of black cut velvet. He moved with a barbaric swagger, self-disciplined yet ruthless, and, as he approached, his eyes raked Noelle.

The insolence of his inspection sent angry flames coursing through her blood. How dare he look at her like that!

Every nerve, every fiber of her slim body went taut as fury drove out her fear, and an astonishing rush of anticipation filled her. It was as if everything she had learned, absorbed, performed, up until this moment of time had all been to prepare her to do battle with this man.

Confidence surged through her. She would choose every word, every glance with expert care. She had been given the weapons she needed to fight him, and she was determined to emerge the victor.

Slowly, deliberately, she lifted her chin. Their eyes locked, and the recoil from the joining was palpable in the air.

He stopped in front of her and then, unexpectedly, took her hand to kiss, turning it over at the last instant so that it was the soft palm that met his lips. "Your beauty has not been exaggerated."

"Nor has your arrogance," she replied coolly, keeping her anger at the audaciousness of his gesture well in check as she firmly removed her hand from his intimate grasp.

A crooked smile of appreciation crossed his features before he turned his attention to his father. "You're looking well, Simon."

His American drawl was stronger than his father's, somehow alien.

"So you've come back."

"Don't worry. It's not permanent. I'm on my way back to America. I stopped by to meet my new *cousin*."

Noelle did not miss his slight, ironic emphasis on the last word. Constance had told her Simon had no brother, so Quinn knew she was a fraud. But did he know her true identity? Her heart was thudding painfully in her chest, but she forced herself to remain composed as, once again, she came under his scrutiny.

"Aren't you going to introduce me to your niece?"

Noelle spoke before Simon had a chance to comply. "I am Dorian Pope, Mr. Copeland." She waited to see if he would react to the name "Dorian." When he didn't, she went on more confidently, "Surely there is no need for a formal introduction between cousins?"

Brazenly she had challenged him to dispute her claim. She held her breath, waiting for his response.

"I agree. Formality between cousins does seem unnecessary." And then, with feigned innocence, "Let's make a bargain right now to have an intimate relationship."

She clenched her fist in the fold of her gown at his arrogance. All the loathing she had ever felt for him magnified. Still, years of painful self-discipline kept her voice even.

"I am afraid it would be most inappropriate for us to make such a pact. After all, we are not related by blood, since your uncle was merely my stepfather."

Arching his eyebrow, he awarded her an unspoken touché. "I'd forgotten that. Kind of you to remind me."

At that moment Constance descended on them in a flutter of fuchsia ruffles. "You horrid boy! How utterly impossible of you not to have told us you were coming. Will you never observe the most elementary conventions of polite society? I vow, I'm surprised you even bothered to arrive in evening dress." Although her manner was affectionate, Noelle could sense the tension behind her words.

Quinn hugged her warmly. "You never give up on me, do you,

Constance? You're still hellbent on turning me into an English gentleman."

"A futile task, I fear," she replied spiritedly. At that moment the orchestra began to play a waltz. "I beg the three of you to move off the ballroom floor. You're fueling the tongues of every gossip in London."

"Then let's not leave them disappointed."

To Noelle's dismay she found Quinn's strong arm clasped around her waist, drawing her hard against his body. The contact was searing. Nightmare memories engulfed her as she fought for control. He led her into the first steps of the waltz, the corded muscles of his thighs burning through her gown. She tried to back away from him, but he was unyielding, the steely band of his arm perversely drawing her closer until her breasts were pressed hard against his chest. Insolently he looked down on her, his eyes fondling the tender mounds of flesh as they strained upward, threatening to break free from the chastity of the lacy bodice. Then, with a twisted smile, he released her to the proper distance as suddenly as he had claimed her. Noelle stumbled; only his strong grasp saved her from falling. Quickly she recovered, once again forcing herself to match his steps.

He was a superb dancer, moving with a lethal gracefulness that belied his size. For a moment she permitted herself the luxury of forgetting who he was, allowing him to twirl her expertly about the floor. Those close by stopped dancing to watch as they glided by; he, the quintessence of maleness, she of womanliness.

Cool feathers of air brushed against her bare skin. Too late, she realized he had led her out into the deserted garden. He stopped moving but did not release her. Instead, with one hand, he pulled an ivory rosebud from her hair and brazenly slipped it into the enticing valley between her breasts.

Just as she reached to pluck out the offending bloom and hurl it in his face, he said softly, "Suppose you tell me what this masquerade is all about."

A shiver of fear crept up her backbone. He had recognized her!

"Masquerade?" she murmured as guilelessly as she could manage, trying to give herself time to think.

Abruptly he let her go. "Don't play the innocent. I have nothing against Simon bedding you, but why is he being so underhanded about it? Other respectable men live openly with their mistresses."

Noelle's thoughts whirled. How stupid of her not to have realized he would interpret her presence in the crudest way possible! She chafed at this additional humiliation.

Then the coolly logical part of her mind took command. No matter how insulting, it was infinitely better for him to think as he did than discover the truth—that she was his wife, owned by him, his chattel. Her mind refused to dwell on even the possibility of so monstrous a thing happening. She would swallow the insult while she made her plans.

"How would you know what respectable men do, Mr. Copeland? I understand from your father that you are a black sheep."

She was disappointed that her shaft did not find its mark. Instead of being offended, amusement showed itself in his wicked grin.

"You understand correctly, madam. What else has my father told you about me?"

Noelle shrugged carelessly. "I vow I don't remember. In truth, I paid little attention; the subject did not interest me."

"And what does interest you, Miss Pope?"

"Almost everything, Mr. Copeland. That is why it is so unusual for me to be as bored as I am at this moment."

With that she turned on her heels and swept back toward the ballroom.

Quinn chuckled as her skirts disappeared through the doorway. She was a spitfire, and a beautiful one at that. A woman like that was wasted on Simon. For a moment the thought of taking her away from his father flashed through his mind, but then he dismissed it. The less he had to do with Simon, the better off he would be.

He walked over to the wall that surrounded the terrace and rested his hands on the stone balustrade while he looked out over the dying garden, where only a few hardy flowers still bloomed in beds scattered with fallen leaves. The muscles in his face tightened. Why the hell had he come back? To anger Simon? Goad him?

When he'd walked out of his father's library almost two years before, revenge had been sweet in his mouth, and he'd sworn to himself that he would never return. Like a nomad, he'd traveled from one shipyard to the next—Amsterdam, Copenhagen, Glasgow—shunning the leather insulated offices to work as a laborer.

Using his strong hands, he had hammered and planed the hulls, resisting the force inside him that yearned to smash the plump shells and reshape them; make them faster, sleeker. He rigged spars and stitched sails, living off what he earned while his fortune lay untouched in a London bank. He'd driven himself until his hands were hard and calloused, until his muscles were taut bands of steel.

And now he'd returned.

Part of it was curiosity. The stories of a beautiful young cousin had met his ears as soon as he reached London. But Quinn knew it was more than that. Contemptuous of his own weakness, he smashed his fist down on the stone balustrade, not even flinching at the bone-crushing impact.

He had wanted to see his father.

Noelle was circling the edge of the floor when Simon spotted her. Catching her by the arm, he drew her out into the back hallway.

"Are you all right?" he asked.

Angrily Noelle shook off his hand. "Isn't it a little late for that?"

Simon looked faintly reproachful. "I know you're upset, Noelle, but you must realize that he was bound to return eventually."

"And I depended on your protection if he did," she snapped.

"You have my protection."

"Oh? I wish I'd been confident of that when he dragged me into the garden."

"He could hardly harm you in the garden. There were a hundred people nearby."

"I don't believe you have even the faintest idea what your son is capable of doing." She dipped her finger into the bodice of her gown, pulling out the bruised rosebud and flinging it angrily on the floor. "Do you know he believes I am your mistress?"

Simon's brows lifted in surprise. "My mistress? Surely you denied it."

"Of course I didn't deny it. He knows I can't be your niece. There is no other way I can explain my presence here. Simon, you must promise me that you will let him keep believing as he does."

Thoughtfully Simon nudged the fallen rosebud with the polished toe of his shoe.

"Promise me," she insisted.

"All right," he concluded, "if it will make you feel better, I promise. Now, let's go back in before we're missed."

"One more thing." Stubbornly Noelle set her jaw. "I want the marriage dissolved now. It must be done quickly, before he discovers who I am."

Impatiently Simon thrust his fingers through his hair. "Noelle, we've been through all this before. You know how complex it is."

"I don't care!"

"You're being totally unreasonable."

"Simon, I'm warning you," she hissed, "you'd bloody well better find a way or I'll tend to that precious son of yours myself, and I'll use a knife."

Her skirt crackled angrily as she whirled away from him.

Simon considered his next move. Somehow he would have to placate Noelle. He dismissed her threat to harm Quinn as a bluff. Women did not kill in cold blood, even a woman like Noelle. No, what really worried him was that damnable pride of hers; it made her unpredictable.

And then there was Quinn. His son consumed women. Impersonally, dispassionately, he used them and then carelessly tossed them aside. To him all of them were expendable because they were so easily replaced. It was obvious that Noelle had intrigued him, but interest was not enough. Noelle's unattainability was the key. Quinn always wanted what he couldn't have, and for now, Simon would make certain that he couldn't have Dorian Pope!

Simon found Quinn in the foyer, his cloak draped across his arm.

"Quinn," he called out with false heartiness. "You can't leave so soon. We haven't had a chance to talk."

"Spare me your camaraderie, Simon. I'm in no mood for a lecture on my behavior the last time we were together. By the way, how is my bride?"

"I saw that she was taken care of," Simon replied evenly. "Come into the library. I have some excellent brandy hidden away. We can have a drink while you tell me where you've been and what your plans are."

"I can tell you everything you want to know standing right here," Quinn said flatly.

The smile faded from Simon's face. "All right. Where the hell have you been for almost two years?"

"I've been traveling. Studying your competition. Now I'm on my way to New York." Quinn paused, knowing how his next words would incense his father. "I've received an offer from Smith and Damon."

With great effort, Simon checked his anger. He'd be damned if Copeland and Peale's fiercest competitor would get his only son!

"They're certainly a fine outfit," he said evenly. "Still, I think you might be happier if you chose to return to Copeland and Peale. I've come to realize I was shortsighted about your experiments. I am now prepared to give you total freedom to carry on your research."

Quinn's eyes were hooded. So, Simon was prepared to swallow his pride to get him back. "I've already accepted Smith and Damon's offer. I leave for New York next month."

"Copeland and Peale is in your blood, Quinn. You're deluding yourself if you think you can turn your back on it." Simon held up a hand before Quinn could respond. "Don't give me an answer now. Just think about it."

"I've made up my mind," Quinn replied brusquely as he pulled on his cloak. Then, as one hand reached for the doorknob, he remembered the enticing young woman he had first seen sheltered in his father's arms.

"By the way, you still have excellent taste in women, Simon. Although I would have thought you'd have preferred someone a little older."

"We are well suited," Simon replied carefully.

"Where did you find her?"

Simon clasped his hands behind his back, his voice as cold as he could manage. "That is none of your business."

Leaning back casually against the door, Quinn did not bother to hide his amusement. "You look like a jealous bulldog guarding his favorite bone."

"Call it what you will, there is something I want you to understand very clearly. Dorian Pope is special. And she's mine."

Quinn gave his father a lazy smile. "We'll see."

With that he went out the door, releasing the gentle strains of the orchestra to the night air.

Chapter Sixteen

The day after the ball brought with it a heavy, chilling fog, so Noelle's new maid, a cheerful girl named Alice, put out a warm frock of pale blue cashmere for her mistress. Noelle had not fallen asleep until dawn, and now, even though it was nearly noon, she felt drained. Pushing back the bedroom curtain, she leaned her cheek against the cold window pane and stared out across the dreary garden. In every swirling ribbon of fog, she saw Quinn's granite-hard face, sleekly carved, infinitely threatening.

The muffled sound of furniture being moved recalled her to her duties. Simon would have left for the office by now. Although the staff was well supervised by Tomkins, she should at least look in; then she would call on Constance. She had been lucky to find the opportunity last night to pull Constance aside long enough to tell her what had transpired with Quinn, but there had been no time for discussion. Today she needed a stiff dose of Constance's good sense.

Noelle draped a fringed shawl printed with salmon roses around the shoulders of her dress and left her room just as the echo of the lion's head door knocker sounded from below. She smiled to herself. So, Constance's curiosity had gotten the best of her; she wasn't going to wait until Noelle called. The knocker sounded again, more persistently this time. Charles must be in the storeroom at the back of the house, Noelle decided as she tripped down the stairs. Smiling broadly, she flung open the door.

Quinn stood on the other side. He looked much as he had the first time she had seen him: massive shoulders straining the seams of his cloak, crystals of rainwater clinging to his raven hair, eyes the color of black onyx mirroring his amusement.

"Somehow I hadn't expected such a warm welcome, cousin. Not that I'm complaining, mind you."

Noelle realized that the smile she had intended for Constance had frozen on her face. "Your father is not here," she snapped. "I suggest you visit him at his office."

As though she hadn't spoken, he gently pushed past her into the foyer. For the first time Noelle noticed with alarm that he was carrying twin valises.

"I'll see him when he gets back." Setting the valises on the black marble floor, he shrugged off his wet cloak to reveal a well cut brown coat, pale buff trousers, and a buff waistcoat fastened with gold buttons. His dark brown neckcloth was intricately tied, but he wore it, and all his clothing, with a careless elegance that clearly signaled his indifference to fashion.

"I'm afraid it won't be possible for you to wait. He is seldom back before six."

"Fine. I'll see him then." With that Quinn picked up his valises and began mounting the stairs.

Panic propelling her, Noelle flew to the bottom of the stairway. "Surely you don't think for a moment that you will stay here."

Stopping in mid-stride, Quinn looked down at her. "As a matter of fact, that's exactly what I think."

"He doesn't want you here."

"Did he tell you that?"

"Not in so many words, but his feelings about you are certainly clear."

"Miss Pope, my father will like nothing better than having me back under his roof. Now, unless you want to end up looking foolish, I suggest you keep that pretty little nose of yours out of my business." With an easy grace, he disappeared around the curve of the staircase.

Gathering her skirts in her hand, Noelle tore after him. She reached the upstairs hallway just as he disappeared into one of the front bedrooms. For an instant she faltered, but the threat of having him living in the same house pushed her on.

She entered just as he set his valises on the bed. Although she had only been in the room once before when she initially explored the house, she remembered it well. All brown and tan, it was a large masculine room dominated by the massive headboard of the bed, gruesomely carved in the shape of a wild-eyed dragon. The enormous head jutted up from the center of the headboard, mahogany thunderbolts flaring from its great nostrils. The figure was overpowering, frightening, and she could not help noting the similarity between the mythical beast and the man whose presence now filled the room.

Shaking off the uncomfortable comparison, she eyed him levelly. "Mr. Copeland, I do not appreciate your patronizing attitude. It is very much my business who stays here. As your father's hostess, I run his household."

"I'm impressed with your efficiency, cousin." A crooked smile curled his mobile mouth. "Are you as conscientious about your other duties?"

She tilted her chin. "I have always subscribed to the belief that any job worth doing is worth doing well." There, she thought, let him make of that what he would!

"I agree. We have something in common."

"We have nothing in common. Now, it will be much easier on us all if you leave."

"I've never been very interested in doing what's easy. I find I like challenges better." Folding his arms, he leaned back against the wall, silently daring her to push him further.

"You don't seem to understand, Mr. Copeland." Noelle's voice was as crisp as footsteps on dried leaves. "You are not welcome in this house."

Marching to the bed, she pulled off a valise. Resolutely she hauled the heavy case to the doorway and set it outside in the hall. Then she went back for the other. When both cases were moved, she planted one hand on her slim hip and glared at him. "Now, if you will be so kind as to leave."

"Cousin, I can see you and I are going to have to come to an understanding." As he uncurled his long frame she took an instinctive step backward, only to feel her spine press up against the bedroom wall. In three easy strides he was in front of her, his legs brushing against her skirt. He lifted his hand and splayed it on the wall next to her head, his thumb just brushing against her hair. Looking down at her, he spoke softly in the lazy drawl she had come to dread.

"I'm staying right here in this house until I decide I'm ready to leave. Even though the landlady likes to pry into things that aren't her business, I happen to like the room. Now, if you're not out of here in thirty seconds, I'll know it's because you want to stay. In that case, I plan to lock this door, strip off your pretty blue dress, and tumble you right on that bed."

Noelle's cheeks flamed in outrage. "You wouldn't dare."

"I'd dare all right, cousin. As a matter of fact, I'm just hoping you'll test me."

With a murderous glare, Noelle jerked past him and marched angrily away. He retrieved his valises from the hallway. As he set them back on the bed he heard the echo of a door slamming at the other end of the house, and he grinned.

Despite her prissy manner, she was a spirited little vixen, and she had stirred him more than he cared to admit. She was also upsetting all of his plans. Just yesterday he had sworn to keep his distance from Simon. Now here he was, a guest in his father's house. It was instinct rather than logic that drove him here today, but he was not going to rest easy until he found out more about the beautiful Dorian Pope.

In her bedroom, Noelle paced the floor, trying to release some of her pent-up rage. He was insufferable, and he was dangerous. Reaching into the bundle at the back of her wardrobe, she cupped her hand reassuringly around the hilt of her knife. Quinn Copeland was going to discover he could only push her so far.

Yanking the bell cord, she summoned Alice and ordered a carriage brought round at once. She needed to talk to Constance now more than ever. Donning a deep blue pelisse and a bonnet trimmed with velvet bows of the same color, she hurried downstairs as quickly as she could, knowing the carriage would not be ready yet but unwilling to spend another moment in the house. The sight of Quinn's cloak lying proprietarily across the settee in the hallway sent fresh spasms of anger racing through her.

Damn him! She yanked open the front door and blindly flung herself out only to crash head-on into a man who had been standing on the other side. Caught off-balance, he toppled backward, his head thumping dully against the metal railing. He lay very still at the bottom of the steps, his body turned to one side. Noelle sucked in her breath in alarm and raced down. Kneeling on the pavement, she bent over the man.

It was Thomas Sully, Quinn's partner in her abduction!

His beaver hat had rolled off to reveal the unruly sandy hair she remembered so well, but his boyish face was paler now, the plump cheeks drained of color. For a moment she was afraid she had killed him, but then he stirred. Carefully she lifted his head and cradled it in her lap. His eyes flickered feebly, shut, and then opened wider as he took in the lovely face that hovered over him. Wonder showed in them but no recognition.

"I'm frightfully sorry," he gulped. "I'm such a clumsy oaf. Did I hurt you?"

Under other circumstances his misplaced apology would have sent Noelle into a paroxysm of laughter, but she was too relieved even to smile. "Don't try to talk."

"Simply dreadful of me to cause you such a fright." He wet his lips nervously, the color rising in his cheeks.

"Please. It's I who should apologize. I'm the one who knocked you down."

"No, I won't hear of it. I stumbled . . . woolgathering. Horrible habit. Are you sure I didn't hurt you? I could never forgive myself."

"Please, no more apologies. I'm perfectly all right, really. Can you stand?"

"Oh, yes, I'm sure I can."

"Then let me help you inside." She dropped an arm behind his shoulders and braced him as he sat upright.

Quinn's voice coming from the doorway startled them both. "I look forward to hearing the two of you explain this."

Dismayed, Noelle gazed upward to see the mocking grin that was becoming so unpleasantly familiar. "I was about to send for a physician," she said coolly, trying to make it evident by her tone that she wanted no further assistance from him.

"No need for that," Tom replied, feeling his head as he stood upright. "I'm feeling better already. Your kindness has worked wonders, Miss . . . ?"

"Forgive me," said Quinn, coming down the steps. "The two of you haven't been properly introduced." To her chagrin, Noelle felt him slip a proprietary arm around her waist. "I want you to meet Tom Sully, a good friend and one of the few Englishmen I can tolerate. Tom, Dorian Pope—my cousin."

"Delighted, Miss Pope. Can you ever forgive me for causing you such a fright?"

"Of course she forgives you," Quinn interrupted. "Dorian has survived many a tumble. Haven't you, cousin?"

Noelle's cheeks burned at his lazy taunt. She tried to pull herself away, only to be drawn closer, her cheek brushing against the wool of his coat, her hip sensing his thigh. "Let's say no more about it, Mr. Sully," she finally managed. "Now, if you gentlemen will excuse me, I have an engagement." Her magnificent eyes challenged Quinn to delay her any longer. With a slight bow, he released her, and she stepped quickly aside. "It has been a pleasure meeting you, Mr. Sully."

"Do you have to go so soon?" Thomas's boyish face was crestfallen. "I mean . . . that is to say . . . of course you must go. I wouldn't think of delaying you. However . . . would it be terribly presumptuous of me on such short acquaintance to invite you to the opera next Saturday? With your uncle's permission, of course. It's *The Marriage of Figaro*."

"Saturday, you say?" Noelle stalled as she tried to think of a polite excuse. He was so friendly and guileless, so obviously smitten with her that she knew it would be kinder to refuse his invitation than to encourage him.

"Impossible, Tom." Quinn folded his long frame into a chair. "My cousin is busy that night. She has an engagement with Simon."

Noelle's delicately arched eyebrow shot upward at this blatant lie. "I fear you misunderstood, *cousin*. My uncle and I have no engagement that night. I should be delighted to attend with you, Mr. Sully. Absolutely nothing could keep me away."

"Smashing! I'll call at eight."

"I shall look forward to it." The carriage drew to the curb. Quinn took her arm and led her to the vehicle. When they could no longer be overheard, Noelle snapped, "Mr. Copeland, your interference is intolerable."

"Since we're so closely related, don't you think you should call me Quinn?"

"I don't think I should have to call you anything. Don't you understand? I want you to leave me alone."

"I was beginning to get that idea. What I don't understand is why."

Noelle yearned to scream the full measure of her loathing at him, but she satisfied herself with a more restrained indictment. "Because I dislike you, Mr. Copeland. I find you arrogant, overbearing, and insolent."

"In addition to being beautiful, you're an excellent judge of character, cousin." With a polite nod of dismissal, he held the carriage door open for her, and Noelle set off for Constance's new residence on St. James's Park.

Constance was still in her dressing gown when Noelle burst into the sitting room.

"He is detestable! I have never met anyone I despise more." One of the blue velvet ribbons on her bonnet came off in her fingers as she yanked angrily at the bow under her chin.

"Faith! What has he done to set you off?"

Restlessly pacing the room, Noelle recounted all that had happened since Quinn had appeared at the ball. "I just hope I can have the satisfaction of being present when Simon boots him out of the house," she finally concluded.

Constance swung her slippered feet over the side of the lavender chaise and then walked toward the window, where she stopped to inspect a fern sitting on a plaster column. "I would not count on Simon evicting Quinn," she finally said carefully. "You will only be disappointed."

Noelle stopped her pacing and stared incredulously at Constance. "Surely you don't imagine that Simon will let him stay?"

"I'm certain of it. Quinn is his son."

"But, Constance, they detest each other. Quinn has been a dreadful son."

"Simon has not been the best of fathers."

"You sound as though you are defending Quinn!" Noelle exclaimed.

"I am not defending him, nor will I chastise him. Noelle, I have the deepest affection for you. Surely you know that."

"Why do I have the suspicion I'm going to hear something I shan't like?" Noelle said dryly.

"Because you're an uncommonly perceptive young woman. However, at the moment you're behaving like a peagoose. Simon won't remain in England forever. What will you do when he leaves? Go to America with him? Stay here and try to make your own way?"

"I don't know, Constance. If you are right about Simon permitting Quinn to remain in the house, I will consider leaving immediately and finding other employment."

"Nonsense! He has been supporting you for almost two years on the understanding that you would repay him by serving as his hostess. Can you have forgotten that?"

"Of course I haven't. I would repay him from my wages."

"Very noble, my dear, and very, very silly. At best you would find a position in a shop or as a governess. In truth, it doesn't bear thinking on. You'd not make enough to live, let alone have sufficient funds to repay your debt."

At the truth of Constance's words, Noelle slumped dejectedly down on the settee. "Nothing at all has changed. I'm still trapped between the two of them. Constance, what happened to make them hate each other so much?"

"I wish I could enlighten you, but I have only the vaguest notion, and that is purely conjecture. Benjamin knew, but he refused to discuss it other than to say it involved Simon's wife. When she died, he felt it best to let the matter die with her."

"Only it didn't die, did it?"

Constance went to Noelle and sat beside her, speaking gently. "Noelle, in truth, you must consider assuming your proper place as Quinn's wife."

"Constance, I cannot believe this of you." She sprang up angrily. "How can you even suggest such a thing?"

"Because I am a practical woman. Faith! Don't look at me so. It's time you opened your eyes. Quinn is very wealthy. As his wife, you would never again have to trouble yourself about anything."

"I don't want his money!"

"Noelle, you must listen to me. Quinn is not an ordinary man, nor is he an ordinary shipbuilder. He has vision. There is a brilliant future in store for him. As his wife, you can share in that success."

Observing the stubborn set of Noelle's chin, Constance sighed. "At least consider it. Not for him and not for Simon but for yourself."

Noelle could see the compassion in Constance's face and knew that she was speaking from her heart. "I wish I could do as you say, Constance, if for no other reason than to please you. But I would rather live the rest of my life as a pickpocket in Soho than spend a day as his wife."

Several hours later Noelle walked from the gray stone building that housed the London offices of Copeland and Peale. The rain that had been falling steadily since noon had stopped, although the day was still gray and cloudy. Across the street, she spotted Fisby's Tea Room and remembered she had had nothing to eat since the night before. She stepped toward the curb just as one of the maroon and black mail coaches, not yet dry from the day's showers, shot by, its rear wheels sending a jet of dirty water over the front of her pelisse. The day that had started out so badly was drawing to an even grimmer conclusion.

Stabbing dourly at the stains with her handkerchief, Noelle thought how right Constance had been when she had warned her that Simon would not send Quinn from the house. Constance had even predicted his words.

"He is my son," Simon had said. Then, when Noelle had pressed him about the divorce, he had again put her off with vague promises.

"A plank of wood ter 'elp yer cross the street, mum?" Two dirty ragamuffins, a boy and a girl, stood at her side, carrying a long board. Noelle's mind slid back in time to two other children who had carried a board on rainy days and looked for wealthy customers to help across streets.

"Thank you," she said, managing a smile. When she was across the street, she pressed a shilling on the surprised urchins. "Buy yourselves a kidney pie and some gingerbread." The little boy thanked her and even managed an awkward bow before the two scampered off.

Noelle chose an inconspicuous table in the rear of the tea room and soon had a sliver of lemon tart and a steaming cup of tea in front of her. She took a slow sip and pondered the mystery of the animosity between Quinn and Simon. What had happened to make Quinn hate his father so? She rubbed her temples wearily.

"Did you know Quinn is back?"

Noelle's eyes shot to the adjoining table, where two women were seating themselves. All that she could see of the one who had spoken was the back of a well-cut silk pelisse. It was the other woman who held Noelle's attention. In her early thirties, she was extravagantly beautiful with hair as black as a raven's wing and a small mole clinging seductively near the corner of her left eye.

"How do you know that Quinn is in London?" she asked with smoldering excitement, the trace of a foreign accent lending a mysterious allure to her voice.

"I saw him riding in Rotten Row not more than two hours ago."

"Was he alone?" The black-haired beauty tried to make her question seem unimportant, but the tension around her skillfully rouged mouth betrayed her.

"Oh, Anna!" The other woman pronounced the name with a soft "a." "Surely you are not going to be as foolish about him now as you were the last time he was in London."

"It is not foolishness! He obsesses me."

"You and half the other women in London."

"But he doesn't come back to other women as he comes back to me."

"Why does he have this hold on you, Anna? We've both been with many other men. None, perhaps, quite as handsome but, still . . ."

"Because he is exciting, dangerous." Anna lowered her voice, but the words were still audible to Noelle. "I want him, but he will not be owned. He is immune to all the tricks that a woman uses. If I pout, he laughs. If I rage at him, he is indifferent."

"And in bed?" The other woman leaned forward in her seat. "How is he in bed?"

Anna's eyes clouded, and her lips parted seductively as she stared unseeingly past her companion. "Like no other. He makes hard, desperate love to me, and I forget everything else. The next time, I vow that I will hold back, make him plead with me. But I know I am lying to myself. He touches me, my strength disappears, and I give him everything."

Noelle could listen to no more. She did not even bother to count the coins she threw down on the table, so desperate was she to escape overhearing any more of the woman's repugnant confidences.

Much to Noelle's relief, Quinn was not present for supper that night, nor did she hear him return to the house, although it was well past midnight before she turned down her light.

Chapter Seventeen

"Miss Catherine Welby to see you, ma'am."

"Whatever for?" Noelle wondered aloud as she glanced at the clock on her desk. It was barely ten o'clock, hardly an appropriate hour for a caller to present herself, especially one who had been as consistently unfriendly as Catherine Welby.

"Show her to the drawing room, Tomkins. And I suppose you had better send in tea."

As the butler closed the door behind him, Noelle reluctantly set aside the stack of invitations she had been answering and banged the lid of the desk shut, rattling a china shepherdess perched on the top. Normally a job she detested, the task had today provided her with an excuse to seal herself away in her parlor until lunch. By that time, she calculated that Quinn would have left the house, and she would have avoided, at least for the morning, another encounter with him.

The heels of her slippers clattered noisily when they hit the marble of the foyer. Automatically she muffled her steps. He had barely been in the house for twenty-four hours, and she already felt like a prisoner.

Smoothing her dress, she entered the drawing room. "Miss Welby, how nice to see you."

"Do call me Catherine, and I shall, of course, call you Dorian," her caller bubbled effusively as she patted the place next to her invitingly. Noelle sat reluctantly, putting as wide a distance between them as the limited dimensions of the settee and common politeness would permit.

"I just know we shall be the best of friends, Dorian. We have so much in common." She then began chronicling the most recent of her social activities.

Noelle barely listened as she tried to puzzle out the motive behind the unexpected call. She and Catherine Welby had attended several of the same functions; however, they were hardly friends. The fluffy little blonde had barely spoken a dozen words to her, and those had been begrudging.

"I beg your pardon?" Noelle returned her attention to her unwelcome caller, aware that she had missed something.

"I asked if you would like to ride with me in the park next week."

"'I'm sorry, but I don't ride."

"You don't ride?" Miss Welby's astonishment could not have been greater if her hostess had just announced her escape from a Turkish seraglio.

"I was raised in India, you know." Noelle adopted a faintly superior air, as if that should explain everything.

"Oh? Quite so."

There was a brief pause, and then Miss Welby plunged into an account of a new riding habit she was having made, describing each tuck and trim in painstaking detail. Noelle was suppressing a yawn with the utmost difficulty when tea arrived.

"Tell me something about yourself," Miss Welby commanded as she took up her cup.

"There's little to tell. My parents died in India several years ago, and my uncle has graciously offered me his home."

"So sad to lose your parents. But how lucky you are to have such a kind uncle."

"Yes, he has been wonderful to me."

Miss Welby's saucer eyes, as innocently clear as a cloistered nun's, peeked over the rim of her cup. "And had you met your dashing cousin before you arrived in England?"

"No, we had never met."

"What a surprise he must have been to you."

"You can't imagine," Noelle responded dryly.

Footsteps were faintly audible in the foyer, and Miss Welby's eyes slid covertly to the door. When the steps continued down the hallway, she could not quite conceal her disappointment.

"Is your cousin an early riser?"

"I am afraid I do not know him well enough to be familiar with his personal habits."

"Miss Cynthia Rowland to see you, ma'am."

Tomkins had barely finished announcing her when Miss Rowland swept into the room, her ribbons fluttering. "Dorian, I had a simply marvelous time the other night. You must persuade your uncle to have another ball soon. Now, tell me about your cousin. Is it true he killed a man in a duel and fled from America to escape being arrested? One hears such stories about him."

Noelle took a deep breath and tried to suppress her annoyance. These silly girls were using her to get a glimpse of Quinn! Was there to be no end to the complications he brought into her life?

"Miss Priscilla Fargate and Miss Cecily Lambreth-Smythe, ma'am." Tomkins's expression was one of faint bewilderment.

By the end of the morning, Noelle had received six female callers. When the last had finally been shown out, her head was throbbing, and her temper was frayed. Storming out of the drawing room, she found Quinn standing in the foyer, speaking with Tomkins.

Noelle marched up to the butler and planted her hand on her hip, pointedly ignoring Quinn. "Tomkins, if any more unmarried ladies come to call, you are to put them in the drawing room and summon Mr. Copeland to receive them. I am no longer at home."

With that she shot Quinn a chafing glare and stalked down the hallway to her parlor.

To Noelle's relief, for the next few days she saw little of Quinn. He was gone much of the time and did not return to take his meals with them. However, life in Northridge Square did not settle back into its familiar pattern. There was a vague feeling of dysphoria —of lives shifted from a comfortable fulcrum and not yet rebalanced. Simon was particularly attentive to her, bringing her small gifts, taking her riding in his carriage, teaching her to play backgammon and vingt-et-un. But, as he volunteered nothing about her divorce other than vague, dismissive references, their relationship was strained.

For his part, Simon was not a happy man. The dream of a spring afternoon in Sussex, of Constance, warm and responsive beneath him, was never far from his mind. Now they saw each other only in the company of others, and Constance's unfailing courtesy was like a knife stabbing away at him.

And then there was Noelle. He was experiencing vague pangs of conscience about manipulating her in his determination to see her in place as Quinn's wife.

But the dream of a Copeland dynasty governed him, and as was his habit, he subjugated his emotions. Sensing Quinn's interest in Noelle, he set aside his plan to force the marriage. If it became necessary, he could still arrange for their abduction and then announce to society that they had eloped. But for now he was content to let events follow their own course.

The gaslights of Covent Garden flooded their box as Act Two of *The Marriage of Figaro* romped to its high-spirited conclusion. Thomas fixed Noelle with a worshiping gaze. "Are you enjoying the performance, Miss Pope?"

"Very much."

"I think the soprano who is singing Susanna is especially fine, don't you?"

"Yes, she is very appealing."

"I cannot tell you when I have enjoyed an evening more."

"The performance is certainly an excellent one, Mr. Sully."

"I was not referring to the opera."

Reaching over, Thomas covered the back of her hand with his own. "Miss Pope, I must tell you that—"

"Tom, old chap, I told Basil it was you." Two uniformed members of the Light Dragoons arranged themselves on each side of Noelle, demanding an introduction. Much to Thomas's annoyance, they did not leave until the interval was over.

As the curtain rose on Act Three Noelle caught sight of Quinn in a box one tier below. He was listening attentively to a woman whose face was in shadow. A slim hand rested possessively on his thigh. When the woman turned her head, Noelle saw that it was Anna, the raven-haired beauty of the tea room. Leaning forward, she whispered intimately in his ear.

Noelle listened to the rest of the opera with concentrated attention but would have been hard pressed had she been asked to describe it. She applauded vigorously at the end and agreed with Thomas that it had been an exceptional production. He had just settled her cape around her shoulders when he spotted Quinn and waved to him. "So the baroness is in London," he chuckled.

"Baroness?" Noelle inquired offhandedly as they stepped out of the box.

"Anna von Furst, one of the most beautiful women in London and also one of the wealthiest. She and Quinn have been friends for some time."

His pause before "friends" was barely perceptible, but Noelle did not miss it. "And what of the baron?"

"He seems to keep to his schloss in Bavaria. Suffers from dyspepsia or some such. Anyway, one seldom sees him."

It was almost dawn before Noelle fell asleep that night, and she still had not heard Quinn's footsteps coming up the stairs.

Chapter Eighteen

Noelle hurried through the Haymarket, an eddy of light reflecting off the skirt of her emerald dress as she passed under a gas streetlamp. This was her first visit to Soho since the day she had attended the opera with Thomas Sully, and that had been over a week before. She had intended to be safely back in her bedroom long before this, her face cleaned of its camouflage of dirt and cosmetics and her clothing once again tucked away in the back of her wardrobe, but one of the children had fallen and punctured her thigh with a jagged piece of wood, so Noelle had stayed to remove it and comfort the child. Now she was uneasily aware of the throngs of people pushing about her, ready to supply the nocturnal vices the Haymarket offered so abundantly. She thought of her warm bed, a hot bath. Ahead of her the crowd was thinning out. Her steps quickened, and she sighed with relief. It would not be much longer.

It was then that she saw him. He was much too far away for her to make out his features, but she knew instinctively that it was Quinn. He was stopped before a group of children who were turning somersaults and walking on their hands in the hopes of earning their dinner. She watched as he flicked his hand toward the children and knew by the way the urchins began to scamper about that he had thrown them a handful of coins. She froze, waiting to see what he would do next. To her consternation, he began to amble in her direction.

Desperately she glanced about her for a place to hide and then remembered she had passed by an alley only moments before. Quickly retracing her steps, she slipped into the dark mouth of the alley and pressed herself against the wall. She would wait here until he passed.

"Wot are yer doin' 'ere, me lovely? This is no place ter find customers."

Fingers as plump as sausages fastened around Noelle's arm, and she spun around to look into small weasel eyes cushioned in pillows of fat.

" 'Ow 'bout warmin' me bed tonight?"

"Take yer bloody 'ands off me," Noelle growled, the accent of the streets natural to her as she marshaled her defenses to combat this additional danger. She tried to pull away, but the fingers only bit deeper into her flesh.

" 'Ere, now, 'at's not bein' very friendly." From the pocket of a gaudy plaid waistcoat draped with chains and stained with the noisome remnants of past meals, he pulled out a folded bank note, holding it up between his first two fingers.

"There's more where this come from if you an' me get on."

"I ain't interested." Noelle nodded her head in the direction of two prostitutes passing the entrance of the alley. "Take yer business over to them, why don't yer?"

"Because I've taken a fancy ter you."

With that he jerked at her arm, dragging her farther back into the darkness. Noelle doubled up the fist of her free hand and swung at his jaw, barely feeling the bone, cushioned as it was by a thick layer of fat. He let out a soft grunt and then swung at the side of her head with his open palm. The blow momentarily stunned her.

"So, yer likes it rough, do yer? Yer'll get plenty of that where yer goin'."

Noelle shook her head to clear it, dimly aware of the crowds milling near the entrance of the alley who were oblivious to the drama being played out so close to them. She knew she must act. Abruptly she let her knees buckle, and as she dropped she slipped her free hand under her skirt and pulled out the knife that was strapped to her calf. Before her abductor could react, she thrust it upward and pointed its tip at his throat. He dropped her other arm, fear flickering in his eyes as he felt the deadly point touching his flesh.

"You scum," she spat out. "Next time you'd better think twice afore ya put yer 'ands on a woman wot says no." With a flick of her knife, she lightly scored the length of a fatty fold. A line appeared like a piece of red string around his neck.

"Yer cut me," he whimpered, his great jowls quivering.

"Yer lucky I didn't kill ya."

She backed away from him, thankful that her long skirts hid the trembling in her knees. The past two years had changed her more than she had realized, and the sight of the blood she had deliberately drawn sickened her. "Now get out of my sight," she ordered.

A fist unexpectedly darted out from behind her, slashing down agonizingly on her wrist and sending her knife flying. Great hands grabbed her arms and pinioned them behind her while a knee crashed into the small of her back. Blinding pain tore through her body.

"Not so fast there," her unseen assailant growled. "I don't like the way yer been treatin' me friend."

"Wot took yer so long, Georgie. Like to kill me, she did." The fat man rubbed the back of his hand along the bloody line encircling his neck. "Look wot the bitch did ter me." He held up the crimson smear.

"I should of killed ya," Noelle hissed.

Again, the knee slammed into her back. Despite herself, she screamed as searing shafts of agony raced through her body. The viselike grip on her arms tightened cruelly until she felt as if her shoulders were pulling from their sockets.

"Any more from you, and I'll snap yer back in two." The voice of the man called Georgie rumbled threateningly in her ear. "Let's get 'er to the boat. She's the last of the lot. We'll make a pretty penny from this night's work."

Noelle tried to focus through the pain. These men were white slavers! They were members of one of the gangs who prowled the streets of London, looking for young girls to ship to the most infamous brothels of Europe, brothels where no desire was too perverted, and the most twisted of appetites could be satisfied.

The fat man leaned over and picked up her knife from the ground. "Not so fast, Georgie. I got a score to settle with this one."

With the handle of the knife clenched in his fist, he held up the shiny blade inches from Noelle's horrified gaze.

"I'm gonna carve me initials in that pretty face of yers."

" 'Ere now, don't be markin' up 'er face. We'll lose money on 'er. Do it someplace wot won't show as much."

The little weasel eyes glittered maliciously at her, and then

Noelle watched, terror-stricken, as the cold steel slid between her breasts and sliced open the bodice of her gown. With a flick of the blade, he pushed aside the fabric and exposed first her right breast and then her left. His thick lips hung slack as his eyes fastened on her.

"Would ya look at this, Georgie," he leered.

Noelle whimpered as she felt the sharp tip of the knife trace the bottom curve of her breast, not yet breaking the skin but menacing in its purpose. The fat man circled the knife up to the top and then began a slow descent toward the coral tip.

"I think this'll be a good spot, don't you, Georgie?"

A scream tore from Noelle's throat as the point of the knife touched her nipple.

There was the sound of racing footsteps, and Noelle found herself flung down as a dark figure threw himself at Georgie. Dimly Noelle saw the fat man abandon his struggling partner and scurry out of the alley. She wasted little thought on him, however, as Georgie's powerful fist caught her rescuer in the jaw and sent him staggering.

She saw the powerful shoulders and lean thighs clearly outlined by the light from the street. A dreadful recognition filled her, and with trembling fingers she tightened the shawl that covered her head.

Quinn quickly recovered from Georgie's blow and sidestepped just in time to avoid another. The men struggled silently, their faces indistinct in the dimness of the alley. Quinn was the taller of the two, lighter than Noelle's burly assailant but more agile. He delivered a series of savage blows, fighting with an intensity that his opponent could not match.

Georgie was breathing heavily, his strength obviously flagging under the single-minded assault. With one last burst of energy, he pushed past his attacker and fled from the alley.

Quinn approached her, his chest heaving from the exertion of the brawl. "Are you all right?" He loomed over her as she huddled down in the dirt.

She was suddenly conscious of her uncovered breasts and pulled the edges of her cloak together, keeping her head down.

"I'm fine," she murmured. "Thank yer for 'elpin' me."

"Let me make certain they didn't hurt you." Quinn reached

down and slipped a hand under her elbow. As he pulled her up, the dim light from the street fell fleetingly on her face.

"It's you!" he exclaimed.

She ducked back into the dark shadows of the alley so he could not see her clearly. Whom had he recognized? she wondered desperately. The pickpocket or Dorian Pope?

"I won't hurt you," he said, mistaking her withdrawal for fear. "Christ! I don't even remember your name. It was different —French."

He hadn't seen through her disguise! "Just call me 'Ighness, the same as everybody else." She lowered her pitch so that her normally husky voice sounded gruff.

With the back of his knuckle, he wiped away a thin trail of blood that trickled from the corner of his mouth. "How long has it been since you've had a decent meal?"

"I eats when I'm 'ungry."

"Somehow I'd hoped you'd make better use of the money I left you, but you're no better off than you were."

"I likes me gin too much," Noelle whined, as an idea, born of desperation, sprang into her mind. "Besides, there ain't much else left for me, thanks ter you. Georgie, 'e'd marry me all legal and proper if I wasn't already married." Inwardly Noelle winced at her choice of name, but it was the first one that had occurred to her.

"Why do you want to marry him?"

" 'Cause we're gonna 'ave a baby, ducks, that's why. 'E's a good bloke, 'e is. Wants to be a proper dad." With difficulty she let out a sly cackle. "Least it won't be a bastard. Georgie and me spent many a night laughin' over it. A rich bloke like you bein' the legal father of our baby."

Noelle could not help feeling a flash of admiration for Quinn. He did not betray by so much as the flicker of an eyelid the dismay her news must be causing him.

"And if you were not married to me, you would be able to marry your Georgie, is that right?"

"Blimey, yes," Noelle managed, tensing for his response.

"All right. I'll make a deal with you. I'll see what I can do about legally ending our marriage."

It was all too easy. "And wot's my part of this deal?"

"You'll make no claims on me, and you'll give me your word that you'll stay away from the gin shops."

"The gin shops!" Noelle exclaimed, so startled by his strange demand that she could barely absorb the fact that her plan was working.

"The stuff they sell around here is deadly. It has sulphuric acid in it. That's a poison, Highness; it'll hurt your baby."

This was a side of Quinn Copeland she had never seen. She had no time to ponder it, however, for he was not finished with her.

"Do I have your word?"

"I wouldn't want to do nuthin' that would 'urt me babe," she muttered. "And as fer the other, you're the last person I'd want anything from. I'll do wot yer say."

"Good. Now, take this. See that you get some decent food." He thrust a wad of bank notes into her hand. "Buy some meat, fruit. None of this goes for gin, do you understand?"

"I give you me word, didn't I?"

"Where can I find you when I'm ready?"

Noelle thought rapidly. "There's a man named Bardy. Yer can leave word with 'im." She gave him directions to the lodgings.

Quinn began brushing away some of the muck that clung to his evening clothes. "If you'll excuse me, Highness, there's a faro game waiting for me. Try to stay out of trouble."

As suddenly as he had appeared, he was gone.

Noelle rushed back to Northridge Square and was soon sinking down into the steaming water of the tub, closing her eyes as the soothing warmth eased the soreness from her back and arms. Outside her window, the wind howled, giving fierce warning of an impending storm; inside, everything was quiet. Noelle had the upper floors of the house to herself. Simon had gone to Birmingham for the week, the servants were asleep far below in their rooms, and Quinn's faro game would keep him until the early hours of the morning. She had the peace she needed to sort out all that had happened to her tonight.

Working the fragrant soap into a lather, she laughed softly as she realized she was finally going to be free of her hateful marriage. Quinn's wealth would surely produce a speedy divorce and a secret one as well. He was no fool; he had quickly seen the advantage of ending the arrangement. Simon would still believe him married, but Quinn would have freed himself from any responsibility for a wife who could only cause him trouble.

Thoughtfully she washed herself, wincing when her soapy fingers touched her arms. Faint purple marks were already beginning to appear. She reminded herself that if it had not been for Quinn's intervention, she would never have escaped so lightly. Although it did not even the score between them, she knew that she owed him a debt.

A frown puckered her forehead as she slid deeper into the water, but it was already losing its comforting warmth. Sighing, she stood and stepped out of the tub. As she dried herself she resolved to repay him by being more pleasant. Now that she knew she would soon be free, she could afford to be friendlier.

Pulling on a sheer beige dressing gown, she went to the mirror and began brushing her hair. Outside, the storm broke with a fury, and a faint crash sounded from the other end of the hallway. Setting down her brush, she slipped out of her room to investigate.

The hallway was chilly after the cozy warmth of her bedroom, and she hurried along, sticking her head into the empty rooms as she passed. They were all closed tightly against the force of the storm. She hesitated when she reached Quinn's door, then turned the knob.

A blast of wind struck her as she stepped into the empty room. The window opposite the bed was open, and rain was blowing in, soaking the draperies and the floor. Sidestepping a broken vase, Noelle dashed across the room, the chilling rain slashing against her body and soaking through her dressing gown. She pulled down on the window, but it refused to budge. Positioning herself directly in front of it, she yanked with all her strength and pulled it shut just as a bolt of lightning flared in the sky.

Stepping away from the window, she looked down at herself. She was drenched. Only her hair and the back of her gown were dry. Even her feet were squishing in a puddle of water. She grabbed a towel from Quinn's dressing room and mopped up the area around the window, finally spreading the towel over the wet floor. The maids could clean up the rest in the morning. All she wanted to do now was to return to her room, put on a dry gown, and slip into bed.

A great clap of thunder rattled the window panes, and at the same moment, the door swung open, and Quinn stepped in. The dim light from the hallway lapped the room and then disappeared as he shut the door. She sucked in her breath sharply, the small sound like a gunshot in the quiet room.

"What are you doing here?" he asked.

Noelle breathed a silent prayer of gratitude that it was dark, and he could not see how thinly clad she was. "I—I heard a crash. The —the wind knocked over that vase. Your window was left open, and the rain blew in. I—I've been trying to clean up the water." When he did not respond, she continued her flustered explanation. "I didn't expect you home so early. It's barely midnight. I imagined your card game would keep you until much later."

"How did you know I was playing cards?"

Noelle laughed nervously. "Isn't that how you gentlemen always end your evenings?"

"Not always."

Slowly he advanced into the room. A flash of lightning from the window behind her momentarily illuminated his handsome face, and Noelle found something unexpected stir deep within her. The mocking smile she had come to expect was not there; his expression was less guarded, the harsh planes softened.

"Excuse me. I must get back to my room." As she turned to slide past him her gown brushed against his hand.

"You're wet."

"The rain—I got soaked when I was closing the window."

"Here, let me get you a towel. You're shivering."

"No!" she exclaimed. And then more evenly, "I'll be all right. Really."

Ignoring her, he pulled a small towel off the washstand and handed it to her. Noelle dabbed at herself and then, unexpectedly, Quinn lit the lamp. The room was flooded with light.

She stood before him, the towel, barely larger than a man's handkerchief, clutched uselessly in her hand. The thin material of her gown was molded to her, revealing far more than it concealed. Wet gauze outlined her full breasts and clung to her lean flanks where the sweet, dark triangle was clearly visible to his exploring gaze.

"Christ, you're beautiful," he said huskily, and it was as if there were a current radiating from him. Every part of her body that was touched by his slumberous gaze came alive with curious warmth.

He took a step toward her, his eyes burning, and slipped his hand behind her neck. With his fingers, he plowed gentle furrows in her hair as he tipped her head up. His breath was hot and sweet, and then his lips possessed her. They were hard and seeking, igniting a flame within her. She felt her own lips part as his mouth became more demanding.

His other hand caressed the small of her back, the fingers strong and healing as they lingered there for a moment and then traveled downward, finally cupping the pliant curve below. She moaned and turned her head from the relentless threat of his kiss, from the heat of his caress, but his lips patiently brushed the valley beneath her ear and then traveled down her neck, igniting tiny fires everywhere they touched.

My God! What is happening to me? Planting her small fists on his chest, she summoned strength born of panic and pushed herself away from him. He released her, and she ran from the room as if all the demons in hell were at her heels.

The next morning, her face was tired and drawn as she stepped into Constance's carriage, a gold barouche with soft jade-green upholstery. The calash top had been put down to take advantage of the day, which had been washed fine by the storm.

"Really, Noelle, you must get more sleep. There are shadows under your eyes."

"I was reading and lost track of the time," Noelle lied, taking a seat facing Constance.

"I fear you are becoming a bluestocking," Constance chastised as the carriage pulled away from the house. "Did I tell you that I have invited Angela Welby and her daughter, Catherine, to accompany us today?"

"Oh, Constance, you didn't! Catherine Welby is the most awful featherbrain."

"Yes, isn't she. But her mother is a charming woman whom I see all too seldom."

Half an hour later when the carriage entered Hyde Park, Noelle was forced to agree with Constance's assessment of Angela Welby. She was a woman of intelligence and humor who could not quite hide her distaste for the frivolities of her daughter.

Catherine had no sooner arranged her skirts around her than she began questioning Noelle about Quinn. Which particular parties would he be attending during the next week? Was it true about the duel? Had the Baroness von Furst actually threatened suicide if he left her again? Noelle turned aside each question firmly, and Catherine soon lapsed into sullen silence, leaving Noelle free to join in the more stimulating conversation of Constance and Angela Welby.

Patches of sunlight flickered pleasantly over the women as the carriage clipped around the perimeter of the park, passing under the October trees, which were awash with leaves of rust and gold. They nodded to acquaintances, chatted comfortably. Noelle felt some of the awful tension within her ease.

"Dorian! Isn't that your cousin riding toward us?"

The excitement in Catherine's shrill voice pierced the peace of the moment, and Noelle's heart made a sickening lurch. Not yet, she thought desperately, I'm not ready to face him. Please, let it be someone else.

Reluctantly she looked toward the man approaching them astride a great ebony stallion. It was unmistakably Quinn. Noelle had never seen anyone dressed for riding as he was. Shunning the proper formal riding attire of the English, he was, instead, wearing a white shirt open at the neck, sleeves rolled just below his elbows, and dark brown trousers. Soft leather boots hugged his calves. He was coatless and hatless, sitting in an oversize saddle. It was outrageous, inappropriate, and infinitely attractive.

"Mr. Copeland!" Catherine's hand shot up into the air. "Mr. Copeland!"

"Don't shout so, Catherine," her mother said.

But the admonition came too late. The driver stopped the carriage as Quinn reined in the powerful stallion and nodded to Constance and the Welby women. "Good morning, ladies." Then his eyes fell on Noelle, his expression inscrutable. Was he looking for some signal from her, an acknowledgment of what had passed between them? Or had he dismissed the entire incident as unimportant?

Noelle willed herself to return his gaze unflinchingly, giving nothing away herself.

"I see you have not given up your barbaric style of riding," Constance sniffed.

"Sorry to offend you, Constance." He grinned. "But I'd feel ridiculous sitting on one of those handkerchiefs you people call saddles."

"How can you object to it, Mrs. Peale?" Catherine cooed, tilting her parasol so that only the most flattering light fell on her face. "I think the saddle is beautiful."

"It's a working saddle, Miss Welby. We Americans stole it from the *vaqueros* of Mexico." The stallion tossed his mane and pawed restlessly at the ground. Quinn patted the animal's massive neck, quieting him. "Easy, Pathkiller."

"Pathkiller? Such an unusual name," Mrs. Welby offered.

"It was the name of a great Indian chief."

Catherine had no intention of letting the conversation get away from her. "You're obviously a fine judge of horses, Mr. Copeland. He is a magnificent animal. Perhaps you might be interested in seeing my new mare. I hope I don't sound immodest if I tell you she is truly exceptional."

Noelle watched to see how Quinn would react to Catherine's transparent maneuvering, but he merely smiled politely.

"I look forward to it." He turned to Noelle. "Would you care to join us, cousin?"

"I wouldn't think of intruding on your outing," Noelle replied evenly.

Catherine quickly jumped in. "Poor Dorian. And we would so love to have had you. You did not know, Mr. Copeland, that she does not ride?"

"No, I didn't. We've never had an opportunity to discuss any of my cousin's shortcomings, Miss Welby, only her talents." This time his expression erased any doubt Noelle might have had. Quinn had not forgotten last night any more than she had.

Chapter Nineteen

Damn it, Simon thought as he took a swallow of weak coffee, why can't the British made a good, strong cup of coffee? It was one of the few disadvantages of living in England.

He leaned back in his chair, stretching his legs out under his desk and gazing with satisfaction at the warm wood and leather of his library. He felt at home here in Northridge Square and over the past few months had come to understand that he did not want to return to Cape Crosse. He would miss the luxuries of English life, his clubs, the slower pace of the London office. Perhaps it was true that America was still a young man's land. And now, with Quinn located, there was no reason why Simon should have to return permanently to Cape Crosse.

He pulled out his pipe and thoughtfully packed the tobacco in the bowl, tamping it lightly with his index finger. A slow smile of satisfaction crept across his face. He had waited long enough for events to unfold by themselves. Now it was time to give the pot a small stir.

Quinn, dark hair still tousled from sleep, was tucking his unbuttoned shirt into fine-ribbed black corduroy trousers when he entered the library. "What the hell do you want so early in the morning? Tomkins said it was important."

"Another late night?"

Quinn yawned in response and slouched down into the leather chair at the front corner of Simon's desk.

"Women or cards?"

"Both, as a matter of fact." He rubbed one hand over his unshaven cheek.

"Coffee?"

At Quinn's affirmative grunt, Simon poured him a cup of the weak brew from a silver pot. Quinn took a swallow and grimaced.

"Why the hell can't this high-priced staff of yours learn to make coffee?"

"Because they don't want to."

Quinn set down his cup, abruptly putting an end to small talk. "Why did you send for me?"

"To give you this." A sheaf of papers slid across the polished walnut top. "It's a contract negotiating your return to Copeland and Peale."

Uninterestedly Quinn picked up the papers, barely glancing at the top page before he flipped the contract down on the desk. "Not interested."

Simon was not particularly surprised by Quinn's refusal, but he continued to press. "Take some time. Look over the contract. If there's something you don't like, make a counter proposal. You'll never get an offer like this from anyone else."

"I'll take my chances. Now, if that's all you wanted from me, I think I'll go back to bed." Quinn began to uncurl his lean frame from the chair.

"Wait!" It was time for the second part of his plan.

"What else, Simon?"

"I want you to stay out of the house tonight."

"Any particular reason?"

"I have a dinner engagement. Strictly business, so Dorian is remaining at home. I think it will be best for everyone if you spend the evening with your baroness. From what I understand, it shouldn't be much of a sacrifice."

"Why are you so anxious to get rid of me, Simon?"

Simon's pipe had gone out. As he relit it the smell of fine Virginia tobacco permeated the room. "Dorian has taken a strong disliking to you. I don't like to see her unhappy."

"She certainly has you by the leading strings, hasn't she?" Quinn drawled. "You're making a fool of yourself, Simon."

"Why don't you be honest," Simon said, cupping the warm pipe bowl in his hand. "You're fascinated with Dorian. A little hard on the pride, isn't it, when a beautiful young woman chooses the father over the son."

"Why are you baiting me?"

"Because I want you to face facts. Everything in this world can't be as you want it to be, and every woman in this world isn't yours for the taking."

Quinn's voice was heavy with sarcasm as he rose to leave. "I'll store that away with all your other fatherly advice."

When the door closed, Simon smiled to himself. He felt quite certain that Miss Dorian Pope would not be dining alone that evening.

It was already dusk when Noelle eased herself through the window and back into her bedroom. She hurried to make certain her door was still locked and then went to the nightstand and lit the lamp, casting cozy shadows about the room. Unfastening her dark cloak and shawl, she uttered a small sigh of relief. With each venture into Soho, she was challenging her luck, and she knew it. But this afternoon's trip had been worth the risk ten times over.

With trembling fingers, she pulled out a crisp piece of folded stationery from the pocket of her emerald dress and once again treated her eyes to the message that had been waiting for her at Bardy's:

Highness,

The matter of which we spoke is progressing smoothly. I will be leaving for America soon and will contact you before I go regarding final arrangements.

Q.C.C.

Noelle laughed, mercurial quicksilver shimmering in the empty room. Finally she was going to be free, the fetters of the marriage that shackled her, broken. A vast ocean would separate her from the man to whom she was now so dangerously bound. She stripped off her pickpocket's disguise and pushed it to the bottom of her armoire; then, standing in her camisole, she reluctantly tore the note into three even strips and tossed them in the fire. The flames licked at the pieces and then devoured them.

Seating herself in front of her mirror, she shook out her hair and giggled at the reflection that laughed back at her. Dirt, kohl, and rouge covered every part of her skin. She dabbed at the mess with a thick lotion smelling of heliotrope and then went to the washstand and scrubbed her face. Only when all traces of Highness had disappeared did she ring for Alice to bring her bath.

As she waited she thought about Simon, and her pleasure was

tempered with caution. Despite his claims to the contrary, she was convinced that he had made no effort to help her end her marriage. Common sense told her to keep her news hidden from him until she had the final papers in her hand. Then, when Quinn was well on his way to America, she would tell Simon of her clandestine trips into Soho, her meeting with his son, and the termination of the marriage. Of one thing she was certain: Simon was going to be less than pleased with the news.

She bathed quickly, slipped into her undergarments, and asked Alice to pull out her new gown of shamrock green. It was more formal than the dresses she usually wore when she and Simon dined alone, but she felt like celebrating, and the gown was especially flattering, its vivid color making her eyes even more lustrous.

Alice brushed her hair until it shone and then, impulsively, Noelle caught it in a snood of fine gold mesh in the style of the Middle Ages. The Gothic illusion was completed when Alice settled the gown over Noelle's head. With a deep V plunging at the neckline and an unusual fullness in the fabric at the front, she was hauntingly medieval.

There was a knock at the door, and Alice returned with the disappointing news that Simon would be unable to dine at home tonight. Sighing over her wasted efforts, Noelle slipped out of her bedroom.

Quinn looked up as she rounded the curve of the stairway. She had not yet caught sight of him, and he watched with admiration as she moved gracefully down the steps.

She was a beautiful enigma. For someone who lived off the pleasures of the flesh, she seemed strangely innocent, even chaste. Somehow he could not imagine her lying in Simon's arms, yet it was not at all difficult to imagine her in his own. He remembered the stormy night when he had found her in his bedroom—how she had trembled under his embrace; his sense of the sweetness of her kiss, and its inexperience.

She saw him just as she stepped down onto the marble floor. The guarded look she always assumed when he was near settled over her.

"What are you doing here?" Her eyes flickered over his impeccable evening attire.

"Waiting to escort you to the dinner table."

"Dinner? You don't take your meals with us."

"Not a very polite house guest, am I? Let me see if I can make up for it." His smile was relaxed, free of mockery, as he offered her his arm.

She hesitated; then, not wishing to appear ridiculous, slipped her small hand into the crook of his elbow. Her body stiffened as they entered the dining room, and she saw the two places set, one at the head of the table where Simon customarily sat and the other, her place, at his right.

"Afraid to have dinner alone with me?" He dropped down into Simon's chair.

"Of course I'm not," she snapped. "Why should I be afraid?"

"You tell me."

"Really, I don't know what you're talking about."

"Then sit down," he said mildly.

There was no way she could refuse without making herself look foolish. With studied nonchalance, she took her place next to him. Quinn picked up the bottle of light Portuguese rosé and filled first her glass and then his own.

"Truce?" he questioned as he lifted his long-stemmed goblet.

There was a disarming boyish charm about him that Noelle had never seen, and she found herself nodding in response and picking up her own glass.

"Here's to the mysterious and beautiful Dorian Pope." He brushed his glass against hers and then took a slow sip.

Discomfited, Noelle lowered her eyes.

"Is it true that you can't ride a horse?"

She shrugged. "I never had the opportunity to learn." Not giving him the chance to question her further, she turned the conversation away from herself. "Tell me about your mount. I've never seen such a horse."

"Magnificent, isn't he? He was bred on a farm not far from Cape Crosse. I bought him when he was a colt."

A maid appeared with a steaming tureen of shrimp chowder that she ladled into small bowls and set before them.

Noelle dipped her spoon into the thick soup. "I thought sailors were notoriously poor horsemen. That doesn't seem to be true in your case."

"Is that actually a compliment, cousin?"

At Quinn's teasing tone, Noelle opened her mouth to give him a scathing set-down, but he lifted his hand, palm outstretched. "Pull back your claws. I apologize."

His grin was so engaging that, against her will, Noelle smiled back.

"I build ships; I don't sail them. The pleasure for me is in the creation—conceiving the idea, making what I build not only seaworthy but fast and sleek. I give birth to a ship, then, when it's launched, let it go so I can create another one." Abruptly self-conscious, Quinn stopped and fingered the stem of his wineglass.

His self-consciousness triggered her own, and she lowered her gaze. Her eyes caught on his bronzed hands. They were large and work-roughened, so unlike the pampered white hands of the London dandies. The tips of his square fingers bore scars where tools had come too close or moved too fast. These were the hands of a man who labored, and they were as hard and unyielding as the materials he used to build his ships.

The maid replaced their soup with tender fillets of turbot. As Noelle raised her fork she realized, uncomfortably, what an act of intimacy it was to eat with another person. The feeling was reinforced as one course followed another: a lobster salad, truffled potatoes, quenelles of pheasant. Their lips opened to receive the food and sip the wine; a knife slipped into a soft morsel and then withdrew; fingers rubbed the stout handles of the silver. The room was mellow with candlelight and their healthy young appetites. A curious languor was stealing over her.

Quinn motioned for the plates to be removed. Silently they watched as the table was cleared and an artfully arranged platter of hothouse fruit was placed between them. Tomkins brought in three decanters on a silver tray: one each of claret, port, and sherry. He positioned them to Quinn's left.

"Anything else, sir?"

"Nothing, Tomkins. We won't need you again."

"Very well, sir." The butler nodded to the maid, and they both left the room, pulling the door firmly shut behind them.

"Sherry?"

"Please."

The amber liquid was delicious on her tongue, and she savored it for a moment before she swallowed.

Whether it was the evening itself or her unconscious sensuality as she held the wine in her mouth, Quinn could not say, but he felt himself hardening with desire as he watched her. His eyes slipped down to the deep V of her bodice, tantalizingly revealing the swells of her breasts.

Their eyes locked dangerously, and then Noelle came to her senses.

"It's—it's time I retired."

"Running away again?" he asked softly.

"No, of course not. I—I'm just tired. Excuse me."

She willed herself to walk slowly to the door, across the marble foyer, up one step, up the next . . .

"Cousin?"

She spun around to see him leaning against the dining room door frame.

"Sleep well."

Despite the evening's chill, her body was burning when she reached her room. Without bothering to light the lamp, she threw off her garments and then, standing naked, freed her hair from the golden snood. The moonlight streamed in through the windows, touching her hair with silver.

She caught sight of her reflection in the mirror. Her body had changed so much. Fuller, more shapely. It was a woman's body, the flesh soft and supple to the touch. Her eyes held onto the reflection, and she moved closer, stopping in front of the mirror. She was conscious of the sensuous brush of her hair across her naked skin and tilted her head to the side, watching a lock fall forward and curl over the top of her breast.

Thoughtfully she lifted her hands and brushed the palms gently back and forth across the coral tips. The sensation sent small, pleasant ripples through her as she stood, dreamily, her eyes closed, her mouth parted slightly. The heat she had felt all evening rose further within her. There was a tightness between her legs—a tingling, a craving for something . . . A face swept across the back of her closed lids—bold and strong with eyes of shimmering black onyx.

She jerked her hands away from her breasts, as though the tender nipples were burning coals searing the flesh of her palms. Her stomach lurched sickeningly at her wantonness. Hastily she yanked a heavy flannel gown over her head and then, ashamed, buried herself in the covers of her small bed.

For the next few days Noelle managed to avoid Quinn. She attended a concert with Simon, had tea with Constance, and turned down a proposal of marriage from a wealthy young viscount with a receding chin and a disagreeable habit of sucking noisily on his front teeth. When Simon came down with a head cold and took to his room, Noelle grabbed the opportunity to make a trip into Soho.

Once again she was unable to make it back before dark, even though she had run most of the way. But this was the last time she would tease fate, she thought with satisfaction. Her dangerous pilgrimages were over.

Leaning against the trunk of the oak at the back corner of the house, she tried to catch her breath before she attempted the climb up to her bedroom window. While she rested she reviewed the simple plan she had conceived to send money to the children without returning to Soho herself.

Under a blanket of ivy just on the other side of the garden wall, she had discovered an old stone urn with a broken base. It lay on its side, its recess deep, dark, and private—a perfect hiding place. Once a week Noelle planned to put whatever money she could spare into the urn. She had instructed Bardy to send one of the children to fetch it under cover of night. She had also charged him to have her papers delivered to the urn as soon as he received them. Noelle smiled at the thought of her precious papers, knowing she would be unable to keep herself from checking the urn each evening, even though it was really too early to expect them.

As her breath came easier she moved through the clump of oaks toward her makeshift vine ladder. A twig snapped. Instinctively she pressed her spine flat against the nearest tree and waited, all her street-wise senses alert, cautioning her that she was not alone in the night garden.

She thought quickly. Her head was covered with a shawl, and the dark cloak hid her emerald dress. It was probably only a servant out for air; the odds were in her favor that she had not been seen.

Suddenly the garden came alive with the crash of footsteps and a rush of motion. From nowhere, a dark form flew through the air and slammed against her with such force that she was thrown from her feet and sent sprawling, facedown, on the ground.

The impact knocked the breath from her body, and for a

moment, her mind refused to function. Finally, with her forearm, she managed to push her chest a few inches off the ground and roll painfully to her side.

Quinn stood over her.

"What the hell are you doing here?" he raged, his eyes afire.

"Comin' ter see ya," Noelle managed, quickly determining that her only hope was to brazen it out with him. "Fine thing it is, knockin' a body off 'er feet." Painfully she pulled herself up, thankful for the inky shadows that concealed her face. Then, as an afterthought, she added, "And me, with a bun in the oven."

Quinn was immediately concerned and started toward her. "Sorry, Highness, but I thought you were a prowler."

"Don't come no closer." Noelle held up her hands to keep him at bay. "The babe's not 'urt, and I don't fancy another brush with yer. Like ta kill me, yer did with yer scurvy trick."

Quinn suppressed a smile. She was a feisty thing, ready to take on the world.

"All right, Highness. Now, tell me why you've come."

"Musta been balmy in me 'ead for even thinkin' of it," she improvised. "Don't yer be suspectin' I 'ad a drop in, neither. Been stayin' away from the gin, just like yer axed me. But Georgie, 'e read yer note ter me, and I made up me mind it would only be proper ter thank ya." She sniffed disdainfully. "If I'd a knowed wot was waitin' fer me, I'd a spared meself the trouble."

"How did you know where to find me?"

"I remembered the 'ouse from afore, when yer brung me 'ere."

Quinn did not bother to hide his suspicion. "That was almost two years ago, Highness."

"I got a good memory, I do." She stuck her small chin in the air in a gesture that was curiously familiar to Quinn although he could not place it.

"I weren't plannin' ter come ter the front door, yer know. I ain't stupid. I was just gonna wait round till yer come out. Anyways, thank yer fer 'elpin' me, and I'll be goin' now."

She turned from him and began walking toward the back gate, expecting at any moment to feel his powerful hand on her arm, spinning her around to face him. When she reached the alley, she could hardly believe her luck. He had accepted her story! She picked up her skirts and began to run, not stopping until she was far from Northridge Square.

For some time Quinn stood in the garden, smoking one cheroot, and then another. Like Noelle, he was a creature of instinct. And now his instincts were telling him that something was drastically wrong. If he could only put his finger on what it was . . .

Chilled to the bone, Noelle huddled in the back alleys of Mayfair for over an hour. Only then did she permit herself to slip back into the garden and climb the vine to the welcome asylum of her bedroom.

Chapter Twenty

The plump breasts of Mrs. Debs, Simon's housekeeper, jiggled like warm puddings as she bustled through the upstairs hallway, making certain the house was being cleaned to her satisfaction. Every spring and every fall, without fail, her vendetta against dirt reached heroic proportions. She ordered carpets taken up, windows washed, drawers straightened, and cupboards cleared. The house was waxed and polished till it shone. No cobweb was safe, no dust mote protected from her keen eye.

As she passed Quinn's door he emerged from his room, dressed in a dark gray coat and trousers.

"Good morning, Mr. Copeland."

"Mrs. Debs." he nodded.

"Will you be gone the rest of the day, sir? We'd like to do your room today if it won't inconvenience you."

Before he could respond, the shrill voice of the maid called out from the adjoining hallway. "Mrs. Debs! Look what I found in the bottom of Miss Pope's armoire, right behind her slippers. Whatever do you think—"

Abruptly she stopped speaking as she rounded the corner and saw Quinn. "Ex–excuse me, sir." She bobbed a curtsy, the cumbersome bundle she carried in her arms making the movement awkward.

Quinn stared at the rough, dark cloth that held the parcel. It looked like a cloak. There was something so familiar . . . He felt a tensing along his spine.

"I'll take that."

The bewildered maid stared at him without moving.

"There now, girl, didn't you hear Mr. Copeland?" Mrs. Debs said briskly, although she was as mystified as the maid.

The girl quickly handed him the bundle.

"Come along now. You've work waiting for you. We'll do your room this afternoon, Mr. Copeland, if that's satisfactory."

He nodded distractedly, and the two women left him.

Once in his room, he set the bundle on his bed. For a moment he looked down on it, his eyes narrowing to dangerous slits. Then with a yank he sent the contents tumbling across the bed. As he had suspected, the dark cloth covering the parcel was a cloak. But the other objects, lying in disarray in front of him, bore mute damning witness to his enormous stupidity.

He saw the shawl with clumps of orange hair sewn to one edge and the small ceramic apothecary pots. But it was the tawdry gown of emerald-green satin that brought a curse to his lips. Tattered black lace at the neck, a jagged seam across the bodice and down the front—the dress was indelibly printed in his memory. As he picked it up in his clenched fist something fell from the pocket, landing with a soft clink at the toe of his polished boot. It was a thin, gold wedding band. The blistering fury that possessed him was like a living entity coursing through his blood.

Dorian Pope and Highness, the Soho pickpocket, were the same woman! The same conniving little bitch!

Enraged, he threw down the gown and stalked the perimeters of the room. One deception after another! Lie upon lie! From the moment he had met her at the ball when she had let him believe that she was Simon's mistress, he had been manipulated just as if he were a puppet. And his own father had been a partner to her plotting!

After the ball, the deceptions had been more subtle. Her breasts pushing against him when they danced. The wet negligee that had molded so seductively to her body. The way she had teased him with her kiss. Her hair, molten honey in the candlelight as they dined. All of it was a lie.

Quinn's rage fed upon itself like a fire burning out of control in a drought-stricken forest. How she must have laughed each time she inflamed him and then fled.

He remembered the night he had rescued her in the Soho alley. She had spewed out one lie after another, and he had believed her. Pitied her.

God damn it! He was a blind fool! Dorian Pope had played him . . . Dorian Pope had . . . No, that wasn't right. It wasn't her name. The drunken night he had married her, there had been another name. It was French . . . Quinn reached into the corners of his memory. Noelle. Noelle Dorian.

He looked down at the wedding ring still on the floor where it had fallen and then picked it up, holding it between his thumb and forefinger. As he gazed at it he realized with blinding clarity how desperate she was to gain her freedom from him. The elaborate masquerade. The way she had cunningly maneuvered him into offering to dissolve their marriage. It all testified to her desperation.

And with that knowledge, Quinn had his weapon to punish her.

The beautiful Dorian Pope was his wife. And, as his wife, she was his possession, subject to him in everything.

Her body was his property to do with as he pleased.

He let the ring fall back into his hand and closed his fist tightly around it; his mouth twisted mercilessly. Within minutes he had put everything except the wedding band back into the bundle and, slipping into her bedroom, returned it to the bottom of her armoire.

Now, to claim what was his. . . .

A shimmering white moon threw shadows over the garden as Noelle slipped out the back door. Dinner was over, Simon had sealed himself in the library, and she could finally steal away to check the urn for a message from Bardy. A paisley shawl draped over her shoulders, she hurried down the moonlit path toward the gate, her thin slippers soundless on the bricks. She shivered as she passed by the clump of oaks, remembering her encounter with Quinn the night before. Once again her luck had held. If it would just stay with her until she got her papers.

Outside the garden wall, all was quiet. She reached under the blanket of ivy, and her hands embraced the cold stone. Inside the urn was a piece of folded paper. Pulse racing, she extracted the note and tilted it toward the generous moonlight.

Highness,

Our business will be concluded tonight. Be at the Boar's Head Inn off Gough Square at 11:00. My carriage will meet you.

Q.C.C.

Eleven o'clock! It was well past nine now, and Gough Square was at least an hour's walk. If only she had been able to look in the urn sooner.

She rushed back into the house, pausing for a moment to compose herself before she knocked on the library door.

"Come in."

Simon was working at his desk, neat stacks of papers arranged on each side of him.

"I just wanted to say good night, Simon."

He looked up and smiled fondly at her. "Going to bed already?"

"I'm tired. I didn't sleep well last night." That part, at least, was true.

"You do look a little pale. Why don't you sleep late tomorrow? I don't want you to get sick."

Noelle agreed and then, after bidding Simon good night, raced to her room, dismissed her maid, and locked the door. She frowned as she pulled the bundle from the bottom of her armoire. Several pairs of slippers were on their sides. The maids must have been cleaning. She had to be more careful, find another hiding place.

And then she smiled. After tonight, she could burn these clothes she detested. She thought of the vow the emerald gown represented, her vow to avenge herself on Quinn Copeland. Now the thought of revenge seemed like a child's fantasy. For the moment all that was important was to be free of him. Tonight was a time of endings; tomorrow, new beginnings.

A sharp pain was piercing her side when she reached Gough Square, a few minutes past eleven. She found the inn at the entrance of a narrow lane that opened off the north side of the square. Its sign, carved in the shape of a boar's head with twin tusks jutting from its snout, creaked on rusty hinges as it swayed in the chill breeze. To her dismay, there was no carriage waiting.

She paced back and forth in front of the inn, the hospitable sounds from within making her uneasy. Despite the dirt smeared on her face, with her eyes rimmed in kohl and her cheeks covered with rouge, she was sure to be accosted by one of the inn's patrons if she had to wait much longer. She pulled the dark cloak more tightly around her and then with a sigh of relief saw a large black carriage pull up.

The driver looked down at her. "Are yer waitin' for Mr. Copeland?"

Noelle nodded and, without giving him a chance to hop down from his seat, opened the door herself and stepped into the empty interior. The carriage moved out into the square.

Leaning her head back against the seat, Noelle pulled open one of the silk curtains and stared out unseeingly. Her body ached with exhaustion; so little sleep last night and then her furious race against the clock to arrive here by eleven o'clock. If only she were not so tired; more alert for this final, all-important encounter.

Not until the carriage turned north on Tottenham Court Road did Noelle begin to feel uneasy. Where were they going? For the first time she wondered why Quinn had not met her himself at the Boar's Head Inn. Why had he not just handed her the papers and been on his way? She realized that in her haste after she had found the note, she had abandoned her customary caution, had not stopped to consider any of the implications of the message.

By now she was thoroughly alarmed. They had cleared the northern edge of the city, and the driver still showed no signs of slackening his pace. She pounded the palms of her hands on the barrier that separated them. The only response was the crack of the whip and the furious pounding of the horses' hooves on the macadam highway.

Trapped inside the carriage as it raced through the stygian night, Noelle fought to control her panic. She forced herself to think rationally. There was really no way she could have been found out. If Quinn had guessed her identity in the garden, he would never have let her go so easily. And she had not seen him since, so there was nothing she could have done today to give herself away.

For a moment her furious speculations turned to Simon. Could he possibly have told Quinn the truth? But Simon was still in bed when she had returned from her shopping this morning, and Quinn had already left the house.

Looking for some clue, she mentally reviewed everything that had passed between them since their reunion at the ball, but there seemed to be no rational explanation for what was happening. That terrified her more than anything else.

Then it occurred to her that he might be deliberately frightening her. He was showing her how easily he could have her abducted. This must be his way of making certain she understood what the consequences would be if she tried to blackmail him. Of course! That was it! He was trying to insure himself against Highness's larcenous ways.

Noelle felt somewhat calmer, but by the time another hour had passed and they still had not stopped, she was almost frantic. An image of the slippers turned over on their sides in her wardrobe flashed in her mind just as the carriage drew to a jarring halt.

She waited for the sound of Quinn's firm, booted stride, but heard only the shuffling steps of the coachman as he came round to open the door. For an instant she hesitated, but the thought of spending another moment alone with her torturous speculations was more than she could bear.

Ignoring his outstretched hand, she jumped down and looked around her. They were at the side of a deserted road, the flickering carriage lamps too dim to penetrate the dense forest that surrounded them. Pyramidal forms of fir and pine were dwarfed by the leafless skeletons of beech, alder, and oak; their trunks, obsidian columns, primitive sentinels that seemed to warn against any human invasion.

Noelle glanced nervously toward the coachman, who was tending the horses. Shoulders hunched, he hummed tunelessly as if the sound might ward off lurking spirits. Once again her eyes scanned the night forest. Suddenly she saw a distant sulphurous glow as a lantern was lit. There was someone in the forest, well back from the road among the trees.

Noelle turned to the coachman. "Where's Mr. Copeland?"

"Me orders was to bring yer 'ere." With that scant bit of information, he climbed back up on his box, settled himself comfortably, and then tipped his hat down over his eyes.

For the first time Noelle noticed what might once have been a path. Narrow and overgrown, it led roughly in the direction of the light. She seemed to have no other choice but to follow it. Hesitatingly she stepped into the forest, the knife strapped to her leg her only comfort.

A branch yanked at her shawl, and she quickly pulled it more tightly beneath her chin before her own hair could tumble out. The footing on the path was treacherous. She stumbled, skinning the heel of her hand as she tried to catch herself. An owl flew in front of her, and she let out a small gasp. Noelle was a creature of the city, and the night forest was as foreign to her as a distant planet.

Still, she kept pushing herself toward the light. The light meant her papers, her freedom.

After what seemed an eternity, she stepped into a small clearing. The lantern she had been following was swaying from the branch of a stunted beech. As it moved it cast grotesque shadows over the barren area. Tied to a tree was Pathkiller, Quinn's ebony stallion. His owner was nowhere in evidence.

Suppressing her fear, Noelle moved out into the middle of the clearing.

"Welcome, Highness." His voice was low and menacing in the eerie stillness of the night.

Noelle whirled around as he stepped off the same path she had just traveled, almost as if he had first lit the lantern and then circled back to follow her.

He walked toward her, dressed all in black, a cheroot clenched between his white teeth. The swaying lantern cast jagged scars across his hard, reckless features, and a tremor of primitive fear clutched at Noelle. This was not the man who had rescued her in the alley or the dinner companion who had charmed her over Simon's table. This was a stranger—ruthless, unpredictable, and deadly. As he spoke his lips barely moved.

"Sorry I can't offer you a drink, but I'm fresh out of gin."

Summoning her courage, Noelle spat out at him. "Why did you 'ave me brought way out 'ere in the middle of nowhere?"

"Because I wanted to. And I always do what I want."

His hand shot out like a striking serpent and grabbed her arm, pulling her toward the lantern's glow. Noelle struggled against him, turning her head away from the condemning light.

"You're a little hellcat, aren't you?" He chuckled unmercifully at her efforts to free herself from him as he dragged her underneath the lantern. Clasping her chin in his rough hand, he turned it inexorably toward the light. When the full glow fell on her face, he held it still, tightening his hand around her small chin as if he planned to crush the bone. Then, without warning, he let her go.

With the unique courage of a survivor, Noelle lashed out at him. "What the bloody 'ell do ya think yer doin'?"

"Just getting a better look at you, Highness. So I can remember you." The glowing ember at the end of the cheroot cast a bloody shadow over his relentless mouth.

"All right. Yer've 'ad yer fun. Now 'and over me papers."

With excruciating slowness, he withdrew a piece of folded paper from an inside pocket. "Is this what you want?"

"Yes," she snapped. Her hand hastily reached out for the document.

"Not so fast," his taut lips admonished as he pulled the paper back, out of her reach. And then, incredibly, he took the cheroot from his mouth and brushed one corner of the precious document with its glowing tip. Tiny tongues of flame lapped its edge.

"No!" It was an animal cry, primitive and heart-rending.

He dropped the burning paper and then ground it into ash with the heel of his boot.

"No!" Noelle threw herself at him, pounding his massive chest with her small fists. "Why?" she screamed.

He pushed her away from him as easily as he might a small child. "Let's just say I've reconsidered."

"You've what?" she gasped in outrage, the macabre glow of the lantern carving skeletal hollows in her face.

"I've decided we're going to stay married, Highness. For a while anyway."

"But yer don't want ter be married ter me," she cried desperately. "Yer too good fer the likes of me. I'm nothin' but a gin-soaked pickpocket."

"Oh, I wouldn't call you that." Slowly his hand reached for her face.

Dear God, no, she begged silently, motionless with fear.

Deliberately his finger traced her eyebrows, the familiar tilt of her nose, the side of her cheek. Terror was etched in her golden eyes as she stood frozen under his touch.

"No, I wouldn't call you that at all." His voice rose dangerously. "I'd call you a sly . . . conniving . . . greedy . . . little bitch!"

With one savage jerk, he pulled her shawl from her head. Like spilled honey, her hair cascaded over her shoulders. Quinn grabbed her by the arms and shook her roughly. Her cloak came undone and fell to the ground. Once again she stood before him in the emerald dress.

The unleashed fury of his voice sliced into the night. "Just how long did you think you and Simon could make a fool of me?"

"I wasn't trying to make a fool of you," she sobbed desperately, looking into eyes as intense as a prowling beast.

"Then just what were you trying to do—Noelle?"

At the sound of her real name on his sneering lips, panic stole her reason, and she began a deadly struggle.

Within seconds he had pinned her arms behind her back. "You're my wife, and I'm claiming what is mine. I own you!"

"No!" she screamed as she broke free of his grasp and ran, her hair streaming out behind her.

Hurling himself through the air like a springing panther, he grabbed at her knees, pulling her feet out from under her. They both fell to the ground. He rolled her over on her back and held her down, using one knee to separate her legs. Then, with an expert hand, he reached under the skirt of her emerald gown and began his exploration. She felt his hand climb up her calf and flailed her legs wildly. She fought like a wild animal, tearing at his shoulders and neck with her nails, biting at anything that came near her mouth.

Then she felt his weight ease itself from her body. He rose slowly, a bloody scratch marring his rugged cheek. Noelle lay still on the hard ground, her bare thighs exposed where the skirt of her gown had been pushed up. Huge and forbidding, his legs outspread, he stood over her. One of his hands rested on his hip, the other held the object of his search, Noelle's knife.

"You didn't really think I'd forget, did you?" he jeered contemptuously.

Noelle rose painfully and stood before him. Even the cheap dress and garishly applied cosmetics could not hide her wild beauty, and for a moment he considered taking her right there in the clearing.

Her chest was still heaving from the exertion of their struggle, but she pushed her shoulders back and lifted her chin haughtily. "What are you going to do with me?"

"Now, that's an interesting question, Mrs. Copeland."

She flinched as if he had struck her. "Don't call me that."

"Why not? It's your name." He advanced on her and, through clenched teeth, growled, "You're my wife, and I don't intend to let you forget it so easily this time."

With that he picked her up and slung her across his shoulder, heading back toward the carriage. She pounded her fists against his back, but he did not break his stride. With one hand, he opened the carriage door and then, leaning over, dumped her unceremoniously inside.

"I think it's time we had a long, overdue honeymoon, don't you?"

With a curt nod to the coachman, he stepped back and watched the carriage start down the road. Noelle's screams hung like discarded memories under the leafless trees.

When all was finally still, Quinn walked back to the clearing. Picking up her cloak, he mounted his horse, and with a quick tap of his heels he took off to join the speeding carriage on its long trip northward.

Chapter Twenty-one

For the next two days, they traveled as if the devil were at their heels, stopping only for food and to change horses and drivers. At a prosperous coaching inn near St. Albans, Quinn arranged to have his stallion brought on at a more leisurely pace, and for the rest of the trip he sat on top of the carriage with the coachman. He frequently took the reins himself, driving at such a breakneck pace that several of the coachmen made solemn vows never again to hire themselves out to an American. He seldom slept, and when he did, it was only for an hour or two.

Inside the carriage, Noelle spent the night and the next day staring blankly out the window. She did not see the towns they passed through or the changing landscape. She saw only Quinn's face as he raged at her, *"You're my wife . . . I own you!"*

When he opened the carriage door and tossed in her cloak with a parcel of food, she did not look at him. The cloak lay where he had thrown it even though her lips were tinged blue with cold; the food went untasted. She was permitted to leave the carriage each time they stopped to change horses, but even the lively scenes in the inn yards failed to catch her attention. Her mind refused to consider the future. She did not let herself think about their destination or what would happen when they reached it.

On her second night in the carriage, she finally slept. At dawn, she awakened, bruised and aching, but once again with a clear mind. She had been incredibly stupid not to have fled from Simon's house the moment Quinn had returned. Stupider still to have ignored the warning of the slippers. But it was useless to waste time berating herself. She had to form a plan!

At dusk, they stopped at the Rose and Crown, a ramshackle inn with broken shutters at the windows. Quinn opened the door of the carriage. His face was seamed with weariness and marred by the scab from her scratch, but his eyes were as alertly chilling as always.

"Get down. We're going to eat here."

"I'm not hungry," Noelle sneered.

In a flash he had roped his arm around her waist and jerked her to the ground. "Next time, don't argue."

She smoldered with resentment as they entered the dingy inn. He walked into a large room at the side, but Noelle stayed back in the shadows of the hallway and watched him. Inconspicuously he took a seat at the end of one of the trestled tables that ran perpendicular to a soot-darkened fireplace.

With the exception of an old crone who was waiting on the tables, the room was filled with men—laborers, poor farmers from the district, and one group of men so rough and ill-kempt that it was impossible to believe they labored at any honest trade.

Noelle took stock of her appearance. She had wiped some of the rouge from her cheeks with a petticoat ruffle and run her fingers through her hair to tidy it, but she knew that with her hair still undone and the emerald dress sticking out under the edge of her cloak, she hardly looked respectable. Still, this might be her last chance to escape.

Taking a deep breath, she framed herself in the doorway, straightened her spine, and in her most measured tones addressed the group. "Pray you, could someone come to my aid?"

The innkeeper eyed her suspiciously as he set down a heavy trencher bearing a juicy joint of mutton. He was a man of stolid disposition with a limited intelligence that had no tolerance for contradictions. To him, things must always be as they seemed, and a woman who spoke like a lady and looked like a goddess but wore the clothes of a trollop did not fit into his scheme of things. He did not dare disrespect, but neither did he accord her the solicitude he reserved for the few members of the Quality who were forced to patronize his inn.

"Wot seems to be the problem, missy?"

"I fear I am in the most dire of straits." From the corner of her eye, Noelle could see Quinn watching her, amusement flickering in his eyes. He wouldn't be laughing for long, she thought with satisfaction.

Helplessly she pressed her fingers to her cheek. "I have been abducted," she cried, her voice quivering dramatically. "Stolen from my parents' house by an unprincipled rogue who intends to compromise me." The room was filled with some sympathetic mutterings, and Noelle pressed home her advantage. "My father, knowing his vile reputation, refused him permission to court me. Now he has taken his revenge." She allowed a tear to trickle down her cheek.

One of the men, a farmer by his clothing, rose from his table and walked toward her. "I got a daughter not much older'n you. I'd kill any man who played fast and loose with her."

"Aye! Only a spawn o' Satan would pull such a scurvy trick," offered another.

Noelle nodded her head and wiped away the tear with her littlest finger.

"Hold!" the innkeeper cried as he eyed her skeptically. "I want to know wot a lady like you claim to be is doin' dressed in clothes such as those?"

There was a low muttering, and a few heads nodded in agreement. Then the room fell silent, everyone waiting for her response.

Noelle's inventive mind went dry. She saw Quinn fold his arms across his chest and lift a dark, expectant brow. In desperation, she pressed her hands to her heart.

"Oh, please, kind sir. I beg of you not to press me. The explanation is so humiliating, so sordid, I could not bear the shame of revealing it. Let it suffice that I barely escaped with my virtue. Oh, if only my dear father were here to help me!" With that she buried her face in her hands and began to sob so heart-rendingly that only she heard the soft chuckle coming from across the room.

The mood of the patrons turned threatening.

" 'Ere, now, don't be bullyin' 'er." A man in a gray smock punched an accusing finger toward the innkeeper.

"Yer as bad as the scum wot carried 'er off!" shouted another.

"Aye! By the cross of blessed Jesus, you're a hard man, Hadfield."

As a dozen men roared their displeasure the innkeeper beat a hasty retreat to the kitchen.

Noelle gave them a teary smile. "You've all been so kind." And, then, with a small sob, "I'll never forgive myself for endangering you as I have!"

"Wot's this?" the man in the smock said. "And 'ow could you 'ave put a room full of grown men in danger."

"Oh, sir, even twice as many men would be no match for the one who has stolen me. I mean no offense, but he is a man of immense cunning and almost superhuman strength."

The men at the tables visibly bristled with offense at her words, and the ill-kempt group of ruffians who had thus far remained silent rose as if one body. Noelle saw that Quinn was no longer smiling but was regarding her with wary respect. Satisfaction welled inside her as she drove home her final shaft.

"What a fool I was to put you all in the path of the American's wrath!"

It was as if the room exploded.

"American!"

" 'E's a bloody Yankee!"

"Curse the bastard!"

"By God, no one will ever say a dozen God-fearing Englishmen weren't no match for one scurvy American!"

"We'll show 'im?"

"By the time we've finished with 'im, 'e won't be carryin' off any more innocent young girls!" snorted a bearded man with a cast in one eye.

"Aye!"

"Let's at 'im!"

The group of ruffians moved toward her. "Where is the blackguard?"

At the blood gleam in their eyes, Noelle hesitated.

"I'm right here."

He was the only man in the room still sitting. Slowly he got up from the table and then inclined his head slightly toward the astonished patrons.

Finally the bearded man detached himself from the group. "I think you'd better come outside with us, Yankee."

"I'd be glad to," Quinn replied coolly, "but let me introduce myself first. I am Quinn Copeland, and this lady is Highness—one of the most famous whores in London."

Noelle gasped in outrage.

"What kind of greenhorns do you think we are?" one man shouted.

"Aye. We're not as easily taken in as that!"

Quinn planted one foot casually on the bench in front of him and picked up his tankard of ale. "I don't blame you for being skeptical. Highness has been deceiving men since she was eighteen."

"Eighteen! She can't be more than that now."

Quinn looked at them solemnly. "The lady is thirty years old. Remarkable, isn't it?" He gestured offhandedly toward her with his tankard. "Of course, it's much easier to tell by her body than her face."

A dozen sets of eyes turned to study her, and Noelle felt herself going pale with rage. "It's a lie!" she shouted.

But the men weren't so certain, and Noelle saw their suspicion. Lifting her head high, she blazed at Quinn, "You are a scoundrel, sir. First you ruin my young sister, and now you ruin me."

"Very good, Highness, but it won't work," Quinn drawled. "These men are much too shrewd to be taken in by your lies."

The man in the gray smock stepped forward. "Suppose you let us decide that for ourselves and tell us what yer doin' with 'er."

"All right. Although I admit I'd rather keep my foolishness private."

Quinn threw some coins down on the table. "A round of ale for everyone."

The innkeeper crept cautiously from the kitchen, and he and the old crone began refilling the men's mugs. Noelle watched with growing trepidation as Quinn stepped over to the fireplace and leaned an arm on the mantelpiece.

"Two nights ago I was in a tavern in London. Highness approached me, and we agreed on a price. Let me tell you, gentlemen, she was worth every farthing." He grinned toward the outraged Noelle. "As I was getting ready to leave for York the next day and had too much of your good English ale under my belt, I invited her to come with me. She said I would have to pay her ten pounds to make the trip. Like a fool I agreed.

"Once we were past London, she told me ten pounds wasn't enough, and I'd have to pay her more. We argued until this evening, when she swore that I must pay her twenty-five pounds or she would make me regret the day I was born. Twenty-five pounds," Quinn growled, well knowing that these men had never seen so much money at one time in their lives. "What is there between a woman's legs that is worth twenty-five pounds? I refused, of course, and now she's making good her threat. So you see, gentlemen, what a stupid fool I have been to be taken in so easily by a woman."

Noelle could see he had the sympathies of some of the men, but others still looked doubtful.

One of the farmers looked toward her. "What do you have to say to this, miss?"

Once again she permitted a small tear to escape. "I have been gently reared, sir. I don't know the art of protecting myself against such black lies."

The man in the gray smock approached her. "You tell us yer still a virgin?"

Noelle swallowed hard. "Yes."

"Let 'er prove it, I say. Get the midwife. She will tell us if the girl's maidenhead is still in place. Then we'll know if she is speaking the truth."

Noelle shrank back in dismay as the men applauded the suggestion by banging their empty tankards loudly on the wooden tables.

"I don't think that will be necessary. Do you, Highness?" Quinn said softly.

Miserably Noelle shook her head.

There were muffled growls and curses as the mood of the men turned ugly. Too many of them had known the treachery of whores, and they did not like being taken in again.

The bearded man grabbed at Noelle's cloak and yanked it off. "Leave 'er with us, Yankee. We'll teach 'er some manners!"

Fear clutched at her as she saw several more of the rough-looking men advancing toward her.

"Aye. She'll 'ave a bit more respect for men when we've done with 'er."

"Won't be so quick with 'er tricks next time."

Quinn laughed easily and walked through the men until he stood directly behind Noelle. With one arm, he caught her body in a band of steel; her shoulders were pressed back into his hard chest.

"I'm tempted to take advantage of your offer, but to be truthful, I have my own score to settle with her." With that he pushed his hand inside the bodice of her dress and began fondling her bare breast.

Noelle wanted to die from humiliation as his thumb touched her nipple, and the leering men cheered him on. She tried to pull away, but the arm around her was unyielding.

"That's the way, Yankee."

"Aye. She'll hum a different tune when ya 'ave 'er on 'er back."

Noelle pressed her eyes shut against Quinn's rough, debasing caress. His harsh laughter rang in her ears. The men's comments became coarser, their suggestions more obscene. Finally Quinn removed his hand and slapped her on the rear. "If you'll excuse me now, gentlemen, I feel the urge to finish what I've started."

There were more ribald cheers. Then Noelle felt her cloak once again settle over her shoulders and a powerful grasp steer her from the room.

As the night air brushed against her face Noelle sensed the change in Quinn. He dragged her over the broken cobbles of the courtyard with menacing purpose, the easy, laughing indolence of the taproom gone.

"You damned little fool. You almost got yourself raped and me killed with your stupid tricks."

She spun to face him, an angry retort ready, but the savage fury etched on his face stopped her. His lips were rimmed white with rage; a muscle twitched in the corner of his cheek.

"You still haven't learned, have you? You're not going to get away from me until I'm finished with you." With iron talons he caught her shoulders and gave her one vicious shake. "If you ever try anything like that again, by God, I'll thrash you within an inch of your life."

He hurled her into the carriage and slammed the door shut with such force that the entire body shook on its springs. Noelle heard him climb to the top, and then the carriage lurched forward so suddenly that she was thrown to the floor. Pulling herself back up on the seat, she clutched furiously at the strap that hung near the door.

She had no doubt from the breakneck pace at which they were traveling that Quinn was holding the reins, but never had he driven so recklessly, letting the wheels come within inches of the deep ditches that ran along each side of the road, violently careening around curves until she was certain he would kill them all. Finally he let up on the pace, not because he cared about her comfort, she thought bitterly, but only to spare the horses.

As her wheel-born prison carried her relentlessly northward, she began to cry in earnest—at first in angry frustration over the failure of her escape and, finally, from fear of what lay ahead for her.

Chapter Twenty-two

By afternoon of the next day, Noelle guessed that they were somewhere in the northern part of Yorkshire. Puffy clouds like smoky pillows raced across the windswept sky. They had long since left the highway behind them for a sparsely traveled dirt track barely wide enough for the carriage to pass. The landscape was more desolate than anything Noelle had ever seen, with endless stretches of moorland and rocky slopes where only a few desperate trees clung to the windswept surfaces. It was a harsh, forbidding land, and they seemed to be its only inhabitants.

A chill drizzle was falling from the leadened skies when the carriage finally stopped. Unable to bear another moment inside, Noelle opened the door and stepped down into a world where the air was raw and pungent, and every sound was muffled by thick gray mist and the vast emptiness of the moors stretching in front of her. Facing out on the moorland, like ancient gnarled warriors, was a line of bleak hills. Jagged rocky scars marred the lower slopes; the upper slopes were obscured by the mist.

At first she did not see the small cottage, it was so much a part of the rocky crag that rose like a gray monolith behind it. No vines softened its rough stone exterior, no trees draped over the thatched roof. This, then, was their destination.

A whip cracked. Noelle whirled around just in time to see the coachman turn the carriage around and then disappear down the same road they had just climbed. She stood alone with Quinn.

Ignoring her, he picked up his valise and disappeared through the door of the cottage. She stood uncertainly outside, cold and desperately unhappy. A gust of wind, still raw from the North Sea, lifted up her cloak and snapped it behind her. The knife edge of the blast cut through to her skin. Reluctantly she walked to the cottage and stepped inside.

To her consternation, she saw that the interior was only one room. Although it was plain, it was clean and more comfortable than the primitive exterior had led her to expect. Braided rugs were strewn across the planked floor, pewter plates rested on a shelf; there was a cupboard, a table of rough-hewn pine, several comfortable chairs, and a large bed covered with a quilted spread.

Quinn was hunched in front of the fireplace, lighting the coal that rested on the grate.

"Shut the door," he barked.

Noelle gave it an angry shove with her foot, and the door slammed with a satisfying bang. Quinn did not seem to notice. She walked over to one of the cottage's three windows and stared out. It was empty and frightening.

He came up behind her and wearily rubbed the dark stubble that covered his jaw. "You won't be able to see anything until the mist lifts, and that won't be before morning, if then. Sometimes it hangs on for days."

"For days," Noelle exclaimed, knowing she could never get away until it cleared. "But that's impossible!"

Quinn sighed. "I think we'd better get a few things straight, Highness. Whether the mist lifts now or next week doesn't concern you, because you're not going anywhere. There isn't a village for thirty miles, and the only other person around is the old woman who takes care of this place. You can run off any time you like, but the chances are you'll die out on those moors, because I'm not going to chase you. My horse won't be here for another day, and besides, I'm too damned tired. Now, you do what you want. I'm going to bed."

He tugged off his boots and sprawled, fully clothed, across the bed. Within seconds he was asleep.

Noelle wandered restlessly about the cottage. To her distress, she saw that it was well-stocked with provisions, as if Quinn were planning a lengthy stay. A large, flat cheese rested on a shelf; two fresh loaves of bread wrapped in clean white cloths were beside it. There were bottles of wine, a basket of eggs, bins full of vegetables and fruit, flour, sugar, and spices.

She sat down in a comfortable armchair and tried to think clearly. Quinn was right. It would be suicide to try to escape over the moors. Following the road the carriage had taken to bring them here was equally foolish, since there was no village nearby.

Besides, even if there were, no one was going to shelter a wife from her legal husband.

Her husband. The sight of him asleep on the bed brought back the painful memory of that long-ago night in the inn when he had claimed her. She remembered the awful pain of it. How did married women survive that brutal assault night after night? How would she survive it?

The fire was warming the room, and Noelle leaned back in her chair and unfastened her cloak. She was so tired. If she could just shut her eyes for a moment, perhaps something would come to her. . . .

She awakened to sounds of movement in the cottage. Through half-parted lids, she saw Quinn walking toward her, tucking a clean white shirt into a pair of fawn-colored trousers. An empty hip bath, its tin sides still wet from his bath, sat in front of the fireplace. He looked down at her, buttoning his shirt as he spoke.

"Are you hungry?"

The sight of him, freshly bathed, banished her drowsiness, and she nodded. "What time is it?"

"Almost midnight."

Midnight! She'd been asleep for hours! Longingly she looked toward the empty tub. She was filthy. If only there were some privacy in this cottage so she could have a bath herself.

From a brick oven set in the side of the fireplace, Quinn pulled out an iron pot and carried it over to the table where two places had been laid. There was already a bottle of wine and a loaf of bread sitting in the middle.

"Come eat," he said flatly. "The old woman left a pot of stew for us. Tomorrow I'll catch some trout if the mist has lifted."

The delicious fragrance coming from the stewpot drew Noelle to the table. As she sat, Quinn filled her glass with a deep red burgundy. The stew was excellent, with hearty chunks of lamb and vegetables in a thick gravy.

While Noelle ate she found herself unobtrusively studying Quinn. How different he was from the gluttons who gorged themselves at the fashionable dinner tables of London—extolling, with full mouths, the merits of every dish; swilling wine, one glass after another; stuffing rich desserts into already overstuffed gullets.

Food obviously meant little to Quinn. Now he ate sparingly, and when he was done, he pushed his plate away and leaned back in his chair, watching her.

Noelle took a few more bites, and then, her appetite gone, put down her fork. "What about Constance and Simon? They'll be frantic with worry."

"I left a note. Not that I care whether Simon worries or not, but I didn't want Constance upset. She's fond of you. Damned if I know why."

He poured himself another glass of wine and took a slow sip. "I'm curious. Just what did you blackmail Simon with to make him go along with this scheme of yours? Was it only for money, or did you threaten to expose our marriage to his friends?"

Noelle's jaw dropped. "Blackmail Simon?" she gasped. "Is that what you think?"

"You don't expect me to believe this was his idea, do you?" Quinn sneered. "The man who was obsessed with having his son marry only the most well-bred of women?"

"You surely don't think it was mine?" exclaimed Noelle.

"That's exactly what I think."

"Well, you're wrong. It was Simon's idea from the beginning."

Quinn laughed, a bitter sound that had no vestige of merriment. "You're a little liar. I've seen Simon's books, and for the past two years he's been paying you quite generously."

"But that wasn't blackmail money," Noelle argued desperately. "That was my salary as his hostess."

"You can call it a salary if you want, Highness, but the rest of the world calls it blackmail." He took a final swallow of wine and then rose contemptuously from the table. "It's obvious you wanted to take Simon for everything you could and then disappear. But I spoiled your plan, didn't I, Highness, by coming back."

Noelle was furious at the unfairness of it but could see no way to defend herself. For the first time she realized he was still calling her "Highness." It was as if Dorian Pope had never existed, and he saw her now only as the scheming London pickpocket who had entrapped him. That knowledge frightened her more than anything else. Although Quinn had often been insolent to her when he thought she was Dorian Pope, he had never actually hurt her. The same could not be said of his encounters with Highness.

She realized that he was preparing a bath for her in the tin tub in front of the fireplace. The steam rose, warm and welcoming, as he added a pot of hot water. Noelle took a deep, steadying sip of wine.

"I am quite capable of pouring my own bath water," she said icily.

With one quirked eyebrow, he dismissed her comment and returned to his task. When he was done, he lit a cheroot and sprawled into one of the chairs near the tub, stretching his long legs out in front of him. The cheroot clenched in the corner of his mouth, he lazily undid his front shirt buttons, revealing the strange disk gleaming silver against the thick mat of dark hair on his chest.

"I think it's time we started our honeymoon, don't you, Highness?"

Her mouth was dry, but she met his gaze unflinchingly. "My name is Noelle."

He expelled a thin stream of smoke. "Well, Noelle," he sneered, "get over here and take off your clothes for your husband. You need a bath."

"I don't intend to bathe in front of you, Quinn."

"Why not? You've done it before."

"Yes. And my memories of it are not pleasant." With as much dignity as she could manage, she said, "I would like you to go outside."

"I'm sure you would. Now get out of that dress."

Something inside of Noelle snapped, and she jumped up. "I won't undress in front of you just because you tell me to. If you want this dress off me, you'll have to rip it off like you did before."

Quinn didn't respond, and his very composure sparked her even more. "Well? Go ahead! You're stronger than I am. I can't stop you! Go ahead and rip it off like the filthy savage that you are!"

His eyes turned into black flints with the force of his rage, and he sprang from his chair. Frightened by the wild look on his face, Noelle gripped the edge of the table in front of her.

But he did not come toward her. Instead, he turned on his heels and walked over to the foot of the bed, where his coat lay smoothly folded.

Noelle had won! He was going outside, and she would have the privacy she demanded. Not daring to let him see her gloat, she picked up her wineglass and drank, closing her eyes with a silent sigh of satisfaction.

When she opened them, she was staring into the barrel of a silver pistol.

He held it lightly in his hand, pointed directly at her. "I don't have to rip off your dress after all, do I, Highness?"

Noelle flicked the tip of her tongue across her dry lips, her eyes glued to the gun as, slowly, she lowered the glass to her side. "You—you wouldn't really use that . . ." she muttered shakily.

In answer, there was a deafening report, and the wineglass exploded into a thousand razor-edged slivers.

"Now, strip!"

His voice was as lethal as the pistol he held, and Noelle knew, unmistakably, that she had lost another battle. Stiffly she walked over to the fireplace and, with her back to Quinn, began to unbutton her dress.

He put one boot up on the low chest at the foot of the bed, the arm holding the gun resting easily on his bent knee. "Turn around so I can watch you."

Slowly she did as he said.

When Quinn saw her stricken face, he felt a hollowness in the pit of his stomach. God damn her! Why did she make him feel as if he were the one in the wrong?

He silently cursed himself for pulling the gun on her, even though it was no longer loaded. It had been a stupid thing to do, and he should never have let her taunting infuriate him so.

Damn it! None of this would have happened if she hadn't deceived him. Standing there, clutching that ridiculous green dress together with her fingers, playing the frightened virgin when she'd undoubtedly shared her favors with half the men in London. Perhaps even his own father.

"Get on with it," he barked, gesturing toward the dress with the barrel of his gun.

She slipped the garment down over her petticoats.

"Throw everything in the fire."

"But I don't have anything else to wear."

"Do as I say. I don't want any reminders."

The smell of scorched cloth filled the cottage as the flames consumed the emerald-green dress. Noelle pulled off her petticoats, and they joined the blaze. Only her chemise was left. With her hair hanging loosely about her shoulders, she slowly lowered the straps of the torn chemise and, finally, the garment itself.

She stood naked in front of him.

Quinn had been with his first woman when he was fifteen, and since then there had been so many he had lost count. But never had he seen a body as perfect as hers, a body he wanted more to possess.

She made no attempt to cover her nakedness, but letting her arms hang loosely at her sides, she lifted her head proudly and met his gaze. "May I get into the bath now?" she asked, her quiet dignity making him ashamed.

He nodded his head abruptly. He'd gotten what he wanted, but the victory was empty. As she slid into the steaming water he angrily pitched his gun down on the bed and, with a muttered oath, strode from the cottage, leaving her alone with her bath.

Noelle was asleep when he finally returned, tired and cold from his self-imposed exile. He lit a small stub of candle and, in spite of his sour mood, chuckled softly when he saw his pistol lying on the floor, well imagining her fury when she discovered the gun was empty. The little hellion had undoubtedly torn the cottage apart looking for the ammunition he had wisely hidden away in the stable. She probably didn't know the first thing about firing a gun, but that wouldn't stop her. Nothing, he knew, would give her more satisfaction than drilling a bullet into his heart.

With a frown, he sat down on the side of the bed and pulled off his damp leather boots; then he lifted the quilt and looked at her sleeping form. Although her shoulders were bare, the rest of her was tightly wrapped in a brown wool blanket that she was clutching together at her breast.

He grunted with annoyance. Even in her sleep, she was trying to guard herself against him, trying to play the innocent. What a bitch she was—a dangerous, beautiful bitch.

You can sleep well for now, Highness, he thought, as he blew out the candle and climbed in next to her. Things went your way tonight. But from now on I make the rules. If I want you, I'll take you. And, if I don't—well, that's my decision, too. He turned his back on her and fell asleep.

When Noelle awakened the next morning, the cottage was empty. Perhaps he hadn't come back! She quickly sat up in bed, only to have her hopes dashed by the cheerfully crackling fire on the grate. Listlessly swinging her bare feet over the edge of the bed, she stood, the blanket still wrapped around her like a warm brown cocoon. It was then that she saw the imprint of a head in the center of the pillow next to hers.

She stared down in disbelief. He had spent the night in bed with her! Turning her back on the bed, she went to the fire and knelt down on the braided rug in front of the comforting flames. Once again she was struck by the unpredictability of the man to whom she was so unwillingly married. When she had railed at him, he had threatened to rape her; when she had defied him, he had forced her to shed her clothes at gunpoint. Yet in the end, he had not touched her. Every time she lost her temper, he got the best of her. It was only when she held herself aloof that she seemed to have an edge.

She bit at her lip thoughtfully. If she could curb her temper, she might be able to—not control him, for he was too barbaric to be controlled—perhaps hold him off. Yes, that was her best hope. Like a knight donning armor, she would assume an air of chilling politeness.

A small voice inside her warned that her volatile nature could not be so easily bridled, but Noelle refused to listen and turned her thoughts, instead, to finding something to wear. In an old walnut bureau, she discovered the neatly folded contents of Quinn's valise but nothing else. Her forage in the chest at the bottom of the bed was more fruitful. Beneath blankets sprinkled with dried lavender, she found some stockings, a boy's jacket and cap, and a flannel nightgown, much too large for her slim figure but certainly more comfortable than the blanket she had wrapped herself in last night. There were also two pairs of small, buff-colored breeches.

Noelle tried on each pair. They fit her like a second skin, comfortable but molding to every curve and hollow much more intimately than she wished.

The chest refused to yield up a shirt, however, and Noelle was forced to take out one of Quinn's. If only he had left me my chemise, she thought, as she slipped the soft white shirt on over her bare skin. Even though she was tall, it fell almost to her knees. After rolling the long sleeves up to her elbows, she gathered the hem of the shirt around her waist and then tied the points into a knot at the front.

Through the window, Noelle could see that the mist had lifted, and the day was fine. Anxious to explore, she washed quickly and brushed the tangles from her hair. Since she had no pins to put it up, she thrust the honey strands under the cap she had found and was just picking up the dark brown jacket when Quinn walked in, carrying a pair of trout.

The corners of his mouth twitched as he took in her garb, his eyes lingering on the breeches that revealed only too well her womanliness. "Well, boy," he mocked, "what have you done with the viper-tongued wench who was here when I left? Never mind. I'd rather not know. I'll just count myself lucky that she's gone and I have a stout lad like you to gut these trout." With that he slapped the fish in Noelle's hands and turned his back to her as he took off his coat.

Noelle stood fuming, a fish in each hand, her resolve to keep her temper in check forgotten. Viper-tongued wench, indeed!

The first trout caught Quinn on the back of his neck, the second glanced off his shoulder.

"Why, you little hellion!" He spun around and came toward her, a wicked gleam in his eyes.

Noelle felt herself being lifted up and then thrown on the bed behind her. Her hair swarmed around her face, blinding her as the cap flew off. Before she could comprehend what was happening, Quinn had tossed her across his knees and had slapped his open palm down hard on her buttocks.

The breeches offered little protection as he punished her dainty rear. She flailed wildly, shrieking every curse she had ever heard and a few she invented on the spur of the moment. Finally, when her buttocks began to burn just as hotly as her temper, she fastened her teeth into the back of his calf and bit down with all her might.

With a howl of outrage, he threw her back on the bed and pinned her down with his weight. "You still haven't learned your lesson, have you, Highness? I'm afraid there's only one way I'll tame you."

As her eyes blazed murderous golden hatred at him, he was acutely conscious of her breasts, unfettered beneath the thin white fabric of his own shirt. Tantalizingly they pressed into his chest, and he felt his lust growing, urging him to claim his wife at last.

With one jerk, he split open the white shirt to the knot at her waist, laying bare her heaving breasts.

The nostrils of his bold nose flared.

With a scream of rage, Noelle tried to pull herself from him, but he caught a great handful of her hair and twisted it through his fingers, rendering her immobile.

"Animal!" she shrieked. "You're a filthy, rutting animal. A foul —" Quinn silenced her vitriol with his lips, but there was no tenderness in the way he pillaged her mouth. He took his own time with his savage kiss, and only when his lips and tongue were satisfied, did he go about the business of pulling the breeches from her writhing legs. When it was done, he reached down and grasped one slim leg, ready to wrench it apart from the other so he could expose her woman's core. Then he heard a sob, more animal than human.

At the sight of her eyes, wild with fear, his stomach lurched with self-disgust. It had been a game to him, but she was clearly terrified. Instinctively he let go of her hair and pushed himself back from her, but she did not seem to notice his withdrawal.

"Please," she sobbed, oblivious to her nakedness. "I'll do anything you say. Don't rape me. Please." Over and over, wildly, sometimes incoherently, she begged him to spare her.

Finally his proud wife had been brought low, but the taste of it was sour in his mouth.

He stalked the moor for hours. My God, she was poison! At one moment, all fire—pulling knives from under her skirts and spewing profanities with breathtaking ease. Then, like quicksilver, she became an ice maiden—beautiful and distant, impeccably correct. And finally, the terrified creature who had begged him for mercy.

With a black scowl, he decided to return her to London as soon as possible. He would deposit her on Simon's doorstep and then leave for New York as he had planned. He had clearly misjudged her sexual experience, and there was no sense in wasting his time with her when the world was full of easier prey; women eager to spread their thighs for him—boringly, predictably.

But he wasn't ready to send her back. She'd gotten into his blood, and he had to sample her before he could be free of her. For a moment he considered returning to the cottage and finishing what he had started. The hell with her pleas! He had always been patently selfish in his relationships with women, and he saw no reason to make an exception of her. Then he rejected the idea, not merely because it was distasteful, but because it damaged his pride. Since when did he have to force a woman to satisfy the ache in his loins! He wanted to feel her trembling under him, not with fear but with passion.

It was then that he decided to employ the charm he possessed in abundance but seldom made the effort to use. A seduction would be amusing. He'd bring her, willing and eager, to his bed. Then the spell would be broken, and he could dispose of her as easily as he had all the others!

Quinn threw back his head and laughed, his white teeth flashing in the sun.

The brush of cold air on her bare thighs brought Noelle back to the present, and she realized she was alone. Once again she had been spared, but the knowledge brought her no satisfaction. Slowly, she pulled herself up, lethargically fastening the few remaining buttons on her shirt as she remembered how she had humiliated herself . . . begged him . . . made him take pity on her.

Dear God, why couldn't she have borne his assault silently, with some measure of dignity! What a coward she had become, unable to bear what countless other women had been enduring since time began.

She looked down at her breeches turned wrong side out on the floor and wished with all her heart that he had not spared her. This way, his revenge was complete. By witnessing her with her spirit broken, without the courage to endure his intimacy, he had finally conquered her.

She pulled on her breeches, wincing as the fabric cupped her tender buttocks, and went outside. Climbing the steep hillside behind the cottage, she was too miserable to enjoy the freedom of moving with legs unencumbered by petticoats and full skirts. When she reached the top, she stopped to catch her breath and looked down. The cottage seemed even more isolated today than it had yesterday, although lit by the rare autumn sunshine, the barren moors had an awesome beauty. In the distance, she could see Quinn's figure stalking the black earth as if he were its master, no doubt reliving the way she had humiliated herself, reveling in her cowardice.

Then she knew without question what she must do if she were

ever to be able to live with herself again, and with that knowledge an icy crust encapsulated her heart.

Despite her resolve, it was not until some time after she had seen Quinn return to the cottage that she could bring herself to enter. He was seated at the table, enjoying one of the trout that had figured so prominently in her downfall, and he politely invited Noelle to join him.

Warily she eyed the hard wooden seat of the chair and quietly refused.

"Not hungry?" he asked innocently as he saw her small hand steal unobtrusively to her abused backside.

She shook her head. "Perhaps later."

Reaching for the loaf of bread on the table, he tore off two chunks and placed a large piece of fish between the slices. He rose from the table unexpectedly and came to her, steering her toward the door. "Come on."

She nibbled on the sandwich while they walked along a path that ran off from one side of the cottage. He chatted easily, as if nothing had ever happened between them, telling her how he had found the cottage and of the old woman who maintained it for him. Despite herself, she listened, amazed that this charming man who was conversing so entertainingly was the same one who had tried to ravish her.

Just as she finished the last bite of her meal, she saw a lake ahead, so small that its far edge was easily visible. It lay even with the plane of the moor, its surface gray and smooth, reflecting the darkening sky and a lone twisted tree growing near its shore.

"Ravensdale Tarn," Quinn told her. "Those are gulls' nests in the rushes on the edge."

"It's beautiful. So still. I didn't know there were lakes on the moors."

"There aren't many. This is one of the most dangerous because it's so deep, and you can't see it until you're right on top of it. At night or when it's misty, the lake is completely invisible. A lot of sheep have been drowned in this water. Even a few men."

Noelle looked at him sharply. Was this his way of warning her not to try to run away from him? But his expression told her nothing, and she eased herself down onto the spongy turf.

Drawing her knees under her chin, she spoke quietly. "I have something I want to tell you." Each word crept painfully out of her solemnly set mouth. "I have decided I'm ready to become your wife." There, she had said it. There was no backing off now.

But he seemed not to have heard her. He only stared out across the flat expanse of water, his forearm resting against the twisted tree trunk, and watched as a gull circled the edge of the lake before gracefully landing near its nest.

Finally he turned to her dispassionately. "What's that supposed to mean—'become my wife'?"

Damn him! He wasn't going to make this easy for her!

"It means that, for the present, I am prepared to . . . to fulfill all of my obligations."

"Are you, now?" he mocked, returning his attention to the lake.

"Yes," she declared, with a toss of her honey mane. "I'm no coward, Quinn Copeland, despite what happened today. And I intend to prove it to you."

His voice was steeped in sarcasm. "And am I supposed to be grateful for this act of bravery on your part?"

Whatever else he was ready to say was cut short by the sound of a man's voice calling faintly in the distance.

"Come on, Highness. I have a surprise for you."

An old man was unloading Quinn's heavy saddle and another smaller one from the back of a wooden cart that stood near the cottage. Tied behind the cart were two horses—Pathkiller, Quinn's magnificent stallion, and a small chestnut mare. Noelle stopped where she was and took in the beautiful animal. As if aware she was under inspection, the mare turned her head toward Noelle and returned the appraisal with warm, liquid eyes. Then, satisfied with what she saw, she pricked up her ears in friendly salute.

As a child, Noelle had sometimes collected a few pennies by standing on the curb and holding horses for the gentry, but other than that, her contact with animals had been unpleasantly limited to rats or the vicious stray dogs that roamed in packs through the alleys of London. Now she fell hopelessly in love with the beautiful animal that stood in front of her.

The horse whinnied softly, as if impatient for her to come near, and Noelle closed the distance between them. Tentatively she reached up and slid a hand down the mare's warm, silky nose, enchanted with the intelligence she perceived in the animal's expression. As if in response, the mare gave Noelle's shoulder a gentle nudge.

She was so captivated by the horse that she didn't notice Quinn coming up behind her.

"It looks like you've made a friend."

Noelle stroked the dark chestnut mane. "What's her name?"

"That's up to you. She's yours."

Thunderstruck, she stared at him.

He turned to untie the horses. "Don't worry. I'm not expecting gratitude. I won't have a wife who can't ride."

She was torn between the desire to fling the unsolicited gift in his face and the knowledge that she couldn't bring herself to part with this beautiful horse. Then the cart clattered its way down the lane.

With the reins of both animals in his hand, Quinn watched the warring emotions so clearly raging on Noelle's face.

"I'll have to shoot her if you don't take her. Nobody else would be stupid enough to buy that bag of bones."

"Shoot her!" Noelle choked. "Are you blind? She's the most beautiful—" The devils dancing mischievously in his eyes stopped her before she went further. She planted her hands on her slim hips and gave him a withering glare.

"Not only is your sense of humor misplaced, it is decidedly macabre."

"Whatever you say, Highness." He grinned. "Now, let's get these horses bedded down."

They led the animals to the tiny stone stable behind the cottage, where Quinn put them into separate stalls, each of which held a bale of straw. He showed her how to rub down the chestnut and then went to tend Pathkiller.

Noelle listened uneasily as the ferocious stallion kicked an iron hoof against the thin wooden partition that divided the stalls. The stallion was a magnificent animal, but she couldn't imagine going into a stall alone with him.

"Give her some oats before you leave," Quinn called over to her. "Tomorrow you're going to have your first riding lesson."

So he was going to teach her to ride. A throb of excitement shot through her at the thought of sitting on the back of this beautiful horse.

"I'm going to call you Chestnut Lady," she whispered as she

rested her cheek against the animal's sleek neck, "and I'll learn to ride you like the wind."

A scene of quiet domesticity greeted Quinn when he entered the cottage that night after having checked the horses. The lamps were glowing warmly, and a crackling fire cast cozy pumpkin-colored shadows about the room. At the center of the tranquil scene was Noelle, laboriously sewing on the buttons that Quinn had ripped from her shirt that morning. The ends of her hair, still damp from the quick bath she had taken while he was in the stable, curled over the modest bodice of the flannel nightgown she had found in the chest. She looked like little more than a child with her bare feet tucked under the folds of the voluminous nightgown and her forehead knitted in concentration.

Only the slight trembling in her fingers gave away her agitation. So, Quinn thought, she's planning to go through with it. He jerked his coat off and flung it over the back of a chair.

The last button secured, Noelle reluctantly set aside the shirt and, keeping her eyes averted from Quinn, drained the half-empty wineglass sitting next to her. It was her fourth glass, and she was feeling definitely light-headed. Still, she needed whatever courage the bottle could offer if she were to keep her resolve. The wine was young and raw, and as it slid down her throat she shivered. Looking for something else to do, she spotted a plate that had fallen over on the shelf and straightened it, almost knocking another over in the process. Afterward she folded her shirt, returned the needle and thread to the chest where she had found them, and then brushed her hair. When her scalp was tingling from the force of the brush and her hair crackling around her head, she finally stopped and meticulously secured it in a long, loose braid.

The pungency of Quinn's cheroot filtered through the room, and Noelle poured another glass, despite the fact that her head was now floating and her fingertips growing numb. Taking a deep swallow, she closed her eyes in a silent, intense prayer to a God whose existence she had so often questioned in poverty and then forgotten in prosperity. Please, she prayed, give me the strength to go through with this. I have to prove to him and to myself that I'm not a coward. Don't let me be humiliated again.

The room seemed to tilt as she willed her feet to move to the bed. She slid in, encased in her flannel cocoon. Don't let yourself think about it, she admonished. Don't look at him. Just shut your eyes and imagine you're somewhere else. She pulled the quilt up to her chin and clenched its top edge between her fingers to keep the room from moving.

"I'm ready now," she managed, her tongue cumbersome from the alcohol.

Whatever she had expected, it was not the sardonic bark of amusement coming from across the room.

"Save your sacrifice, Highness. I'm going to sleep in the stable. I prefer women who enjoy lovemaking, not one who has to fortify herself with a bottle of wine before she has the courage to get into bed."

Noelle tried unsuccessfully to raise herself up on one arm. "I have pl–plenty of courage. Don't have to fortify myself to find it. Said I would do my duty." The words would have been more defiant if they had not been slurred.

Quinn walked over to the bed and looked down on her. "Your 'duty' doesn't interest me. I don't take unwilling women, but I'll be damned if I'll put myself to the test by sleeping next to you at night."

"Since when have you developed scru–scruples?"

"It doesn't have anything to do with scruples. I just don't have a talent for rape."

"That's not how I remember it from our wedding night!"

"That was different, and you know it."

"Why? Because you thought I was a whore?" A large, wine-induced tear slid from the corner of her eye as she remembered her mother. "Whores are people, too. They have feelings."

"Oh, for Christ's sake! Go to sleep." He pulled his coat back on and headed for the door. "And don't wear that damned braid to bed anymore."

Dimly aware that she was not thinking clearly, she pulled herself up with as much dignity as she could manage. "If you don't like it, husband, then I shall take it out immediately."

With great difficulty, she put her feet over the side of the bed and stood, her stomach queasy at the sudden movement. "Whatever you say, I'll do. You're my lord, my master. Wives must please their husbands, mustn't be cowards." She stumbled across the room toward him, unbraiding the single plait with clumsy fingers as she moved.

Her stomach lurched, and she realized with horror that she was going to be sick. In that instant, Quinn picked her up and carried her outside. By the time the spasms overcame her, he was holding her head over the back of a clump of bracken. When her stomach was finally empty, he carried her back into the house and put her to bed. Then he left her.

Noelle lay wakeful for some time. The embarrassment she would normally have felt at being sick in his presence was somewhat tempered by her realization that he intended to leave her alone. She had made her gesture; he had refused it. Now she could live with herself. Her eyes began to feel heavy, and when she finally fell asleep, it was in the middle of the bed, her arms stretched luxuriously above her head.

Chapter Twenty-three

"Wake up, Highness. That scurvy little mare of yours is ready to be ridden." Quinn's voice was bright with good humor. "Put on your breeches and let's get started."

"No," Noelle moaned as she brought a limp palm to her forehead, trying to soothe away the throbbing reminder of last night's wine. "Not today. Maybe tomorrow."

"Out of that bed before I drag you out!"

Painfully she inched her eyes to narrow golden slits and saw him standing at the foot of the bed. A lazy smile parted his lips, but the determination in his eyes made it clear that he would do as he threatened if she defied him.

With a protracted groan, she rose from the bed and staggered toward her clothes. She pulled her breeches on under her night-gown and then, as Quinn turned his back to go to the fire, hastily took off the enveloping garment and slipped into her shirt. After she had finished a bitter cup of coffee he thrust into her hand, she felt somewhat better. For the first time she noticed a package on the table. "What's this?"

"Open it and see."

Inside was a pair of riding boots, the same warm, chestnut-brown as the mare he had given her yesterday. Noelle stroked the soft, pliable leather regretfully. "I know your gift is kindly intended, but I won't accept any more presents from you."

If she expected him to be upset by her refusal, she was disappointed. "My intentions weren't kind at all. Just practical. Or were you planning to ride in those silly slippers? Now, be outside in five minutes. I'll bring your horse around."

Five minutes later, conspicuously clad in her new boots, a sullen Noelle was waiting in front of the cottage. Her foul mood vanished, however, as soon as her mare came into sight.

She extracted an apple from her pocket. "Good morning, Chestnut Lady. Pretty Chestnut."

"Hold it out with your palm flat," Quinn told her. "Otherwise, she might take a few fingers with it."

Noelle did not bother to inform him that an animal with Chestnut's obvious intelligence was perfectly capable of distinguishing between fruit and fingers.

"When you're back in London, showing yourself off in Rotten Row, you'll undoubtedly insist on riding sidesaddle like the rest of the foolish women there, but here you'll ride astride," Quinn declared as he checked the girth and lowered the stirrups. "Riding sidesaddle is the easiest way there is for a woman to break her neck. It's a stupid custom."

Privately Noelle was delighted, but her capitulation in the matter of the riding boots made her perverse. "No gentleman would actually expect a lady to straddle a horse."

"You're probably right. But since I'm not a gentleman, I expect you to do more than sit on her back like a pretty ornament. Unless you ride astride, you'll never really feel the power of the animal or know the excitement of control."

He looked down at her wryly. "Or are you afraid you won't be able to manage her?"

Noelle's small nostrils flared defiantly. "Teach me to ride your way. Then ask me if I'm afraid."

By early afternoon, when Quinn finally called a halt to her lesson, she was making confident circles around the cottage with her spine straight, stomach tucked in, and arms close to her sides. Noelle was quick to point out that the formal riding style he insisted she adopt was markedly different from his own easy slouch in the saddle.

"Americans ride differently," was the only explanation he offered, but she suspected that he was as capable of riding in the English manner as the best horseman in London.

Their time together was markedly free of strain. Quinn patiently explained each new step and willingly answered all the questions her fertile mind produced. He was unfailingly charming as well as generous in his praise of her accomplishments, and Noelle, lulled by his amiability and basking in the approval of so demanding a teacher, wondered if she had misjudged him.

* * *

Before Quinn fell asleep that night he thought back over their day together. For some time now he had been aware of her intelligence, but it was not until today as they had eaten lunch at the edge of the tarn that he had taken the time to probe its dimensions. What he had discovered amazed him.

In a short period of time, she had acquired an education that was vastly superior to that which most women acquired over the course of a lifetime. He knew of only one other female with such intellectual scope, and, in Noelle's remarkable education, he detected the fine hand of Constance Peale.

He frowned and shifted in the straw. It had been somehow easier to think of his wife as an unscrupulous pickpocket than as a beautiful woman whose intelligence would do credit to a man.

After four days of lessons, Quinn declared that Noelle was ready for a longer excursion and they set off after breakfast. Noelle tucked her hair under the boy's cap she had found and unaware of Quinn's assessing gaze, swung a slender leg expertly across the saddle.

They set out across the moor, through stretches of bracken and gorse, across shallow becks strewn with water-smoothed rocks. Noelle, the child of London's crowded slums, reveled in the untenanted vastness of it. Throughout the morning, she found herself laughing, partly from the sheer joy of being outside on Chestnut's back but, just as often, from a story Quinn told or a joke he made. Once again she found herself letting down her guard and responding to his charm.

Toward noon, they came upon the ruins of an abandoned abbey. Their voices were hollow echoes as they dismounted and companionably explored the crumbling stones that, three hundred years before, had housed the pious enemies of Henry VIII.

Noelle stared at the one remaining upright wall with its six perfect Gothic arches empty against the sky. Captive to the mood of the place, she took off her cap and absentmindedly shook out her hair. As Quinn watched the honey strands catch the sunlight his resolve to have her on his own terms became indurate. He came up behind her. "You can almost hear the priests petitioning God for Anne Boleyn's damnation, can't you?"

"They were doomed anyway, I think. She was just the catalyst.

Henry's pride wouldn't allow him to be subject to anyone, not even a pope." The breeze picked up the ends of her hair as she turned to him and added quietly, "But then, you understand all that better than I, don't you?"

He laughed, softening the hard line of his mouth. Since he had left London, he had not bothered to shave, and the beard which now covered his jaw made him look more the pirate than ever. She was once again struck by how ruggedly handsome he was.

"Poor Highness," he said softly. "Are you afraid I'll have you beheaded?" Eyes shimmering with desire that he made no effort to conceal, he picked up a silken curl and held it between his fingers.

It was as if a current ran from his hand along the strands of hair and into her mind, paralyzing it. She could not summon the will to pull her eyes from his. He brought up his palm and rested it possessively on her cheek, gently outlining the fine bone with a work-hardened fingertip. Slowly his hand moved, igniting whatever it touched—setting fire to the delicate line of her jaw, the slim column of her throat, and the little hollow at its base, warming the nape of her neck as he caught it in his caress. The delicious heat held her prisoner, and she offered no resistance when he pulled her toward him and lowered his hungry mouth to hers. Tremulously her lips opened and she received his tongue. The heat of him engulfed her. Fastening her arms around his shoulders, she surrendered to the power of his kiss.

Quinn triumphed in the nectar of her mouth and the surrendering softness of the supple body pressing into him. She was returning his fire with her own. Then, with a gentle pressure on her shoulders, he pulled away from her and brushed the hair back from her delicate face with his fingers.

"Let's finish our ride," he said softly.

Noelle's eyes clouded in confusion. Finally she stammered, "I —I'd like to ride by myself for a while."

Quinn hesitated. He did not like the idea of her riding alone. Although she was proving to be an exceptional horsewoman, she was still inexperienced. However, she was not a woman to be kept on a tight rein, so, with some misgivings, he acquiesced.

"Keep that line of cliffs in front of you and don't stay out too long. The mists come up fast."

Noelle nodded and mounted Chestnut, her vision blurred with

unshed tears. Tapping the sides of her boots lightly into the mare's flanks, she left the abbey and her husband behind her.

Her mind and body were in turmoil as she flew across the hard earth. It seemed she didn't know herself at all anymore. The panic that clawed away at her at the very thought of a man's embrace was still as much a part of her as the air she breathed, but Quinn seemed capable of lulling that fear in her, of making her blood surge through her veins like wildfire, consuming everything in its path.

Why was it this man alone who was capable of making her forget all reason—a man so savage, so dangerous that every instinct warned her he would destroy her? The emptiness around her offered no answer to her agonizing questions.

She pushed her horse on, too absorbed in her misery to notice the plunge in temperature or the ominously darkening sky. Just as the cold, blanketing mist enveloped her, she snapped her head up and remembered, too late, Quinn's warning. She tugged on the reins, and horse and rider came to a stop in the swirling gray opaqueness.

Noelle looked around her, desperately trying to get her bearings. It seemed as if the cliffs had been on her right, or had she changed direction without being aware of it? Which way should she go now?

Sensing her rider's uncertainty, Chestnut laid back her ears and sidestepped nervously, the billowing clouds from her nostrils mingling with the misty swirls.

"Easy, girl. Easy. Let's try this way."

They set off, Noelle hunched over Chestnut's neck as they chiseled their way deeper into the mist. A freezing drizzle began to fall, and she prodded the reluctant mare on. The rain brought its own dangers, but perhaps it would clear away the mist so she could check her direction.

Before long the drizzle had soaked through her jacket and breeches to her skin, and she was shivering with the cold. Her fingers grasping the reins were stiff and numb, and she tried to flex them to restore their feeling. Desperately she peered into the thick, blanketing mist, but she could barely see Chestnut's nose, much less the cottage.

Then, with a blinding flash of lightning, the skies opened, and a driving rain assaulted them. Terrified by the noise, the mare threw her head down, jerking the reins from Noelle's stiff fingers. Frantically she grasped the wet mane just as a second bolt of lightning split the heavens. The gentle mare, stricken with terror, reared, pawing the rain-lashed air with slashing hooves, and then bolted with Noelle clinging desperately to her back.

The rain stung her cheeks with its force. Her wet hair slapped across her eyes as she futilely clawed for the reins. Then, in the blue phosphorescence of another jagged thunderbolt, Noelle saw, to her horror, that their blind groping had taken them to the very banks of Ravensdale Tarn. She barely had time to grab a breath before she was catapulted into the deep waters.

The slamming impact tore her from the mare's back, and the frigid water closed over her head. Wildly, she thrashed her arms, desperately clawing through the water's weight for the surface. Her head broke through, and she glimpsed her horse in front of her. With a heroic effort, she flailed at the water. Her frozen fingers brushed against Chestnut's leg but slipped off as the mare pulled away, instinctively swimming for the shoreline.

Again and again, the relentless waters towed her under. Arms numb with cold, she fought the inky blackness until she had no strength left. Then, as she surfaced for the last time, she gulped the air too greedily and, instead, sucked in the poisonous water.

A curious lassitude possessed her as the wall of water sealed itself for the last time over her head, and she plummeted down into the bowels of the tarn. As if in a fantasy, her body was no longer hers. She sensed her hair floating around her head like a corona around the sun. While her lungs burned, her body lost its weight.

She accepted the inevitability of death.

Something hard slammed into her ribs . . . jerked against her . . . hurting . . . angry . . . Pulling at her. Forcing her up. Breaking through into the cleansing air. Into the sanctified, life-giving air.

She was dragged to the bank of the tarn and held while her body rejected the water it had swallowed. Then she sank into unconsciousness.

Chapter Twenty-four

She was lying naked on her stomach. Everything was soft and safe. Hot, orange flames flickered on the other side of her eyelids. Bit by bit, part by part, an encompassing warmth was stealing the ice from her body.

Something soft, like a towel, slid along her naked spine. Up. Down. Along her arms, shoulders, down her spine again, across her hips, caressing each smooth buttock, stroking her long, slender legs.

So soft, so warm. The icy core inside her began to thaw as warm, warmer, each limb absorbed the delicious soft stroking.

Then, warm flesh, warmer than hers, cupped her shoulders and gently turned her so that her front was offered up. The textured softness brushed her face, her neck, then her chest. It circled the globes of her breasts, touched her nipples, then moved onto her flat stomach, kneading it with softness. Again, the warmer flesh touched her, this time on her thighs, moving one limb a fraction apart from the other so the softness could caress her thighs, knees, calves, every toe.

In her delicious warm languor, she lifted up one arm and then the other, delighting in their lightness, the way they responded to her wishes. She stretched them out above her head, arching her back like a contented cat in the hot summer sun.

Abruptly, cruelly, the stroking stopped. She muttered an incoherent sound, not really words, just a throaty, quiet protest. There was a soft chuckle, and then it was no longer the softness stroking her but warm breath, teasing her nipples into aching hardness; warm flesh rubbing the hollow cave of her stomach, brushing the soft fleece that marked her womanliness.

Then nothing.

Again she moaned, arching her back, seeking the warm flesh, protesting.

The soft chuckle. A blanket slid up over her nakedness. "Oh, no you don't, Highness. You'll have to open your eyes first. I want you awake when I make love to you."

His arm slid behind her bare shoulders, lifting them. A burning liquid hit her lips, her tongue. She coughed as it slid, molten, down her throat. He put her head back on the pillow, and her eyes opened.

Lying next to her, Quinn was propped up on one arm, his bare chest glowing bronze in the firelight. The towel with which he had dried her lay discarded in front of him. He took a slow sip from the remaining brandy and then gazed down at her, a lazy smile lurking at the corners of his mobile mouth.

"Welcome back."

Noelle turned her head to the side and looked around her. They were lying on a soft pallet in front of the fireplace. Quinn was naked; only his hips were covered by the corner of a blanket.

Memory washed over her—the storm, the tarn, her desperate struggle reaching for her horse's leg only to have it slip away. . . .

"Is Chestnut safe?" she managed.

"A hell of a lot safer than you. That damned nag almost got you killed. That and my stupidity. I should never have let you go off alone." He shifted his weight and the curious silver disk he wore reflected the flames. "I tried to follow you, but I lost you in the mist. I knew you were headed roughly in the direction of the tarn. It was just luck that I got there in time."

"It was my own fault. You warned me, but I didn't pay attention to where I was going. And then the storm frightened Chestnut, and she bolted."

Quinn saw Noelle shiver. "Here, drink some more brandy."

Once again he raised her head. As he held the glass to her lips some of the liquid trickled out the side. She drank, and then he lowered her back to the pillow, enjoying the play of the firelight on her hair. A small amber droplet clung to the corner of her moist mouth. Slowly he lowered his head and captured it in his kiss.

Almost instantly he felt her stiffen under him. He pulled back, placing a quieting finger over her lips before she could voice her protest.

"Your time has run out, Highness," he said huskily. "I'm going to make love to you now."

Little golden pinpoints of fear flecked her eyes, and he could see by the way her fingers convulsed around the edge of the blanket that she had just realized she was naked and completely vulnerable to him.

Her eyes darted to the brandy bottle sitting a few feet away.

"Not this time. Tonight it will be just the two of us in this bed. A man and a woman who want each other."

"No," she whispered, "I—I don't want you."

With firelight dancing in his eyes, he eased the blanket from her clenched fist and slid it down to her feet. Then he touched her face and began lightly stroking away the fear-etched ridges. His mouth followed his fingers, and, finally, with gentle urgency, he claimed her parted lips.

Noelle breathed in the virile scent of him, tasted the hint of brandy on his tongue, felt the roughness of his beard against her cheek. She wanted to protest her nakedness, his invasion of her mouth, but the sweetness of it stole her words.

Then his mouth traveled from her lips to the curve of her shoulder. His hand crept up her naked side to her breast, thumbing delicious circles around the coral areola and then lightly brushing the tiny bud at the tip.

She moaned at the sensations that his touch generated and heard a muffled exclamation, low and deep in his throat. He lifted his head so that he was staring deeply into her eyes, promising with his own what was to follow. And then his mouth descended to a tender coral bud, tonguing it and then sucking deeply, teasing first one, then the other—relentlessly persistent until her head thrashed from side to side on the pillow.

Again the muffled exclamation, low and triumphant. Was it laughter? Passion?

His mouth possessed her once more. His hand moved down her body, brushing the silken fleece but not stopping this time, going on to touch private places. No need to part legs already open.

His body covered hers, and she accepted its weight, her traitorous arms locking around his shoulders. Her flesh was on fire, waiting, yearning, eager when his rigid manhood probed at the entrance of her secret core.

"Open your eyes," he commanded. "I want to see you when I take you."

Afraid he would stop if she disobeyed, she did as he ordered, opened her eyes and locked them with his. She hated him then as she saw his triumph. Hated herself more for having obeyed. He was not making love to her, he was conquering her. This was his revenge. It had all been a calculated seduction.

"I told you I'd claim what was mine." And then he filled her.

"No," she sobbed, wanting to fight him. But it was too late. He moved inside her slowly, relentlessly. Watching her. Boring her with his eyes and his manhood. She felt her body climbing, overcoming her will. She reached. Toward what? Ached. Release. Please. Whatever. Sweet, blessed . . .

The crescendo of her passion captured her and carried her to shattering, humiliating fulfillment. She was barely aware of his shudder as he finally allowed himself his own hot, liquid release.

Long after he had moved her from their place in front of the fire to the bed and fallen asleep beside her, Noelle lay awake, shamed by her body's unrestrained response to someone she detested. The nagging fears about her own nature that she had tried so hard to dismiss had borne ugly, bitter fruit.

Quinn had forced her to acknowledge his complete domination of her body. He had threatened her at her most primitive level, and she hated him for it. Even more tragically, she hated her own healthy body.

The next morning when she slipped out of bed, she was careful not to touch him, knowing now that the slightest graze of skin upon skin might ignite a fire over which she would have no control. She washed and dressed quickly, dispassionately studying his sleeping form the whole time. He slept as aggressively as he lived, throwing the span of an arm over the place where she had been lying, angling his long frame across the bed to keep his feet from dangling off the end, encompassing the bed, making it his own just as he did everything else.

"Noelle?" A muscular forearm shaded his eyes from the gray light of morning.

She ignored him, viciously yanking on her boots.

"Highness, take off those damned clothes and get back into bed."

"Must you modify every noun with a profanity?" she sneered. "I realize you didn't have the benefits of a British education, but that's hardly an excuse for the limitations of your vocabulary."

Something resembling a snort came from the bedclothes. "You talk too much. Come over here."

"So you can maul me again? No, thank you."

He lifted himself up on one arm, the covers falling uncomfortably low at his waist. "So it's 'maul' now, is it? I don't remember having had to pry your legs apart."

She winced at his vulgarity but kept her voice coldly steady. "No, you didn't. And I'll never forgive myself for that."

He sighed with exasperation. "For God's sake, Noelle, you're a healthy woman. You enjoyed a good tumble in bed. There's nothing wrong with that. I made love to you, and you responded."

"No," she spat out. "You weren't making love to me; you were conquering me. Forcing me to acknowledge your superiority. Well, I don't acknowledge it!"

His laugh was soft and bitter. "Why, you little hypocrite! You regret having enjoyed it, don't you?" He rolled off the bed and grabbed the discarded towel, wrapping it around his hips as he advanced on her. "You would have liked it better if I had raped you. Then you could have been a victim."

"I was a victim! You took my choice away."

"You wanted it. The way I see it, you made your choice."

"No!" she exclaimed. "I couldn't help it. It was you! You . . ."

"I made you want it? Well, then, good," he drawled.

"There was nothing good about what you did to me."

Quinn studied her for a moment and then shrugged uninterestedly. "Have it your way." He sauntered over to the bureau and pulled out a clean shirt. "I need to get back to London. I'm leaving today, and I don't want you slowing me down. There'll be a carriage coming for you tomorrow."

Noelle was incredulous at his pronouncement. "This is all part of your pattern, isn't it? You take what you want from women and then discard them." She rushed over to him and grabbed his arm, her fingers biting into the thick tendons. "Well, there's a difference this time, because I yearn for nothing more than to be one of your discards!"

He flicked off her restraining fingers, and mockery flooded his eyes. "I wouldn't plan on it quite yet if I were you."

"Damn you!" Noelle raged. "What do you want from me?"

"You still don't understand, do you? You're mine, and I don't give up what I own unless it's on my terms."

Her face was engraved with bitterness. "These last few days, I thought I had misjudged you. Now I see how stupid I was." She fled from the cottage before he could see her tears.

Quinn stared at the open door. "Maybe I was the one who was stupid," he said softly.

When she returned to the cottage, he was gone. For the rest of that afternoon, Noelle attempted to ride out her anger on Chestnut Lady's sturdy back. With reckless abandon, she thundered across the moors, trying to forget her pain.

It began to rain late in the day, and she hurried back, unwilling to risk being caught again on the moors in a storm. The cottage was warm and dry, but it offered nothing in the way of diversion —no books, no pen and ink. Nothing to distract Noelle from her painful memory of Quinn, bringing her ecstasy such as she had never known, even as he sneered at her.

In the amber glow of a single candle, she lowered herself onto the bed, dropped her head into her arms, and wept.

A loud knocking startled her awake, and stiff with cold, she snapped up in bed, surprised to find sunlight flooding the room. The knocking sounded again. She stumbled to the door, her hand rifling through her mass of uncombed hair.

The coach Quinn had promised was waiting outside, the heads of its team of horses almost invisible behind the steaming clouds of their warm breath in the cold air. On the threshold of the cottage stood a spindly middle-aged woman whose sharp features clearly hallmarked an inquisitive nature.

"Mrs. Copeland?" she queried, taking in Noelle's unusual garb with equanimity.

"Yes."

"Ah, excellent. We have found you, then, with no difficulties." She pushed past Noelle into the cottage and deposited a small valise and several dress boxes on the table. "I'm Edwina Tipton. Your husband, dear Mr. Copeland, made my acquaintance through the rector of our parish and asked me to accompany you back to London."

"Oh?"

"He instructed me to tell you that your horse will be brought on by a groom. What a charming man!" she twittered, oblivious to the fire in Noelle's eyes. "I vow, you are certainly the luckiest of women to have such a husband, blessed not only with a most pleasing countenance but a sympathetic nature."

"I must ask you to enlighten me, Miss Tipton," Noelle said coldly. "How did you learn of my husband's sympathetic nature?"

The woman looked startled. "Why, when he told me of your condition, of course. Dear Mr. Copeland felt it necessary to confide in me. He gave me every assurance that your fits were only temporary and that under no circumstances was I to permit you to dwell on your current instability."

"Fits!" Noelle sputtered with outrage. "Why, that despicable . . ."

"Now, now, Mrs. Copeland. We mustn't upset ourself."

She pulled the lid off one of the boxes on the table. "Here, just look what I've brought you. We have a superb dressmaker, originally from London, of course. Dear Mr. Copeland purchased these clothes to replace those you destroyed during one of your little . . . spells." She did not seem to hear Noelle's muffled growl as she opened one box after another, extracting a hat, shoes, two dresses, even hairpins. "Unfortunate, of course, to have thrown your entire trousseau on the fire, but, then, the more unpleasant aspect of matrimony is certain to produce some strange behavior in any sensitively reared bride."

Just at that moment, Miss Tipton pulled out undergarments so intimately revealing that even she blanched. She dropped them as if the very act of touching anything so seductive would compromise her.

For the first time in days Noelle smiled and then commented wickedly, "As you can clearly see, my husband has animal appetites."

But Miss Tipton was not so easily daunted. "Nonsense, my dear! Your husband is a wonderful man who cares for you. I'll fix some tea while you dress, and then we'll be off. I know it is your fondest wish to be reunited quickly with dear Mr. Copeland."

"It is my fondest wish, Miss Tipton, that dear Mr. Copeland's soul will rot in hell."

Other than a brief sympathetic glance, Noelle's companion ignored her remark and resumed her bright prattle, a practice she was to continue throughout the long journey back to London. When the outer limits of that city finally came into view, Noelle breathed a silent prayer of thanksgiving, for she knew that another day of hearing about "dear Mr. Copeland" would have sent her leaping across the carriage to throttle her traveling companion.

Chapter Twenty-five

Simon was tired when he reached Northridge Square. He had been away for several days, trying to track down a rumor that the Royal Navy was preparing to commission three new frigates. It had been an unsatisfactory trip, aggravated by his worry about Noelle. Quinn's curt note, delivered by messenger the morning that they disappeared almost three weeks ago, had done little to relieve his anxiety. He knew his son too well to have any illusions about how Quinn would react to the deception.

The trip from which he was returning had come at an unfortunate time. There had been too many hours alone in his carriage with only his own thoughts for company, and he did not particularly like what he was finding out about himself.

"Good evening, sir," Tomkins said as he opened the front door for his employer. "I trust you had a pleasant journey."

"Damned unpleasant, as a matter of fact. Has there been any word from my son yet?"

"Yes, sir. Mr. Copeland returned two days ago."

"He did, did he? I want to see him right away."

"Certainly, sir. He's in the drawing room."

Simon gave his hat and coat to Tomkins and went to find his son. As the door opened Quinn looked up lazily from the copy of the *Evening Mail* he was reading.

"Welcome back, Simon."

"Where's Noelle?"

"Not even a 'hello'?"

"Is she upstairs?"

Quinn set down his newspaper. "She's not here."

"Damn it, Quinn! Don't play games with me. If you've hurt her . . ."

"You'll what? Don't forget that she's my wife, Simon. Thanks to you I can do what I want with her."

With a sigh, Simon slumped down into a chair near the window.

"You don't like that, do you?" Quinn taunted. "It's what you wanted all along, but now that you have your victory, it doesn't mean much, does it?" He picked up a glass of brandy from the table next to his chair and swirled it slowly in his glass. When he spoke, his words were low and accusing. "Why is that, Simon? Is it because your feelings about your son's wife aren't fatherly at all? Was it really a deception when you both let me think she was your mistress, or had you been sleeping with her all along?"

"You bastard!" Simon exclaimed, leaping up from his chair. "You should know the answer to that better than anyone. After what you did to her the night you married her, she could barely stand to be in the same room with a man, let alone have one touch her."

"But I'll bet you tried, didn't you?" Quinn said, and even he did not know whether the bitterness in his voice was directed at himself or at his father.

"No, Quinn, I didn't."

The two men were silent for several minutes, and then Quinn spoke. "I'm afraid I did Noelle an injustice. I was too quick to blame this whole scheme on her. I can see that she didn't have to do much persuading to convince you to fall in with her ideas."

"I was the one who did the persuading, not she. It was my plan. Neither Noelle nor Constance wanted to go along with it."

Quinn laughed sardonically. "Constance, I'll believe. But it's useless to try to shield Noelle. I know her calculating nature too well."

"I'm beginning to realize you don't know her at all. In spite of the life she was leading, Noelle was a sensitive young girl when you found her, and she still is."

"Spare me your lectures, Simon, and pour yourself a brandy. I have something else to discuss with you."

"First tell me if Noelle is all right."

"For God's sake! You're acting as though I've murdered her! She's on her way back from Yorkshire now. She should arrive tomorrow."

Simon poured his brandy and sat down. "Were the two of you able to adjust yourselves to the situation?"

"That's none of your business," Quinn snapped.

Simon avoided meeting his eyes. "What else do you want to talk about? I'm tired. I want to go to bed."

"This won't take long." The trace of a smile touched his lips. "I've changed my mind about returning to Copeland and Peale."

"Are you serious?"

"I am if you accept my terms."

Simon understood his son too well, and now he knew the importance of treading carefully. "I believe I presented a proposal to you several weeks ago. That offer is still open."

"Not good enough," Quinn grinned. "If you want me back, you'll have to do better than that."

"Stop playing cat and mouse with me! Tell me what you want!"

Quinn went to a small desk in the corner of the room where he pulled out a sheaf of papers. "It's all in this contract."

He waited patiently while Simon read it through. When he was done, his lips were tight with anger.

"You're out of your mind! You know I'll never agree to two of these conditions."

"Which ones, Simon? There are a number of them."

"You know very well which ones I'm talking about. Giving you an equal partnership as well as total control of the Cape Crosse yard."

"Have it your way, Simon. I withdraw my proposal. It was everything or nothing." Quinn stood and turned toward the door.

"Sit down," Simon hissed. "At least give me the courtesy of letting me explain myself!"

Quinn looked down at Simon for a moment and then, with a shrug, lowered himself back into his chair.

"It is premature of you to expect an equal partnership with Constance and myself," he insisted, struggling to keep his voice level. "Eventually, of course, I'd planned to make you a full partner, but hardly now."

"The only way you were going to give me an equal partnership was in your will. You're a healthy man, Simon, and I don't intend to sit around waiting for you to die."

He leaned back in his chair and studied his father coolly. "But that's not what really sticks in your craw, is it? It's the idea of relinquishing control at Cape Crosse."

"I built that yard from nothing. Nothing!" Simon's fist slammed down on the table next to him. "Now it's one of the best operations in the world. I've already asked you to manage it. That should be enough."

"Simon, that shipyard can't function with both of us running it." All the mockery was gone from Quinn's voice. "You're a good businessman; I don't pretend to be your equal. But now you have to step aside and let me build our ships my way. In the next twenty years the China trade is going to become more important than anyone dreamed, but the richest prizes will only go to the fastest ships. We have to be ready."

"Even if I wanted to accept your offer, I couldn't. You forget that I have a partner."

Quinn's response was his revenge for the part Simon had played in his conspiracy with Noelle. "Constance has already signed."

Simon's hand shook as he flipped back through the pages of the document to the end. There it was in her fine copperplate — Constance Peale.

Neither man spoke. Finally Simon wearily rubbed his eyes with the tips of his fingers. He was growing tired of the struggle, of trying to shape events to suit himself. Now Quinn was paying him back in the same coin.

Slowly he finished his brandy. Quinn deserved his revenge; he'd earned it. Simon got up from the chair and took the contract to the desk. His hand was firm as he dipped the pen in the inkwell and put his signature on the line next to Constance's. He passed the document on.

"Don't underestimate yourself. It seems you're more of a businessman than either of us thought."

"I was playing with a stacked deck, Simon, and we both know it."

Long after Quinn had left, Simon sat in the drawing room, too drained to move. When he finally took his watch from his pocket, he saw it was nearly ten o'clock. Slowly he pulled himself up and started for his bedroom, his hand trailing wearily behind him on the banister. He was irritated when the door knocker sounded. Who could be calling this late?

Her beauty, as always, caught him unprepared. "Noelle!"

"Hello, Simon."

She was expensively outfitted in brown and cream velvet. She wore a spencer the color of warm mocha. The jacket was cut fashionably short, covering only the bodice of her gown. It was softly edged at the neck and wrists with beige mink. Fetchingly angled over one finely arched brow was a pert velvet toque whose mocha and cream plaid matched the skirt of her traveling dress.

As she stepped smartly past Simon her graceful carriage hid her dismay at seeing him so soon. She had a score to settle with him, but she had hoped to postpone it until she was rested.

The coachman appeared at the door and brought her valise into the foyer. "Will there be anything else, madam?"

"Please see that my companion reaches Ludgate Hill as soon as possible."

With a nod and a respectful bow, he left the house.

"I—we didn't expect you back tonight," Simon said uneasily. "I'm glad you're home, Noelle."

"I'm sure you are." Her voice was chill and distant. "You finally have what you've wanted all along, don't you?"

The footsteps of one of the servants approached them from the back hallway.

"Let's go in the drawing room, where we can talk."

"I'm tired, Simon. I want to go to bed now."

"Please, Noelle." He took her arm and rather forcefully guided her through the double doors into the drawing room. "I must speak with you before you get away from me."

"What can you possibly have to say to me after all that's happened?"

"That I'm sorry."

She pulled off each of her gloves with a crisp snap. "Oh, come now, Simon. You're no longer dealing with an innocent. How can you be sorry when you've planned so long for this moment?" Looking at him contemptuously, she tossed her gloves down onto the settee. "You've made me into the perfect wife, haven't you? Well-dressed, well-educated, possessed of all the social graces. Only the best for your son!"

"Try to understand. I was convinced the two of you would come to care for each other."

"Are you insane?" Something inside Noelle snapped, and the composure she had tried so hard to maintain crumbled. "I'm frightened of him! Can't you understand that? I always have been. He is wild and unpredictable. Your son is a savage!"

Simon winced as if she had slapped him, but her own suffering was so keen, she had no room in her heart for his. "You were going to tell him, weren't you? If he hadn't discovered who I was, you would have told him yourself!"

Simon's silence condemned him.

Her fisted hands shook in front of her with the force of her pain. "You promised you would protect me! Why? Why did you do this to me?"

Unable to bear the sight of her anguish, Simon turned his back on her and walked to the window, but her reflection stared back at him accusingly in the glass. "There's more, Noelle."

"What do you mean?"

As he spoke his finger traced the edge of the window pane that framed her image. "I announced your marriage to the papers last week."

"Oh, Simon, *no*!"

"It's created a scandal, of course. Everyone believes you've eloped. London's talking of nothing else. To make it worse, the daughter of a prominent banker tried to kill herself when she heard the news. Fortunately she wasn't successful. But she left a note that has made things more complicated than I ever imagined they would be. She accuses Quinn of promising to marry her. You're portrayed as a seductress. It's all very sordid."

Reluctantly Simon turned to face her. "I'm so sorry. I didn't mean for it to happen this way."

Noelle barely heard his words. "I will never forgive you for this."

She fled from the room. Now all she wanted was to be alone. Like a wounded animal, she needed to curl into a tight ball, shut out the rest of the world, and tend to her injuries. She was almost to the stairs when Tomkins's voice stopped her.

"Madam. Please forgive me for not having attended you when you arrived. We did not expect you until tomorrow, and I was preparing to retire."

"It's all right, Tomkins," she managed. "You had no way of knowing I would return early."

"Nevertheless, madam, let me apologize. I would also like to take this opportunity to extend to you the best wishes of the staff and myself on this most auspicious occasion."

Not trusting herself to speak, Noelle merely inclined her head.

"Your valise has already been taken to your new room. I'm sure you'll be relieved to know that Mrs. Debs personally supervised the transfer of all your clothing and personal effects. Mr. Copeland was most specific. He wanted everything ready before your arrival."

Something of what she was feeling must have shown itself on her face because the butler's expression became faintly puzzled.

"Tomkins?"

"Yes, madam."

"Which Mr. Copeland?"

"Why, your husband, of course, madam."

The dragon carved into the mahogany headboard of his bed seemed to laugh at her dismay. They had moved her entire armoire into his spacious room. Her underthings were stacked neatly in a chest in the dressing room; her hairbrushes leaned intimately against his. A crystal perfume vial stood next to a china shaving mug.

"You certainly don't look like a boy any longer, Highness."

Noelle jumped, twisting around at the sound of Quinn's voice. The well-groomed man in the immaculately cut gray suit seemed almost a stranger, so accustomed had she become to seeing him in an open shirt, faded trousers, and riding boots. Only the beard was a reminder of the man who had kept her imprisoned in the cottage in Yorkshire.

Quinn's thoughts were taking much the same course as he surveyed his elegantly coiffed and gowned wife. He took in the way her body filled the dress he had purchased, her breasts swelling beneath the creamy bodice as he had known they would, the tightly nipped waist—a gown well suited to his masculine taste. Still, he knew he was going to miss those breeches. His eyes traveled her body, remembering the hips and shapely backside hidden under the plaid skirt.

"I want my things moved back into my own room."

He chose to deliberately misinterpret her statement. "Why? Are you planning more trips down the vines?"

"How did you know about that?"

"It wasn't hard to figure out. The only thing I don't understand is why you kept going back. Somehow I don't think it was to pick pockets."

She hesitated. If she told him the truth, he would undoubtedly scoff at her. Still, what did she care what he thought? Defiantly she tossed her head. "I used to take money to some of the children."

The callous response she had expected did not come. "Tomorrow I'll arrange for a less dangerous way to send them money."

Once again he had thrown her off her stride. To hide her confusion, she stormed at him, stamping her foot and telling him not only that she refused to stay with him in this room, but that she would not remain in the same house with him! He said nothing, merely crossing his arms over his chest and listening to her.

The more Noelle raved, the more she knew she was hopelessly trapped. Only when she realized how ridiculous she sounded did she finally fall silent. As much as she detested Quinn, as much as he frightened her, returning to her old life terrified her more. These past two years had strengthened her mind and her body, but they had also weakened the primitive instincts that had ruled her existence on London's streets, and she was now certain she could no longer survive in the netherworld she had left behind. It seemed all her choices had been taken from her except one—being Quinn Copeland's wife.

There was amusement on his face, but it was not altogether unsympathetic. "The trouble is, Highness, you weren't born to this life. If you were, it would be easier for you to accept the idea of a marriage of convenience. It happens all the time to well brought up young ladies."

"I feel as if I've been bought."

"In a way, you have. But then, so have I."

She felt a dawning of hope at the bitterness in his words. "You were going to get a divorce!" she exclaimed. "Why not now?"

"It takes an act of Parliament to get a divorce in England."

"Then how—"

"How was I going to arrange it?" He looked at her levelly. "All records of our marriage were simply going to disappear."

"And now that Simon has announced it, that's impossible," Noelle slowly concluded.

Quinn didn't answer, and his very silence fueled her anger.

"You should have done it while there was still time!"

"Don't you think I haven't told myself the same thing a hundred times in the last few days!"

"And what about the scandal you've caught me in? Everyone

believes we've eloped. A young woman almost died because of you!"

Quinn laughed harshly. "I met that particular woman once in my life, and it was in the presence of at least ten other people. I don't even remember what she looks like. But I'll tell you this about her —she had very active fantasies."

Noelle sighed and pressed the tips of her fingers to her eyelids. She had no idea whether he was telling the truth or not, and for the moment she was so weary from the long trip that she couldn't seem to bring herself to care.

When she opened her eyes, it was to watch Quinn pull something from the drawer of a small table next to the bed. He brought it to her, cupped in the palm of his hand.

It was a small, black velvet jeweler's box.

"Open it."

She removed the lid. Nestled in white satin were two rings. One was the simple gold wedding band she had hidden away so long ago in the pocket of her emerald dress. The other was the most superb ring she had ever seen, a magnificent topaz surrounded by rows of sparkling diamonds.

Quinn took the gold band from the box and placed it on her left hand. "This is for the sake of propriety." Then he slipped the mammoth topaz onto the same finger. "And this is in defiance of it!"

"I—I don't want to wear it," she faltered.

"All of London expects us to go into hiding, and I'll be damned if I intend to give them that satisfaction." His black eyes challenged her. "Now, what about you? Are you going to lock yourself away here, or do you want to fight them with me?"

Noelle's thoughts whirled. She had done nothing wrong, and she didn't care what any of them thought. She would go where she pleased! "I'll fight them." A faint smile curled her lips. "But on one condition."

"What's that?"

"You'll sleep on the daybed in the dressing room."

Quinn shrugged. "I'm too big to fit on it, but if you want to sleep there, go ahead. I'll take this bed."

Noelle had not expected it to be so easy, and she was instantly suspicious. "And do I have your promise that you won't molest me in any way?"

"Of course."

She looked at him distrustfully, and he grinned.

"The world is full of willing women, Highness. Unwilling ones are too much bother. Now, are you with me or not?"

Slowly Noelle nodded.

"Good! We begin tomorrow night. The Atterburys are giving a ball."

"Were we invited?"

"Of course not."

The trace of a frown furrowed Noelle's brow. "I hope Madame LaBlanc finished my new ball gown while I was gone. I don't want to have to wear anything white this time."

Quinn's laughter shattered the room.

"May I ask what you find so amusing?" Noelle said haughtily.

"Nothing. Nothing at all."

Chapter Twenty-six

Despite his weariness, Simon slept little that night, and with the first pale light of the gray November dawn, he finally gave up the struggle and rang for his bath. It was barely eight o'clock when he found himself standing alone on the doorstep of Constance's town house. He had no business being there. Not only was it much too early to make a call, but the new boundaries of their relationship, although unspoken, were abundantly clear, and he was about to step over them. Still, he could no more have stayed away than he could have let himself starve to death. He had to see her.

The butler was incredulous over Simon's request. "I beg your pardon, Mr. Copeland, but I can hardly have her maid awaken her at this hour."

"If she doesn't, I will."

The servant's frosty tones bore clear witness to his disapproval. "Very well, sir. If you will wait in the drawing room, I will have Mrs. Peale made cognizant of your presence."

Simon had barely circled the room twice before Constance flew in. The emotions he had been keeping under such tight restraint threatened to break free at the sight of her small form clad in the barest wisp of a robe of silver and blue striped silk.

"What's happened, Simon? Is it Noelle? She's hurt?"

"No, no. She's fine. I'm sorry, Constance. I didn't mean to frighten you by arriving so early. It's just that—"

"You didn't mean to frighten me!" As she pushed herself forward her robe fluttered open to reveal an ice-blue negligee. "You have finally overstepped yourself, Simon! How dare you demand admittance to my house in the middle of the night. Bully my servant! Nearly send me into a spasm! I won't have it! Do you hear me, Simon Copeland? This time you have pushed me beyond my limit. I want you out of this house immediately." She pointed a shaking finger toward the door. "Do I make myself understood?"

In spite of himself, Simon grinned. Here was the Constance he knew so well. The thought of having her change back into a polite stranger was suddenly more than he could bear. With deliberate insolence he settled himself in a chair, crossed an ankle over his knee, and looked up at her.

"You'll have to throw me out."

Pain twisted inside Constance at Simon's familiar overbearing manner. He sat in front of her, so maddeningly arrogant, a mirror image of his son. The Copeland men! One of them seemed determined to ruin the person she looked upon as a daughter. The other was breaking her own heart.

Her voice quivered, but she did not lower her gaze. "Very well. If you insist on behaving like a ruffian, I shall be forced to treat you as such." She reached out toward the bell.

"I wouldn't advise it, Constance, unless you plan to call them all, because, I'm warning you, it will take more than one to throw me out."

There was a moment of silence, and then Constance's hand dropped back by her side.

"I have something to say, and I'm not leaving until I'm done." Simon cleared his throat, giving himself time to search for the right words, but they wouldn't arrange themselves in any proper order and so he chose the wrong ones.

"You shouldn't have signed Quinn's contract without consulting me," he snapped. "It was a clear violation of our partnership agreement."

"Fiddlesticks! I was well within my rights, and you know it."

"Legally, perhaps, but certainly not morally. You should have told me what you were planning."

"Very well, Simon, I stand corrected. I was remiss. Now, would you be so good as to leave."

"No, I won't!" In anger and frustration, he leaped up from the chair and went to her, towering over her tiny frame. "I don't give a damn about the contract! As a matter of fact, I'm glad you signed it. Quinn should have been made a partner years ago, but I was too stubborn to see to it. He's a better shipbuilder than either Ben or I ever dreamed of being!"

Imperiously he thrust his fingers back through the gray at his temples and into the darker hair behind. "Damn it, Connie! I've bungled everything so badly. You tried to warn me, but I wouldn't listen."

"Tell me what happened," she said softly as she took a seat on the settee, putting aside her own torment to deal with his.

"Noelle returned last night. I'd never imagined she would be so bitter." He slumped down into an oval-backed armchair across from Constance. "I don't know what happened between the two of them while they were gone, but it wasn't good."

"I'd gathered as much when Quinn came to see me. Your interview with him did not go well?"

"It was a disaster. Among other things, he accused me of having less than fatherly feelings toward Noelle."

Constance fingered the single pearl button at the neck of her robe. As much as she was afraid of the answer, she had to ask. "What are your feelings toward her?"

"She's my daughter." Simon did not miss the trace of skepticism on her face. "Oh, I won't lie to you, Connie. I'll admit I sometimes have had to remind myself of that, but it's only because she's so beautiful, so proud. I doubt that any man could completely resist her." He shook his head ruefully. "Any man, that is, except my son. I was so sure he'd fall in love with her! But he believes she engineered the whole scheme even though I told him I was the one responsible. Connie, I'm actually afraid for her. Now that their marriage has been revealed, I can't protect her from him. Quinn is ruthless with anyone who wrongs him. He doesn't know how to forgive."

"Simon, would you tell me what happened all those years ago between you and Quinn?" The question had been impulsive, but now that it was out, she did not attempt to withdraw it. "I don't mean to pry, but there's so much I don't understand."

Simon cupped the polished wooden curves of the chair arms with the palms of his hands and looked at Constance, sitting so serenely before him. Surprising what a restful woman she was, despite her flighty manner. Not always jumping about like so many females. It was peaceful being with her. Why had it taken him so long to realize how much he loved her and how much he wanted her love in return? Now she was asking him to peel away all his carefully acquired layers of self-protection and reveal the most shameful part of his life.

"I'd like some coffee."

It arrived so soon after Constance had summoned the maid that he concluded her well-trained staff had anticipated the request. He drank most of one cup before he began his story, and then he told her everything. Even after so long a time, the pain was still real and Simon's face was as pale as Constance's when he finally finished.

"I'm glad you told me," she said. "It's not a pretty story."

"Now you see that my son has much to forgive."

"Yes, he does. But I think I am not entirely wrong when I say you are no longer the same man."

"You're dealing with me too kindly, Connie. Especially in view of what I've done to Noelle."

"You're a businessman. You can't deny your own nature, Simon. You must, however, learn to temper it."

"It's not an easy lesson. I'm too accustomed to taking what I want without regard for the wishes of others." There was no mistaking his meaning, and the afternoon in Sussex was once more before them.

"That's why I really came to see you, Connie. I could no longer let that day stand between us. My behavior was inexcusable."

This was not at all what Constance had expected. "Your behavior?"

"Why, the way I made love to you. You're a woman of refinement and sensitivity. To have thrown you on the floor in the middle of the afternoon, taken you so abruptly—it was despicable of me."

The ice-blue negligee rustled softly as Constance rose from the settee. "Simon, let me make certain I understand. You are not apologizing for having made love to me, merely for the place and manner in which the act was performed."

"Well, yes, I suppose you could put it that way."

"And you were not repulsed that I gave myself to you so —freely?"

"Repulsed!" Simon shot up from his chair, finally comprehending how disastrously he had misread her. "I love you, you muddle-headed woman! Of course I wasn't repulsed!"

And then she was in his arms.

"Oh, my dear Simon! My dear, dear man! You may make love to me on the floor of the drawing room or in the attic or even atop the dining room table if you choose." The green eyes that looked up at him suddenly brimmed with tears. "Do you remember how Benjamin used to tease you about being the perfect husband for me? He must have realized then how ill-suited I would be for unmarried life. Since he knew I would outlive him, I believe he was trying to accustom you to the idea of taking his place."

"Did you just propose to me, Connie?" Simon teased gently.

"Why, yes, I suppose I did. Do you mind terribly?"

He ran his hand slowly down her back, feeling the small ridges of her spine through the thin blue and silver silk. "I don't mind at all."

A tremor passed through Constance's body. "Simon, did you not say that a woman of refinement and sensitivity should not be taken as abruptly as you did before?"

He buried his face in her fragrant hair. "That's what I said."

"Well, then," she whispered, "pray tell me how I should be taken."

Simon looked down at her. "Like this," he murmured as he drew her body against his and kissed her tenderly, searching her mouth for a desire that matched his own.

He was not disappointed.

Chapter Twenty-seven

Noelle tried to compose herself as she fastened her chemise and then slipped into the petticoats Alice handed her. In less than an hour she and Quinn would appear, uninvited, in Lady Atterbury's ballroom. She no longer held any illusions about what that would involve.

The anger that had been growing inside her since her trip to Madame LaBlanc's once again threatened to break through, and she drew a deep, steadying breath. That morning, she had avoided Quinn by closeting herself with Mrs. Debs and catching up on the business of the household. After lunch, restless and irritable from her confinement, she had decided to pick up the new ball gown herself at Madame LaBlanc's and at the same time order a riding habit so she would be properly outfitted when Chestnut Lady arrived. The thought of riding sidesaddle did not appeal to her, but she would just have to manage. In the meantime she would order the most elegant and expensive habit that Madame LaBlanc could fashion and have the bill sent to her husband as quickly as possible. Quinn was going to learn right away that everything in this farce of a marriage could not be on his terms!

As Noelle stepped from the carriage two young women with whom she was slightly acquainted came out of Madame LaBlanc's shop. Her own greeting went unspoken as they looked her full in the face and then deliberately turned their heads away without saying a word.

The message was abundantly clear. Mrs. Quinn Copeland was not to be recognized by London society.

Furious at the snub, Noelle issued explicit orders to Madame La Blanc concerning the construction of the riding habit. After scolding her for an action that would only aggravate the scandal, the dressmaker had laughed wickedly and promised that the garment, with the requested modifications, would be completed quickly.

A loud sneeze distracted Noelle from her thoughts. "I'll finish dressing myself, Alice. Go to bed now and don't wait up for me. After a good night's sleep, that cold of yours will be much better."

"Are you sure you can manage, ma'am?" Alice's question was punctuated by a noisy sniff.

"I'm sure." Noelle smiled. "Now, get along before you have me sneezing, too."

As the maid scurried gratefully from the room Noelle sat down at her dressing table and inspected her hair. Alice had followed her wishes exactly, and the result was just as she had intended. Shunning the dictates of fashion, her hair was drawn up into a chignon with only a few tawny curls at her temples and the nape of her neck to distract from the smooth line. It was a style that had been out of fashion for years, but Noelle did not care; it suited her rebellious mood to be different. Besides, the arrangement was flattering. As she dusted a light film of color over her pale cheekbones, the magnificent topaz ring caught the lamplight and winked its agreement.

Noelle looked over at her new gown of bronze satin laid out on the daybed. It was simple, and yet with its unusual color and cut, magnificent. The only real ornamentation on the gown was at the hem, where a design of velvet flowers in the same rusty hue as the dress fabric had been appliquéd. It was the bodice, however, that made the dress such a success. It was cut in a wide, plunging V from the center of the shoulders down to the waist. Filling in the vast, open area were several layers of light bronze gauze.

Thoughtfully Noelle got up from the dressing table, walked over to the gown, and fingered the sleek satin. With the memory of today's snub fresh in her mind, she impulsively unfastened her petticoats, slipped off the chemise that Madame LaBlanc had designed to go under the garment, and then refastened her petticoats, so she was naked from the waist up. Only then did she settle the gown over her head. Holding it together in the back with her fingers, she smiled at the effect. No one could actually see through the gauze, but still, the gesture had made her feel better. Now, could she fasten the long row of hooks in the back by herself?

"Need some help?" Quinn drawled, leaning with his accustomed arrogance against the doorjamb. His pirate's beard and tousled blue-black hair contrasted handsomely with his gleaming shirt and well-cut waistcoat of white Marseilles.

"Yes, please," Noelle replied stiffly. "Alice has a cold, and I sent her to bed."

Quinn stepped behind her. "It'll be my pleasure." Slowly his index finger slid down her bared spine. With a small shiver, Noelle put her hands at her sides and forced the fabric of the garment to meet at the back. Taking his time, Quinn worked his way up from the bottom, slipping each hook through its tiny velvet loop.

"You haven't lost your nerve, have you? Tonight won't be easy, you know."

"So I'm discovering." She told him about the incident at Madame LaBlanc's.

"Does their approval mean so much to you?"

"You don't know me at all, do you?" Unwittingly she had echoed Simon's very words to Quinn the night before. "I don't give a fig for their opinion, but I won't be able to rest until I make certain they understand just that."

"All right, Highness. If you want to shock them, you might as well make a job of it."

Before she could stop him, he had reached out and yanked the entire gauze insert from the front of her dress.

"Quinn!"

"Shut up and look at yourself!" Roughly he turned her to face the mirror. "You're the most beautiful woman in London. No one can take that away from you."

He was right. Never had she looked better, even though the gown was now scandalously revealing. The V in the bodice had been cut so wide that the inside curves of both her breasts were completely exposed. As she stared with dismay at her reflection something heavy and cold fell into the warm valley. It was a plain square-cut topaz suspended from a long gold chain.

Quinn chuckled as he fastened it. "In case they're so blind, they miss your assets, this will draw their attention back to their oversight."

Noelle opened her mouth to protest, but Quinn's words silenced her.

"Pick up your chin, Highness. With you in that dress and me at your side, they'll know for certain that neither of us gives a damn what they think!"

The ball in honor of Leora and Dabney Atterbury's twentieth wedding anniversary was well under way before Simon was able to claim Constance for a dance. Since his arrival, he had been subjected to a deadly combination of thinly veiled barbs and unsolicited advice, and the effort to keep himself in check was stretching his temper thin. Constance, in the meantime, was handling the situation far better than he—telling everyone within earshot how happy the match had made her and how satisfied Simon was that Quinn had chosen his own dear cousin to marry, reminding everyone that the new couple were not related by blood —in short, giving the whole scandalous affair at least a veneer of respectability.

"I don't know how you manage it so well, Connie," he growled as she slipped into the curve of his arm. "All I want to do is shove my fist in their smirking faces!"

"Of course you do, my darling. But that's because you're only slightly more civilized than a mountain goat."

Simon smiled softly down at her. "I didn't hear any complaints from you this afternoon."

"I lower my standards when I'm undressed," she whispered back.

They danced with great contentment for some time, secretly celebrating their discovery of each other. Although neither had put it into words, both were strangely reluctant to announce their future plans quite yet. Plenty of time later for wagging tongues to have their day, hanging the news out like so much laundry on a public clothesline. Speculating. "Her husband's barely been dead for two years, you know." For now, it was theirs alone.

As they left the dance floor one of those brief moments of silence that sometimes unaccountably falls on a large gathering came over the assemblage. The butler's sonorous voice inserted itself into the breach.

"Mr. and Mrs. Quinn Copeland."

As if in one body, the eyes of the guests turned to the doorway. No one spoke. No one moved.

The couple stood at the top of a trio of black marble stairs, Noelle to the side and slightly in front of Quinn. Proudly, even arrogantly, they stared down at their peers, by their imperiousness silently daring anyone to utter a word of censure. The glow from the chandelier caught Noelle's gown and turned it to molten bronze, then touched the topaz pendant and set it glittering wickedly on her bare flesh. There was a muffled exclamation as the gathering took in the gown that plunged to her waist and exposed the inner curves of her breasts, unmistakably accented by the golden stone.

Then Quinn lifted his hand. Lightly, possessively, he rested it on his wife's shoulder so there would be no misunderstanding. She was his.

To Noelle, it seemed they stood there forever. No one watching could suspect how her heart was racing, how much she longed to be anywhere except where she was.

Then Constance's voice rose above the stunned silence of the room. "Leora Atterbury, what a cunning creature you are, inviting these naughty newlyweds. Not a person here guessed your surprise. I vow, it has quite made your ball! Ah, well, who can blame you for wanting to be the first to snag them. Dabney, how lucky you are to have such a clever wife. I'm positively green with envy for not thinking of it myself."

Leaving her host and hostess bewildered but pleased, she made her way to Noelle. "My dear, you will set a new fashion with that outrageously flattering gown. I'll wager there will be a dozen like it by this time next week. Now come along, both of you. I know Leora and Dabney will insist you lead the next set."

Constance's audaciousness proved to be more successful than even she had dared hope. In a closed society boredom was a greater enemy than scandal, and it was not long before the guests were vying for the attention of the notorious couple. Afterward, the women bestowed whispered dispensations on each other.

"Scandalous, of course. But really, what is one to do? After all, the Atterburys did invite them."

There was only one guest who held back. Miserably he watched the bridegroom, and only when Quinn was finally alone, did he approach. They spoke quietly for a few minutes. Quinn laughed. The guest's manner became agitated. Finally he jerked himself away from Quinn and strode purposefully toward the bride.

"Miss Pope—that is, Mrs. Copeland, may I have the next dance?"

"Why, Mr. Sully!" Noelle smiled. "What a pleasant surprise. It's good to see a genuinely friendly face." And then she looked at him more closely. "Is something the matter?"

"I—please!" he blurted out. "Could we go somewhere to talk?"

"Why, yes, of course."

As he led her out through a side door and into a small anteroom, Noelle wondered what had made Tom Sully so distraught. She knew he had been attracted to her but was certain his feelings ran no deeper than infatuation, so he could hardly be too upset about the marriage. What, then?

She took a seat in a low-backed Windsor chair. "Suppose you tell me what is wrong."

He paced about the small room, stopped, looked at her, and his eyes fell to her breasts. He flushed and looked back up at her face, struggling to keep his gaze from dropping again. "It's so difficult. I —I cannot credit such an action. He has placed you in an impossible position."

"Who has?"

"Your husband!" He spat out the last word contemptuously, his plump cheeks shaking with anger. "I tried to talk with him earlier, but he told me to mind my own business. Said he knew what he was about. When I threatened to tell you myself, he only laughed. Dorian, please believe me. I'd as soon put a knife through my own heart as hurt you this way."

Noelle was becoming genuinely worried. "Tell me what this is all about. The longer you delay, the more you are alarming me."

"All right then, here it is." He nervously twisted a large silver signet ring as he spoke. "Almost two years ago, Quinn and I were on our way to meet Simon. It was late. We'd both been drinking rather more than usual, and we ended up wandering out of the Haymarket into a street—little more than an alley, really—where we were accosted by a pickpocket. . . ."

Noelle listened with dismay to his story. How stupid of her not to have anticipated this. Of course Thomas was distraught. He believed Quinn was married to two women at the same time!

As he concluded, Thomas knelt down on one knee in front of her and took her hand in his. "Dorian, I wish I were not the one who had to tell you this, but you must understand—your marriage is neither legal nor binding."

"Thomas, I'm afraid you are mistaken. The marriage is, unfortunately, both legal and binding."

"Dash it!" he exclaimed. "I'm giving you the facts. You must believe me. It's the truth!"

Torn between laughter and tears at the awful irony of it, Noelle reached out her free hand and put it on his upper arm. "I knowed yer was speakin' the truth, ducks. I was there when it all 'appened."

Thomas's jaw went slack. He stared up at her, not even blinking, so dumbfounded was he by her revelation. Finally he closed his mouth, then opened it to speak, forgot what he was going to say, and closed it again.

"My God, Sully, you look like a salmon about to propose!"

Furiously Thomas dropped Noelle's hand and jumped up off his knee. "Devil take you! I've half a mind to call you out! Why didn't you tell me the truth instead of letting me make a bloody jackass of myself. You knew I would keep it quiet."

Quinn rambled into the room, smiling crookedly. "Sorry, Tom, but I couldn't resist. My little pickpocket's changed quite a bit, hasn't she?"

This was too much for Noelle. "I'm not your little pickpocket, and I think you've treated Mr. Sully abominably!"

As she swept from the room the topaz swung back and forth on her bare skin like an indignant pendulum. Little pickpocket, indeed! When she reached the ballroom, she rounded the corner too sharply and bumped up against the back of a pale pink dress.

"I'm sorry. How clumsy of me."

"Why, Dorian, what a surprise!" As she turned Catherine Welby's smile was sweet, but her saucer-blue eyes were cold. "You're in such demand this evening, I hadn't thought to have the opportunity to offer you my best wishes."

"Thank you, Miss Welby," Noelle responded politely while she glanced surreptitiously around her for a means of escape.

"I've already congratulated your husband, but perhaps it's really you who should be congratulated. Fancy stealing your own cousin right out from under our noses."

"In point of fact, we are not actually cousins." Determined to avoid an encounter that could only be unpleasant, Noelle began to move away, but Catherine had no intention of letting her go so easily.

"I must say, I admire your strength of character. I vow, I don't know another woman who would be able to endure public censure so calmly."

"The opinion of others means little to me."

"Come now, Dorian, you needn't pretend with me. We're friends, and as a friend, I must tell you that there has been some wicked talk."

"Oh?"

"The worst kind, I'm afraid." She lifted a plump white hand to shield her vindictive whisper. "It's rumored that you married so quickly because you are—*enceinte!*" Her eyes traveled to Noelle's slim waist. "Dreadful, isn't it? Naturally I have assured everyone it is untrue."

"How kind of you," Noelle said dangerously.

"Well, you know how cruel gossips are."

"Yes, Miss Welby, and I know who they are, too."

There was no mistaking Noelle's meaning, and the fixed smile faded from Catherine's face. Quinn Copeland was the most fascinating man she had ever met. It was infuriating enough that he hadn't returned her interest, but now, to see him wed to a nobody was more than she could bear.

"Just remember, Mrs. Copeland, it's one thing to catch a husband, but it's quite another to hold him." With a smirk, she pointedly nodded toward the ballroom floor.

Following her gaze, Noelle saw Quinn take a woman in his arms and lead her out for a waltz. It was the raven-haired Anna von Furst—drawn, haunted, and eerily beautiful. Unsmiling, the couple's eyes joined, and then Quinn and the baroness began wordlessly moving in the perfect rhythm of a man and a woman who know the responses of each other's bodies intimately.

Gradually Noelle realized others were watching her, waiting to see how she would react to the slight. Fixing a bright smile on her lips, she excused herself from Catherine and accepted an invitation to dance with a handsome young viscount of somewhat tarnished reputation. If Quinn did not care with whom he was seen, neither did she.

Not long after that the Baroness von Furst left the ball. Even so, Noelle did not see her husband again until midnight, when he appeared at her side to escort her into the dining room and then promptly turned his attentions to a ruddy-faced woolens manufacturer from Leeds. The tables were ladened with every possible delicacy, but Noelle ate sparingly, taking only a small portion of lobster salad and another glass of champagne.

"Will you save a dance for me?"

It was Simon, somewhat abashed, but still determined.

As Noelle looked up at him she realized her bitterness had been replaced by an emotion that was considerably more painful—an aching sense of betrayal. "I'm sorry, but I'm promised for the rest of the evening."

Simon seemed to have anticipated her refusal. He spoke so softly that no one standing nearby could overhear. "It's funny, isn't it, how people delude themselves. I thought I would be able to give you to my son without losing you myself."

Inexplicably Noelle's eyes filled with tears. "I wasn't yours to give, Simon."

He nodded, and then, before he left her side, he reached down and softly squeezed her hand.

The gesture made her infinitely sad. It was as if he were saying "You are my child, and I will always care for you no matter what has happened between us."

For the rest of the ball Noelle was never still. She rushed from one set of arms to another, drank glass after glass of champagne, and flirted outrageously. It made no difference who her partners were as long as she could keep dancing.

Quinn shunned the ballroom for the faro tables that had been set up in the library. It was not until he had won nearly three hundred pounds that he went to claim his wife.

She looked as though someone had just made love to her. Her laughing face was flushed from dancing, a lock of hair had escaped from her chignon and hung down behind her ear, and there was a sheen of moisture between her breasts. As Quinn watched, the mustachioed officer who was holding her let his hand slip from her waist to the top of her hip and leaned forward to whisper something in her ear.

Quinn made his way across the floor. "I'll dance with my wife now."

"See here, Copeland . . ." The officer thrust out his chin belligerently, but his words trailed off at the dangerous glitter in Quinn's eyes, and he hastily backed away.

Quinn scooped his wife into his arms, pulling her so close to him that he could feel the hammering of her heart through his shirtfront. In response to the handsome couple commanding the center of the floor, the bored musicians nodded conspiratorially at each other and deliberately began picking up the tempo of the music. At first it was so gradual that no one noticed, but then one couple after another began to feel the effects of the quickening pace and fell back. Finally the tempo was frenzied, and Noelle and Quinn danced alone.

They spun about the floor, their clothing flashing bronze and black. Her champagne laughter bubbled up at him. Eyes blazing with self-confidence, she dared him to keep up with her in this accomplishment at which she had now become the master. He tightened his grip in answer to her challenge.

She tossed her head, and her hair shook free from its confines, cascading about her shoulders. As they flew faster it spun wildly about her, slapping at Quinn's cheeks and stinging them like tiny whips. His body quickened with desire. The music came to a final crescendo, and he crushed a handful of untamed mane in his fist, pulling her head toward him and lowering his hard mouth to hers.

To Noelle, the kiss seemed part of the dance. Indeed, it was as violent as the music had been and as ragingly exciting. It was barbaric and so blatantly erotic that the onlookers were stunned.

Only Quinn heard the soft moan when he reluctantly unfastened his mouth from hers. She shuddered as some vestige of self-control returned to her. With a courtly bow, he picked up her hand and brought it respectfully to his lips, then led her from the floor.

On the way home in the carriage, Noelle fell victim to the early morning hour and the champagne that had so beclouded her judgment, and was asleep long before they reached Northridge Square. Quinn carried her into the house and, with his teeth grimly set, deposited her on the narrow daybed. As he left the dressing room he firmly shut the door between their rooms.

The next day all of London was gossiping about Quinn and Noelle and the passion that blazed so uncontrollably between them. They were said to have ravished each other in the center of the Atterburys' ballroom. Noelle publicly ignored the comments and privately swore to drink no more champagne. In the meantime she and Quinn were the rage of London. A party could not be considered a success without the Copelands in attendance.

The fashionable elite never seemed to tire of speculating about them. A few sharp eyes had noted that the glow was back in the Baroness von Furst's lovely cheeks. Others commented that although the Copelands were seen everywhere together, they seldom spoke. The mystery of it all was delicious.

As Constance had predicted, Noelle became a fashion trend setter. This fact was brought home after the Atterburys' affair when she and Quinn attended a ball in the Berkeley Square residence of Lord and Lady Whitney. Lady Whitney herself greeted them in a violet gown cut open to the waist. As Noelle stepped into the ballroom she quickly counted seven other dresses of different colors and fabric but with the same bare bodice.

The fashion followers were, in turn, inspecting Noelle's new gown with smug superiority. It was a simple black crepe completely covering her from neck to hem. There were sly whispers. The gown was well cut, certainly. The little pearl choker collar quite pretty. But, really, it was all so plain and unoriginal.

It was only as Noelle passed through them that the guests saw the dress had no back. The smooth line of her spine, the contour of her shoulder blades, the glowing ivory of her skin, had all been daringly exposed to a point several inches below her temptingly slender waist.

From that time on, there was a line of carriages at the door of Madame LaBlanc's establishment. The new customers were graciously accommodated by Madame's ever-increasing number of assistants while the sly Frenchwoman reserved her considerable creative energies for the woman who was making her the most important dressmaker in London. Noelle Copeland was an original in both spirit and fashion, and Renée LaBlanc was going to make certain her client would not be outdone.

Noelle was not the only one being imitated. All over the city, young gallants were growing beards and clenching thin cheroots between their teeth. It was a pitiful imitation, however, for no matter how hard they tried, none of them could match the swaggering self-assurance of Quinn Copeland. They were all left feeling slightly foolish when, just as their beards reached a respectable length, Quinn shaved his off. One afternoon the couple appeared in Hyde Park. She was leading her pretty chestnut mare, he his ebony stallion. It was only when she mounted that the onlookers saw that the full skirt of her royal-blue riding habit had been cunningly split at the center, forming two side legs. From that day on, Noelle Copeland rode astride.

The weeks passed. No sooner had the gossip from one episode died down than another reared its tantalizing head. There was even a rumor that Quinn Copeland was supporting a group of urchins in one of London's most disreputable tenements. Drawing rooms buzzed, dinner tables sparkled. Never in recent memory had a season been so entertaining.

In Northridge Square, however, things were not quite so gay. Except in public, Quinn and Noelle saw little of each other. Most nights he would escort her home only to leave her at the door. In the morning Noelle would awaken to find the covers on his bed undisturbed. He made no attempt to explain his absences, and she asked no questions about them.

There was one matter, however, about which she did question him, and that was the future. Surely he did not intend their farcical marriage to go on much longer? But no matter how hard she pressed, he refused to commit himself. She could not understand his perversity, especially since she was certain that he chafed to be away from Northridge Square and all that life there entailed.

Something else puzzled her. Last October, shortly after Quinn had reappeared in her life, Simon had told her that his son had accepted a position with a firm of shipbuilders in New York City. If that were true, what was holding him here now? And why had he and Simon, despite the animosity between them, been closeting themselves in the library with ledgers and stacks of files?

She still had not mended her tattered relationship with her father-in-law, so she could not ask him about Quinn's plans. There was always Constance, but Noelle found one excuse after another to postpone discussing the problem with her. Finally she admitted to herself that she was afraid of what she might hear, for there was always the horrifying possibility that Quinn was actually planning to take her with him.

In December, Simon left for the continent, and Noelle found herself missing his booming orders to the servants, the way his laughter filled the house when his friends came to call, and, unreasonably, the sense of security his presence seemed to give her. Even Constance could not help dispel Noelle's loneliness, for she too had left the city.

It was another departure, however, that had a more immediate effect on Noelle's life. Her sleek figure swathed in black silk, Anna von Furst was seen abruptly leaving London one morning. The next day, the newspapers announced that the Baron Otto von Furst had died in a hunting accident in Bavaria.

More frequently now, after the dinner parties and balls and assemblies were over, Quinn and Noelle would climb the stairs to their bedroom together. Whenever it happened, Noelle's heart would thump frantically. Was this going to be the night Quinn would try to open the door that separated them?

It became more and more difficult to repress the memory of the time in Yorkshire when he had made love to her. As if reading her thoughts, Quinn would stalk her with scowling eyes, but he made no attempt to touch her. They snapped at each other over trifles. Noelle was sharp with the servants. Quinn got into a fight at the faro table. Things could not go on as they were much longer.

Chapter Twenty-eight

Ever since the gentlemen had finished their cigars and brandy and joined the ladies in the drawing room, Hugo Meade, the Marquis of Blystone, had been pressing his thigh hard against hers. Noelle barely noticed. Not even Quinn's grim scowl from across the room could penetrate her good humor. Just when she thought she could not bear living another day with him, everything had changed.

It happened so unexpectedly. Tonight, on the way to their third dinner party of the week, Quinn had abruptly announced he was going to leave London in two days to assume permanent control of the Cape Crosse shipyard. Noelle, he declared, would stay here. He had set up a generous bank account for her so she could purchase her own residence and maintain her current style of living. Although there could be no divorce, they would no longer be together.

Noelle's heart sang. She was finally to be free of him!

The marquis's pressure on her thigh had become so relentless that Noelle was recalled to the present. With a shock, she realized he had been murmuring endearments to her.

". . . adoration for you. All evening your beauty has sparkled like the finest wine waiting to be sampled by a true connoisseur."

"Really, Lord Blystone, you should not say such things." The arm of the sofa pushed up against her other thigh as she tried vainly to move away from him.

"Don't pretend with me," he pursued. "I know you return my passion. We must arrange to be alone so I can show you how much I love you."

Before she could snatch them away, he had caught up her fingers and brought them to his lips.

"Get your hands off my wife, before I break them."

The marquis dropped her hand as if it were a viper. Noelle had no idea how long Quinn had been standing behind them listening, but from the menace in his voice, it had been long enough.

"I hate to interrupt such a tender moment, Hugo, but I'm taking my wife home now, and if you so much as look at her again, I'll kill you." He grabbed Noelle's arm and none too gently pulled her up. With everyone watching them, he propelled her toward the doorway as if she were a disobedient child. Through stiff lips, Noelle thanked her hostess, all the while trying to hide her humiliation.

She kept her silence throughout the short carriage ride home. The unshed words struggled to be released, but she held them back, waiting for the moment when there would be no coachman to overhear her. Quinn did not even glance in her direction. Finally they stood alone in the dimly lit foyer at Northridge Square. As Quinn shut the front door Noelle unbridled her fury.

"How dare you humiliate me like that!"

"Don't push me tonight," he scowled blackly. "If you're smart, you'll just get out of my sight."

"I'll get out of your sight, all right, as soon as I tell you what I think of your manners!"

"I'm warning you, Highness . . ."

"And I'm warning you! You're a selfish, egotistical, arrogant bastard!"

"And you're a cheap little man-teasing bitch!"

Noelle swung at him then. She drew back her fist and smashed it full force into his jaw. Quinn should have seen it coming. Under other circumstances, he would have. But the unaccustomed jealousy that had been eating away at him all evening like a maggot had dulled his reflexes, and so he caught the full force of her blow.

Noelle sucked in her breath as she realized the folly of what she had done. Dear God, he would kill her! Catching her skirts up above her calves, she flew up the stairs, propelled by her fear.

There was a pounding. She did not know if it was her own heart or his footsteps behind her. Her mind raced. A key? Was there a key in the bedroom lock? She reached the top step, the hallway; her body sensed his presence behind her and, with a desperate lunge, she threw herself toward the door. It seemed a miracle when the knob turned in her hand. She shot inside and pushed against it. The latch caught. She reached for the key, began to turn it . . .

The door crashed in on her with such force that she was knocked from her feet. The floor underneath her shook as the heavy oak slammed shut. Lying in a pool of spilled satin on the dark rug, she heard the key turn in the lock. There was a whimper—pitiful, like a child's. With a curious detachment, she wondered who was in the room with them, and then realized the sound had come from her own throat.

Quinn loomed over her, one hand balled into a fist at his side.

"You're going to pay for that in the only way you understand."

Locking his eyes with hers, he raised his hands to his lapels and slowly pulled off his evening coat, flicking it over the chair next to him without changing his position. Then he began unfastening his waistcoat, slipping the jet studs one by one into the palm of his hand. There was no waste in his movements. Each action was deliberate, unhurried, and filled with purposeful menace. He pulled at the knot of his white neckcloth.

"For weeks now I've kept my distance from you. I've paid your bills and let you go on your way. Lately I've been asking myself why. And you know, Highness, I couldn't come up with a good answer."

Noelle watched with deadly fascination as his shirt slowly parted, revealing the powerfully muscled chest she remembered so well. It was only when his hands dropped to the waistband of his trousers that she overcame her paralysis. With a cry she leaped to her feet and dashed toward the door, but like a whip his arm snapped out and coiled around her.

"Oh, no, you don't! Not till I'm through with you."

He yanked off her cloak and then picked her up and unceremoniously tossed her onto the bed. She gave a yelp of pain as her elbow slammed into the mahogany dragon's head, but Quinn ignored her cry. Throwing himself down beside her, he gripped her slim shoulders and flipped her over onto her stomach, then planted his knee in the small of her back.

"With what this dress probably cost me, I'll be damned if I'll rip it off!" Only when he had unfastened each hook did he pull the satin gown from her struggling form. His patience wore thin, however, when it came to her petticoats, and they were soon in a torn heap on the floor.

She lay on her back before him, only pantaloons and a thin white chemise covering her flesh. In the struggle to remove her clothing, her hair had come undone and now it streamed about her, iced by the winter moonlight pouring in through the window.

For a moment Quinn stared down at her. There was something different about the way she looked. It nagged at him. And then, in an instant, he saw what it was. The beautiful eyes that blazed up at him were full of fury and loathing, but they held no terror. She hated him, that was certain, but she seemed no longer to fear him.

With the fascination of a scientist testing a hypothesis, he reached down and cupped her breast through the thin material of the chemise. She spat out an angry oath and kicked at him furiously. He chuckled. And then his amusement died in a groan of pain as one of her blows landed on his tender jaw.

With a growl he fell on her, using the pressure of his muscular body to still her struggles, slamming his mouth to hers in a kiss that was more an assault than a caress, grinding his hard lips, wanting to hurt. She fought against him, clawing at his back with her nails, arching her body in a futile attempt to push him off. He felt her first tremors of panic and, unaccountably, his anger fell away. Losing their desire to injure, his lips began ministering to her bruised mouth. There was a subtle change in her responses. Although the heels of her hands still dug into his shoulders, trying to push him away, her slowly parting lips delivered a different message.

He kissed her temples, her ears, enjoyed the slim pillar of her throat. When he brought himself back to her mouth, his tongue no longer had to invade, it was welcomed. Now her body moved under him with a different rhythm. His erotic senses told him his hands could move further without meeting resistance, that her breasts yearned to be stroked until the tender tips ached and strained for more.

Her response brought his own desire to a frenzy, but he held himself in check, stroking her arms and throat before he slipped down the straps of her chemise, kissing the line of her collarbone and shoulders before claiming her breasts. Even as they both lay naked in a bath of moonlight, he listened to her body, taking his cues from her response. When his kiss voyaged below the line of her waist to her stomach, and he sensed the subtle overture of fear, he replaced his mouth with his hand and smiled to himself as her muscles once again relaxed.

Then everything changed. He felt the subtle pressure of her hands on his shoulders, signaling that she no longer wanted him over her. Cautiously he shifted his weight so that he was lying on his side, facing her. For a moment she was still, and then her soft hand reached toward him and he finally understood. She wanted access to his body.

His breath was ragged in his throat as her fingers began their first tentative exploration of the muscles of his shoulders and chest. Although her movements were cautious and inexperienced, he could not remember when a woman's touch had excited him more. With a barely audible moan, he rolled onto his back. Her fingers touched the hair on his chest and then found a nipple, hard and flat, so different from her own. He shuddered, and her hand jerked away. Willing himself to lie still, he waited for her. Hesitantly she returned to test her power. His breath quickened as her cascading hair teased his bare flesh. Her hand made its way to his stomach, traveled across its flat plane, and descended unsurely. He felt her tremble, and then her fingers touched the very pulse of him. With a wince, she drew back her hand from his size, and the fear he had vanquished with his patient caresses once more took her prisoner.

He began again, gentling her with his kiss, firing her with his touch. He heard his voice murmuring reassurances to her. When he finally felt her quiver, he knew that her thighs were ready to part freely, and she would receive his manhood as willingly as her mouth was receiving his tongue.

He entered her slowly, whispering all the while that he would not hurt her. Her body began to move. Checking his own raging desire, he shifted his weight so she would not have to bear it all and adjusted his rhythm to hers. Giving instead of taking, his own pleasure mounted. She whimpered and tossed her head to the side. He buried his face in her fragrant hair as they climbed together. And for a time in the moonlit room, their bodies made their minds forget how to hate.

"Get out of bed," he snarled.

Noelle shifted and finally managed to open her eyes far enough to see Quinn standing over her, bathed and dressed. An ugly scowl marred his features as he reached down and snapped the covers from her warm flesh.

"I said get up!"

She sat up with a jerk, her hair tumbling around her face and shoulders. "What are you doing?" she sputtered.

His eyes narrowed to dangerous slits. "You'll be rid of me in another day. Until then, do what I say. Be dressed and downstairs in twenty minutes." He spun around on his heels and stomped from the room.

Noelle sat stunned. Was this the same man who had made such tender love to her last night? Who had held her? Kissed her? She thrust her fingers back through her tangled hair and dug the heels of her hands into her temples as she tried to push back the memory of how naturally she had responded, how eagerly she had traced the hard lines of his body with her fingers.

In the wake of Quinn's contempt, shame overwhelmed her. Her husband was an experienced lover, and she was an innocent. His mistress was gone. He had needed a woman. Why hadn't she understood that? It was all very simple really.

But it was not so clear to the troubled man who stalked the black and white marble floor at the base of the staircase. Not clear at all, for the sweetness of her lovemaking the night before had shaken him more than he cared to admit.

"You're five minutes late."

She paused on the landing and, summoning all her will, met his glaring eyes with cold disdain. "If you had awakened me five minutes earlier, I would have been on time."

"Why don't you save those high-and-mighty airs of yours for the marquis. Remember that I know what a hot-blooded bitch you really are!"

It would have been less painful if he had slashed her across the face with the back of his hand. Sickened, he watched shame etch itself on her ashen cheeks, and then he dropped his gaze. "The carriage is waiting for us," he said gruffly. "Constance is back, and she's sent a message asking us to call on her immediately."

They traveled like strangers—Noelle staring stonily ahead and Quinn brooding out the window.

"You look pale, my dear. She doesn't look well, Quinn."

As soon as Noelle had stepped into the drawing room, she had noticed an air of suppressed excitement clinging to Constance as tenaciously as the fragrance of her perfume. Now, even as she fussed over Noelle's pallor, she was darting expectant glances toward the door.

"I own I would feel better if you were not leaving for Cape Crosse so soon. Crossing the ocean is dreadful enough without being ill at the same time."

Somehow Noelle was not surprised to find that Constance assumed she would be accompanying Quinn to America. She was a practical woman, and practical women did not abandon their husbands. Besides, even though she was discerning about other people, Noelle had long ago realized that Constance possessed a blind spot where Quinn was concerned.

Just as she began to explain that she would not be leaving, the door of the drawing room opened and, to her astonishment, Simon entered. Why wasn't he in France? she wondered.

Her curiosity did not go unsatisfied for long. Simon greeted them, and after apologizing for being late, he slipped his arm around Constance and quietly announced that they had married.

There was a strangled exclamation from Quinn, and then he clenched his jaw, his face darkening. Noelle wanted to slap him. Couldn't he, even for a moment, set aside this vendetta with his father and wish them well?

Trying to distract them from his rudeness, Noelle rushed to Constance and embraced her, finding the right words even though there was little happiness inside her. Impulsively she turned to Simon and hugged him, too. He grinned like a schoolboy at the gesture, and she felt oddly ashamed of her recent treatment of him.

"You're wrong, Quinn," Constance said softly, slipping away from Simon and going to his son.

"About what?" His eyes were brooding and his lips set in stone.

"He loves me."

Quinn arranged his face in a semblance of a smile and embraced her affectionately. "Of course he does. He couldn't help but love you." But the glare he shot Simon over the top of her head was filled with venom.

"He doesn't believe you, Connie," Simon said with surprising equanimity.

"Of course he doesn't, and really, Simon, one can hardly blame him."

Noelle felt as if she had been cast adrift in a strange land where the inhabitants spoke an unfamiliar language. Constance read her thoughts.

"Noelle believes we've all lost our senses."

She disengaged herself from Quinn and, taking her place behind a well-ladened tea tray, picked up one of the china pots. "Sit down, Noelle. Simon. If you must pace, Quinn, step back from my new vases. They were frightfully expensive, but I simply couldn't resist them. Have a croissant, Noelle, and some tea. Simon, tell me if that's not enough cream."

When everyone was served, Constance turned her attention to Noelle. "Quinn believes that Simon has married me only to gain back control of the company. Don't you, my dear?"

"I confess it crossed my mind," Quinn said dryly from the other side of the room. And then, more vehemently, "Damn it, you deserve something better!"

"But I don't understand, Constance," Noelle interjected. "I thought you and Simon were equal partners."

Constance shot Quinn a disapproving glance. "Your husband appears to be a member of that unfortunate breed of men who believes women need know nothing more about their husband's occupation than the name of the firm. Really, Quinn, I had expected better of you."

She returned her attention to Noelle. "Last month, Quinn became an equal partner with Simon and myself, each of us owning one third of the company."

Suddenly Noelle understood why Quinn was so disturbed. "And when a woman marries," she said thoughtfully, "she no longer can keep title to her personal property. It all passes to her husband. So Simon now controls the company."

Constance emitted a triumphant whoop. "There! You see, Quinn, all she needs is to be headed in the proper direction. Very good, my dear. The law is ridiculous, of course, and an insult to all women, but it is the law. However, in this case, I circumvented the law by selling half of my shares before Simon and I were married."

"You can't do that!" Quinn exclaimed hotly. "It's illegal. No shares can be sold outside either of our immediate families!"

"That is why I sold them to your wife."

Noelle was flabbergasted. "What do you mean, Constance? I never purchased any shares of Copeland and Peale from you."

"Oh, but you did, my dear. And in the future, you really must remember to read whatever you sign. It is most foolhardy to set your name to anything you haven't thoroughly investigated even when it is put before you by a trusted friend in the form of a petition to raise the minimum working age to nine years."

"But I've never given you any money."

"Of course you have. Remember your foolish insistence on paying me while you were with me in Sussex? I put that money aside, intending to return it to you. When I decided to sell my shares to you, I simply used it for my own purpose. With your signed permission, I might add."

Noelle was thoughtful as she tried to piece together what Constance was telling her. This meant that Simon now controlled one third of Copeland and Peale in his own right and one sixth through Constance's remaining shares. Quinn controlled the same, one third in his own right and one sixth through the shares Constance had given her. What an amazing woman she was! With one bold stroke, she had neatly restored the balance of power between father and son.

"How much money did Noelle have?" Quinn asked, looking at Constance with considerable admiration.

"Nearly fifty pounds."

He almost choked. "You sold sixteen percent of the best shipbuilding firm in the world for fifty pounds?"

"Forty-eight pounds, five shillings, and sixpence!"

Quinn threw back his head and laughed. Only Noelle did not join in. She knew she should tell her very kind, very generous friend that she wouldn't be going to America and would never see the shipyard, but she couldn't bring herself to spoil Constance's happiness quite yet and neither, it seemed, could Quinn. She would wait until tomorrow.

"Before I turn these papers over to your wife," Constance said as she accepted a heavy envelope from Simon, "I must ask you to make the same agreement your father made."

"What's that?"

"This is Noelle's property. Legally, of course, you can take control just as Simon can take control of my property. But I am asking you to give me your word that you will not do that. Noelle must vote her own shares."

"But that's ridiculous!"

For once Noelle found herself in agreement with her husband. Still, what did it matter? Quinn would be gone soon, and he could do anything he wanted with the shares.

Quinn shook his head in disgust and turned away. "Constance, I've always respected your judgment, but this makes no sense. Noelle knows nothing about building ships."

"You will teach her."

Quinn confronted his father. "Why did you agree to this nonsense?"

"I didn't at first, but when I stopped raving and began listening to Connie, I discovered she made sense. She doesn't deserve to lose all of her decision-making power just because she's decided to marry."

"Of course she doesn't. But you can hardly compare Constance's value to Copeland and Peale with Noelle's."

"Noelle has more value than either Constance or I," Simon snapped. "She'll be bearing the heirs to the company!"

Noelle shot up from her seat, but before she could speak, Constance caught her by the hand.

"Simon has been tactless as usual. Naturally we hope you will have children, but that is your business, not ours. The fact is, Noelle, you are blessed with both courage and common sense and will certainly be an asset to the company. Well, Quinn, will you give your word that she controls her property in her own right?"

A faint prick of foreboding stung Noelle as Quinn turned and studied her with dark intensity. What was he waiting for? Why didn't he just agree and get it over with? He knew she would not hold him to his promise.

"You have my word."

Constance placed the envelope in Noelle's hand. "Welcome to Copeland and Peale, my dear."

Quinn excused himself from the room. Noelle took another cup of tea and questioned Simon and Constance about their wedding. The three of them smiled over London's reaction to this second elopement in the Copeland family and then discussed Constance's planned move back to Northridge Square.

When Quinn returned, Constance invited them to stay for lunch, and he accepted with alacrity. As they settled themselves around the table Noelle noticed that Quinn's black mood had vanished. He teased Constance, treated his father with courtesy, and was even polite to her. It was as if a great weight had been lifted from his shoulders, and it made Noelle very uneasy.

Her apprehension grew when they returned home to an unusual flurry of activity. Tomkins held one of Quinn's valises in his hand as he opened the front door for them. They stepped inside just as two footmen were descending the stairs, one at each end of a trunk. When they passed her, Noelle glimpsed a wisp of bronze satin peeking out from beneath the closed lid.

Her eyes flew to Quinn, but he had already disappeared down the back hallway. She ran up the stairs and into her bedroom, where Alice was fastening the last straps on one of three trunks scattered across the floor. The door of Noelle's armoire stood open, its empty maw telling her everything. Quinn had sent word ahead to the servants, telling them to pack all her things. He planned to take her with him!

She finally located him in her small blue and peach sitting room at the back of the house. He had never been in this room, and now it added to her outrage to see him trespassing among her things, holding one of her books in his hand.

"I thought you might want to take some of these with you."

"I'm not going anyplace, Quinn."

He continued as if she hadn't spoken. "Your taste in books surprises me. Bacon, Locke, Samuel Pepys. Not a single one of Mrs. Radcliffe's melodramas. But then, you've managed to surprise me from the beginning, haven't you, Highness?"

Noelle refused to be distracted. Defiantly she crossed her arms and glared at him. "I'm making my own choices now, Quinn. It's over. You've had your revenge for everything you think I've done to you. You've abducted me—"

"Abducted you?" He set down the book he was holding and lifted a dark, mocking eyebrow. "You're being melodramatic. A man doesn't abduct his wife. She goes wherever he tells her."

He was baiting her with his arrogance, deliberately trying to make her angry. But she wouldn't permit him to have that advantage over her.

"I'm to remain here. We've settled it."

"Things are different now," he shrugged. "I've sent a note to

Constance telling her we've had a last-minute change of plans and are sailing early."

"Nothing is different. You can have my shares in the company. Do whatever you want with them. I release you from your agreement."

"I gave Constance my word, not you."

"Your word!" she sneered contemptuously. "Your word means nothing. You keep it only when it suits you."

His voice remained infuriatingly cool even as his eyes narrowed determinedly. "You're going to come with me to Cape Crosse."

"Cape Crosse is your home, not mine. I'm English. I don't belong in America. I belong here."

"You hate this life as much as I do. I've been watching you, Highness. You enjoy the company of the coachman and the kitchen maid more than anyone you meet in society. You don't belong here with this swarm of parasites. You belong with people who make their own way. America is a new country, sometimes a dangerous one. There's room for independent spirits."

Then he was next to her, catching up her shoulders in his hands, his voice barely a whisper, his closeness sapping her strength. "Come with me, Highness. Come with me of your own free will."

She recoiled from the strange, hypnotic appeal of his vision. "No! It's my life. Mine! I make my own choices!"

"You're my wife." His lips barely moved as he hissed each word. "The choices are mine."

"Never!" She pulled away from him and ran toward the door, but he caught the back of her dress and spun her around so violently that her chin slammed into the hard muscle of his shoulder.

"There are two ways we can do this, Highness. You can walk to the carriage like the lady you pretend to be, or you can leave it up to me." His fingers tightened ruthlessly on her arms as he gave her one warning shake. "Which will it be?"

In answer, she drew back her foot and kicked at him with all her might.

"Have it your way," he muttered through clenched teeth. Pitching her roughly over his shoulder, he carried her into the hallway, past the gaping servants, and out the front door.

Noelle did not make it easy for him. She pounded him with her fists and then sunk her teeth into the tendons of his back. He let out a muffled curse and cracked his hand down hard on her buttocks. As the carriage pulled away from the house on Northridge Square, she still felt the sting of it.

Chapter Twenty-nine

Afterward, Noelle could never quite remember the details of that nightmarish week when she lay helplessly ill in their cabin aboard the packet *Dorsey Beale,* her stomach violently rebelling against the relentless pitching of the ship. Most of the time Quinn left her alone, hiring a young immigrant girl from the ship's steerage to attend her during the day, and at night slipping quietly into the dark cabin, not even bothering to light the lamp that swung from the center beam as he undressed and climbed into the narrow berth across from her.

On the day after Christmas, when she still showed no signs of improvement, he announced he was taking her topside. She summoned enough energy to frame a protest but was too weak to resist when he wrapped her warmly in a blanket and carried her up to a chair on the deck. The frigid air soon set her teeth chattering, but for the first time, her stomach was quiet. From that point on, she made a steady improvement, spending as much time walking in the salt air as she could, even when the wind buffeted her so strongly, she could barely push one foot in front of the other.

One night as she sat on the edge of her berth, brushing her hair, the door of the cabin swung open to admit Quinn. It was unusual for him to desert the ship's gaming tables so early, but when she looked up to see his eyes boldly raking her body as if she were naked instead of wearing a modest nightdress, she understood that he had finally decided to claim her.

He crossed the cabin with an easy confidence that filled her with dread even as it excited her. Before she knew what was happening, he pulled her up into his arms and crushed his mouth to hers. Perhaps it was the suddenness of it, but for whatever reason, her body responded, and she felt her limbs turn to liquid.

Just as he opened the top of her nightdress to his caress and the last vestige of her will was slipping from her, the memory of his cruel taunt their final day in London returned to shame her: *"Don't forget, I know what a hot-blooded bitch you are."*

It was true! All he had to do was touch her, and she was ready to give herself to him!

"No!" she cried, pushing herself back from him. "I don't want your kisses. If you're going to take me, just get it done with. I won't try to fight you anymore. But I'll not have you caress my body just so you can mock me afterward if it responds!"

Quinn had the grace to look slightly abashed. "I was angry with you. I didn't mean what I said. You know that."

It was the closest thing to an apology she had ever heard from him, but the hurt was too deep. "I don't know anything of the kind!"

He took her by the shoulders then, his eyes colliding with hers. "Your body is beautiful and healthy. You should never be ashamed of it or let anyone, even me, make you ashamed of it." Abruptly he turned away and spoke so softly, she barely heard the words. "That night was probably the only good thing that has ever happened between us."

"You're wrong, Quinn," she immediately retorted, disturbed by the intensity of his tone. "Nothing good has ever happened between us, and it never will."

When he turned back to her, his face was coldly impassive. "You're right, of course. Now get into bed. It'll be as you want it."

He took her then, impersonally and silently, night after night while she lay motionless beneath him. He was careful not to hurt her but there was no tenderness, no joy for her or, she soon realized, for him. Perhaps that was why she made no effort to stop him. No matter how dearly acquired, she finally had a small measure of revenge.

Each night after he left her berth for his, the disturbing question that had been lying dormant in her mind since he had carried her from Northridge Square and thrust her into the carriage surfaced to demand an answer. Why had she not escaped from him when she had the chance? Could it be that she hadn't wanted to leave? It was a ridiculous notion, she told herself, and tried to put it out of her mind.

During the day Quinn's behavior was courteous. He began to seek her out, at first chatting politely as he walked with her around the frigid decks, and then, with the captain's permission, initiating her nautical education by leading her through every part of the ship. He pointed out stays and shrouds, hatch coamings and quarter knees, explaining the function of each and talking of the differences between this vessel and ones built by Copeland and Peale. When he spoke of his ships, it was hard for Noelle to reconcile this fascinating man with the one who had abducted her—not once, but three times—shamed her, bullied her, and was now taking her away from all she knew to the primitive land that was his home.

When was it they first began to talk of other things—politics, philosophy, even themselves? He told her a little about his boyhood, and although he did not mention either Simon or his mother, she sensed he had lost his childhood early, something she understood only too well. Was that why she found herself speaking about the children in London's tenements, sharing her outrage that such conditions could exist in a city that was supposed to be civilized?

It was not long before she came to realize what a well-educated man her husband was. In addition to having been schooled by private tutors, she learned that he had spent an unhappy year at Eton before he had been sent down as incorrigible. Still, he had received a university education at William and Mary, a small college in Virginia, where he had been an outcast among the wealthy sons of Southern planters because of his outspoken criticism of slavery.

They frequently went to the ship's hold, in which Pathkiller and Chestnut Lady were being comfortably transported.

"Don't be surprised when we arrive if you find the house needs some tending," he said one day as they entered the stall. "I haven't been home for over three years, and Televea has been closed."

"Televea?" She held out a piece of carrot in the palm of her hand for Chestnut Lady.

"It's a Creek word meaning 'home.' Simon bought the house from a Creek merchant who had made a fortune in cotton but overextended himself and was forced to sell off his house and his land."

"Do you mean an Indian?"

Quinn smiled. "Don't be so shocked. The Indians in Georgia

don't carry tomahawks anymore. Some of the pureblood still wear turbans and leggings, but most of them dress like the white man."

Noelle was surprised to learn that the Cherokee nation had its own constitution and its own alphabet. Instead of the crude huts she had imagined Indians lived in, there were farms and churches, schools for the children.

"The Indians have become very civilized," Quinn said, his mouth twisting slightly at the corners.

"But isn't that for the best?"

He picked up a brush and began stroking Pathkiller's black coat. "They thought that by adopting the white man's ways, they'd be able to keep their land, but it was a foolish hope."

"How do you mean?"

"Treaties were made, then they were broken. The Cherokees have very little land left them. A tiny corner of North Carolina and Tennessee, a small piece of Alabama, and the very northern tip of Georgia. And now, what little they have has been taken, too."

Thoughtfully he fingered Pathkiller's mane, the brush idle in his hand. "Last May Congress passed the Indian Removal Bill. All of the eastern tribes—the Seminole, the Choctaw, Chickasaw, Creek, and the Cherokees—were ordered to give up their homeland for territory in the west, territory that they don't want."

"Does no one speak out for the Indians?"

Quinn nodded. "A few. But it hasn't changed the outcome."

"And so," Noelle said thoughtfully, "the Cherokees have to abandon their homes for an unsettled land. Have they gone yet?"

"Barely two thousand of them. The rest—more than sixteen thousand—have stayed, hoping for a miracle."

"Do you think there will be one?"

"It's been a long time since I've believed in fairy tales, Highness. The Cherokee nation is going to be broken."

Sensing how deeply the injustice troubled him, Noelle reached out and gently touched his arm. "I'm sorry, Quinn."

For a moment he looked at her, and then he nodded curtly and walked away.

That night, Quinn did not cross the cabin to her berth; nor the next. Long after he had fallen asleep, Noelle lay awake trying to understand why it was becoming harder and harder for her to keep her hatred for Quinn burning as fiercely as before. Could it be because she was strangely fascinated by him? Of all the men she had ever met, he was the only one who had never bored her.

She remembered the night she had returned from Yorkshire and confronted Simon. "I'm frightened of him," she had declared. "Can't you understand that?"

But had she been completely honest? It was true that Quinn moved through life with only the thinnest restraint on the violent side of his nature. It was also true that, too often, she had been the target of that violence. But she had lived on the cutting edge of danger since she was seven years old. While his treatment of her was abominable, in some perverse way it was not as dehumanizing as being fawned over by men who knew nothing more about her than that she was beautiful.

Without quite knowing it she made her decision. For now, it would be Cape Crosse, Copeland and Peale, and Quinn. She needed time to adjust to this new country. But most of all, she needed time to settle her relationship with her husband. As long as she felt any ambivalence toward him, she would never be free of him, no matter how much geographical distance might separate them. As for the future, she had a good mind and a strong body. She would make her own way whenever she chose.

PART FOUR

The Copeland Bride

Chapter Thirty

Savannah, one of the busiest ports in the South, lived up to its reputation the mild morning in late January when Quinn and Noelle debarked from the *Dorsey Beale*. Merchant ships anchored beside brigs and paddle steamers. Sloops darted in and out of the bustling harbor while barges and flat-bottomed boats made their way to and from the mouth of the Savannah River on their journeys for the wealth of cotton and tobacco. Wagons pulled by workhorses and teams of oxen lined the piers as burly roustabouts unloaded cargo from deep within the holds of the ships. Carriages and wagons for hire dotted the waterfront streets, their drivers mulling about in small groups, waiting for the hefty fares they anticipated from the wealthy first-class passengers leaving the ship.

After he had supervised the safe debarkation of Pathkiller and Chestnut Lady, Quinn hired one such carriage. Normally, he explained, they would travel between Savannah and Cape Crosse by boat, but today there was a sou'wester blowing, and it would be just as fast overland.

The trip took them over rough roads and crude wooden bridges that looked as if the slightest breeze would sweep them away. They ate a silent dinner at an inn along the road and arrived at Televea at dusk. The carriage traveled down a narrow brick-paved lane thickly edged with pines. The lane stretched for some distance before it opened into a clearing with what had once been a magnificent white frame house sitting high on a rise.

It had been built in the federal style with the center well-balanced by a tall hipped roof and, flush at each end of this main section, narrow one-story wings. Graceful windows set in recessed arches were framed by shutters that had once been black and shiny but were now faded and, in several cases, hanging loose from single rusted hinges. Overgrown boxwood and azaleas encircled a long porch supported by four simple square columns, which, despite peeling white paint, still lent their dignity to the rest of the house.

After the coachman had taken the horses around to the stable and come back to unload the luggage, Quinn and Noelle walked up the steps to the porch, which was bare except for an abandoned bird's nest piled with droppings and a rattan rocking chair with a faded chintz cover.

The muscles in Quinn's jaw tightened. "Welcome to Televea," he muttered as he stepped into the deserted foyer. "There aren't any servants. I'll have to hire some." He lit a lamp that stood on a candlestand just inside the door. Elongated shadows flickered up the walls to the high ceiling and over a worn Persian rug, which was centered on what had once been a beautiful inlaid parquet floor. The coachman looked around curiously as he brought the trunks inside and followed Quinn upstairs with them. When the man was gone, Quinn lit a cheroot and began to wander from one room to the next, as if he had forgotten her. Curious to see the rest of his house, which had been so ill used, Noelle followed him.

In most of the rooms furniture had been pushed to the center and placed under dustcovers. The curtains in the drawing room were faded; the windows in the sitting room hung bare. Everywhere there was the smell of must. In the wing at the left of the house was an empty ballroom with a columned arch that opened into a conservatory where glass walls swept in a graceful semicircle. Although the panes were unbroken, they were so darkened by grime that they were opaque.

The right wing held a long, narrow dining room. An American eagle had been carved into the plasterwork of the once-white mantelpiece. Over the fireplace was a richly detailed painting of a pair of quail signed by the American naturalist John James Audubon.

Noelle could contain her curiosity no longer. "On the ship you told me that Televea had been closed since you left, yet Simon was in Cape Crosse less than a year ago. Where did he stay?"

Quinn pushed aside a pile of rags with the toe of his boot. "He owns a house near the shipyard."

"But why did he let this beautiful house deteriorate so badly?"

"Because he hates it," Quinn said impassively.

"Then why didn't he sell it?" she persisted.

"He did. I bought it from him before I left London."

Noelle looked around the gracefully designed room, wishing, for the hundredth time, that she knew what had happened between Quinn and his father. "How could anyone hate a house like this?" she said, almost to herself.

Planting the heel of one hand against the dusty mantelpiece, Quinn stared down into the cold cavity of the fireplace. "You ask too many questions, Highness, about things that aren't any of your business."

She left Quinn wandering about the house and went upstairs, where she found her trunks in a dusty but pleasant room that adjoined the master bedroom. A search of the wardrobe revealed a pile of sheets. While she made up the bed she thought how grateful she was that Quinn had not demanded she share his room. Still, as she was going through her trunks for a nightdress and robe, she realized she was unconsciously listening for the sound of footsteps. But there was only silence from the other room.

Below in the kitchen, Quinn sat with an open bottle of whiskey. The sight of Noelle walking through the rooms of Televea had disturbed him more than he wanted to admit. Why hadn't he left her in London as he had intended? His loins ached with the desire to possess her. Only his memory of those punishing nights on the ship when she had so stubbornly held herself apart from him kept him from claiming her now. If she weren't so damned beautiful . . . But then, it was more than her beauty. Everything about her seemed to affect him.

He took another swallow. He was goddamned if he would let it go on this way any longer! When he decided he wanted to father a child, he'd bring her to his bed. Until then, he'd take his comforts elsewhere. Noelle would bear his children, run his household. That was all!

The next morning, as Noelle sat at the kitchen table, sipping a cup of tea, a knock sounded at the door, distracting her. She opened it to find a group of six women, three white and three black, assembled on the back stoop.

"Miz Copeland?"

"Yes?"

"I'm Dainty Jones, your new cook."

It was a moment before Noelle found her voice. Dainty Jones was the tallest woman she had ever seen and certainly one of the thinnest. She had closely cropped ginger hair, its color the only reminder of her Scots-Irish ancestors, and ruddy skin stretched tight over angular bones. Her face was shaped much like an hourglass—broad at the top, sunken at the cheeks, broad again at the chin—and her accent spoke of the backlands.

"How do you do, Miss Jones," Noelle finally managed.

"Call me Dainty."

Shouldering her way into the kitchen, she continued her introductions. "This here's Bessie Pugh. That's Grace Mahoney. She's good with a needle, so you better take her as your maid. Them two is Favor and Evangeline Patterson. They don't have no experience, but they're hard workers. That one bringin' up the rear is Earline Wilcox. She's shy of strangers, so I 'spect you better leave her stay in the kitchen and help me. Mr. Copeland said the men'd be over tomorrow to start work on the outside."

Although Noelle did not know it at the time, it was not customary to have servants of both races in the same household. But in Cape Crosse, those who wanted Copeland wages had to be willing to work together.

She surveyed the group of women who stood assembled in the kitchen. From the towering Dainty Jones to the ebony-skinned Patterson sisters, they were a far cry from the proper English servants of her experience. But she couldn't allow herself the luxury of misgivings. Constance was not here to help her, and she certainly had no intention of running to Quinn. She had a household to manage, and she was going to have to do it by herself.

By the end of her first week at Televea, Noelle had absorbed herself in the challenge of restoring the beauty of the old house, taking time out only to write Constance a long letter describing her new household and her unorthodox servants. She did not mention Quinn at all. As the days passed, she flew from one place to the next—attic to storeroom, kitchen to bedroom, directing her servants at their tasks, sometimes stopping to sweep a floor or scrub out a corner herself.

She began with four rooms: the dining room, drawing room, and two front bedrooms. They were scoured from floor to ceiling, rugs were beaten, floors polished, windows washed. Years of accumulated grime were removed from the lovely parquet floor in the front hallway. The furniture was uncovered and rubbed with lemon oil and beeswax until it shone.

The servants proved to be good workers, and Dainty Jones's cooking contradicted her skeletal form. Soda biscuits and griddle cakes, pies and Indian puddings, a Brunswick stew full of butter beans and red pepper—all of them poured generously from her fragrant kitchen.

True to his word, Quinn sent a small crew of men to restore the exterior of the house, and it was soon festooned with ladders and scaffolding. On the days when the winter rains fell, Noelle pulled the workers inside to paint and do carpentry.

She rarely saw her husband during those first exhausting weeks, and he made no attempt to enter her bedroom. Other than approving her progress in the house and agreeing to take her to Savannah as soon as he could get away so she could make the purchases she needed to finish the job, he had little to say to her.

One day she overheard the maids gossiping about a woman named Kate Malloy who ran an illegal gambling house for the upper-class gentlemen of Cape Crosse and its environs. From their conversation, she gathered that a game of poker was not all that was available at Kate Malloy's. It had been difficult for her to imagine a man as virile as Quinn going for long without a woman, and now she suspected that all his late nights were not being spent at the shipyard. So much the better, she told herself. Let Quinn take his lust elsewhere. Nothing could make her happier!

Several weeks after her arrival, an incident occurred that left Noelle vaguely uneasy. She was behind the house, shaking out a small Oriental rug she had found on one of her forages to the attic when she looked up to see a strange man standing near the smokehouse, watching her. He had a barrel chest, thick, powerful limbs, and a head that was abnormally small for so large a man. She could not see the color of his hair, hidden beneath a battered felt hat, but she could see his eyes. Small and malevolent, they bored into her. For a moment neither of them moved, and then the stranger spat insolently into a pile of dead leaves at his feet and disappeared back into the trees.

That evening, she mentioned the incident to Quinn. He made inquiries among the men who had been working at the house that day, but no one else had seen the stranger. Within a few days, she had put the encounter out of her mind.

Noelle learned from Dainty that the women of the community and nearby plantations had agreed among themselves to postpone calling until she was settled. "You can bet they don't like waitin', Miz Copeland," Dainty said, chuckling, one morning as she sank the heels of her bony hands into a mountain of bread dough. "But they're too polite to do anythin' else. Any female in this part of Georgia who's older'n fifteen or younger'n fifty has set her sights on Mr. Copeland at one time or 'nother, and now curiosity's eatin' away at all of 'em faster'n maggots on week-old meat. They want to see the woman who finally managed to catch him. Oo-ee!" Dainty chortled. "They sure is some curious ladies jes' waitin' fer the chance to set their eyes on you!"

Chapter Thirty-one

One day, while the workmen were eating their lunches in Dainty's kitchen, Noelle stepped into her sitting room to survey their progress with the painting. As she studied the ceiling moldings high above her, she saw a section they had missed. The heavy ladder was off to the side a bit, but she calculated she could reach it if she rested her weight on one foot and leaned out.

After loading a brush with paint, she hitched up her skirts and carefully climbed the ladder. When she reached the top, she held on with the tips of her fingers and, leaning far out with the brush, she dabbed at the offending spot.

"Good God!"

His voice startled her so that she nearly lost her balance. As it was, she dropped the brush, which promptly smeared the freshly painted baseboard.

"What the bloody hell do you mean sneaking up on me that way!" she exclaimed. "Just see what you've made me do!"

He moved over to the base of the ladder and looked up at her with amusement. "If I'd known you were so handy with a paintbrush, Highness, I wouldn't have hired all these workmen."

"Why are you home at this time of day?" she snapped.

"I left some papers in my bedroom." He grinned up at her. "Are you planning to stay up there all day?"

"I was just coming down," she said stiffly as she began descending the ladder, trying not to catch either her skirt or her petticoats. The business was made more difficult by Quinn grinning up at her, obviously enjoying his unrestricted view of her lacy underthings.

"I should come home during the day more often. I had no idea I was missing so much."

"Don't be infantile," she flared, stepping down off the last rung.

She was about to sweep from the room when she stopped herself. This was the perfect opportunity to confront him. It galled her that he had forced her to come to Cape Crosse so he could fulfill his promise to Constance, yet now that she was here, he hadn't once mentioned showing her the shipyard. If he thought that after all that had happened she was still willing to turn over control of her shares to him, he was about to be reinformed.

"I want to visit the shipyard."

"Don't you have enough here to keep you busy?"

"It's not a matter of keeping busy, Quinn," she said sweetly, knowing that even if he wanted to, he wouldn't break his word to Constance. "I just want to keep an eye on what's mine."

She could tell by the cold look that settled around his eyes that he didn't like her comment; however, he nodded begrudgingly. "Have one of the men bring you around tomorrow."

Her face as she turned to leave the room did not quite conceal her pleasure over the small victory. "I'll do that, Quinn."

With a groom to lead the way, Noelle rode Chestnut Lady the two miles to the shipyard. She had taken particular care with her appearance that day, coiling her hair low on her neck in a simple but elegant arrangement that she set off with tortoiseshell combs. She chose a fawn riding habit trimmed with dark brown piping and, as a final touch, settled the topaz ring on over her wedding band.

The shipyard was larger than she had imagined and bustling with activity. There were ships in various stages of construction, each one surrounded by piles of wood and mountains of fresh shavings. Lining the yard were at least a half-dozen buildings, some a single story open at the sides, others taller and enclosed. The sound of iron being hammered told her one belonged to the shipsmith; another she guessed to be a warehouse. She watched a wagon pull up at a third to receive a load of canvas through the door of the loft. At the end of the yard was a wharf where a large ship with a team of workmen crawling through its rigging was anchored. The smell of wood shavings, tar, and old hemp permeated everything.

"Afternoon, Miz Copeland."

"Why, hello, Carl."

The flaxen-haired Swede who had done some work at Televea

the week before blushed with pleasure that she had remembered his name. "If you're lookin' for Mr. Copeland, he's over watchin' the planking. I'll go tell him you're here."

"No, don't bother. I'll go over myself."

Noelle walked toward the group of men Carl had indicated and watched them curiously. They were standing at the base of the frame of a ship, its bare timbers towering over them like the rib cage of a giant animal skeleton. Off to one side, fires burned under large kettles that were shooting their steam into long enclosed boxes.

While Noelle watched, there was a cloud of white steam as one of the boxes was opened and two men wearing leather gloves reached in with hooks to extract a steaming plank of wood. As it whipped loosely in the air, pliable from the moist heat, they climbed up to the exposed ribs at the bow of the skeleton ship and, before it could stiffen, began clamping it down so that it conformed to the curve of the frame.

"I don't like the way that one looks, Pat. Take it off and try another strake."

As Quinn moved around the front of the frame he caught sight of her, his admiring glance telling her that the extra pains she had taken that morning with her appearance were worth the effort.

"Take over, Pat. Any more of that wood looks green, you let me know."

As he approached, Noelle shielded her eyes with her hand from the wintry midday sun. "I don't want to pull you away from your work, Quinn."

"I'm done here. It's a good time to show you around." He led her to a large frame building at the front of the yard. Over the doorway was a wooden sign with intaglio letters of shining gold:

COPELAND AND PEALE, SHIPBUILDERS
CAPE CROSSE, GEORGIA
LONDON, ENGLAND

Noelle looked up at the sign and smiled. "I see the British have been put in last place as usual."

Quinn laughed. "Old Tim told me that when Simon first had the sign hung, it read the other way around and kept disappearing. He'd have a new one made and, within a day, it'd be gone, too.

Finally he took the hint and changed the order of the towns. Nobody's touched it since except to repaint the letters."

For the first time, Noelle noticed a small group of men standing to the side.

"Afternoon, Boss."

Quinn took Noelle by the arm and led her over to the men, and he introduced her. It was a pattern that was to repeat itself as they made their way through the yard, leaving each man anxious to go home and tell his wife that he had met Mr. Copeland's bride that day.

As the afternoon progressed she found that she remembered much of what Quinn had told her while they were on board the *Dorsey Beale*, and now it was surprisingly easy for her to make the mental connection between the incomplete structures before her and the finished ship. When she correctly identified a carling and then a breast hook, she felt as much satisfaction as she had the day she had finished *Robinson Crusoe*.

"So you finally decided to let her visit us, Quinn."

Noelle turned to see a pleasant-faced young man in a frock coat walking toward them.

"Noelle, this is Julian Lester, our business manager."

"It's a pleasure to finally meet you, Mrs. Copeland."

She liked him immediately, and they were soon calling each other by their first names and chatting about the responsibilities of his position.

"You can't imagine how glad we all are to have Quinn back. I do much better with ledgers and contracts than with caulking mallets and lathes. Simon and I are much the same. That's why we've needed Quinn so badly."

"Julian exaggerates," Quinn said. "He's done a fine job these past two years."

"I'm just glad it's over now, and we can settle down to building the best ships on the North Atlantic." He turned toward the sloop behind them. "We'll be launching her soon. Why don't you come and watch?"

"I'd like that," Noelle answered.

As he was ready to leave them, he said, "My wife will never forgive me if I don't ask you if you're ready for company, Noelle."

"I'd enjoy meeting her," she assured him. "Just warn her that she may have to crawl over ladders to get in the front door."

After Julian Lester left them, Quinn led her out to the wharf and then, taking her hand, helped her onto the anchored frigate. His hand felt comfortable as it clasped hers, cool and strong, a little rough from the work it had been doing. She made no protest when he did not immediately let her go.

"These masts are made from spruce. We float the trees down the river and finish them smooth in the spar shop. Sailors are superstitious, so we never step a mast without putting a silver coin under its butt."

Abruptly he craned his neck and pulled away from her. "No, Frank. You need more tension on that stay. Slack off on the shroud!"

As quickly as that, he had forgotten her and was at the ratlines, climbing up into the rigging as easily as if he were mounting a staircase. Noelle watched him for a while and then began wandering about the frigate, speaking to the men as she passed but being careful to stay out of their way. She heard Quinn's laughter and looked up to see him climbing even higher, supremely confident in this world of which he was the undisputed master.

Later, as she rode toward Televea, she reviewed the afternoon. The shipyard fascinated her, and she vowed that she would go there frequently and learn all she could. As she rounded a sharp bend in the road Chestnut nickered and tossed her head nervously. Noelle reached out to pat her neck. "There now, Chestnut. What's the—"

Suddenly a horse shot across the road from a stand of trees on the side. As Chestnut began to rear, a large fist reached out and clamped itself around the bridle, bringing the mare back under control. "Need some help, little lady?" The voice was sneering and unpleasant.

Noelle jerked around in her saddle. Her heart lurched as she stared into the small, malevolent eyes of the man she had seen standing by the smokehouse at Televea. "What do you think you're doing?" she demanded, her hand instinctively tightening on her riding crop.

Insolently he doffed his felt hat, revealing thin, straw-colored hair. "Jes' wanted to pay my respects to the bride." His eyes slid down over her body. "Looks to me like you coulda done better than that bastard Copeland."

Noelle glanced uneasily at the hand still clamped around her bridle. "Who are you?" she asked, keeping her voice cold and even.

"Name's Baker, little lady. Luke Baker." He studied her expressionless face. "That name don't mean nothin' to you, does it?"

"Should it?"

"Jes' thought your husband mighta mentioned me. Him and me go back a long way."

Suddenly Noelle remembered a conversation she had overheard between Simon and Quinn during those last days in London. "You're the man who was suspected of setting fire to the warehouse, aren't you?"

"Don't know nothin' about no fire." He grinned unpleasantly as he said it, and Noelle decided that he was lying.

"Let go of my horse, Mr. Baker," she snapped. "This instant!"

His small eyes raked over her. "Tell me, little lady," he jeered. "You ever get lonesome at night? I hear between the shipyard and Kate Malloy's, your high-and-mighty husband don't spend a lot of time at home."

Noelle lifted her riding crop and slashed it down across the fist that held the bridle. Baker gave a startled yelp of pain, but to her dismay, did not release his grip. "You little bitch," he snarled, jerking the crop from her with his free hand. "You're gonna pay for that."

"No, Baker. You're the one who's going to pay."

In their struggle, neither of them had heard Quinn approaching on Pathkiller from the other side of the bend. Baker stared at the pistol trained at his heart. Slowly he released his grip on Noelle's mount.

"Put that gun away, Copeland. I ain't done nothin'."

Quinn did not take his eyes off Baker. "You're wrong, Luke. I sent one of my men for the sheriff as soon as I heard you'd been seen lurking around the yard. You're going to be spending some time in jail."

Baker licked his lips nervously. "What for?"

"Trying to burn down my shipyard last year," Quinn scoffed

contemptuously. "What happened? You couldn't get to me so you went after the shipyard instead?"

"You're bluffing," Baker sneered. "I wasn't anywhere near that shipyard. And I got witnesses to prove it."

"I've seen your friends, Baker, and I don't think their word will count much with a jury. Besides, I've got my own witnesses. Ned McLoughlin and Carl Bremer saw you that night."

Baker stared impotently at the gun trained so unwaveringly upon him. "You're lying! There weren't any witnesses to that fire."

"Oh, but there were. We knew you'd show up again as soon as you heard I was back from England. Ned and Carl have just been biding their time, waiting to tell their stories to the judge." Noelle saw fear flickering in Baker's eyes. "You're not a stupid man, Baker," Quinn said, "but you've let your hatred for me ruin your judgment. You should have stayed away."

Baker could no longer contain his rage. "You son of a bitch!" he screamed, drops of spittle collecting in the corners of his mouth. "Stay away? After you killed my brother?"

"Your brother attacked an unarmed man."

"He was an Injun!" Baker spat. "You killed a white man for an Injun!"

Quinn's eyes narrowed dangerously, and Noelle saw his muscles tense. Later she wondered what would have happened if the sheriff had not ridden up at that moment with some of the men from the shipyard.

After they had taken Baker away, Quinn turned to her. "Are you all right?"

She nodded. "Baker was the man I saw near the smokehouse."

Quinn dismounted and picked up her riding crop from the road. "I suspected it was him, but I wasn't sure. Until today, nobody else had seen him. Then, right after you left the yard, one of the men told me somebody thought they'd spotted him near the gate." He rested his hand on the back of her saddle and handed the crop to her. "You should have waited for the groom to ride back with you, Noelle. I've told you I don't want you riding alone around here."

"Don't try to put a leash on me, Quinn Copeland," she flared. "I can take care of myself. I had my knife in my boot and was just waiting for the chance to use it." Without waiting for a response, she dug her heels into Chestnut's flanks and galloped off down the road.

Chapter Thirty-two

The next afternoon, Julian Lester's wife, Emily, came to call. In appearance, she was much like her husband, with the same soft brown hair and hazel eyes. As Noelle led her through the completed rooms she found herself warming to her as quickly as she had to Julian.

"You've done so much here," Emily marveled as they returned to the drawing room. "Televea is going to be even more beautiful than it was when I was a child."

"I didn't realize you'd lived here so long, Emily."

"Oh, my, yes. At Darcy Hall, not a mile away. Goodness, I spent almost as much time at Televea as I did there. Of course, we all did. We were drawn here like bear cubs to honey."

"Why was that?" Noelle asked, trying to imagine this house full of children.

"Because of Amanda. We all loved her."

Although Noelle had never heard her name, she knew Emily must be referring to Quinn's mother. "Tell me about her. Quinn speaks so little of his childhood."

"Oh, Noelle, she was something, 'deed she was. We all had secret guilty dreams about our parents disappearing. Not *dying*, mind you." Emily laughed. "We were too civilized for that. Just mysteriously disappearing for a while so we could come to live at Televea.

"Our mothers all called her 'Poor Amanda' because her servants took advantage of her, and she couldn't keep house. They'd give her their recipes for furniture polish or tell her how to get the muddy tracks off the stairway carpet. She'd just laugh and tell them she was too busy playing with her son and keeping her husband happy to have time for such foolishness. Oh, my, how they used to sigh over her. But they loved her, too. She'd delivered most of their babies."

"What did she look like?"

"There's a painting of her somewhere. I suppose Simon took it down after she died. She wasn't beautiful, not like you are. But she was striking. Strong features. Dark hair that she always wore in a sort of braided coronet on her head and, oh, my, you never saw a woman who cared less about clothes. Why, she'd take us into the woods, wearing a new dress, and before you'd know it, she'd be dragging her hem in the mud at the riverbank while she showed us how to catch fish without poles. Simon used to complain that he had to build an extra ship every year just to replace the clothes she ruined. He'd always laugh when he said it, though, and we knew he didn't really mind."

Emily smiled, and there was a faraway look in her eyes. "We all envied Quinn so much. They treated him differently than our own parents treated us. They were always touching him, I remember. Every time he walked by, one of them would rumple his hair or hug him or sometimes just pat his arm. I remember one day Simon kissed him on the top of his head in front of the other boys. How they all teased him! But he only laughed and said that if they didn't mind themselves, he'd tell Simon to kiss them, too."

Emily sighed. "Of course, it all changed after she died."

"How did it happen?"

"Malaria. It was real bad that summer. What a sad time that was. Nothing ever stays the same, I guess."

She gave a small embarrassed laugh. "Goodness me, Noelle, I sound just like Julian's Aunt Cornelia with my reminiscing. He says I've been acting strangely ever since I discovered I was in the family way." There was pride in her voice as she confided that after seven years of marriage, she and Julian were finally expecting a child in the summer.

"I hope it doesn't take so long for you and Quinn. It would be nice to have our babies close together."

Noelle smiled noncommittally, glad now that she had not shown Emily the upstairs of the house. Somehow, she doubted that her new friend would understand why she and Quinn were sleeping in separate bedrooms.

After Emily had gone, Noelle poured herself a cup of tea and wandered distractedly into her sitting room, her footsteps echoing on the bare floor. She ambled over to the front window and gazed thoughtfully out. She didn't see the hedges that were now clipped back from the walk or the brick driveway that curved so gracefully up to the front of the house and no longer had weeds growing between its cracks. All she saw was Amanda Copeland.

How vivid Emily had made her. Was that why, now, she seemed so close? Did she know, even from her grave, what a hard, driven man her son had become, hating the father he had once loved, happy only with his ships? Was she trying to reach out to Noelle? Tell her to help her son?

Abruptly Noelle set down her cup and made her way, as if by instinct, to a room she had entered only once before. It had been a nursery, she guessed, before it had become a schoolroom. Among the dusty trunks and old chests, she found the evidence of her husband's boyhood: primers with childish pictures and misspellings in the margins; a wooden ark; a battalion of lead soldiers, their bright red uniforms chipped and faded. There was an airy wooden cradle with spindle sides and, behind it all, as she had somehow known it would be, the painting of Amanda Copeland, carefully wrapped in layers of protective cloth.

It was a full-length portrait of a woman wearing a red dress with a white fringed shawl draped over it. At the base of her throat hung a small silver disk, the same one that Quinn now wore. Emily had described her well: black hair, a strong nose, dark eyes set a bit farther apart than fashion dictated.

Noelle sat for some time studying the portrait and thinking about the woman Amanda Copeland must have been. Finally she replaced the cloth and left.

Quinn had left word with the grooms that Noelle was only permitted to ride to the south and east of the house, not into the wooded area that bordered the rear. The restriction had begun to chafe at her even before the incident with Luke Baker. Now that he was safely in jail, she decided there was no longer any need for such caution. And so, the afternoon after Emily had made her visit, Noelle impulsively turned toward the woods, ignoring the groom who called out to her from the stable door. Chestnut Lady's hooves silently crushed the sprouting seedlings that had unwisely sought haven on the narrow path. She wouldn't go any distance, she decided; just far enough to ease her resentment.

She had been exploring the clearing for some time, humming tunelessly to herself and wandering around the ruins of an old cabin before she realized she was not alone. Her first thought was of Baker. As the icy, prickly warning of danger shot down her spine, she was conscious of how well the dense overgrowth had shut out the strength of the late afternoon sunlight and of how far she had strayed from her tethered mare.

Still humming softly, she bent over and adjusted her riding boot as if there were something wrong with the heel and, at the same time, slowly extracted her knife from the other boot. Sliding it into her pocket, she began casually making her way toward her horse.

She still had some distance to go when a twig cracked ominously close to her. She began to run, darting around the back of a clump of cypress in a rapid change of direction designed to lose her pursuer. She wove through the trees as agilely as she had once run through the twisting streets of London. But she was city bred, and she had not counted on the small roots growing loosely above the surface of the sandy loam; roots thin, but strong, and ready to snare the leather toe of a riding boot.

The side of her hip hit first. Just before the rest of her body slammed against the ground, she felt her hair snag on the jagged crown of a severed tree trunk. Turning to free herself, she sucked in her breath. There, planted firmly on the ground next to her, was a pair of moccasins.

Her heart hammering, she pulled herself up, first noting the buckskin leggings and then the rifle slung across the front of a tuniclike homespun shirt before her eyes fell on his face. All that Quinn had told her about the Indians adopting the ways of the white men fled from her mind as soon as she saw the series of concentric circles tattooed on one broad cheek and the silver disks hanging from his ears. He looked surprised at the knife she thrust toward him.

"Don't come near me!" she shouted, beginning to back away toward her mare.

But he didn't heed her warning. As she saw him prepare to spring she jerked her body to the right. He had already made the leap in the direction of her movement before he realized she had tricked him. Flipping the knife over into her left hand and pulling herself back, she caught him on his side with the blade, just below the bottom rib.

It was only a glancing blow. The Indian looked down at his side, more startled than hurt at the crimson stain spreading slowly on the side of his tunic.

"You've drawn blood," he said. "A woman."

It was somehow startling to hear English words come from his mouth, even though she already knew many of the Indians spoke English.

"You threatened me!" She kept the knife blade pointed toward him. "Why were you spying on me?"

"You were running toward the swamp."

Cautiously she lowered her knife, still holding it firmly in her fist but beginning to feel foolish. Something in his straightforward gaze told her he was speaking the truth, that he had been trying to protect her, and it was merely her prejudice that had made her assume she was being attacked.

"I am Wasidan. And you are the white woman Kalanu has married."

Kalanu? Did he mean Quinn? "I'm Noelle Copeland" was all she said.

"Yes. Get your horse. I will lead you back to Televea. You should not have come in this direction; the swamps are dangerous."

Quinn raced toward the woods, his face a thundercloud as he dug his heels into his stallion's already lathered flanks. He'd been a fool to leave orders as if he thought she would obey them. How could a stable boy keep a leash on her when he hadn't been able to do it himself? At least the boy had had the sense to send for him. Quinn would not let himself think about what would happen if he were too late.

He had barely entered the trees before he saw them coming toward him, Wasidan in the lead, riding a biscuit-colored mare, and Noelle following on her chestnut. The relief that coursed through him was quickly replaced by an anger that he struggled to set aside as his old friend spotted him and raised an arm in greeting.

"Kalanu, my friend. It is good to see you."

"And you, Wasidan. It has been too long."

They clasped hands as their horses drew alongside each other. It was then that Quinn noticed the red stain on Wasidan's tunic.

"You've been hurt."

"It's only a scratch. Your woman is as fierce as the wolf."

Quinn's eyes, hard and cold, flickered over her. With a tug on the reins, she swung past the two men and headed toward the stable. She had handed her horse over to the groom and was walking back to the house when he caught up with her, his fingers digging into her arm.

"I'm not done with you yet," he growled through tight lips. "I'll see you inside after I've spoken with Wasidan."

She stepped from the tub and patted herself dry before she wrapped her wet hair with the towel Grace handed her. Quinn had still not returned to the house, even though she had waited downstairs for over an hour before she came to her senses and marched furiously to her room. What was she doing cooling her heels like a kitchen maid? He could just wait for her!

Even the hot tub water could not soothe away her anger. This time he had gone too far. His arrogance had actually put her life in danger! He should have told her it was swampland behind the house instead of issuing those mindless orders to the groom.

She slipped a mauve silk robe over her still damp body and pulled the sash tight around her waist. "The blue muslin will do for tonight, Grace."

Suddenly the front door slammed with a vengeance. Only Quinn could enter a house so violently. Noelle instructed Grace to tell him she would be downstairs presently, but the girl's hand had barely touched the knob before the door was thrown open.

"Go downstairs," he ordered the startled maid.

"She stays right here. You can go down and wait until I'm dressed."

He jerked his head toward the door. "Get out of here, Grace." Nervously the girl did as she was ordered.

"What in the hell did you think you were doing?"

His jaw was taut and his lips barely moved as he challenged her. Dimly he realized that his anger was out of proportion to her deed, but he couldn't forgive her for the fear she had sent racing like poison through his veins when he had discovered she was in danger.

"Can't you follow simple instructions? Do you always have to defy me?"

Noelle's eyes flashed golden currents of belligerence even as one part of her registered how achingly handsome he was—head thrown back, legs spread wide apart, hands resting in fists on his hips.

"How dare you come in here accusing me! I don't follow orders that have no explanation."

"I don't need to give you any explanations."

"By not telling me that was swampland, you put my life in jeopardy."

"You put your own life in jeopardy and the life of my friend with your damned knife!"

"Your friend," she scoffed. "That savage attacked me!" This was not only unfair, but untrue, and Noelle knew it. Still, she did not take back what she had said, because she saw the words had fallen on him like the lash of a whip. A terrible excitement built within her at the dangerous narrowing of his eyes. Propelled by loneliness, by a bedroom door whose latch was never tested, by an unspeakable yearning for something more than distant politeness from this man, she deliberately pressed him.

"You sicken me with your talk of how persecuted the Indians have been. If this is a sample of what happens when they live near the white man, I think the government is right to move them all away." Lifting her chin, she walked toward him with measured steps, calculating her words as she went. "They're filthy savages, Quinn, no matter how you try to disguise it. They're a threat to every white woman who strays farther than her front porch."

"So, the little guttersnipe who cheated and lied her way out of the slums is now judging other people!"

"People!" she jeered, her moist lips trembling with the danger and excitement of what she was doing. "They're animals!"

"Are we, now?"

Her breath caught in her throat. "What are you saying?"

"If I'd realized it was so important to you, I'd have told you long ago that I'm Cherokee, but, frankly, it didn't occur to me."

"I don't believe you!" It was a lie. She did believe! Amanda's portrait had already told her the truth, had already warned her of the madness of inciting him.

"You don't want to believe me because you're afraid."

"I'm not afraid!"

"You should be," he sneered, his mouth thinning into an ugly line of contempt. "You've heard what Indians do to white women."

Jerking the towel from her head, he entangled his bruising hands in her mass of damp hair. "Does it frighten you now, Highness, having a savage so close to your beautiful hair? Can you taste the fear in the back of your mouth like cold metal against your tongue?"

He twisted his fingers around the long piece of silken hair growing from her crown. "This is where the Cherokee takes a scalp. Only this place. Sometimes the victim even lives to tell about it."

"Get your hands off me," Noelle cried out.

"It's too late for that."

Dropping her hair, he pushed her back against the wall and split the fragile silk of her robe. The fabric fell to her waist, where the knotted sash kept it from going farther. His eyes raked her nakedness, then he slid his hands roughly down her neck, past her shoulders to her breasts.

"Look at my hands on you. See how white your flesh is against mine. Even your nipples aren't as dark as my skin."

She shuddered as she looked down at his massive dark hands and watched the calloused palms knead her tender tips.

"It's not just the sun that has stained my skin. It's the blood of the Cherokee."

She swung out at him with her fists and began spitting out inflamed, exciting oaths until his mouth clamped down hard on hers, and he parted her lips with a tongue that was unwilling to please but eager to punish. Like a vixen, Noelle bit down. When he jerked back from her, his eyes black with fury, she ran, knowing that no matter how swiftly she fled, he would catch her.

He tore off the sash of her robe when he spun her around, and the fabric snared her ankles, sending her naked body sprawling to the floor. Before she could bring herself up, he had placed himself between her prone body and the door. She watched helplessly as he removed his clothing. He had told her she should be frightened of him, and now, too late, she was.

He moved toward her. His arm grasped her around the waist and hurled her to the bed. She thrashed helplessly under him while he foraged her mouth in a crushing assault filled with the passion of rage and tasting of the blood she had drawn when she bit him. His legs pried hers open, and then he reared back and poised himself to enter her. As she felt him ready to ram his anger deep within her, tears clouded her vision. How ugly this had become, this wild assault to which they had led each other.

Closing her eyes, she turned her head to the side and braced herself for the searing pain of an entry for which she was not yet ready. He was suddenly still, and the room echoed with the sound of their ragged breathing. Instead of the brutal invasion that she feared, his hands found her breasts, and her tears began to dry as, despite her fear, the coral buds hardened under his rough caress. She felt his touch slide down her sides and brush through the soft, tight triangle at the juncture of her thighs. Then she moaned as he invaded her with his touch, testing her desire in the only way he could trust.

His lips began teasing her nipples, then biting them, bringing her such agonizing pleasure that she thought she would go mad. His mouth moved on to her smooth belly, her thighs, cutting into the tender skin, biting and sucking at her flesh. She cried out his name as, intimately, he violated her with the wrath of his tongue.

He brought her to the brink of fulfillment and then pulled away, leaving an aching void that yearned to be filled. Their eyes clashed —locking, hating, wanting. Imperiously she arched her hips, and he drove himself into her with all the remaining force of his anger. Wrapping her legs tight about him, she strained against his body, pulling him down and parting her lips so she could taste the rugged planes of his face with her tongue and teeth. She was barely conscious when she sobbed her fulfillment, and he shuddered convulsively within her.

Later, when he sat up and dropped his legs over the side of her bed, she reached out a restraining hand and touched his arm. "Quinn, I didn't mean what I said earlier," she whispered miserably. "I've guessed for some time that you were Indian from Amanda's portrait and the silver disk you wear. I'm sorry. I deliberately goaded you. It was wrong of me."

Without a word, he disappeared into the dressing room.

Noelle fell back on the pillow and stared up at the ceiling. What devils had driven her to that desperate madness? It had been insanity to incite him as she had. Suddenly she began to shiver. Turning on her side, she drew up her knees.

From his bedroom, Quinn heard her moan. He rushed in to find her huddled in a tight ball under the covers. Her hair was a tangled mass, and he carefully brushed it back from her ravaged face, then he eased the blankets from her body. He sickened as he looked down.

"My God, Highness." His voice was ragged. "Look what I've done to you."

Even as he tucked the covers back around her, he couldn't erase the memory of the faint red marks marring her beautiful flesh. "I should never have brought you here. We're poisoning each other."

She turned her face into the pillow and began to sob. He slid his arms under her and gently carried her in her blanket cocoon to a chair, where he held her in his lap and stroked her hair. After a while, he began speaking softly to calm her, first talking about everyday things and then telling her stories of his boyhood. He spoke of treasure hunts, of teasing Emily and taking his lessons with Julian, of Amanda climbing trees with him, fishing, teaching him to track and use a bow and arrow, of everything except the feelings churning inside him.

It was as much the gentle closeness of him as it was his words that quieted Noelle. "I wish I'd known your mother," she finally murmured into his damp shirtfront.

"She would have liked you, Highness." He smiled. "She liked unconventional women."

"Will you tell me about her, Quinn? Really tell me this time."

"What would you like to know?"

Everything! she wanted to say. Everything that has been hidden away from me, that has made you a bitter, driven man. But instead she only asked, "How did she and Simon meet?"

Quinn was quiet for so long that she didn't think he was going to answer her question, but she was wrong. His answer, however, left her stunned.

"Simon bought her."

"Oh, no!" She began to tremble again.

Carefully Quinn eased her down into the chair and disappeared through the dressing room. He returned with a glass of brandy, which he held up to her lips. When she had taken several swallows and was steadier, he moved to a wing chair across from her. Stretching his legs out in front of him and sipping from the remaining brandy, he told her the story of Simon and Amanda, all of which he had not learned himself until after his mother's death.

Quinn explained that Amanda's father was a white trapper, her mother a pureblood Cherokee. She was raised in her mother's village near the Georgia-Tennessee border. Her parents died within a short time of each other when she was fifteen, and her father's brother, a miserly man named Carter Slade, came for her. He took her to his farm near Augusta, where he worked her from dawn until long after dark.

One evening, Simon appeared at the Slade farm, leading a lame horse. He asked for shelter and, for a price, Slade agreed. That night, Slade saw Simon watching his niece, and when she left the room, he asked if he wanted to buy her.

At first, Simon had laughed. It was illegal; Cherokees hadn't been sold into slavery since they had fought with the British during the Revolutionary War. But Slade insisted that as a Cherokee, Amanda would honor any agreement a member of her family made.

And so, Simon Copeland, a man who didn't believe in slavery, a man who had never owned a slave, bought Amanda Slade for five hundred dollars.

Simon never knew what Amanda felt when she learned she had been sold, but as Slade had predicted, her honor demanded that she keep the infamous agreement. And so, the next morning, she turned her back on the past and went off with the handsome stranger who now owned her.

Even then, Simon wasn't an impulsive man. He was horrified at what he had done and didn't permit himself to touch her, yet each day he grew more fascinated with her. It was Amanda who finally went to him, giving her love freely, asking for nothing.

"It was a bittersweet moment when Simon realized how much he loved her in return. He was an ambitious man who had planned to make an advantageous marriage, and Amanda had neither money nor background to recommend her. To make matters worse, even though her father was white, she considered herself Cherokee.

"Quinn, none of what you've told me explains your bitterness toward Simon. Even if he did buy her, he took your mother away from a horrible life. From what Emily told me, he was a wonderful father to you, a loving husband—"

"Oh, he was a loving husband, all right!" Quinn exclaimed bitterly. "Everyone in Cape Crosse will tell you that. And a wonderful father. If you press them, even my friends will tell you I've been an ungrateful son to have turned against him. Christ! If I've heard once about Simon taking me everywhere with him on that bay of his, I've heard it a thousand times."

"Then why?" Noelle's eyes pleaded with him to finally tell her the truth, but when she saw the pain etching itself so deeply across his features, she almost wished she had kept her peace.

"He didn't marry her, Highness," Quinn finally said. "Not until a few hours before she died. She was his slave until the end."

"He didn't marry her!" Noelle exclaimed. "What reason could he have had?"

"You should know the answer to that better than anyone. She wasn't a suitable Copeland bride. No family, no education." He stared into the depths of his glass and muttered, "Nothing but a loving heart."

Then he told her how he had overheard the brief, hushed ceremony, trying not to let himself understand what it meant but knowing, without question, that, at the age of twelve, his world had come to an end. Later, when his mother called him to her, she sensed that he had discovered the truth.

"She told me that I mustn't blame him. Said it hadn't been important to her. But I've never been able to forgive him. It was only the threat of having her die leaving me a bastard forever that finally forced him to marry her."

He stood up and walked over to the fireplace, staring down into the dying embers. "After the funeral, I ran away to the Cherokees."

"Did Simon come after you?"

Quinn nodded. "But it took him over a year to find me, and then I was so filled with hatred that he couldn't trust me in the same house with him. That's when he decided to send me to England to stay with the Peales and go to school."

A silence fell between them that Noelle finally broke. "I'm sorry, Quinn," she said simply.

Brusquely he rejected the pity in her voice. "I'm leaving at first light tomorrow for Milledgeville. Wasidan asked me to try to make the governor see reason."

"But you told me there was no hope, that the Cherokee removal to the west was inevitable."

"It's a fool's errand, Highness. But I can't say no to him."

Sleep eluded her that night, and she was still awake at dawn when she heard Quinn riding off. She threw herself from the bed and pulled on her riding habit remembering his words as she did.

"We poison each other," he had said, and he was right.

The bricks were still wet with dew as she cantered down the drive toward the road. Her thoughts turned to Simon. She sensed that he had suffered more than Quinn wanted to recognize and that he was a wiser man now. Instinctively she understood that Amanda had forgiven him even if Quinn hadn't. She wondered if Quinn was capable of forgiveness, tortured as he was by the past, torn by the two conflicting halves of his nature—the proud Cherokee and the master shipbuilder.

Simon . . . Amanda . . . Quinn . . . They had managed to snare her in the tangled web of their lives and make her part of them.

Chapter Thirty-three

After that morning, Noelle had little time to indulge in introspection, for following Emily Lester's example, her new neighbors began to arrive at the door. She soon found that between returning their calls and making frequent visits to the shipyard, she was no longer able to supervise the house and the servants by herself. As had become her habit, she turned to Dainty Jones.

" 'Spect I'd better see if I can find Nathan Davis. Used to work for Miz Burgess 'fore she died. He's the man for the job all right."

And so Nathan Davis was installed as majordomo of the household to double as Quinn's valet when he returned. A gentle man with chocolate skin and a trace of a limp in his left leg, he commanded the respect of the rest of the servants without ever lifting his voice.

Quinn's abrupt departure meant that he could no longer take her to Savannah, and for this Noelle was grateful. The intimacy of a journey together was more than she could have borne. Still, with the main body of the house nearing completion and a wardrobe that desperately needed to be supplemented with dresses more suitable to the Georgia climate, she had to make the trip. When she discovered that Copeland and Peale's own sloops made regular runs to Savannah for supplies, she announced that she was going along and invited Emily to accompany her.

The trip to Savannah helped Noelle temporarily put aside her unhappiness. With Emily companionably beside her, she bought upholstery and drapery fabrics to take back with her, as well as lightweight cambrics and muslins for her dresses. She returned to Televea to find that Quinn was back from Milledgeville, his trip as unsuccessful as he had predicted. Life progressed as usual.

Luke Baker was convicted of arson and sent to the state prison. Quinn immersed himself in his work at the shipyard. The weeks passed and Noelle's bedroom door remained firmly closed. Slowly she was discovering that the longing of her own body was the most formidable enemy she had ever faced.

Even though she had been warned, Noelle was unprepared for the first onslaught of summer. The Georgia sun burned saffron in the sky, and the air was heavy with heat. She discarded all but one of her petticoats and began wearing the new pastel muslin dresses Grace had finished. Nathan hung the beds with mosquito netting and set out lemonade and iced tea in sweating pitchers that puddled on the silver trays that held them.

Emily, whose body was now proudly swollen, laughed when Noelle complained. "Honey, you'll be looking back on this as a cool spell when August comes."

Noelle grew to appreciate Televea more than ever when she discovered how much more comfortable it was than the homes of her neighbors. Not only was it exceptionally well shaded, but it had been built on a slight rise to catch the breeze. Why was it, then, that it was becoming more and more difficult for her to fall asleep, even though her bedroom was cool? Why was it that she paced the floor each night, back and forth, until exhaustion overcame her?

One morning she was sitting in the kitchen, reading a cheerful letter from Constance and eating her second slice of fresh bread heaped with the damson plum preserves that Georgina Sinclair had brought with her when she had come by the day before.

"You gonna end up plump as Miz Sinclair if you don't watch yourself," Dainty scolded. With her sleeve, she wiped away the faint beads of perspiration that had formed on her upper lip. "First she brings you them pecan pies, then that lemon pound cake, now it's damson preserves. All outta jealousy, if you ask me. She wants you to end up like her!"

"You just don't like her because she said your hickory nut cake was heavier than hers." Noelle laughed, licking a spot of jam from her fingers.

"Go on and laugh. But you jes' watch. I'll bet my great grampa's britches that next week she'll show up with somethin' else." Drying her hands on the tea towel she kept tucked in the side of her apron, she leaned back against the sink. "Still, I guess there's no need to fret. Except for me, I never knowed anybody could eat as much food as you and still stay so thin. You ain't breedin', are you?"

"No, I'm not, Dainty Jones! And when are you going to learn that servants aren't supposed to ask such personal questions?"

"It's all part of my job," Dainty sniffed, not the slightest bit cowed by Noelle's reprimand. "Women who are breedin' need special food to strengthen their blood."

Noelle could clearly see that a lecture on the feeding of pregnant women was forthcoming, and to forestall it, she said, "Dainty, I've decided to have a dinner party. Televea is almost finished, and I think it's time we showed it off. What do you think? Can you manage it?"

Dainty pursed her lips, clearly offended by the question. "I may not be one of your fancy-dancy Frenchified cooks, but I reckon I know a thing or two about puttin' on a dinner party!"

Noelle suppressed a smile. "Fine. I'll leave it to you. Let's say two weeks from Saturday. Plan on eight couples."

Her gown was the color of the inside of a seashell shot through with silver. Somehow, it seemed just right for this special night, which was, she knew, not hers but Televea's. The weather had even been kind that day, and the breeze coming into the house was cool and fragrant from the afternoon's thundershowers.

She straightened one of the curls that teased the corners of her eyebrows and then, as the clock chimed a quarter before the hour, hesitantly went to the door of Quinn's room and knocked. Hearing nothing but silence from within, she opened the door. A lamp was burning, his evening clothes were laid neatly on the bed, but the room was empty. Their guests were scheduled to arrive at any moment, and Quinn wasn't home from the shipyard!

Furiously she stomped down the stairs into the drawing room. She had left a note on his desk last evening, reminding him he must be ready by nine o'clock. Was it too much to ask that this once he could come home before midnight? How humiliating for her to receive their first guests alone.

Just then she heard the front door slam, and she rushed out to see Quinn mounting the steps two at a time, muttering a vile oath under his breath while he yanked his neckcloth loose with one hand and unbuttoned his shirt with the other. Shaking his head, Nathan followed at a slower pace.

She shut the door and sank down into one of the newly upholstered drawing-room chairs, relieved that Quinn was home but still angry with him. To distract herself, she took inventory of the refurbished drawing room.

The pale yellow love seats and bright green carpeting reminded her of lemon sherbets resting on a bed of mint. To accent the lighter green cast of the marble in the mantelpiece, she had selected a paper for the walls with spiraling stripes of the same shade. It was a satisfying room, formal but comfortable, and cool even on the hottest of days.

Nervously her eyes traveled above the mantelpiece. Just that morning she had made the decision, but now she was beginning to have second thoughts. Perhaps on this one issue, she should have consulted him.

It was not long before the doors burst open and Quinn, resplendent in black and white evening attire, entered. His eyes found the portrait of his mother immediately and then darkened ominously as his gaze moved to his wife.

Noelle thrust up her chin defiantly. "This was her home, Quinn. She belongs here."

The sound of voices in the hallway prevented his response.

"Noelle, you found it!" Emily exclaimed as she and Julian stepped into the room with her brother and his wife following closely behind. "Edwin, look! Amanda's back."

Edwin Darcy gazed at the painting over the fireplace. "So she is. That's a portrait of Quinn's mother," he explained to his wife, Madeline. "She was a remarkable woman."

"Do you remember the time she helped us build that raft?" Julian laughed.

Quinn smiled, and Noelle saw that the tension had ebbed from his face. "My first attempt at designing a boat. We had a little trouble keeping her off the banks as I remember, but she was sturdy."

More couples arrived, and their reminiscences were cut short. Soon Nathan appeared at the door to announce dinner. The house glowed with beeswax and candlelight, and Noelle felt a surge of pride as she and Quinn led the way to the dining room and the couples took their places around the lavishly set table. She had discovered that of all their guests only Julian and Emily Lester; Emily's brother, Edwin Darcy; and Wheeler and Thea Talbot remembered Televea when Amanda had been its mistress. The rest had either not known the Copeland family well or arrived after Amanda's death.

The wives who had watched the transformation of Televea taking place described it to their husbands, and the men who were seeing it for the first time were lavish in their praises of what Noelle had done. Quinn looked about as if he, too, were seeing it all with fresh eyes, and when Noelle glanced his way, he lifted his glass and, to her discomfiture, silently toasted her.

Dainty Jones had clearly made up her mind that no one would forget her meal. There were oysters on the half shell, a salad filled with watercress and hearts of palmetto, roast suckling pig, and wild duck stuffed with apples. Biscuits and breads appeared with sweet potato soufflés, onions in cream, and baked celery laced with almonds. Each course had its own wine, and the servants saw to it that all the glasses were kept well filled.

"Steam, Quinn. That's the future. Not sail." The voice of Ralston Witt, president of Cape Crosse's only bank, rose above the other conversations at the table. "Copeland and Peale's going to fall behind if you're not careful."

"We've built several steamships in London already, and we're building another one now," Quinn said, "but the fuel for an ocean voyage takes up so much room, there's no space left for cargo. It's just not profitable yet. Besides, the engines need a lot of improvement before they'll be practical for longer runs."

Witt looked skeptical.

"It's true, Ralston," Julian said. "They're not really that reliable yet."

"Nonsense!" Witt insisted. "Steamships have been making river voyages for years."

Setting down her fork, Noelle smiled politely at her quarrelsome guest. "As I see it, steam is fine for river traffic or coastal voyages, Mr. Witt, where the boats can stop and take on fuel. But it'll be years before a steamship can make the China run competitively. When that does happen, Copeland and Peale will be ready. But until then, my husband will keep building faster sailing ships." She picked up her wineglass and sipped, not unaware of Quinn's faint look of admiration.

"My, my, Noelle!" Georgina Sinclair exclaimed. " 'Deed I had no idea you were such an authority. The rumor I heard must be true."

"What rumor?"

"Why, that you've been spending your spare time at the shipyard."

"I do try to spend one or two afternoons there every week."

"Mercy! Whatever for?"

"I like it. I think women need to take more interest in business."

"Well, whatever do you do?" asked Thea Talbot, clearly astonished. "Are you helping the clerks with their correspondence or working on the accounts?"

"Hardly." Julian laughed. "Last week she was in the shop, rolling oakum with old Tim Mahoney. The week before that she bullied Ned MacLaughlin into letting her climb into the rigging of the *Polly Shay*."

Quinn dropped his fork on his plate with a clatter that sounded to Noelle like an explosion, but which no one else seemed to have noticed.

"Oh, Noelle, you didn't!" Madeline Darcy emitted an approving tinkle of laughter. "Quinn Copeland, I do believe you've finally met a woman who's more than a match for you!"

Protected by the presence of their guests, Noelle lifted her head and bestowed a grin on him that was so full of mischief that against his will Quinn laughed.

"You may be right, Madeline. But I wouldn't put any money on it just yet."

The heat slowed down work at the shipyard, and at Quinn's request Noelle began to accept many of the invitations they received. She grew fond of the Darcys and Talbots, but it was with Emily and Julian Lester that she was the most comfortable, and the two couples spent an increasing amount of time together. Emily was now large enough to be self-conscious about appearing in public, so the couples restricted themselves to informal picnics and quiet dinners at each other's homes. They talked about books and politics, shipbuilding and roadbuilding, teased each other and laughed about unimportant things.

When they were all together, the Lesters provided a buffer between Quinn and Noelle so that for the first time they could enjoy each other without having to be perpetually on guard. Noelle learned that her husband liked horseracing and dogs, that he disliked cockfighting. Quinn grew more and more fascinated with his wife's quick intelligence and lively wit. If the Lesters noticed that their friends were often curiously formal with each other and never touched except by accident, they kept their observations to themselves.

In July, Julian and Emily's baby was born. They named her Lydia Mae and asked Quinn and Noelle to be godparents at the christening that was planned for the end of August.

Wasidan was frequently at Televea that summer, and Noelle grew to look forward to his visits. It had not taken them long to overcome the awkwardness of their first encounter, and they had since become friends. From him, Noelle learned much of the customs of the Cherokee people as well as of their present struggles. She also discovered that it was Wasidan Quinn had rescued from Luke Baker and his brother.

The Bakers and several of their cronies had seen him one day as he fished in the stream that ran near Televea. They were drunk and began taunting him. Despite the fact that he was unarmed and outnumbered, Wasidan fought them, but the man overpowered him and strung him to a tree. They were torturing him with their knives when Quinn came upon them.

The summer advanced, and the heat settled heavily over Cape Crosse. Each day Noelle pushed the limits of her strong young body—swimming in a small pond she had discovered in the woods behind the house, riding, walking for miles, hoping that exhaustion would drive away the demons that seemed to have taken possession of her at night. It had been five months since the angry night Quinn had last made love to her, and all she could think of as she lay sleepless in her bed were his strong hands on her starved flesh. She began nourishing her old hatred of him, letting it grow along with her need.

Hour after hour, her footsteps traced the perimeters of her quiet room. Sometimes she imagined she heard another set of footsteps echoing from the other side of the connecting door, but she knew only too well that it was her imagination. She had learned enough by now about Kate Malloy and her infamous establishment to be certain that all of her husband's late nights were not being spent at the shipyard.

When Quinn did not come home, she began slipping from the house to the dark stables and taking her mare out with only the moonlight to guide her through the now familiar countryside. Each time she rode, she seemed to find her way past the lane that led to Kate Malloy's.

And if he is there, who do you have to blame but yourself? she thought torturously. You've made it clear that the only way he can have you is to rape you. But Quinn is as proud as you are, and unless you torment him to it, he's not going to touch you.

She knew there was another way. She could go to him, give herself freely, but her pride would not let her. At least now she had his respect even if she had nothing else. If only, she wished, there were a way she could go to him and still keep her pride.

Chapter Thirty-four

"Lydia Mae Lester, I baptize thee in the name of the Father, and of the Son, and of the Holy Ghost."

The minister's voice echoed resonantly within the walls of the small wooden church as he made the sign of the cross on the tiny forehead of the baby nestled comfortably in Noelle's arms. Lydia Mae smiled toothlessly at her new godmother, and Noelle hugged her in return. She was a beautiful baby, and at the moment, Noelle wished without reservation that she were hers. She looked up at Quinn standing next to her and saw that his face had softened. Their eyes caught, and for a brief moment, there was a union between them.

It was then that Noelle knew what she would do.

A hot afternoon rain began to fall as they made their way back to Televea, and the inside of the closed carriage was stifling. Noelle fanned herself with her gloves and thought about what she would say as she watched little rivulets of rainwater sweat down the window beside her. They rode in silence until the carriage turned into the driveway leading to Televea.

"She's a beautiful baby, isn't she?" Noelle made her voice as casual as she could.

"Yes, she is."

"I've never seen anyone as happy as Emily and Julian."

"They've waited a long time for that child."

Noelle stared straight ahead. "Have you ever thought about having children?"

"I've thought about it."

When he said nothing more, Noelle knew this would be even more difficult than she had imagined. Surely he understood. Why did he have to make it so hard for her?

"Yes: I—I suppose most people have thought about it," she faltered.

His eyes, cold and demanding, caught her. "Highness, what are you trying to say?"

Noelle's tongue flicked out over her dry lips. "Only that— This afternoon when I was holding the baby, I—I realized I was being very unfair to you. We've been married for two years. Of course, we don't have an ordinary marriage, but still—it would be cruel of me to deny you children."

As suddenly as it had started, the rain stopped, leaving the air even heavier than before and the atmosphere in the carriage more oppressive.

"So. Once again you're prepared to do your duty."

"No! Not—not duty exactly. It's just that . . ." She tried to hide her confusion. "I think it's time we had a child."

Abruptly the carriage stopped. "You do, now." The contempt in each word was so unexpected that she recoiled.

"It—it really doesn't make any difference," she said miserably, wishing she had never started this. "Just forget—"

"No. No! Put in your order!" He grabbed her by the shoulders and pulled her toward him, beginning to shake her slowly and methodically. "Do you want a boy? A girl? Fair? Dark? Tell me what you want!"

"Stop it!" she screamed, covering her ears against his taunting.

He pulled her hands away and jerked her to within inches of his face. "I won't stud you, Highness!"

The carriage came to a halt, and with a cry of humiliation, Noelle yanked herself away from him and jumped out, stumbling as she ran toward the house.

Quinn stepped to the ground more slowly, watching her with tortured eyes as she disappeared inside. He knew he had never wanted her as much as he did at that moment, but his anger and the sheer force of his will kept him rooted to the spot. She would come to him honestly, or she would not come at all. There would be no more excuses, only her own admission that she wanted him.

Despite the heat, Noelle shut all the windows in her bedroom and pulled the draperies closed until only a thin shaft of light penetrated the dim room from one window where the draperies did not quite meet at the center. Overcome with hatred and humiliation, she could think of nothing except sealing herself away from him, from the servants, from everyone, even herself.

Her dress was damp with perspiration, torn at the hem where she had caught it when she leaped from the carriage, and she pulled it off along with her petticoats, leaving them all in a crumpled heap on the floor. Her hair came undone as she was undressing, and it clung to her damp body and curled in moist tendrils at her hairline. Clad only in pantaloons and her thinnest chemise, she threw herself on the bed and cried. The temperature in the room rose with the final force of the afternoon heat.

When she could cry no more, she rolled over onto her back and threw her forearm over her burning eyes, trying to shut out her mortification as she repeated the scene in the carriage over and over in her mind. The room gradually darkened, but evening provided no relief from the heat now trapped inside.

It was nighttime when a knock sounded at her door. Noelle lay silently. When the knocking continued, growing firmer and more insistent, she snatched a porcelain vase from the table next to her bed and hurled it at the door. The footsteps quickly retreated.

The interruption opened her wound once again, and shame and the suffocating heat of the room choked her until she could barely breathe. She lay motionless, arms at her sides, sweat trickling down between her breasts, drawing one conscious breath after another. A mosquito landed on her bare leg, but she didn't bother to brush it away even when she felt the sting of it drawing out her blood.

The door in the adjoining room opened and then shut. She heard the sound of his movements, water splashing, and, finally, the creak of the bedropes. Dragging herself from her bed, she began to pace the room, her chemise so wet that it was transparent, her hair tangled honey falling to her waist over glistening shoulders.

Six steps in one direction. Eight in the other. She was almost demented from her hunger for him, her need to have him and still keep her pride. Back and forth. One . . . two . . . three . . . four . . . One step after another.

Dear God, her desperate thoughts raged, he has driven me to the brink of insanity, poisoned me, but I must have him. I must have his fingers burning into my flesh. My hands on him, kneading muscles like steel. Touching him. Tasting him.

Propelled by a force stronger than her pride, she found the

doorknob that separated them twisting in her hands. The moonlight streamed in the open windows of his room, and the fresh air was cold against her wet flesh. He propped himself up on one elbow and watched her come toward him, the sheet that covered his bare chest slipping down to his waist.

She stood at the foot of the bed in a shaft of moonlight so he could see her clearly, so there would be no misunderstanding. Her fingers tugged at the thin blue ribbon that held the bodice of her chemise together. As it came undone in her hands she locked her eyes with his and opened the garment slowly until she had unveiled the gleaming mounds of her breasts to him. Only then did she bend over and peel the damp chemise off.

Even when she was naked, she did not move, did not try to hide from the burning eyes that branded her flesh. Instead, she reached to the back of her neck and, with both of her hands, lifted the weight of her hair high so that nothing was hidden from his gaze.

His nostrils flared, and she felt a flash of triumph. Let him reject me now, her hatred cried.

With her hands still holding up her hair, she walked toward him with the slow seductiveness of Eve and then set one knee up on the side of the bed. "I want you," she said huskily.

With a dark moan, he reached out toward her, but she evaded him. Now it would be on her terms. Slowly she leaned across his chest, lowering herself until her burning nipples were pressed against his cool flesh. Thrusting her fingers roughly into his thick black hair, she clamped his mouth to hers, plunging her tongue between his teeth.

With only her instincts to guide her, she made love to him so agonizingly, so expertly, that when she was done, he could only crush her to him, unable to bear the thought of having her steal away from his side.

That night, she dreamed that her bed was on the side of a vast, rocky hill where low-flying curlews swooped toward her, their wings batting at her face, flying closer and closer until, one by one, they tangled themselves in the wild mass of her hair. She jerked awake to find Quinn's arm pinning her down as he slept, his fingers painfully entwined in the strands of her hair.

With a slow sigh, Noelle released the tension of her nightmare. As her breath warmed his cheek Quinn stirred. His hand released its grip on her hair and slid down her body, cupping itself around one of her breasts. She felt him grow rigid against her leg, and then she was conscious of little else as she gave herself up to the sensations he was arousing.

It was much later when Noelle pulled herself from bed. She smelled of sweat and sex, and all she could think of was getting away from the piercing eyes that watched her so intently and sinking into the tub she had heard Grace filling in the next room.

As if he were reading her thoughts, he climbed out beside her and tilted her chin up. "Ever take a bath with a man before?"

"I certainly have not," she flared, presenting a picture of offended dignity so incongruous with her wild abandonment in bed that Quinn laughed and scooped her into his arms.

"We'll have to do something about that."

She told him his behavior was odious and demanded that he put her down that very instant, but he ignored her half-hearted struggles and lowered them both into the water.

It was a big tub, but it hadn't been designed to hold two people, especially when one of them was as large as Quinn. He draped a dripping calf over the side and watched with amusement as, avoiding his eyes, she lathered a washcloth and began efficiently scrubbing herself.

"You're missing the point, Highness." He grinned, taking the soapy cloth from her and setting it aside. He lathered his own hands and washed her that way, lingering so long on the most sensitive parts of her body that, with a gasp, she finally grabbed the soap away and began to wash him.

She studied his body with open fascination as she slid her hands over him—the rippling muscles, the faint white marks along each side of his spine where his skin had stretched taut when he had grown too quickly as a boy, a jagged scar on his calf.

Not long after they had finished washing each other, they found themselves on Noelle's bed, their bodies leaving a wet imprint on her pale blue bedspread as they satisfied each other in a fashion as old as time.

It was nearly noon when Quinn propped himself up on one elbow and gazed down at her.

"Are you sure the shipyard won't fall apart without you?" she teased.

But he didn't smile. With a question in her eyes, she reached up toward his cheek. Gently he stopped her hand. "Which way is it going to be, Highness?"

"What do you mean?"

"I mean that from now on, you'll either be in my bed every night as my wife, or you'll stay the hell away from me. You can't have it both ways anymore."

"I'll think about it," she snapped, even though she knew what her answer would be.

"Do that. You have until tonight."

Chafing at his arrogance, she watched him get out of bed and walk to the door that connected the two rooms. "Quinn."

He turned.

"If I do decide to share your bed, don't think anything else has changed between us!" It was her pride speaking, and she immediately regretted her words.

"That's fine with me, Highness. We both know how we feel about each other. Nothing that happens between us in bed, no matter how good, is likely to change that."

His words proved to be too prophetic. At night, they were like two bodies with one mind, joining together with total abandon —nothing held back, nothing feared. But during the day, the hostilities between them escalated. The memories of past betrayals were too fresh.

Although neither would admit it, both were afraid of the terrible attraction that drew them together. They were increasingly cruel to each other, sometimes even trading caustic jibes in the presence of the servants. As the summer ended, their lovemaking grew more violent. It was as if it were a sickness that had spread out of control, advancing beyond their bodies to devour their minds.

Chapter Thirty-five

In September, the activity at the shipyard returned to normal, and Noelle began spending more time there, although she never searched out her husband, and for his part, he ignored her presence. One day she stepped into Quinn's office to shed the short jacket she had worn over her riding skirt, for the day had grown warm. Tossing it on a chair, she noticed a new wooden half model sitting on his desk. She picked it up and, as she ran her fingers along the smooth line of the hull, she felt a spark of excitement. The shape was sleeker than anything she had ever seen, its bow leaner and its breadth much further back than was customary. She knew that a half model was the first step toward building a ship. If Quinn had made a model, he must be getting ready to start.

"What the hell are you doing in here! Put that down!"

She jumped and the model slipped from her hand and fell to the floor, knocking out the pins that held it together and sending the wooden layers scattering. It was a simple matter to reassemble it, but Quinn clenched his fist in anger, his eyes turning the color of gun metal. He hated the constriction he felt in his guts whenever he came upon her unexpectedly. Why the hell couldn't she stay home where she belonged—out of his way, out of his life, out of everything except his bed!

"*God damn it!* Look what you've done! You have no right to be in here!"

"I have every right to be in here, and don't you forget it," she stormed, so hurt by his attitude that she paid little heed to what she was saying even though she realized he was dangerously angry. "I may not own as much of this company as you do, but I own part of it, and I want to know why you didn't tell me you were getting ready to build this ship!"

Her attack was so audacious that for a moment he was

speechless. Finally he choked, "Are you seriously suggesting that I should be accountable to you!"

Noelle saw she had cornered herself and looked for a graceful way out. "I—I didn't say you were accountable, but I do think you should have kept me informed, especially about something as important as this ship."

"Why, you presumptuous little vixen! I'll keep you informed all right!"

He sent her tumbling back into a chair and then, hovering over her, set his foot up on the seat beside her, heedless of the muddy print it was leaving on her skirt. "In the next three years I'm going to build the fastest sailing ship the China Seas have ever seen, and no one is going to stop me. Now, is there anything else you want to know?"

"When do you start building her?"

Quinn felt a glimmer of reluctant admiration at her refusal to back down. "We begin lofting the plans this month." He took his foot off the chair and jerked his head toward the door. "Now, if that's all, I suggest you get yourself home, where you belong."

Angrily Noelle shot up from the chair. "Home and into bed, isn't that what you mean?"

"You said it, not me. But then, I guess you're the best judge of your own character."

"You bastard!" She drew back her arm to slap him, but this time he saw the blow coming and grabbed her wrist, holding it firmly between them.

"By God, if you hit me again, I'll beat you within an inch of your life! I mean it, Noelle. Don't push me any further!"

When he let her go, she stomped from the room and then deliberately spent an hour watching the men sheathe the hull of a sloop with copper before she permitted herself to leave.

That night, their lovemaking was more frenzied than ever as Quinn brought her to one shattering climax after another, but when it was over and they had each moved to separate sides of the bed, she felt hollow and unfulfilled. She was so tired of fighting him! Would it always be this way between them? Their rage disguised as pleasure; their lovemaking full of anger because both of them hated the weakness that was driving them together. A tear slid soundlessly from the corner of her eyes onto the pillow.

"Would you like to hear about the ship, Highness?" Quinn's

voice was so low that for a moment Noelle thought she was imagining it.

"If you'd like to tell me," she said softly.

"I'm going to call her an American clipper."

"Clipper. It's a good word. I like it."

"She'll be big—seven hundred and fifty tons—and full rigged. There'll be no gilt on her, no ornament, nothing to distract from that long, thin hull."

He spoke on into the night of his plans, his hopes, and even his worry that Wolf Brandt, the man who had commissioned her, might not be able to find a crew when she was finally ready to go to sea. Sailors, he told her, were deeply superstitious, and a ship so radically different in design from any they had ever seen would invoke their most primitive fears.

"Does Mr. Brandt understand this?" she asked.

"Yes. But when you meet him, you'll see that he's a man who likes to take risks. If he can man her, he knows she'll make him a fortune."

"Quinn?"

"Hmm?"

"If you don't want me at the shipyard anymore, I won't come."

Incredibly he slid his arm under her and gently drew her to his shoulder. "The men like having you there. They think you bring us good luck."

"And what about you?"

It might have been his chin that brushed across the top of her head, but suddenly, Noelle wanted to believe that it was his lips.

"Go to sleep, Highness."

His voice was so gentle that her heart constricted and, in that instant, Noelle knew that she loved him. The unexpectedness of it staggered her. She squeezed her eyes shut and, willing her body to lie still within the strong circle of his arms, tried to tell herself it was an illusion, but the truth was written so clearly inside her that she couldn't deny it. She loved him, had loved him for a long time.

When did it happen? Was it as long ago as that storm-ridden night in Yorkshire when he had pulled her from Ravensdale Tarn and then made love to her, or since they had come to Televea? Had it happened in the passion of their lovemaking or in quieter moments as he had spoken of his Indian heritage or described his ships?

The awful irony of it was not lost on her. She had committed the same folly as dozens of other women. She had fallen in love with Quinn Copeland. But she was much more vulnerable than any of them, because she was bound to him in the eyes of both man and God.

The next evening, their carriage took them to the home of Wolf Brandt. He had issued a dinner invitation only that morning, and Quinn had accepted. As the carriage neared the northern edge of Cape Crosse, Noelle tried to calm herself by recalling what Quinn had told her about the man, but all she could remember was that he was a bachelor. She seemed to remember Quinn telling her Brandt was renting a house that Edwin Darcy owned, but she wasn't certain. Everything had been so muddled for her since last night that nothing seemed to make sense any longer. To add to her confusion, Quinn had been different with her since the moment, not a half hour ago, when he had come up behind her in the hallway as she was making a final check on her appearance in the mirror.

"Don't touch anything, Highness. You're perfect."

She had dressed with special care in a lace-trimmed gown the color of old gold doubloons. It was a romantic dress with something about it that conjured up Spanish ships and plundered treasure. The two of them together, she in her gilded dress and Quinn with his buccaneer's swarthy good looks, seemed as though they belonged in an earlier time.

Now, as Quinn helped her down from the carriage, his hand held hers a fraction of a second longer than necessary. She looked up into his eyes and wondered how she could have ever thought them cold. There was something there he had never before permitted her to see. Was it tenderness? Affection? Had he too tired of the war between them, of the verbal skirmishes, the bed that was too often only another battlefield? Noelle's lips curved tentatively and Quinn smiled in return, his face looking younger than she had ever seen it, almost boyish.

Whatever might have happened between them was cut off by the sound of the front door opening as Wolf Brandt himself stepped out to greet his guests. As soon as Noelle saw him, she was certain she had met him before. Only a few inches taller than she, he was an attractive man in his late thirties with fair hair and gray eyes. None of his features was extraordinary, but there was an elegance about his manner that stirred her memory.

"Quinn, welcome! And Mrs. Copeland. I'm so glad that you could come."

While he ushered them into the house, Noelle tried to recall when she had last heard that faint Germanic accent. There was something so familiar about the way he turned his *w*'s to *v*'s, his *th* to *z*.

After the butler took her wrap, Brandt surveyed Noelle with such open appreciation that she was amused. Wolf Brandt was obviously an accomplished flirt.

"Mrs. Copeland, you are even more enchanting than I have remembered."

"So we have met before. I thought as much."

"But of course. And you don't remember." He flicked his palms open and closed in an elegantly despondent gesture. "You see, Quinn, how sad life can be. Unlike you, I am one of those unfortunate men whom beautiful women quickly forget."

Quinn gave a snort of amusement, and Noelle smiled. "Somehow I doubt that."

"I will jar your memory. We were introduced at an unpleasantly overcrowded ball in London. The Atterburys', I believe."

"Of course," Noelle lied. "How could I have forgotten, Mr. Brandt."

"You will call me Wolf. It is short for Wolfgang, you know. Hideous name! Only my sister is permitted to call me that. Come, let us go into the drawing room. She is waiting for us."

Noelle's attention was caught by a pair of exceptionally fine Sèvres vases sitting on a table, and so she did not see Quinn's thunderstruck expression or the apologetic shrug Wolf Brandt gave him. She did, however, notice that just before her host reached out his well-manicured hand to open the drawing-room door, he swept her with a faintly pitying gaze.

Like a beautiful, deadly spider, the Baroness Anna von Furst sat in the exact center of a white satin sofa. She was a study in black and white. The black crepe gown that molded to her body was dramatically slashed to reveal one alabaster shoulder and the luscious top of a single white breast. Her hair was pulled back from her face in shining raven's wings, her eyes and lashes so sooty, they looked as if they would leave stains on her white skin. She wore no jewelry, no feather or flower. Only her lips, red as fresh blood, moist and predatory, gave color to her ensemble.

"And so, Wolfgang, you finally bring our guests to me. I have been waiting."

In the face of Quinn's betrayal, Noelle could not move. Just as she had discovered her love for him ánd deluded herself into believing that things could be different between them, he had brought his mistress to Cape Crosse to flaunt before her!

She was dimly conscious that he was walking toward Anna, but since his back was toward her, she couldn't see the angry white line that traced the edge of his lips as he took her hand, nor did she hear the frost in his greeting.

With a gentle yet insistent pressure on her arm, Wolf Brandt propelled her into the room. The baroness's eyes flicked over Noelle lazily, and then in a manner neither hostile nor friendly, she said, "What a pretty child you are. I had forgotten."

At the subtle barb, anger flooded through Noelle, blurring the edges of her pain. "But I have not forgotten you, Baroness," she said. "You don't look as well as you did in London. I can see that the loss of your husband has weighed heavily on you."

Noelle caught the slight crinkling at the corner of Quinn's eyes, and it fueled her fury. So he found it amusing to see two women sparring over him! How amused would he be when he saw she didn't care?

The butler appeared at the door to announce dinner, and Anna rose quickly and slipped her arm through Quinn's. With a brilliant smile, Noelle turned to Brandt.

"Wolf, you must tell me how you like Cape Crosse. Do you find it frightfully dull after London?"

His gray eyes raked her appreciatively. "No longer, my dear Mrs. Copeland. No longer."

Unlike Quinn, Wolf Brandt was a man who was content with himself. He was wealthy, handsome, and had no hidden devils tormenting him. He observed the world through a slightly jaundiced, but never bitter, eye, amused at the follies of others, but somewhat detached from them. Men sometimes confused Brandt's fastidious ways with effeminacy, but they were wrong. He was a man who liked beautiful things and liked them in their proper places, but he was also an accomplished lover who derived as much pleasure from bringing a woman to fulfillment as he did from his own release.

It never occurred to women to doubt his masculinity. They knew that he was that priceless rarity, a virile male who genuinely loved women and, more important, who understood them. Brandt recognized what escaped so many other men, that a woman's emotions were her strength, not her weakness, and it never occurred to him to try to reason away her feelings. It no longer surprised him, however, when he saw other men make this mistake, for he had long ago accepted the fact that most men did not understand women as he did.

As the beautiful Mrs. Copeland held out her wineglass to him to be filled for a third time, he knew that Copeland certainly did not understand his wife; nor, it occurred to him, did she understand her husband. He steadied her trembling hand with his own as he poured her wine, not missing the dark scowl that came over her husband's face. The situation intrigued him. There was a magnetism between them that was so palpable, the air was heavy with it, yet they were letting his sister's scheme drive them apart.

Quinn Copeland was foolish, Brandt decided. All he needed to do was take his beautiful wife in his arms and tell her that Anna no longer meant anything to him. But this he would not do. He was a proud man who would see his own life crumble around him before he would bend that pride. And the exciting, tawny-haired woman who had been flirting so outrageously with him ever since dinner had started was much the same. It was a volatile combination of personalities running out of control, and if one of them did not bend, the collision could be tragic.

Brandt twisted the stem of his glass in his fingers, considering his own place in all of this. If Copeland decided to treasure this delicious creature as he should, he vowed he would leave them alone despite the fact that she intrigued him more than any woman had in years. But if the shipbuilder were foolish enough to continue making her unhappy—well, then he, Brandt, would be waiting close by.

As Anna whispered a laughing comment to Quinn, Noelle leaned forward and offered a tantalizing glimpse of her breasts to her handsome dinner companion. She was rewarded by the sight of her husband's face tightening in anger.

"This wine is excellent, Wolf." She smiled provocatively over the silver rim of her glass. "Did you bring it with you?"

"But of course. I always travel with my own stock. This particular vintage is from my vineyard near Rheims."

"I had no idea your business interests were so diversified."

"The vineyard is my pleasure, not my business. A man should never confuse the two."

Speaking easily and requiring nothing from her in the way of response, he described the beauty of the land and the small château that graced the property. She gazed at him intently, nodding her head in the proper places but concentrating only on the hushed conversation and intimate laughter coming from the other side of the table.

Wolf was saddened by the triumph that flushed his sister's lovely face as Quinn slipped his arm across the back of her chair. His darling, magnificent Anna with her raven hair and alabaster skin. Wise about everything except this one man. Victory was not going to be as easy as she thought. The shipbuilder loved his wife even if he would not admit it to himself. Still, that was undoubtedly a point in Anna's favor. This complex man would not succumb to love easily.

"Ladies, perhaps you will excuse Quinn and myself. We have a small bit of business to discuss, then we will join you in the drawing room."

There was only the briefest hesitation before the beautiful Mrs. Copeland rose gracefully from the table and glided from the room, leaving his sister in her wake. Wolf smiled to himself, wishing he could be an observer of what was to come. It would be most interesting to see how they would deal with each other.

In the drawing room, Anna wandered over to the corner table, where she picked up a piece of jagged white coral and idly turned it over in her hands. "You're really quite charming, you know," she said.

"I beg your pardon."

"I have been studying you. You're lovely. But, of course, Quinn has always been surrounded by beautiful women." Anna's scarlet lips curved in a sly smile. "Now he is quite angry with me for having shown myself openly to you despite his orders. But he knows I'm not a woman to be kept locked in the attic." With a touch as light as the thread of a spider's web, she placed her fingertips on Noelle's arm. "In the end, it will be easier for both of us because we will not have to pretend."

Noelle could feel her heart breaking, but she clung to her dignity. "You will do well to stay out of my way, Baroness. I do not have the advantage of generations of impeccable breeding, and my inferior blood sometimes makes me behave rashly. Now, if you will excuse me, I feel the need for some fresh air." With her head held high, she swept from the room.

Anna drew a deep breath. For an instant, she looked older than her thirty-two years, but at the sound of footsteps approaching the door, she sank down on the sofa and languidly draped one hand over the arm.

"Where is my wife?"

She smiled lazily. "Where is Wolfgang?"

"Don't assume everyone has your talent for intrigue, Anna."

"What an ugly scowl, *liebchen*. You must stop it at once, or you will frighten me."

The grim line of Quinn's mouth relaxed. He was fond of Anna, and despite her teasing manner, he knew she was suffering. "This time Wolf is innocent. I just left him alone in the dining room, looking over some papers he has to sign."

"Too bad." Anna pouted. "It would have made things so much easier." She stood and walked toward him, arching an amused ebony brow. "Who knows? It may still all work out."

The line of his mouth was firm, but not unkind. "Don't do this to yourself, Anna. Everything is over between us. We agreed to that in London."

She pressed herself to him, the hardness of his body against hers making her voice husky with desire. "I never agreed to anything, *liebchen*. I have not yet tired of you."

Gently he skimmed the raven softness of her hair with his hand. "I have enough complications in my life without adding another. Accept the fact that we can never be together again."

"Never?" she murmured, tracing her fingers upward along the lapels of his jacket and then sliding them along his neck into the black hair that curled over the back of his collar. "Perhaps you are being too hasty." She pulled his head toward her parted lips and brought his mouth hard against hers.

The kiss was pleasant, and Quinn responded to it, but too soon he realized that Anna's ripe body was not stirring him as it once had. With something akin to anger, he caught her in a closer embrace and drove his tongue into the moist cavern of her mouth.

Noelle watched from the open doorway, wanting to tear herself away but unable to move. She grabbed the door frame for support.

"My beautiful swan, you do not need to see this." Coming up from behind her, Wolf Brandt slid an arm around her and drew her toward him.

Quinn brought up his head just in time to see his wife disappear in Brandt's arms. Furiously he disengaged himself from Anna and stalked toward the door.

"*Bitte*, Quinn. Please wait." The languid air was gone as Anna ran after him and clutched at his arm. "Where are you going?"

"Where do you think?"

"You are not a man to grovel before a woman," she exclaimed. "What will you do? Tell her you did not enjoy kissing me? She will know that's a lie!"

"Damn it, Anna, shut up!" He began to pull away from her, but she threw her body in front of him.

"Leave her to my brother, Quinn. You saw at dinner how he fascinated her. It is like that sometimes. A thunderbolt! A woman cannot always help it when her heart strays. Don't make a fool of yourself!"

Refusing to listen to any more, he pushed her aside and darted from the room only to find the hallway empty. By the time he thought to look outside, it was too late; a carriage was already pulling away from the house.

Brandt quietly stepped from the deep shadows of the porch. "I had my driver take her home."

"You had no right."

"And you, my old friend, had no right to humiliate her as you did. Do you not even care how she feels?"

"This is none of your business, Brandt," Quinn snarled.

"There you are wrong. We have known each other for a long time, and, while we have never been intimates, we have always respected each other. Is that not true?"

"You have one minute. Get to the point."

"Proud and impatient." Brandt smiled. "Excellent qualities in a businessman, but not so good in a husband, yes?"

"Like I said before. This is none of your business."

"But I must have my say, because I am now involved."

"How do you figure that?"

"*Ach!* You Americans! It is obvious, is it not? I find myself attracted to your wife. She is the most desirable woman I have met in a long time, and she deserves to be cherished." The amusement faded from his gray eyes. "I give you fair warning, Copeland. Mend your ways or I shall do my best to take her from you."

Quinn's voice was flat and unemotional. "I'll kill you if you try."

"Any other man, yes. But not me, I think, because I have warned you. You are a fair man, and you'll know that you have only yourself to blame if you lose her."

"Your time's up, Brandt."

Without another word, Quinn strode to his carriage, rousing the napping coachman with a none too gentle kick before he pushed him to the side and grabbed the reins himself. Gravel sprayed from the wheels as the carriage tore off down the drive.

Quinn was halfway to Televea before he changed his mind and turned the horses toward Kate Malloy's, where he got quietly and thoroughly drunk. When he got home, he found his own bed empty and the door that connected their rooms firmly locked against him.

Grimly he pulled back his foot, ready to break it down, but then he stopped himself. What was the use? She had seen him kissing Anna, and he was damned if he owed her any explanations. She wasn't going to lead him around on a leash like a trained dog! It was time she understood that he didn't need her. God damn it, he didn't need anyone!

Chapter Thirty-six

Wolf Brandt and Anna von Furst were quickly accepted by Cape Crosse society. The women of the community were delighted to have a baroness in their midst, even one as aloof as Anna, but they barely knew what to make of her handsome brother, who kissed their hands so elegantly and smiled at them in a way that sent blood rushing to their cheeks.

Even Emily Lester was not unaffected. One November afternoon, she laughingly confided to Noelle, "You know how I love Julian, but I declare, that Mr. Brandt gives me naughty thoughts. The same ones, as a matter of fact, that I had about Quinn when I was sixteen!"

Noelle laughed with her but then quickly changed the subject, for she didn't want to discuss either her husband or Wolf Brandt with Emily. Since the disastrous evening with Brandt and Anna, she and Quinn had barely seen each other. At the few social functions they could not avoid attending, the strain between them was almost intolerable. Riding in a closed carriage at his side, walking into a room on his arm, sitting across the dinner table from him, all of these were difficult enough, but even worse were those moments when something happened to amuse them both, and they would catch each other's eyes in an instant of total communication only to remember what was between them and quickly turn away.

Noelle decided that she could no longer remain in Cape Crosse, but having made her decision, she did no more.

November turned into December. It seemed that wherever they went, they met Wolf and Anna. Noelle was forced to admit that there was no way she could fault Anna's behavior in public. She treated Noelle politely and was as formal with Quinn as she was with the other men in the community. No one suspected that they were more than acquaintances. As for Wolf Brandt, Noelle was growing to depend on him more each day.

They came across each other so frequently when she was riding Chestnut Lady that they no longer bothered pretending the meetings were accidental. She felt easy with him. He made no demands on her, never pressed her for more than she was willing to give, never touched her except to take her hand when they met. When she was with him, she felt the sadness lift from her and, along with it, the sense of lethargy that seemed to have claimed her. Something of it must have shown in her face, because when they would meet at the shipyard, she could feel Quinn's eyes boring into her, watching the two of them, the warning clear in his cold, probing gaze. More than anything, Noelle wanted to fall in love with Brandt. Then, she knew, Quinn would have finally lost his hold on her.

It didn't happen. Instead, she came to the painful realization that her love for Quinn had more than one easy dimension. She loved the body of him, the taste and feel and sex of him. But those were all transient and, given time and distance, would surely fade. It was the deeper facet of her love for him that she knew would not be given up so easily, for she had come to love the man he could be if he were only free of the bitterness that shackled him, the bitterness that turned honest laughter into mockery, pride into arrogance, and anger into contempt.

January came and with it, Wheeler and Thea Talbot's ball. As Noelle left the bedroom where the women were straightening their gowns and touching up their hair, she heard a soft giggle. Peering around the corner to investigate, she saw a small towhead pressed against the far edge of the railing that circled the stairwell. It was a good hiding place. The corner was dark, and there was a skirted table that concealed her from the view of the well-dressed guests who passed in the hallway below. She spun around as she heard the rustling gown behind her.

"You needn't look so guilty," Noelle whispered. "I won't tell on you."

Eight-year-old Elizabeth Talbot regarded her shyly. "I just couldn't go to bed until I'd seen everybody."

"No, of course you couldn't," Noelle solemnly agreed.

"You look like a princess, Mrs. Copeland."

"Thank you." She smiled, noting with some amusement that "princess" was not the easiest word to manage for a little girl who had two front teeth missing.

"I never saw a dress with feathers on it. They look like they're tickling your chest."

"They are, Elizabeth," Noelle said, laughing, for the fine snowy plumes were indeed pleasantly tickling her shoulders and the swelling tops of her breasts. She pulled up a small wooden stool and sat chatting quietly and looking out over the hallway below with the child.

"There's Mr. Copeland!" Elizabeth exclaimed as the butler admitted Quinn.

The excitement in her voice told Noelle that the little girl had a childish crush on her husband. It seemed that youth offered no immunity to his fascination.

"Why didn't he come with you?"

"He had to work late, so I traveled with Mr. and Mrs. Darcy."

"I think Mr. Copeland is the handsomest man in Cape Crosse. Do you think he is?"

"Well, I—yes, I suppose he is."

They sat silently and watched the brightly colored pattern of people pass beneath them, their thoughts traveling in remarkably similar directions. As the orchestra began to play Elizabeth's small, bare feet tapped out the rhythm on the carpet. Finally, unable to resist the music, she stood and spun around, her nightdress billowing out to reveal thin, pale calves.

"When I grow up, I want to marry someone just like Mr. Copeland and go to a ball and wear a white dress with pretty white feathers on it and have silver slippers on my feet and dance and drink champagne and—"

"What's this? I thought all of the beautiful women were downstairs."

Mortified, Elizabeth stopped where she was. Blushing to the roots of her pale hair, she dropped Quinn an awkward curtsy.

Quickly Noelle came to the child's rescue. "Doesn't Elizabeth move gracefully? It's a shame children aren't permitted in the ballroom."

"Perhaps we'll just have to move the ballroom up here. May I have the pleasure of this dance?"

Elizabeth's eyes flew to Noelle. She smiled her encouragement.

Quinn bowed solemnly and then took Elizabeth in his arms. She was such a tiny child and he so large that Noelle should have been amused, but she wasn't. Instead, she felt tears gathering behind her lids at the courtesy and gentleness with which he led the young girl in the long white nightgown through the steps of the dance. If only this side of him didn't exist. If only she could go back to the days when she had simply hated him. Loving him was so much more painful.

After Quinn had gone back downstairs, Noelle found she was reluctant to leave her quiet refuge with Elizabeth. She was still there when Wolf and Anna arrived. The butler removed the crimson velvet cape that covered Anna's matching gown. Noelle watched as the baroness's jet eyes scanned the gathering until they alighted on Quinn, standing just inside the arched entryway to the ballroom. She turned to greet the Talbots, and then began to make her way casually through the crowd, occasionally stopping to greet an acquaintance or admire a gown. Only Noelle could see that she was forging a determined path toward Quinn.

Wolf, too, was searching the crowd. Noelle bid an affectionate good-bye to Elizabeth and made her way down the stairs. He was waiting for her at the bottom.

"Tonight you look more than ever like my beautiful swan."

He swept her into the ballroom and out onto the polished floor. She saw Quinn drain the contents of the glass he held and then pull Anna into his arms.

"My friend Quinn is not happy to see his wife so much in my company."

"I don't care!"

"*Ach!* Don't lie to me, my sweet. You care very much. Unfortunately so do I."

When the dance was over, Wolf fetched her a glass of champagne. She had barely tasted it before Julian claimed her, and from that point on, the evening whirled around her in flashes of light and color. The atmosphere in the ballroom grew heavy with the hot pack of bodies, but she would not let herself stop moving. She laughed and danced with every man she knew except her husband. Wolf led her out for a waltz and held her much closer than he should, but she was past caring, because Quinn was once again dancing with Anna.

Midnight came, and he still had not approached her. Her anger grew at his rudeness. If they did not dance together at least once, everyone in Cape Crosse would know by morning that something was wrong between them.

He finally came to her just as Wolf was ready to escort her, for the third time, onto the floor.

"I'll dance with my wife now, Brandt."

"But of course, my friend."

It was the most miserable dance of Noelle's life. He held her as far from him as he could and did not say a word. When it was over, she fled from his side and ran up the stairs and down the hallway, dashing blindly into an empty bedroom.

She stood in the dark for some time, trying to steady herself. Somehow she was not surprised when Wolf entered the room and silently walked over to her.

"My poor darling. You are having a bad time of it, and I am afraid I am only going to make it worse." Gently he tilted up her chin and kissed her.

Although his kiss ignited no fires within her, it felt good to be in his arms, and so she made no protest when his lips traveled down the column of her neck, nor when his hand found her breast. What a far way I have come, she thought, from the young girl who was sickened by the mere thought of a man's touch to the woman standing here passively allowing someone I care for, but don't love, to caress me.

She sensed him in the room an instant before he jerked Wolf away from her. There was the sound of fist smashing into bone, and then Wolf lay still. Noelle let out a cry of rage mixed with fear and tried to run to him, but Quinn caught her by the arm.

"Enough! Your whoring is done for tonight!"

Driven by the image of Brandt's hand on her breast, he pulled her from the room and dragged her down the back steps of the house. The carriages were clustered around the stable while their drivers, trading tales and spitting tobacco, huddled together against the windy night. As soon as she noticed the men, Noelle stopped struggling and forced herself to walk quietly at Quinn's side. Her attempt at dignity crumbled, however, when she saw that Quinn had not traveled to the Talbot home in a carriage, but had ridden Pathkiller.

Whipping an arm around her waist, he mounted the stallion, pulling Noelle up with him. Before the startled eyes of the coachmen, he spun the animal out and carried his wife off as if she were plunder captured in an outlaw raid. They tore into the night, the chill wind loosening her hair and cutting through the thin white silk of her gown. When they reached Televea, Quinn rode directly to the darkened stables and dismounted, drawing her down with him.

"Let me go!" she cried, struggling against the arm that was still clamped like a band of steel around her waist.

"Not just yet!"

With a mighty thrust, he pushed her inside the stable, sending her sprawling down into a pile of straw. He banged the door shut and lit a lantern that hung on a hook. It swung about, sending crazy shadows writhing across the walls and bringing back to Noelle the memory of the nightmare encounter in the forest clearing when he had unmasked her.

She crouched in the straw, trying to force her mind to think clearly while Quinn put Pathkiller in a stall. If she tried to run away, he would catch her, and it would only go harder. Somehow she must reason with him; she must reach the part of him that was just and compassionate.

Her brave hopes were shattered, and horror took their place when she lifted her eyes and saw him standing in the shadows across the stable from her. His immaculate evening dress was barely rumpled by the breakneck ride; the white ruffles on the front of his shirt looked as fresh as they had when he'd entered the Talbots' front door. Only the savage rage that now contorted his features was different. That, and the ugly black whip that dangled in a loose coil from his corded hands. . . .

She froze, her terrified eyes glued to the monstrous weapon. At first he was as still as she, and then he took a step toward her.

"My God, Quinn!" she cried, her fear making the words ragged distortions of sound. "Have you lost your mind?" When he made no answer, she scrambled desperately to her feet.

He advanced on her with deadly purpose. She began to back away, and then, horrified, she watched him uncoil the lash until he held only the stout leather butt clenched in his fist.

"I'm within my rights as your husband."

A scream tore from her throat.

"If you don't want the servants to witness this, I suggest you keep your screams to yourself. Or maybe I'll gag you."

"You can't do this," she sobbed, unable to pull her eyes away from the monstrous lash snaking across the floor at his feet as he moved closer to her. "Nothing happened tonight. Nothing ever happened. I swear it. I love you, Quinn!" The admission was torn from her with all the agony of a stillbirth. "I love you!"

With a howl of rage, he lifted his arm and snapped his wrist.

He had never intended to hit her. It was merely by accident that he even held the whip in his hand, for in his preoccupation with his own despair, he had absentmindedly picked it up from the floor of the stall where one of the stable boys had carelessly tossed it. But when he had seen the fear in her eyes and realized that she actually believed him capable of using the vile weapon on her, he had been powerless to toss it aside. And now in his rage at hearing her swear her love for him when he knew she was only lying to save herself, he struck out.

The cruel tip of the lash sliced through the silk of her gown, splitting the side from the hip down and exposing one slim leg. It did not touch her flesh, but that made no difference to him. Filled with self-loathing, he flung the hateful weapon across the stable.

With a strangled scream, Noelle threw herself after it. "I'll kill you for this!"

The butt was warm from his hand when she caught it up. She jerked her arm back and swung it through the air. The lash caught the corner of his jaw, leaving a thin trail of blood behind. Before she could draw it back again, he snared it in his fist and yanked it from her hand. Lost to reason, she flew at him, going for his eyes with her nails, barely noticing when he restrained her hands.

"You hypocrite!" she screamed. "I was never unfaithful! Not like you! How many women have there been since we were married? Spreading their legs so you could rut between them!"

"That's enough!" he roared. "You even talk like a whore!" Grabbing her by the shoulders, he flung her back into the straw. "Now you'll play the whore for me!"

With a cry that was filled as much with despair as it was with rage, he yanked up her skirt and fell on her. His fingers scraped roughly over the soft skin of her belly as he tore off her dainty undergarments. Instead of cowering, she met his savagery with her own, punishing him as he was punishing her.

When it was over, she turned on her side in the straw, not even bothering to push down her skirt and cover herself. It was he who wrapped her in his coat and carried her to her bedroom. He who gently bathed the inside of her thighs. At the same time he cleansed her, he engraved a picture in his mind that he knew he would carry to his grave.

When he saw that she was finally asleep, he sat down at her small desk. For some time the only sound in the room was the scratch of a pen moving across paper. When he was done, he read what he had written.

My dear Noelle,

I said we were poisoning each other and tonight has proved the ugly truth of those words. What has happened has convinced me that we can't remain together any longer. I will arrange for your passage back to England and see that you're provided for.

I'm not asking your forgiveness, because I know you won't be able to give it. The only way I can begin to make amends is to give you the freedom you've always wanted, and so I will contact my attorney about a divorce. Now that we're in America, it should not be difficult. You'll soon be free to marry Brandt if you wish. He's a good man and will take better care of you than I have.

I received a message from Wasidan today and must go to Washington. I won't see you again.

Quinn

He folded the letter in half and leaned it on the mantelpiece. Then he kissed her closed lids in farewell and left the room.

PART FIVE

Noelle

Chapter Thirty-seven

"Noelle, forgive me for calling so early in the morning. I had to see you."

She felt a stab of guilt as she walked into the drawing room. The last time she had seen Wolf, he was lying unconscious on the floor. But not until minutes ago, when Grace had told her he was downstairs, had she spared him a moment's thought.

He took a step toward her, and she saw the swollen purple bruise. "Oh, Wolf, your jaw!"

"It is nothing. You are the one I am concerned about. Are you all right?"

She drew a tremulous breath. "No, I—I'm afraid I'm not." Her hand shook as she held out Quinn's letter. "Read this."

Wolf took it from her and carried it over to the window. He skimmed the page and then went back to the beginning and read it through again, more carefully. When he was done, he looked at Noelle, standing like a marble statue next to the fireplace, and saw how pale she was, how painfully fragile in her misery.

Walking over to her, he handed back the letter. "Is the thought of never seeing him again so horrible to you?"

"Oh, Wolf, I can't hide from it anymore. I love him."

"Does he know?"

"I told him last night, but he didn't believe me."

"Do you want this divorce?"

"I don't know what I want anymore. Last night I wanted to kill him. Then I wanted to die. This morning, I . . ." Her words trailed off. She made a series of small, tight pleats in the letter and then thrust it deep in her pocket. "There's no rage left inside me now, only sadness and bitterness. Somehow I can't get rid of the notion that it's himself he wants to punish, not me."

"Do as he says, Noelle. Get your divorce and marry me. I will give you the life you deserve."

"How could I do that to you!" she cried. "You're not a man to settle for second best, and one day you'd grow bitter."

Brandt had known that this would be her answer. Still, he would make one last effort before he gave up the dream of having her. Cupping her chin in his hand, he kissed her gently. "I am willing to take that risk, my darling."

"But I'm not," she said softly. "I care too much for you to hurt you like that."

Wolf trailed a finger down her cheek and then walked resignedly over to one of the lemon-yellow settees. "He loves you, you know."

"You're wrong!" she cried. "He detests me."

"No, my darling. At the moment, he detests only himself. To him, loving is a weakness to be conquered. Quinn can tolerate weakness in others, but never in himself. My sister understands this about him. In many ways, she understands him better than you."

"And she'll be here to comfort him when he returns," Noelle snapped.

"No, she will not. Come sit down next to me, my darling. I am about to do something noble, and it will be easier for me if you're close by."

She looked at him quizzically and then did as he asked.

"I have not been entirely honest with you, partly from loyalty to my sister and partly from my own selfishness because I wanted you for myself. But now I think it is only fair to tell you that Quinn did not send for Anna and that they have not slept together since she arrived."

"I don't believe you. Anna told me herself that—"

"She lied to you." Wolf caught Noelle's hand and held it tight. "I am taking Anna away with me. We leave for Savannah tomorrow and then for France next week. I promise you, you will not have to worry about my sister again."

Noelle looked at him incredulously, trying to take in what he was saying. "Why are you doing this? She will hate you."

"Even my sister must someday bow to the inevitable, and I will not permit her to destroy herself any longer. When she is no longer angry, she will realize I am right. Anna is a realist, you see, and she already knows that Quinn loves you." He stood and gazed down at her. "I must go now."

Not trusting herself to speak, Noelle held out her hand, and he brushed it with his lips. *"Auf Wiedersehen.* Good-bye, my beautiful swan."

Later that evening, Dainty clucked her tongue in disapproval as she set a basket of eggs on the kitchen table ready for tomorrow morning's breakfast. "I don't like it one bit, Miz Copeland. A man's supposed to be with his wife, not galavantin' all over God's creation."

"It's not for you to like or dislike, Dainty Jones, and I'm sure you've eavesdropped enough in this household to understand why Mr. Copeland is needed in Washington. Now, I'm going to bed!" Noelle stalked from the kitchen, banging the door behind her.

Dainty shook her head sadly as she took a last swipe at the table with her dishtowel. That young 'un needs some tendin' to, she thought to herself. And ain't no cook in the world can give it. No siree, it's her husband she needs!

When Noelle reached her room, she pulled a small valise from the back of her wardrobe and resolutely placed it on the bed. She would go to Savannah now—tonight. Later she would send for the rest of her things. The longer she put off leaving Televea, the more difficult it would be for her. Wolf was wrong. Quinn didn't love her.

She packed the valise quickly, not giving herself time to think or to feel. When she was done, she fastened the straps and started toward the door to call for Nathan. But as she passed the fireplace something caught her eye.

There on the mantelpiece near the spot where she had found Quinn's note lay the disk of beaten silver that he always wore around his neck, the disk that had once been Amanda's. Slowly she picked it up and cradled it in the palm of her hand. The metal was cold. Tears she had refused to give into all day now began to fall freely. She knew how much this necklace meant to Quinn, and yet he had left it for her. Was it possible that he did love her? Or was this merely his way of telling her how sorry he was?

Long after the house was quiet and the servants were asleep, Noelle was still awake. She sat in her bedroom, fully dressed, the necklace lying in her lap. Finally she picked it up and slipped it around her neck. As she tucked it inside her dress the silver disk slid down between her breasts, where the metal nestled, warm and comfortable.

Slowly she walked to the bed and unfastened the straps of her valise. For the past three years of her life, all the good and all the bad were tied to one man. If she left now, she would never be at peace with herself because she would never know the truth. When she returned to England, it must be with the certain knowledge that Quinn did not love her.

She had nearly finished unpacking when she heard a pounding at the front door. Uneasily she glanced at the clock. It was well past midnight. Who could be calling at this hour? As she hurried down the stairs she met Nathan coming from the back of the house, hastily pushing his arms into the sleeves of an old robe. He reached the door before her and opened it.

Noelle had never seen the small, wiry man who stood on the other side nervously shifting his weight from one foot to the other. "I gotta see Mr. Copeland right away!" the man exclaimed.

Quickly Noelle pushed Nathan aside. "I'm Mrs. Copeland. Tell me what's wrong."

The man's eyes darted into the hallway behind her. "You get Mr. Copeland, ma'am. I got a horse waitin' for him. There's a fire at the shipyard."

"Dear God, no!" Noelle whispered, and then, sharply, "Nathan! Get as many of the men as you can. I'm going ahead." Not bothering to fetch her cloak, she brushed past the stranger and raced across the porch toward the horses at the bottom of the front steps.

"Wait!" the man cried. "I came for Mr. Copeland!"

"My husband isn't home," she declared as she caught up her skirts and mounted the nearest horse. "Hurry! There's no time to argue." She did not wait to see if he followed her.

As she reached the edge of the pine trees near the main road, her mind was racing. How long ago had the fire started and how far had it spread? There was a new cutter they were getting ready to— Without warning, two horses shot out from the night shadows on either side of her. She jerked back on the reins as they blocked the road. "What do you think you're—"

"Son of a bitch!" a familiar voice exclaimed. "Where's Copeland?" Even before she could make out his features, Noelle knew it was Luke Baker.

Another horse drew up behind her. "He wasn't there, Luke. She took off 'fore I could stop her." It was the stranger who had come for Quinn.

Fear clawed at Noelle as she looked around at the unshaven faces of the three men who surrounded her. There was no fire at the shipyard. It was a trap. Somehow Luke Baker had escaped from prison and come after Quinn.

Bracing herself, she dug her heels into her horse's flanks. But she was too late. Baker had anticipated her movement. He swung out his forearm and caught her painfully around the waist. He jerked her to his own horse just as hers shot out from beneath her. "Now, that wasn't too smart, little lady," he sneered. "You didn't really think I was gonna let you go that easy, did you? Get that horse, Greeley. We got a long way to ride. Looks like we can't get Copeland, but I gotta feelin' she's gonna do jes' fine."

"No!" Noelle clawed at the knotted muscles of his lower arm. "No! Let me go!"

"Shut up!" He jerked hard against her ribs, sending the breath rushing from her body. "You're comin' with us, little lady. When your husband finds out I got you, it'll be better than killin' him like I planned. He knows me well enough to figure out what I'm gonna do with you."

Noelle's struggles grew more frantic, and Baker landed a sharp, ringing blow on the side of her head. "Fightin' won't do no good," he jeered. "You belong to me and my boys now. And we're gonna treat you real fine."

They traveled the rest of that night and for the next two days keeping off the roads so they wouldn't be spotted, sleeping in snatches. The men were like rodents, she thought, skulking at the perimeters, afraid of open spaces and daylight. Other than a few vulgarities when she went into the bushes to tend to the needs of her body, they did not molest her, but she knew it was only the speed at which they were traveling that protected her.

The second day of riding was even more difficult for her than the first as they drew nearer the mountainous area of northern Georgia. The insides of her thighs were chafed and raw, and her wrists throbbed from the ropes that bound them to the pommel of her saddle. Her hair had come undone and hung in tangles down her back, and her green cashmere dress was ripped at the shoulder. She was also colder than she could ever remember with not even a shawl to protect her from the January chill.

She discovered they were heading west toward St. Louis, and her spirits sank even lower. Images of her knife lying uselessly in a drawer in her bedroom at Televea haunted her. She tried to distract herself by studying the three men and thinking about escape. Of the three, the one called Otis seemed to be the least ominous. He was large and burly, but dull-witted. Greeley, the man who had come looking for Quinn, was barely taller than she, but there was a furtive intelligence about him that made her suspect he was nearly as dangerous as Luke Baker. As for Baker, he terrified her. He seemed somehow less than human. She learned that he had escaped from prison the week before, killing a guard in the process. She tried not to think about what would happen when their pace slowed.

It was barely dark on the second day when they pulled into a clearing surrounded by pines and Baker announced that they would make camp for the night. "By now we lost anybody might of tried to come after us. I think we can take it easy for a while, don't you, boys?" Noelle's stomach lurched as Greeley and Otis hooted out their agreement.

Baker pulled her from her horse and tossed her down on the edge of the campsite, first making certain her wrists and ankles were tied securely. Before long, the men had built a fire and begun drinking.

She did not know how long she lay there, her cheek pressed against the frozen ground, her body screaming in agony from the tight ropes. They finished one bottle after another, bragging drunkenly about the money they were going to make in the spring, robbing the trappers who were on their way to St. Louis to sell their furs. She tried to ease the pressure on her wrists and ankles by shifting her weight.

"What's the matter, purty lady? Those ropes cuttin' into you?" Baker took a swig from a bottle Greeley passed to him and then wiped his mouth with the back of his hand. "Don't you worry none. Won't be long before I untie you. Then you gonna be able to stretch all you want."

Noelle tried to shut out their obscene laughter.

"What're we waitin' for, Boss?" Otis staggered to his feet. "Let's strip her and see what we got!"

Baker lashed out with his foot and kicked him viciously in the side of his leg. "Siddown! You don't do nothin' until I tell you. She's mine! You better understand that from the start. You'll git your turn, but not until I say."

"You bein' a little rough on Otis, ain't you, Boss?" Greeley looked over at Noelle, and she shuddered at the menace in his eyes. "Can't hardly blame him for wantin' a piece of that. Mighty anxious myself. For the past two days she's been lookin' down her nose at us. Treatin' Otis an' me like dirt. Actin' like she's too good for you, Luke."

Fear prickled along her spine as Noelle saw that Greeley's words had found their mark. Baker pushed his huge body up from the side of the campfire and lumbered toward her. His hand crushed her arm as he yanked her to her feet and dragged her over to the campfire.

"Greeley is right, purty lady. I think it's time you made up to us for bein' so unfriendly."

Noelle struggled against him, cursing the ropes that shackled her ankles and kept her arms pinioned behind her. "You disgust me!" she hissed. "You're worse than animals. All of you!"

"Looks like you need to learn some manners," he snarled.

Greeley grinned. "I'll just bet you're gonna teach her some, ain't you, Boss?"

Baker's thick lips curled back over his teeth. He pulled her against his chest and, snaking his arm around her, began opening the bodice of her cashmere dress with sadistic slowness. She felt his fingers unfastening each button until the garment fell down to her waist and only her chemise protected her flesh. Then, with the men cheering him on, he slipped his hand inside and began to fondle her.

"No!" She jerked her head to the side and sank her teeth deep into his arm.

With a yelp of pain, he grabbed her hair and wrenched her head back. Viciously he slapped her across the face, drawing blood where her tooth cut into her bottom lip. Before she could recover, he yanked her back until her shoulders slammed into his chest and split open her chemise. The silver disk hanging around her neck glittered in the firelight as her breasts tumbled out, completely exposed to their hungry eyes.

"Will you look at them," Otis gaped.

"Purtiest sight I seen in a long time." Slowly Greeley uncoiled his wiry body from in front of the fire and approached her, his eyes challenging Baker to stop him. But Baker held her tight and said nothing.

When Greeley was in front of her, he reached out. All the instincts that had helped her survive the streets of London came alive. She heard the wind in the pines, noticed the patches of dark hair growing on the back of his thin hand. Then he caught her nipple between his thumb and forefinger and brutally twisted it. She gasped with pain.

Baker grunted in her ear, "You like it, doncha, bitch! You like what ol' Greeley is doin' to you. Women always like a little pain. Makes 'em hot for it, don't it, Greeley?"

"Why don't we find out."

"Let's just do that. Cut her loose."

Greeley freed her wrists. As the ropes fell off she made herself stand quietly while she tried to move her fingers. Greeley crouched down in front of her and slipped the knife between her ankles. He sawed back and forth until the rope split. At that moment Noelle made her move. With a sudden lunge she dashed toward the horses. Even if they killed her, she had to make the attempt.

"Get her!"

Baker was the first one on her, then Greeley. She fought them desperately, but they quickly overpowered her and dragged her back to the fire.

"Hold her shoulders," Baker snarled. "Otis, get her legs! I'm gonna teach this bitch a lesson she'll never forget."

She felt the cold air on her thighs as he pushed up her skirt and split open her undergarments. They were all over her now. Greeley, pinioning her arms above her head with one hand and groping at her breasts with the other; Otis, his lips hanging slack with lust, spreading her legs.

Baker opened his trousers. Horrified, she watched him lower himself onto her, felt his ugly swollen sex push itself against the inside of her thigh, felt it travel upward . . .

A shot rang out, and Otis fell forward across one of her legs. Abruptly Greeley released the pressure on her wrists just as Baker spun off her, yanking up his trousers while he groped on the ground for his gun.

"Get up, you son of a bitch! I want to see your face when I kill you." Quinn stepped out of the trees, the grim set of his jaw as deadly as the rifle he was pointing toward the men.

Noelle kicked Otis's dead body off her leg and struggled to her feet. Just then Greeley shoved the heel of his hand into her back and sent her sprawling. For one brief second Quinn was distracted. It was all the time Baker needed. He dove at Quinn's legs, and the two of them crashed to the ground, Quinn's rifle slipping from his hands.

From the corner of her eye, Noelle saw Greeley leap toward Baker's pistol. She threw herself at his back. He grunted with the surprise of her attack and tried to dislodge her, but she clung to him, fighting as she'd never fought before, biting and kicking, reaching her fingers around to gouge at his eyes. Finally he shook her off and spun around, his hand clenched in a fist. She stepped back, but it was too late; his blow caught her in the shoulder. She staggered, and then righted herself just as he drew back his arm again. Viciously she brought her knee up and smashed it into his groin. He doubled over, catching her leg as he fell and sending her to the ground.

She saw the pistol—cold, deadly metal just beyond her grasp —and stretched for it and clutched the butt in her hand. As Greeley charged her, she brought it up and fired it directly at him. His face exploded.

She cried out as pieces of it—bits of bone, raw, red tissue —rained down on her naked breasts and arms. And then his faceless body slumped to the ground at her side. She sprang to her feet and stared down with horror at the crimson gore splattered over her bare skin. She could feel it running down her neck, her cheek, splashing off her onto the ground.

Stunned, she lifted her head, barely able to comprehend that Quinn was engaged in a fight every bit as desperate as hers had been, for his own hands were empty while his opponent's held a knife. There were bloody slashes on the sleeves of his buckskin jacket and across his chest where the deadly blade had already found its mark.

She watched the men slowly circle. Baker was clearly the larger, every bit as tall as Quinn but much heavier. He began taunting him, calling him a half-breed and urging him to attack. But Quinn waited, weaving his body back and forth, never taking his eyes off his opponent.

Suddenly Baker lunged. With the speed of a panther, Quinn sidestepped; at the same time he smashed his arm down on Baker's hand. The knife slipped to the ground. Not giving the man a chance to recover, he brought up his fist and pounded it into Baker's chest.

The man staggered, but he didn't fall. Instead, with an agility surprising for one so heavy, he lifted his foot and jabbed it deep into Quinn's abdomen. Quinn doubled over.

Baker seized the moment and brought his hands up, ready to hammer them down on the back of Quinn's neck. Just then Quinn straightened and slammed his fist into Baker's jaw. The huge man reeled. Quinn caught him and began punching him, landing one punishing blow after another. There was a crunch, and Baker's cheekbone crumbled beneath Quinn's murderous fist. Unable to move, Noelle watched as coldly, and with deadly purpose, Quinn beat the man who had tried to rape her until he collapsed into unconsciousness.

Quinn's breathing was labored and uneven when he finally looked over at her. She stood motionless, her hair streaming wild. What was left of her dress hung low on her hips, exposing her waist and the top of her belly. The rest of her was naked and blood-spattered.

Unsteadily Quinn bent over to pick up her torn chemise. Then he went to her and, without a word, began dabbing at her face and body with it, cleansing off the gore. When he was done, he led her into the forest to the place where Pathkiller was pawing restlessly at the ground. From his saddlebags he drew out one of his own garments, a worn buckskin jacket much like the one he was wearing, and handed it to her. She pulled together what was left of her dress and then put the jacket on over the top. When she looked up, Quinn had disappeared.

A moment later she heard the shot.

Closing her eyes, she began to tremble as, once again, she saw Greeley's face exploding over her. Later, when Quinn walked out of the trees, she felt as if she did not know him—a dangerous, bearded stranger, his eyes shadowed by the night, a rifle dangling from one hand, the reins of the horses from the other.

"Did you have to kill him?" she asked listlessly.

He tied the horses to a branch and walked over to his saddlebags. "What did you expect me to do?"

"We could have taken him back. Let him stand trial."

Pulling out a cheroot, he cupped his hands around the tip and lit it before he looked at her. "So he could escape from jail before they got around to hanging him? Is that what you wanted?"

Silently she stared back through the trees and then she shook her head.

"Mount up," he said. "There's a clearing a couple of miles from here where we can make camp for the rest of the night."

Later, as he fashioned a shelter for her from pine branches, she asked him how he had found her. He responded brusquely, saying only that he had returned to Televea to learn she had been kidnapped and had been tracking her ever since.

The winter sun was well up in the sky when she awakened the next morning. Despite everything that had happened, she had slept well. Even Greeley's face did not haunt her deep, dreamless sleep. Now she propped herself up on one elbow and looked at Quinn crouched by the fire, a tin cup in his hand. He had shaved since he had awakened, and his hair was still damp from washing. She drank in the lean line of his jaw, the bold flare of his nostrils, the eyes, deep and unfathomable. He was fierce and splendid. A feeling of happiness and something like peace spread through her at the sight of him so near.

He looked over and smiled. "Afraid I'm fresh out of tea and scones. You're stuck with coffee this morning."

Her mouth curved in response. "Coffee's fine."

He brought her a steaming cup, his smile abruptly disappearing when his fingers brushed against hers. He pulled away quickly and went back to his place by the fire. Her brief happiness in the morning disappeared. "You should have awakened me," she said stiffly. "It must be ten o'clock by now."

"You needed to sleep." He jerked his head toward the trees behind him. "There's a creek back there where you can wash. Dainty put a clean change of clothes for you in my saddlebags."

She set her coffee down and, without looking at him, gathered the clothes and made her way to the creek. As she washed she barely noticed the sting of the cold water on her flesh. She dressed quickly in the fawn riding habit that Dainty had packed and then, more slowly, returned to their camp.

Quinn was saddling Pathkiller. Although he had his back to her, he heard her approach. "We'll take it easy today," he said. "There's an inn about five hours ride from here where we can spend the night."

The question could no longer remain unasked. "Why did you go back to Televea, Quinn?"

For an instant his hands seemed to falter on the girth strap, and then he finished tightening it. "We'll stop every hour so you can rest. I know the owner of the inn. It's a clean place and the food is good."

She touched the silver disk around her neck. "Tell me why, Quinn. I have to know why you returned."

He brushed past her toward the other saddle that lay on the ground. "We'll talk about this later, Noelle. After we're back at Televea."

If he had struck her, he could not have made his feelings more clear. The tears that had been steadily rising in her throat threatened to strangle her. With a low sob, she turned and fled into the trees, running mindlessly, numbed by her pain and her great sense of loss. She did not hear the footsteps racing after her, was barely conscious of his hands on her shoulders snatching her to him, of the roughness of his jacket against her cheek.

"Highness, don't cry. Please don't cry," he whispered hoarsely. "Don't let me hurt you any more than I already have."

She clenched her fists and pressed them against his chest. "Why didn't you send me away long ago instead of torturing me so?" she sobbed. "Is this your revenge? Making me fall in love with you and then tossing me away? Is this what your hatred of me has led you to?"

"Hatred?" He pushed her back from him and gave her shoulders a shake. "My God, you're the most wonderful thing that has ever happened to me. I love you more than I love my own life!"

"Then why did you leave me?" she cried, barely comprehending the declaration she had waited so long to hear.

"For God's sake, what was I going to say to you?" His lips curled brutally, and his next words were laden with mockery. "My dear wife, despite the violence that happened between us in the stable, you must understand that I really love you!"

"Yes!" she screamed. "Yes! That's exactly what you were supposed to say!"

He dropped his hands from her shoulders and, with a savage curse, turned away from her. "Don't you understand? Even if you could forgive me, I could never forgive myself."

Her tears were falling freely now. "Then why did you go back to Televea?"

For a long time he said nothing. When he finally spoke, his voice was quiet and once again under control. "I went back because I had to see you one last time and make sure you were all right." He stared off into the distance. "Marry Wolf Brandt, Noelle. When *he* says he loves you, you'll be able to believe him."

Noelle stood without moving. There was a terrible resignation about Quinn, a slump to his shoulders she had never seen before. Suddenly she realized it was not he who had his revenge, but she. She had finally done what she'd sworn to do so long ago. She had finally defeated him. How many times she had prayed to see him humbled. Now it had happened—and all she could think of was how awful it was and how much she loved him. There was nothing else—no satisfaction, no feeling of vindication, nothing but an overwhelming urge to erase that awful resignation.

"I'm not going to listen to any more of your ridiculous self-pity!" she exclaimed, slashing at her tear-stained cheeks with the back of her hand. "We've both done terrible things to each other. But that's all in the past now. We have the rest of our lives. And if you think I'm going to marry Wolf, you're quite mistaken. I'm not a piece of property to be passed from one man to another. You're my husband, Quinn Copeland. Mine!"

Slowly he turned. She took a step toward him and, instinctively, he reached out. Then his arm fell back to his side. "It's not that simple."

"Yes it is." She closed the rest of the distance between them and, reaching up, cupped his cheek with her hand. "There's only one thing that's important, Quinn. Whether or not you love me."

He turned his head and pressed his lips to the palm of the hand that caressed him. "You know I do. More than my own life. But—"

"Shhh," she whispered, her eyes shining with the depth of her love for this splendid, stubborn man. "It's enough, my darling." Her breath caught in her throat as she saw some of the awful bleakness begin to lift from his face.

"And what if I fail you again?" he asked.

"You probably will." She smiled. "And I'll fail you. We're both imperfect creatures with too much pride. We'll have to learn to trust each other. It won't be easy."

His voice was choked with emotion as he muttered, "You're the damndest woman."

And then she was in his arms, caught in an embrace so full of love that everything else ceased to exist for them. They were alone in the world, two lovers joined at last.

Together, they moved to the shelter of the pine boughs where they shed their clothing and lay together beneath the warm blankets. Slowly they began moving their hands and then their mouths, searching out smooth curves and moist hollows, hardness and softness.

The cold January morning ceased to exist for them as they gave everything to each other—their bodies, their thoughts, their very breath. Climbing . . . passions racing rampant . . . they soared together until they were one.

Chapter Thirty-eight

Their child was born the following October. Whether he was conceived in the stable or in the golden moments of their slow journey back to Televea, neither of them knew, but they both suspected that the violent night in the stable, which had changed everything for them, had also brought them their son. At Noelle's insistence, they named him Christopher Simon, combining Quinn's middle name with his father's first. Christopher had Quinn's black hair and high cheekbones and his mother's topaz eyes. He was a lively, sparkling child, and they gloried in him as they gloried in their love for each other.

Quinn traveled to Washington with Wasidan to plead the Cherokee cause, but to no avail. The removal of the Indians to the west went ahead as planned, and four thousand died in less than a year, nearly a quarter of the tribe. Disease, famine, exposure, and heartbreak killed them. Among the Cherokee, the awful journey from their ancestral home to the new land of Oklahoma came to be known as *nunna-da-ul-tsun-yi*, the trail on which they cried.

Quinn grieved for his people, and his wife comforted him. Their love for each other was healing. Slowly the loneliness and sense of isolation that had been so much a part of both their lives dissolved. Only the subject of Simon stood between them —Noelle pressing Quinn to reconcile with his father, and Quinn, despite his desperate love for her, steadfastly refusing.

By the summer following Christopher's birth, Quinn's American clipper was finally on the stocks. Its keel had been laid, its frame fitted, and even though the exposed ribs were not yet ready to be planked, Quinn's daring new shape was already evident.

That summer, they frequently went to the pond in the woods behind Televea, sometimes alone, sometimes taking nine-month-old Christopher and splashing with him in the cold, clear water.

"Come on, Highness. Get in here before I pull you in!"

When it was just the two of them, she would step naked into the water and swim to him, a flash of silver in the still pond. But when Christopher was along, she contented herself with slipping off her shoes and stockings, hiking up her skirts, and wading in. As her toes sank into the mud at the edge of the pond, she inevitably thought back to those long-ago days as a mudlark, digging her feet in the banks of the Thames for pieces of coal. How far she had come.

When Christopher was with them, she loved sitting on the bank and watching as he and Quinn played naked in the water. Christopher, full of courage and squealing with delight, splashed furiously with his chubby arms and legs, confident that if the water came too near his nose, a strong set of arms would catch him up and hug him close. When he had played long enough, he arched back from his father's glistening, sun-bronzed chest and reached out for softer comfort.

"All right, my friend," Quinn would chuckle, stepping from the water and handing Christopher over to his mother, "I know what you want, and I can't say I blame you."

While she put Christopher to her breast, Quinn would slip on his pants and then sprawl beside her. With their bare feet, sun-darkened skin, and wet, tumbling hair, they looked more like a family of gypsies than the Copelands of Cape Crosse.

They returned home from the pond one July afternoon with Christopher asleep on his father's shoulder. "It was a perfect day, wasn't it, darling?" Noelle said, bestowing Quinn with the shattering smile he'd so often envied others for receiving. Then she kissed him. Christopher awakened and protested. Setting him on the grass to play, they resumed their pleasant pastime, not hearing the carriage until it was nearly up to the house. Noelle reluctantly pulled away from her husband and stepped toward the front of the drive. "Who on earth can this be?"

The carriage drew to a halt, and a groom jumped down to open the door. Noelle saw a small, embroidered slipper emerge, then the hem of a rose-colored gown and then Constance Peale Copeland herself. Her bouncing auburn curls were as thick and lustrous as ever, her emerald-green eyes as sparkling.

"My darling, darling girl!" Flying into Noelle's arms, she brought the familiar fragrance of violets with her.

"Constance!" As she hugged her, Noelle saw Simon step down

from the carriage. Constance gave her another squeeze and then, chattering all the while, swept on to Quinn.

Noelle looked up into Simon's blue eyes. He had not aged at all in the past two and a half years. If anything, he seemed more youthful.

"Hello, Noelle."

She sensed him holding back and remembered the strain between them those last months in London. It all seemed so foolish now. If it weren't for this man, she would have nothing. He was the only father she would ever know, and she loved him.

She stretched out her arms. "Oh, Simon, I'm so glad to see you!"

He swept her up then, pulling her feet off the ground and hugging her until she had to gasp for breath. He finally relinquished her with a kiss and went on to greet his son.

Quinn was turned away from her, so Noelle could not read his expression, but she could tell by the rigid set of his back that nothing had changed.

The moment between the two men did not last long, for Simon spotted Christopher sitting on the grass, a dandelion clutched in his grimy fist.

"Will you look at this, Constance," he exclaimed. "Will you just look at this!"

"Oh, my dear, he's perfect!"

For Simon, the dream was complete. And Christopher, as if he sensed the importance of the occasion, ignored everyone except his grandfather. He held out the dandelion and, solemnly, Simon accepted it; then, kneeling down on the grass, he hugged the child to him.

Christopher soon had enough of that and, accustomed to the delights of his father's pockets, began investigating his grandfather's. It was not long before he held Simon's gold pocket watch.

Noelle turned to her husband, and her smile froze on her lips. He was standing off to the side, once again a stranger in his own family.

She went to him at once. "Quinn?"

It was as if she didn't exist. Staring at his father and Christopher, Quinn's eyes were bleak and hard, and she could read his thoughts as clearly as if he had spoken them aloud. His father had triumphed after all.

Abruptly he turned to leave.

She reached out for his arm. "Please don't go now," she whispered. "They've only just arrived."

"I'll be back later."

Simon stood up. "You going somewhere, Quinn?"

"To the yard. I have to check on a few things before the men go home."

Simon planted a swift kiss on Christopher's head. "I'll come with you."

"Suit yourself."

Without speaking, the two men walked toward the stables. Constance and Noelle exchanged a long, unhappy look.

"Oh, dear," Constance sighed. "I confess I had hoped things would be improved by now. It was a foolish idea of mine, arriving here unannounced."

"Don't be a peagoose!" Noelle said. "I can't think of anyone I'd rather see. Let me deposit this little ragamuffin in the nursery while you freshen up, and then we'll curl up with a pot of tea and have a nice, long chat."

Constance smiled at her fondly. "I'd like nothing better."

Chapter Thirty-nine

"Damn him!" Quinn seethed as he slammed the bedroom door behind them.

"I take it you're referring to Simon." Noelle sighed wearily.

Dinner had been a catastrophe, and the strain was catching up with her. The fact that Quinn had appeared at all was, she suspected, only a mark of his affection for Constance, for he had treated his father with thinly veiled contempt and turned his full attention to his stepmother. Noelle had tried to compensate for his rudeness by entertaining Simon with stories of his grandson, but she knew by the sadness in his eyes that he saw through her efforts.

"He has no business being here!" Quinn jerked off his coat and threw it down on the bed. "Did you see him out there this afternoon, gloating over Christopher as if he were personally responsible."

Noelle's laugh was bitter. "He was, ducks."

"Are you trying to be funny?"

She was immediately contrite. "I'm sorry. Of course not. I'm just tired, that's all."

He stalked into the dressing room, the chasm between them widening. While he was gone Noelle removed her gown and petticoats and slipped on a gold silk robe. She was sitting in front of her dressing table taking down her hair when he returned, still dressed in his trousers with his white shirt open to the waist.

"I want him out of the house tomorrow."

He was spoiling for a fight. Noelle picked up her hairbrush and began jerking it through her hair. "And Constance? Would you like me to throw her out, too?"

"Just whose side are you on, anyway?"

She gritted her teeth. "I'm on your side."

"It certainly didn't seem that way at dinner tonight."

"What are you implying?"

His eyes raked her with their old arrogance. "You're my wife. I expect your loyalty."

"Loyalty! Why don't you say what you mean? You want me to be as rude to Simon as you are. You don't want loyalty, Quinn. You want obedience!"

"Put it however you like."

She slammed her hairbrush down on the dressing table. "You go to hell!"

In two long strides he was at her, pulling her up from the dressing table by her arms, his fingers biting deep into her flesh. The planes of his face were stark and furious.

"Quinn!"

He froze, horrified by his own anger, and then he clutched her to his chest, she who was more precious to him than life itself. "Oh, God, Noelle. I'm sorry. My darling Noelle. Forgive me. I had so much anger inside me when I came upstairs, I was deliberately goading you into an argument."

Noelle's voice was barely audible. "I love you, Quinn. You're more important to me than anything."

"I've got the devil's own temper, Highness, but I never thought I'd see the day again when I'd turn it on you."

She drew back her head and looked up at him unhappily. "Quinn, I have to tell you something."

"From the expression on your face, I don't think I'm going to like it much."

"No, you're not." Her eyes were deeply troubled. "I love Simon. I can't help it, and I won't pretend with you about it. In a strange way, he and Constance gave birth to me, at least as I am now, and I love them both."

Troubled, Quinn moved away from her and dropped down into one of the wing chairs in front of the fireplace. "I guess I don't understand how you can love him after the way he manipulated you."

"Your father is a human being, Quinn, not a god. He makes mistakes like the rest of us. If you could accept that about him, you might finally be at peace with yourself."

A log fell behind the grate, sending up a shower of sparks. "Go to bed, Highness," he said softly. "I'm going to sit up for a while."

He was still in the chair when he finally heard her deep, even breathing. Staring at the dying flames, Quinn willed his own body to relax, but it was no use. He wasn't going to get any sleep tonight. Maybe a drink would help. Maybe two.

As he stepped down into the front hallway, he saw a dim band of light glowing from beneath the closed door of the drawing room. So, he wasn't the only one who was finding sleep difficult. He hesitated only a moment before he went in.

Simon was sprawled in a chair with his back to the door and a half-empty glass dangling from one hand. He had positioned himself in the exact center of the room, where his view of the portrait that hung over the fireplace was unrestricted.

Quinn watched him silently. Simon was wearing a faded paisley robe that had been a Christmas gift from Amanda. God, it had to be more than twenty years ago. Funny he should still remember that robe; even funnier that Simon had kept it. He walked over to a carved Venetian chest that held an assortment of bottles and poured himself a stiff measure of whiskey. Then again, maybe it wasn't so funny.

Simon lifted his glass to the portrait and, without once looking at Quinn, said, "She was a beautiful woman, your mother. Not in the conventional sense, maybe, but in the ways that counted."

Quinn lowered himself to the sofa and stretched his long legs out in front of him, sipping from his drink as if he were alone in the room.

In one motion, Simon drained his own glass and stood up to refill it. "The strange thing is, having a legal marriage didn't really matter to her. Your mother wasn't much for convention. Oh, she went to church on Sunday, but that was only because I insisted. The institutions of religion didn't interest her." He corked the bottle and wandered back to his chair. "She married me in her heart the day I bought her from Carter Slade, and she never again thought of me as anything but her husband. She used to laugh at me when I brought it up. Damn woman. She never did understand what a coward I was."

"Why, Simon?" Quinn's voice was flat. "Why didn't you marry her when you should have?"

"Prejudice." The word, finally spoken, hung between them in

the quiet room. "Blind, stupid prejudice. There was one little part of me that didn't want a wife with Indian blood. Isn't that the goddamnedest, saddest thing you ever heard in your life? One drop of your mother's blood was worth more than all of mine put together."

For the first time since Amanda's death the tight knot of hatred inside Quinn eased. Perhaps it was Simon's honesty. Noelle's words came back to him as clearly as if she were standing at his shoulder. *"Your father is a human being, Quinn, not a god. He makes mistakes like the rest of us."*

Simon went on talking, keeping his eyes on the portrait. "Of course, when you were born, I realized how stupid I'd been. But that was a little late, wasn't it? Even if I had taken Amanda far away from Cape Crosse to be married, there was always the chance someone would have found out. God forbid that people should discover the truth about Simon Copeland; that his only son was a bastard and his wife—not his wife at all. I decided it was more expedient—now there's a word I've always liked—it was more expedient to do nothing, and so that's what I did—nothing."

Quinn leaned forward, all trace of indolence gone from his posture. He had to ask his father why he had finally married her at the end when she was dying. But before he could even frame the question, Quinn knew the answer as surely as if he had looked into his own heart. Simon hadn't been able to bear the thought that Amanda would die without ever having been his wife.

The room was quiet as each man occupied himself with his own thoughts. It was Quinn who finally broke the silence. "I hope Christopher's not going to be as hard on me as I've been on you."

"Oh, no you don't, my boy!" Simon exclaimed, somehow afraid of the curious weakness that was coming over him at his son's words. "Don't you start getting soft on me. Your hatred is the one thing I've always been able to count on. Too many changes aren't good for a man of my age."

Quinn laughed. Whether it was from the whiskey or Simon's words, he didn't know, but he couldn't seem to help himself. Finally he sobered, knowing there was something more he must say. "I've been wrong, Simon. It was wrong of me to sit in judgment on you all these years."

Simon felt a deep happiness well up inside him. He took a sip from his drink and cleared his throat. "That ship you're building, son. You've sure got yourself a winner there. How many knots you figure she'll do?"

The conversation moved on to important things.

The next morning Noelle and Constance met in the hallway.

"Do you know where . . . ?"

"Did Quinn . . . ?"

They saw the anxiety in each other's eyes.

"Oh, dear," Constance finally managed, tightening her lacy green wrapper around her waist. "You don't think . . . ?"

Without another word they rushed down the stairs. Noelle's gold silk robe fluttered around her ankles as she flew into the front hallway. Quinn had been in such a dangerous mood last night, there was no accounting for what might have happened.

"Perhaps Dainty has seen them."

They were on their way to the kitchen when Noelle noticed that the door of the drawing room was ajar. She tugged on Constance's arm, and together they went in.

Only the faintest light penetrated the tightly drawn draperies. The air was close, full of old smoke and stale liquor. Empty bottles lay on their sides on the rug. Quinn's boots leaned against a spindled candlestand; Simon's pipe and a collection of cheroot butts overflowed a fluted candy dish. There were glasses on the floor along with two wooden half models and part of a loaf of bread. The occupants of the room, rumpled and unshaven, were sound asleep.

Simon was lying flat on his back on the settee, his legs dangling over one arm, while Quinn was slouched down into an overstuffed chair, his feet propped up on a table, a half-filled bottle tilting precariously in his lap.

"Faith! No wonder they didn't come to bed. They were in their cups."

"In Georgia, we say they were drunk as skunks." Noelle smiled.

"Do you, my dear? How colorful."

Something warm and joyous began to grow inside Noelle as she surveyed the empty glasses and half models and cheroot butts, all the evidence of easy camaraderie. "Oh, Constance, do you think they've finally set things right between them?"

Constance reached for Noelle's hand, her green eyes suddenly brimming with tears. "Appearances can be deceiving, of course, but it looks hopeful, most hopeful indeed." She gave a tiny, embarrassed sniff. "If a trifle vulgar."

A giggle, as light as air, escaped Noelle. "I don't know if we ought to awaken them. This is the first time I've seen them together in the same room without shouting at each other."

"Mmm. Still, I confess I'm overcome with curiosity." Constance leaned over her husband and touched his shoulder. "Simon?"

There was no movement at all.

She shook him a little harder. "Simon, wake up!"

He mumbled something unintelligible and rolled over onto his side.

"You shan't get away that easily, my dear. Open your eyes."

Simon lifted one heavy lid and stared at her. "Go away." He closed his eyes and went back to sleep.

Noelle laughed. "Neatly done, Constance."

"Very well, you vexatious girl, if you think you have a better way, I am most anxious to see you demonstrate it." She looked pointedly at Quinn.

"All right. Watch this."

Noelle pulled the bottle from Quinn's lap and set it on the table. Then, kneeling down beside his chair, she began gently stroking his cheek with her hand. "Darling, it's time to wake up."

With his eyes still closed, Quinn pulled her to his chest and began caressing her hair. "Oh, Highness," he whispered seductively.

Quickly Noelle extricated herself, but not before the high color had crept into her cheeks.

"Most edifying." Constance's green eyes twinkled with amusement. "Since we can't seem to rouse them, we should at the very least put some order to this disgraceful room. It smells frightful in here, like a tavern of the most disreputable sort!"

Noelle drew back the draperies and opened the windows. The rush of cool morning air accomplished what the women could not.

Slowly Simon began to stir. "Timezit."

"I beg your pardon, my dear?"

He forced his mouth to work. "What time is it."

"Nearly half past eight." As he pulled himself up into a sitting position, Constance placed her hand on her small hip. "Simon, what could you have been thinking of? Drinking all night.

Sleeping in the drawing room. I don't permit myself to imagine what else."

"When I'm feeling better, Connie, remind me to spank you." Noelle giggled.

Quinn opened his eyes a quarter of an inch. "Don't see what's so funny. Man can't drink in peace in his own house. Come here, Highness."

He reached out an arm for her, but she quickly dodged it. "No thank you. I don't trust you this morning."

"Not so loud," Simon groaned as he threw his forearm across his eyes. "Damned domestic brandy."

"Didn't hear you complaining last night." Quinn rubbed his hand over the dark stubble of his jaw.

"Why you miserable—" Remembering the presence of the ladies, he cut himself off and contented himself with grumbling, "Plies me with liquor. Now he criticizes me for drinking it."

Quinn laughed and then winced from the effort. "Damned brandy," he groaned.

Now it was Simon's turn to laugh.

"Simon! Quinn!" Noelle exclaimed. "Will you please tell us what happened?"

The two men exchanged a brief glance and then Quinn rose, somewhat unsteadily, and propped his arm across Noelle's slim shoulders. "We had good whiskey, bad brandy, and interesting conversation. Now, help me upstairs, love."

When they reached the doorway, he turned back toward Simon. "After we've had some breakfast, let's see if we can make it to the yard. I've got a problem I'd like your opinion on."

Constance and Noelle found each other's eyes. They would have to wait until later to discover exactly what had taken place in this room last night, but whatever it was, it had been good. Noelle smiled up at Amanda's portrait and clasped her arm more tightly about her husband's waist.

He brushed the top of her hair with his lips and then looked at his father. "Simon?"

"Hmmm?"

"Let's take Christopher with us."

Reckless abandon.
Intrigue. And spirited
love. A magnificent
array of tempestuous,
passionate historical romances
to capture your heart.

- [ ] **THE RAVEN AND THE ROSE**
  by Virginia Henley   17161-X $3.95

- [ ] **TO LOVE AN EAGLE**
  by Joanne Redd   18982-9 $3.95

- [ ] **DESIRE'S MASQUERADE**
  by Kathryn Kramer   11876-X $3.95

- [ ] **SWEET TALKIN' STRANGER**
  by Lori Copeland   20325-2 $3.95

- [ ] **IF MY LOVE COULD HOLD YOU**
  by Elaine Coffman   20262-0 $3.95